New York Times, number one bestseller **P.C. Cast** is an award-winning fantasy, paranormal romance, and young adult author. She was a teacher for many years, but now concentrates on writing and public speaking full-time. Currently she divides her time between Oklahoma, Grand Cayman Island, and Scotland.

Visit her website at www.pccast.net

Goddess of Love

P.C. Cast

piatkus

PIATKUS

First published in the US in 2007 by The Berkley Publishing Group,
a division of Penguin Group (USA) Inc., New York
First published in Great Britain as a paperback original in 2011 by Piatkus
Reprinted 2011 (twice)

A CIP catalogue record for this book
is available from the British Library.

ISBN 978-0-7499-5356-0

Typeset in Jenson by Hewer Text UK Ltd, Edinburgh
Printed and bound by CPI Group (UK) Ltd, Croydon, CR0 4YY

Papers used by Piatkus are from well-managed forests
and other responsible sources.

MIX
Paper from
responsible sources
FSC® C104740
www.fsc.org

Piatkus
An imprint of
Little, Brown Book Group
100 Victoria Embankment
London EC4Y 0DY

An Hachette UK Company
www.hachette.co.uk

www.piatkus.co.uk

With love for Christine Zika, goddess editor and friend.
I'll miss you!

Acknowledgments

A big thank-you to Shaunee Cole for helping me "schuzze." Really, Twin. I couldn't have done it without your invaluable research.

Thank you to Richard Thomas of the Broken Arrow fire department for technical support. Any fire guy mistakes are mine.

As always I thank my agent and friend Meredith Bernstein.

A big grin and thank-you to my good friend Lola Palazzo, owner of the ever delicious Lola's at the Bowery restaurant, for aiding me in my meticulous, untiring, thorough research of her specialty martinis. Okay, let's just admit it – some research is more fun than others . . .

I would like to give special thanks to Christine Zika, who was my goddess editor for the first five Goddess Summoning books, including this one. Because of her guidance I am a better writer and a more confident storyteller. It is a lovely added bonus that along with being a wonderful editor, she also became my friend. I wish her every success in her new career!

Dear Reader,

Okay, I'll admit it – authors have favorite books. I know, I know, books are like children and we don't always want to admit to liking one better than another, but it's true. The Goddess Summoning books are my favorite children.

As with my bestselling young adult series, the House of Night, my Goddess Summoning books celebrate the independence, intelligence, and unique beauty of modern women. My heroes all have one thing in common: they appreciate powerful women and are wise enough to value brains as well as beauty. Isn't respect and appreciation an excellent aphrodisiac?

Delving into mythology and reworking ancient myths is fun! In Goddess of the Sea I retell the story of the mermaid Undine – who switches places with a female U.S. Air Force sergeant who needs to do some escaping of her own. In Goddess of Spring, I turn my attention to the Persephone/Hades myth, and send a modern woman to Hell! Who knew Hell and its brooding god could be hot in so many wonderful, seductive ways?

From there we take a lovely vacation in Las Vegas with the divine twins, Apollo and Artemis, in Goddess of Light. Finally we come to what is my favorite of all fairy tales, 'Beauty and the Beast.' In Goddess of the Rose I created my own version of this beloved tale, building a magical realm from whence dreams originate – good and bad – and bringing to life a beast who absolutely took my breath away.

I hope you enjoy my worlds, and my wish for you is that you discover a spark of goddess magic of your own!

P. C. Cast

Prologue

Venus was restless.

No. It was worse than restlessness. Restlessness could be calmed by a lovely chilled goblet of ambrosia and ordering a nymph to amuse her. (Which meant anything from plaiting the goddess's hair into an intricate crown of blonde braids to receiving a full body massage from a water nymph – a deliciously sensual experience that was best performed on the seashore. Naked.) But Venus didn't feel like summoning a nymph. And she was already sipping a glass of this season's excellent ambrosia, newly harvested from the Elysian Fields.

Venus sighed and tapped her elegant foot against the smooth marble floor of her chamber in Vulcan's underground palace. She'd retreated from her own golden temple located high atop Mount Olympus (she did have a spectacular view) and come down to her husband's palace for the same reason she had for centuries: to find peace and solace from the exhausting duties of being the most beautiful, most desirable female ever created – of literally being love personified. It usually worked to hide away from the demands of being the Goddess of Love deep within the bowels of Vulcan's realm. After all, it wasn't as if there was anything romantic going on between Vulcan and Venus. The very thought made a musical little laugh escape from the goddess's perfect lips. That had been the point of marrying Vulcan. Well, not the *whole* point. For her, marrying Vulcan had given her an escape from the exhausting job of personifying love. For Vulcan, marrying the Goddess of Love had been validation, an attempt to show the rest of Olympus that he could fit in and be one of them.

Apparently their passionless, loveless marriage had worked better in theory than it had in actual application.

Venus put down her crystal goblet of ambrosia. Now where had that ridiculously cynical thought come from? There was nothing wrong with the arrangement she had with Vulcan. It had been working for centuries, and for centuries more it would continue to work.

With a sudden inspiration, Venus stood up and hurried from the opulent chamber. That's it – she'd find Vulcan. They were, after all, friends. Perhaps he could help her figure out a good love match for Hermes. It was past time the Messenger God had those wings on his golden sandals fired up. Plus there was nothing like a little illicit love to brighten one's day.

Vulcan wasn't hard to find. (Like there were *any* surprises about him – big or otherwise?) He was, as usual, in the center of his realm where the forge of Olympus and the great pillar of flame were located. She entered the room quietly. He was standing before the column of fire with his arms raised. Venus studied him with detached interest. He really was a splendidly built god, though not typically blond and lithe and graceful, as were most of the Olympians. Vulcan was dark and powerful. The rest of the gods shunned him because of his physical imperfection – the limp he'd had for eons. But his lameness was slight. It would hardly be noticed at all if he didn't live amidst the perfection of the golden gods.

Yes, physically he was definitely attractive. Not that *she* had ever felt any desire for him (or he for her, as far as she could tell, and naturally, had there been desire, Love would be able to tell). Venus cocked her head to the side, considering how true it was that desire and passion often had little to do with the physical and much more to do with something as nebulous as a spark that passed between two spirits. And that spark was definitely missing between the two of them.

Venus shook herself mentally. Such thoughts were a waste of time. She was, after all, Love. She could command that spark whenever she wished. So why not command a little fun and games for the flamboyant Hermes? It would be a good diversion for Vulcan, too. He was far too serious and too often did nothing but work, work, work. Venus moved closer to the dark god so that she could see just a little over his broad shoulder where the yellow and orange flames in the sacred pillar of fire were swirling in response to the magic the god was working – whatever that was. Within the flames she caught a brief glimpse of something that looked like the night sky filled with glistening constellations, which was odd but not particularly interesting. Venus had never understood what was so fascinating about the pillar of flame. Of course that might be because Vulcan had never shared details about his magic with her. Hmm . . . She stood there, chewing her lip. She'd never really thought about that before. Then she shrugged mentally. What difference did it make?

'Vulcan!' she called cheerily at his back.

He glanced over his shoulder and gave her a distracted smile. 'Have you been resting well?'

'Actually, darling, I'm terribly bored today.' She walked languorously over to the stone bench positioned near the flaming pillar and reclined gracefully. 'How about you and I cook up something delicious between Hermes and say . . .' She hesitated, considering. 'Between Hermes and Aeolus?'

His attention still on the roiling flames, he answered her in a vague, preoccupied voice. 'Aeolus? But doesn't the God of Winds prefer young nymphs, young *female* nymphs to other immortals?'

Venus waved a hand dismissively. 'Such a small detail. I'll decide on the spell, you decide on the flame that will carry it, and—'

'Forgive me, Venus, but I'm in the midst of some rather important . . .' – the god hesitated, choosing his words carefully – 'research.' He did look at her then, but only long enough to give her a distracted smile. 'Perhaps another time.'

Venus glared at him, although it wasn't as if he noticed her irritation. By Neptune's phallus-shaped trident Vulcan was dull! He'd never been wild and passionate and fun – like, say, Apollo or his twin, Artemis – and that had, in truth, been part of the reason she'd married him. To be safe from passion. Then why did she suddenly find their arrangement (as well as the god himself!) so annoying?

'That's right. I wouldn't want to interrupt your precious . . .' – she fluttered her shapely fingers at the pillar of flame – 'fire research. As usual, you're dreadfully dull. Perhaps another time.' She echoed his words sarcastically. Then the goddess stood up, and with hardly a glace at Vulcan, disappeared in a puff of glittering, ambrosia-colored dust.

By Zeus's beard Vulcan was glad she was finally gone! Not that he disliked Venus. Actually he'd thought of her as a friend for centuries. It was only recently that the friendship had begun to sour. The god sighed and rubbed his forehead. That wasn't Venus's fault. It seemed that lately everything in his life had begun to sour. But the dissatisfaction was his own – with his life. And she was right. He was dreadfully dull.

When had he lost his spark for life? For adventure? *For love?* The last question floated through his mind, surprising him. Love? He snorted. He'd married Love, for all the good it had done him. There had never been anything but respect and friendship between Venus and himself. Of course she'd gone ahead to have countless dalliances, but that had never bothered him. They had an arrangement, not a marriage.

No, his relationship with Venus wasn't what was bothering him. It was his life in general. His gaze drifted back to the visions of the constellations he had summoned within the fiery pillar. They looked so peaceful . . . majestic . . . so free. Longing washed over the God of Fire. If only he could escape to the heavens and leave the tedium of his life behind . . .

And why couldn't he? He was an Olympian. A powerful god. Nothing was impossible for him.

Of course he couldn't leave his realm untended. Vulcan rubbed his face and began to pace back and forth in front of the burning pillar. Who could run his realm were he to leave it forever? None of the other gods would deign to take his position – it was too far beneath them, literally as well as figuratively. He had no flashy view, no frolicking nymphs, no glittering decadence. He controlled the fires of the earth and Olympus. It was an important job, but it certainly wasn't as flashy as, say, pulling the sun across the sky or bringing spring to the earth.

Pacing did nothing to relieve his frustration. He'd walk. That would clear his head. As he climbed the stone steps that led to the surface he tried to concentrate on the positives – he was a god, and even though it would take a miracle for him to be able to retire to the heavens, the Olympians were known for their ability to work miracles.

*　　*　　*

5

The God of Fire walked slowly across the grand ballroom of Zeus and Hera's palace. He could have moved more quickly. His lameness didn't prohibit speed; it just prohibited grace. Over the eons he had learned to be slow and steady to save himself from disdainful looks and muttered insults. How he loathed the immortals and their unceasing passion for perfection. They were shallow and selfish. Most had no comprehension of what real pain and sacrifice and loneliness meant.

Vulcan uttered an oath under his breath. He should have gone to ancient earth and walked through a deserted forest there to do his thinking. What had made him come to his parents' temple? It was stupid of him because the perfection that surrounded him only made his own imperfections more obvious.

'Vulcan? I called after you several times and you did not hear me. Is all well with you, my son?'

He stopped and turned to face Hera, who was hurrying after him. Automatically he relaxed his expression and smiled at his mother. 'All is well. I was just lost in thought. Forgive me for being rude.' He kissed her soft cheek.

'You would never be rude, my son.' Her sharp eyes studied him. 'You seem sad. Are you quite certain all is well with you?'

'Mother, please don't worry about me.' Vulcan forced another smile.

'You know I do.' She drew in a deep breath.

'There is no need. Now I must get back to my realm. It was good to see you, Mother.' He kissed her cheek again, and before those knowing eyes of hers could see further into his soul, Vulcan hurried away. The last thing he needed was his mother – or may all the gods forbid, his father – looking too closely at his life. He followed his own path, chose his own destiny. And he definitely didn't want interference from the king and queen of the gods.

6

Had Vulcan hesitated and glanced over his shoulder at Hera, he would have been surprised to see her circling her fingers in the air, which instantly began to glitter. And had he been listening carefully, he might have heard her whisper, 'I grant my son a single dose of mother love to aid him in whatever it is that is making his heart heavy.'

Vulcan didn't turn around, though, and he didn't listen to his mother's whisper. He definitely didn't notice the almost invisible thread of power that followed him.

Vulcan continued through the palace, intent on leaving before he ran into any of the other Olympians. He still moved slowly, but his gait wasn't awkward and self-conscious. Actually he moved silently, with a strength that was none-the-less obvious because of its pace. He had just come to the exit of the grand ballroom when he heard laughter that was so uninhibited and joyous and musical that there was no doubt at all to whom it belonged.

No. He did not want to face her again today. He stopped and stepped silently into the concealing shadows as Venus approached. She was laughing and having an animated conversation with the Goddess of Spring. Obviously leaving his realm had instantly cured her boredom.

'All right Persephone! I concede to you. After one glimpse of those divine boots, I'm willing to admit that I was too harsh in my judgment of your little kingdom,' Venus said as she laughed.

'How many times do I have to explain it to you? Tulsa, Oklahoma, is not a kingdom, not is it mine.' Persephone's laughter was light and carefree, beautiful in its own right, even though it didn't have the seductive lure of the Goddess of Love. 'Think of Tulsa as you would one of the ancient cities, like Pompeii or Mediolanum, only the sewage systems in Tulsa are better.' She paused and frowned. 'But I cannot say the traffic has improved.'

'Are you telling me that you spend six months of the year in a city with fabulous marbled baths like Pompeii?' Venus asked eagerly.

'No. Sorry. Tulsa doesn't have Pompeii's baths.'

'Then does it have Mediolanum's delicious red wine?' Venus moaned in remembered pleasure. 'Red wine from Italy's Mediolanum region is sinfully rich and wondrous.'

'Uh, no. Tulsa isn't a wine region, although they do import wines from all over the world.' Persephone chewed her bottom lip delicately while she paused and thought for a moment. 'Actually I've found myself falling in love with a drink called a specialty martini. And they are definitely made right there in Tulsa.'

'That only sounds vaguely interesting. Certainly not enough to account for your obsession with that place.'

'I'm not obsessed!'

'Of course you are,' Venus said. 'You spend six months out of the year in Tulsa. And right now it's not even spring or summer there, but you've just returned from yet another visit. You can't fool Love, Persephone. I know obsession when I see it.'

Vulcan assumed the Goddess of Spring would be angered by Venus's words, so he was surprised to hear her respond with good-natured laughter.

'Maybe I am obsessed. And why not? I do adore Tulsa. There's something about walking the streets of a modern city, one where no one recognizes me as an immortal, that is just so wondrously freeing. Think of it, Venus. No one prejudges you by what you may or may not have done for uncounted centuries. No one knows who your parents are. No one cringes in fear if

8

you get annoyed. And here's the best part – no one worships you because you're a goddess. If you're worshipped' – she smiled seductively – 'it's because you're a desirable, intelligent, fascinating *woman*. Can you imagine what a lovely change that is?' Persephone didn't give the goddess a chance to answer. 'And the men! Modern men are different than ancient mortals. They don't have their hang-ups.'

Venus's smooth brow wrinkled in confusion.

'Hang-ups – it means that they don't think like archaic, barbaric dolts. Well, most of them don't. Modern men don't have the prejudices the ancients have; they know how to appreciate women as equals, and that is very, very sexy.'

From the shadows Vulcan watched understanding dawn over Venus's beautiful face at the same instant he felt a shock of something that he didn't recognize at first because the emotion was so foreign to him – hope. What Persephone had said about modern men being different had given him sudden, sweet hope.

'I wouldn't be recognized as Love?' Venus said at the same instant Vulcan realized that he wouldn't be recognized – or judged or shunned – as the God of Fire.

Persephone smiled impishly. 'You could practice your skills of seduction without anyone knowing that you are the incarnation of love.' The goddess sighed romantically. 'Sounds intriguing, doesn't it?'

'It does indeed.'

Yes, Vulcan agreed silently. Not being recognized did, indeed, sound intriguing.

'And don't forget the excellent shopping,' Persephone added, gracefully pointing her toe and holding up her foot so that she could show off her black alligator-skin cowboy boot.

'Persephone, my friend, perhaps you would like to show me around your entertaining little kingdom?'

'It would be my pleasure.'

The two goddesses linked arms and, laughing, walked off in the direction of Persephone's mother's temple, where Vulcan knew Demeter kept open a portal to the modern city Tulsa.

'Fascinating . . .' he murmured to himself. Leaving his parents' temple he hurried to the stairs that would return him into the bowels of Mount Olympus and his own fiery realm. By the time he reached his great hall, Vulcan's mind was buzzing like the brown bees of Greece. Modern men didn't have the ancients' prejudices. They wouldn't even recognize divine Venus as the physical incarnation of love. So it wasn't entirely impossible that maybe, possibly, there might be a modern man in the shining Tulsa Kingdom who could be enticed into stepping into his immortal place. Especially if Love herself was unknowingly involved in the enticing . . .

With a new sense of purpose, Vulcan strode to the heart of his realm, stripping off his toga as he went so that by the time he faced the pillar of open flame that heated the world his muscular body was naked and already glistening with sweat.

He raised his hands, palms open. In recognition of the presence of the Fire God, the orange pillar rippled and flashed. Vulcan closed his eyes and concentrated. Then he began the incantation.

> Fire swirl and burn, strong and clear,
> like passion does love, to Venus stay near.
> Follow Love's sweet path through Demeter's portal,
> search, test, seek, find a modern man who is mortal.

The fire danced around Vulcan's palms like an exuberant child, mirroring the unusual excitement that suddenly burned within his breast. He was so intent upon the spell that he didn't notice the thread of Hera's power that snaked from around his body and joined the pillar, making it flare and swell with magic straight from the queen of Olympus. Vulcan clapped his hands together and completed the spell.

With the unbreakable strength of an immortal's belief,
find a mortal man who can grant me relief!

The pillar of flame exploded with a roar that would have instantly deafened a mortal man. Unscathed, the Fire God watched as a sliver of golden flame, invisible to all except for the God of Fire himself, formed within the pillar and then split free of it to hover in the air in front of Vulcan.

'Go! Do my bidding!' the god commanded. Quick as one of his father's infamous thunderbolts, it dashed from the heart of Mount Olympus. Vulcan knew its path. The questing flame would follow Venus all the way through Demeter's portal and into the Kingdom of Tulsa. There it would seek and search for something it could never find in the ancient world of man – a modern mortal who could take his place as God of Fire.

Vulcan smiled in satisfaction and settled down to wait.

Hera felt the tug of her power being used. She glanced surreptitiously at Zeus. He was busy with Demeter. The two of them were arguing good naturedly over the quality of the ambrosia harvest.

'Dearest, I need to check on some last minute details for the feast this evening. Will you excuse me?'

Zeus nodded and waved absently at her. Demeter caught her eye and Hera winked quickly at her. The Goddess of the Harvest nodded slightly and launched into the ambrosia argument with new zeal. Hera hurried from the Great Hall, sure Zeus was well occupied – at least for a few moments. She ducked into a shadowy alcove and closed her eyes, concentrating on the gift of power she'd given her son.

There! Under her closed lids she could see the thread of invisible fire Vulcan had bespelled. She watched as it snaked through Olympus toward Demeter's temple and then vanished into the portal that led to the modern city of Tulsa. Surprised, Hera concentrated harder, and her consciousness expanded, hooked into the thread of questing fire by the power of the queen of Olympus. Through the spark of connection she saw Venus and Persephone enter the modern world, and she could feel the weight of Vulcan's incantation as it followed the Goddess of Love.

Why was Vulcan following Venus and Persephone? Had he finally tired of that sham of a marriage of his? Hera smiled. She sincerely hoped so. Her son deserved more than the shell of a marriage. With a mother's determination she reached out to the thread of fire that carried the gift of her power and spoke to it.

> Hear my command; do my divine will.
> It is my son's empty heart I wish to fill.
> So seek what cannot be found amongst the gods.
> One who will complete him against all odds.
> He has long been alone, the God of Fire.
> Find that special touch to awaken his desire.

Hera flung out her hands and new power, filled with her words, flew invisibly through Olympus, joining the thread of fire and augmenting its already white-hot strength.

Hera smiled in satisfaction and retraced her steps back to the throne room.

Chapter One

Pea felt a wash of relief, which was quickly followed by embarrassment when she heard the fire siren getting closer. Crap crap crap! What a way to start Saturday morning.

'They're almost here, Chlo-chlo-ba-bo!' she yelled up at the tree.

The pitiful whine that replied from the middle of the winter-bare branches squeezed at her heart, but Pea shook her head sternly at the dog, refusing to give in to Chloe's manipulation.

'Okay, look! How many times do I have to tell you? You. Are. Not. A. Cat.'

A black nose appeared from a top branch of the tree. Behind it Pea could see the glint of bright, intelligent eyes staring down at her.

'Hrumph!' Chloe barked the strange, deep growl sound she made when she was highly annoyed.

'Whatever! You can love cats. You cannot be one.'

Chloe had just *hrumph*ed indignantly at her again when the fire engine glided to a smooth stop at the curb. Pea sighed and gave Chloe one more glare. Then she started to walk toward the men who were climbing out of the traditional shiny red fire truck. Instantly Chloe erupted in a pathetic chorus of whines and yaps. Forgetting all about embarrassment and doggie manipulations, Pea rushed back to the tree.

'Chlo-chlo! It's okay, baby girl. I'm right here.'

'Bring the ladder over here, Steve.' A deep male voice called from close behind her. 'This is the tree.'

'Hurry!' Pea yelled without taking her eyes from the frightened dog. 'She's really scared, and if she falls she's definitely going to break something.'

'Ma'am, cats rarely hurt themselves when they jump from trees. The whole land-on-their-feet myth actually has quite a bit of truth to it,' the voice over her shoulder said.

Chloe whined again.

'Hey, that's not a cat.'

Pea turned to the fireman, an annoyed frown on her face. 'I clearly told the dispatcher that my *dog*—' she began, putting her fists on her waist and letting the worry she felt for Chloe shift over to irritation, but one look at the man had her anger fizzling and her tongue stammering. She felt her cheeks flame with heat. Quadruple crap! It was *him*. Griffin DeAngelo. The most gorgeous man she had ever seen. Ever. Even on TV. He was also the guy she'd been crushing on for the entire past year – ever since she'd walked Chloe by his house (which was just down the street from hers) and seen him mowing his yard. Without a shirt on. And here he was. Standing in her front yard like he'd walked right out of one of her very graphic dreams.

Naturally he wasn't looking at her standing there in her baggy sweatpants and sweatshirted glory, and he hadn't noticed her sudden pathetic inability to speak. He was peering up at Chloe with a quizzical smile tilting his delicious-looking lips.

'How in the hell did he get up in that tree?'

'She's not a he, she's a she. And she climbed,' Pea said.

'Oh, pardon my language, ma'am; I forgot you were there. I'm Griffin DeAngelo, captain of the Midtown Station.' He tapped his helmet in an archaic and adorable gesture of a gentleman greeting a lady.

'I know!'

'You know?' He raised an eyebrow as if to punctuate his question.

'Yeah, you live down there.' Pea pointed down the block directly at his house. Like a stalker. 'Remember, we met at the fourth of July block party last fourth of July, and also at the summer weenie roast and again at the pre-Christmas light hanging neighborhood meeting,' she babbled, sounding exactly like a stalker.

His beautiful forehead wrinkled in confusion. 'I'm sorry, ma'am. I don't remember.'

Of course he didn't. No one remembered meeting her. 'No problem, I'm um ...' She paused as she stared up into eyes that were so big and blue and beautifully dark lashed that she suddenly and moronically forgot her name.

'Ma'am?'

'Dorreth Chamberlain!' she blurted, holding out her hand like a dork. 'And the dog caught in the tree is Chloe.'

He took her hand gently, like he was afraid she might explode at his touch. And why wouldn't he think that? She'd just told him that they'd met three times, none of which he remembered, and she was still standing there gawking at him like a kindergarten kid in a bubble gum factory. And her hair! Pea forced herself not to groan and pat manically at the frizzy mess she'd tied back in her favorite scrunchie.

'Check it out. It's a dog,' said a young fireman who had joined them with two other men carrying an extension ladder.

'How the hell did it get up there?' said another fireman, with a laugh.

Griffin cleared his throat and gestured at Pea.

'Sorry, ma'am,' was mumbled in her general direction.

Pea laughed gaily, gesturing up at the tree, trying hard to sound perky and interesting. 'She climbed!' As usual, none of the men so much as glanced at her.

'Climbed? She must be twenty feet up in that old oak,' one of the unnamed guys said.

'She's a good climber. She's just not a good climber downer,' Pea said, and then wanted to dissolve into the sidewalk in embarrassment. *Climber downer?* God, she really was such a dork.

'Well, let's get her down,' Griffin said. The men went to work extending the ladder, and Chloe started growling.

'What kind of dog is she, ma'am?' Griffin asked her.

'She's a Scottie, but she thinks she's a cat. See, I have a cat named Max, and Chloe is totally in love with him, hence the fact she is clueless that she's a Scottie *dog*. Chloe is in denial. She believes she's a Scottie *cat*. I'm not sure whether to get her another dog, get her some Prozac or take her for a visit to the pet psychic.'

Griffin laughed, a deep, infectious sound that made Pea's skin tingle with pleasure. 'Or maybe you should just invest in a safety net.'

Pea giggled and tried to have one of 'those moments' with totally, insanely gorgeous Griffin the Fireman – one of those eye-meeting moments where a man and a woman share a long, sexy, lingering, laughter-filled look.

Naturally the moment did not happen.

First, her coquettish giggle turned into – horror of all horrors – a snort. Second, blonde and beautiful appeared on the scene.

'Pea! Don't tell me Chloe got caught in a tree again!'

Griffin immediately shifted his attention to her neighbor, who was hurrying up to them, her six-year-old daughter in tow. 'Hi, Griffin,' she said.

'Good to see you again, Stacy,' he said, and tilted his hat to her, too.

Pea sighed. Of course he remembered Stacy – tall, sleek, always together-looking Stacy – even though Pea knew for sure that Stacy had only made *one* of the neighborhood meetings in the past year. With Stacy there was no way in hell gorgeous Griffin would give her another thought. If he'd ever given her a first thought. Even with a kid at her heels, Stacy was ridiculously attractive.

But, surprisingly, the fireman's eyes slid back to her. 'Pea?' he asked with a raised brow.

'Yeah,' she said, shrugging and launching into the short version of her all too familiar explanation for what everyone called her. 'Sadly, Pea is an unfortunate childhood nickname that stuck.'

'Oh, come on! There's nothing wrong with your nickname. Pea's adorable,' Stacy said, grinning at her.

'Yea for Pea!' Stacy's daughter Emili chimed in. 'I like your name. It's cute. But it's not as cute as him.' Emili pointed up at Griffin. 'Are you married? Pea's not married. Maybe you could marry Pea. She doesn't even have a boyfriend and my mommy says that's a shame because she really is cuter than people think she is 'cause—'

Pea sucked in air and felt her face blaze with heat while Stacy clamped her hand over Emili's mouth and tried unsuccessfully not to laugh.

Thank the sweet weeping baby Jesus that Chloe chose that moment to snarl a warning at the young fireman who was positioning the ladder against the tree.

'Chlo! It's okay.' Pea hurried over to the trunk of the tree and looked up at the black snout and bright eyes. Chloe whined.

'Sorry, she doesn't like men,' she said to the fireman. 'I really don't think she'll bite you. But she will complain. Probably a lot.'

'I'll get her,' Griffin said.

'She's all yours, Captain.'

Griffin started up the ladder and Chloe's low, rumbling growl intensified.

'Chloe! Manners!' Pea called up to the perturbed Scottie. *Please, God, please don't let her bite him*, she mentally telegraphed over and over. Until Griffin did something that made Pea's thoughts, as well as Chloe's growls, come to an abrupt halt. He was calling Chloe, but he wasn't calling her like someone would call a dog. He was, unbelievably, kitty-kittying her.

'Come here Chloe, kitty-kitty. It's okay little girl. Come here, kitty-kitty-kitty.'

Dumbfounded, Pea watched her dog's ears lift and her head tilt toward the approaching man.

'Good girl,' Griffin murmured. 'Good kitty-kitty, kitty-kitty.' He held his hand out slowly and let Chloe get a good sniff of him. 'See, you smell her, don't you? That's right, kitty-kitty-kitty, come on down.'

Pea could only stand and stare as Griffin reached into the tree crevice and pulled Chloe, who was still sniffing him curiously, into his arms and began the descent down the ladder.

'Amazing,' Stacy said with a deep breath. 'How did he do that? Chloe hates men.'

'He's too pretty to hate, Mommy,' Emili said.

'Honey, let's keep that for our inside thoughts, shall we?' Stacy said. Then she glanced at Pea and whispered, 'Even though it's totally true.'

Pea pretended not to hear either of them, which was easy. Her entire being was focused on her dream man striding toward her with her dog – who was actually wagging her tail – held firmly in his arms.

'Here ya go, ma'am.' He handed Chloe to Pea.

'Th-thank you,' Pea stuttered. 'How?'

'How?' he repeated.

'The kitty-kittying. How did you know to do that?'

'Just makes sense. You said she thinks she's a cat, and you have a cat, right?'

Pea nodded.

'That's how you call your cat. Right?'

Pea nodded again.

'I figured she'd recognize the call.'

Griffin scratched Chloe on the top of her head, and Pea watched in astonishment as her dog – her man-hating dog – closed her eyes and sighed happily.

'That's just part of it, though,' Griffin said. 'I was counting on Chloe smelling Cali.'

Pea suddenly understood. 'Your cat?'

'My cat.' Griffin gave Chloe one last scratch, then turned back to his men. 'Okay, let's get this loaded up. Have a good day, ma'am.' He nodded politely to her and then to Stacy. He winked at Emili, and then he was gone.

'Em, honey, go on inside and wait for Mommy. I'll be there in just a second,' Stacy told her daughter.

'Are you and Pea going to talk about how pretty that fireman was?'

'Of course not, honey. Now go on.'

''Kay! Bye, Pea.' Emili skipped off to her house, singing a song about lemon drops and unicorns.

'Okay, I'd forgotten how drop dead Mr. Tall Dark and Fireman is. I can definitely understand why you've had a thing for him for ages,' Stacy said.

Pea put Chloe down and the dog trotted over to the tree and began sniffing all around the trunk. 'Do not even think about climbing up there again,' Pea told her sternly. Chloe glanced back at her and snorted. 'I swear that dog understands every word I say,' Pea muttered.

'Hello! Sexy, incredible man. We were talking about him and not your insane Scottie.'

'She's not insane,' Pea said automatically. 'And yeah, he's gorgeous and I might have a little crush on him.'

Stacy rolled her eyes, which Pea chose to ignore. 'But now he's gone. I don't see the point in going on and on about him.'

'Like you haven't gone on and on about him before?'

Pea silently chastised herself for the one or two – okay, ten or twelve – times she'd mentioned to Stacy how hot she thought their neighbor was. 'Whatever,' she said, trying to sound nonchalant and dismissive. 'He's still gone, and there's still no point in talking about how gorgeous he is.'

'The point is, Ms. Totally Single, that he seemed interested in you.'

'Get real, Stacy. He wasn't interested; he was polite. There's a world of difference.'

'Bullshit.'

'Stacy, he didn't even remember me, and today makes the fourth time we've met. Men like him are not interested in women like me.'

'So he has a crappy memory. Lots of guys do. And women like you? What does that mean?'

Pea sighed, and didn't feel up to mentioning that Griffin's memory hadn't failed when she'd walked up. 'Women like me – short, plain, forgettable. He belongs with a model or a goddess. He doesn't belong with me.'

'You know, that's your problem! You defeat yourself before you even start. I've told you before that all you need is a little self-confidence. You're perfectly fine looking.'

Perfectly fine looking. Didn't that just sum it all up? There was sexy Stacy giving her what she really considered praise and encouragement, but the best she could come up with was perfectly fine looking. She studied Stacy – tall and blonde with her great curves, fabulous boobs and those cheekbones that made her face look like someone should carve it out of marble. How could she possibly understand what it was to be so average that you went through life being invisible? She'd never walked into a room and not turned heads. Pea would bet the great raise she'd just got that gorgeous Griffin had already forgotten her. Men always did, but she would also bet that the firemen were discussing her hot blonde neighbor all the way back to the station. And then someone might say something like: 'Oh, yeah, that *other* girl was there, too.' Pea was the other girl. The forgettable girl.

'So will you do it?'

'Huh?' Pea said, realizing Stacy had been talking and she'd not heard anything she'd been saying.

Stacy sighed in exasperation. 'I said, it's not even noon yet. You have plenty of time to go into that fabulous kitchen of yours and bake a big plate of your to-die-for brownies and deliver them to gorgeous Griffin at the station as a thank you.'

'Let me think about that.' Pea paused for half a blink. 'No.'

'And why not?' Stacy didn't give her time to continue. 'Because you have so many men beating down your door to go out with you tonight? Because you're in an incredible relationship with your dream man? Hmm? Which one is it?'

'You know I'm not dating anyone, and thanks for reminding me,' Pea said through her teeth, and then thought *for the zillionth time.*

'Okay, so is it because you don't find Griffin attractive?'

'As you very well know that's definitely not the case.'

'Then is it because you're hateful and rude and you don't believe in thanking the man who just saved your weird Scottie cat's life?'

'Chloe isn't weird and she wasn't about to die,' Pea said.

'She definitely could have broken something if she'd fallen out of that tree.'

'Stacy, it's stupid and pathetic to bake brownies as an excuse to see a man who has no interest in me.'

'He smiled at you and asked about your nickname,' Stacy countered.

'He was being polite.'

'Maybe. Maybe not. If you don't bake the brownies, you'll never know.'

Pea opened her mouth to say no. Again. But Stacy interrupted. Again.

'Take a chance, Pea. Just one small chance. The worst that can happen is that a bunch of overworked firemen will get a treat. On the other hand, maybe your brownies will work magic and you might actually live out one of those fantasies you usually only dream about . . .' Stacy waggled her brows at Pea.

'Fine!' Pea surprised herself by saying. 'I don't have dance class till this afternoon. I'll bake the damn brownies and drop them off on my way to class.'

'Finally I'm victorious with the Pea-and-men issue! Okay, look, be sure you write a little thank you note, too. On the stationery that has your new work title and letterhead.'

'Huh?'

Stacy rolled her perfect eyes. 'It serves two purposes. He'll know how amazingly successful you are, and he'll also know how to get in touch with you.'

'Great. Yeah. Okay. Whatever.' Pea called Chloe and started to retreat up the steps to her homey porch.

'You'll write the note?' Stacy called.

'I'll write the note.'

Chapter Two

She never knew what to wear. How did most women do it? How did they figure out how to put the right clothes with the right hair with the right shoes? (Shoes! That was a truly nightmarish subject! She could never seem to pick out shoes that didn't look like a cross between someone's grandma and someone's cutesy two-year-old daughter.) Pea pulled at her sweater (why did it look so shapeless? She did have boobs. Really!) and checked herself in the rearview mirror of her fabulous new car. Pea groaned. Her makeup looked wrong. She couldn't put her finger on exactly what was wrong about it, but it just wasn't . . . wasn't . . . wasn't anything. It wasn't cute or sophisticated or sexy. And why did the new eye shadow she'd just talked herself into buying yesterday suddenly look orangish instead of the lovely blushing peach color it had seemed to be in the store? Naturally the eye shadow now clashed horribly with her mauve lipstick, which was all over her teeth. Pea rubbed it off vigorously. Then she glanced at her hair. How could the sky be clear and there be zero humidity today in Oklahoma, but her hair was still capable of frizzing out like the puff ball on a dandelion? What had she been thinking when she left it down? With a sigh of resignation, she pulled the scrunchie out of her purse and wrapped it around her hair. Then she grabbed the plate of brownies and walked through the parking lot to the front door of the fire station.

It didn't open. Were they closed? It was Saturday, but still. Fire stations didn't close. Did they? They'd been at her house earlier that day. And fires happened twenty-four seven. No way could they actually be closed. Had she gone to the wrong door? She stood there, chewing her lip and looking around what she had assumed to be the front entrance to the old fashioned brick fire station. Maybe she should just leave the plate of brownies. They were wrapped in aluminum foil; they'd be fine. And she had written a quick thank you note (signed by Chloe), so they'd figure out who they were from, and probably wouldn't worry about being poisoned by them or anything. Did firemen worry about being poisoned by thank you food? Maybe this hadn't been such a good idea.

Pea chewed her lip some more.

This kind of thing was exactly what Stacy had talked to her about time and time again. Stacy wouldn't just stand out here, undecided and pathetic with zillions of questions zinging through her mind. Stacy would have gone to the right door or whatever. Who was she kidding? The firemen would have caught one glimpse of blonde and beautiful through the obviously two-way glass that framed the door (oh, great – were they all in there watching *her* right then?) and there would have been a mass rush to get the door open for her before—

'Ma'am?' The door opened and a man she recognized as one of the guys who had carried the ladder to the tree looked out at her.

'Oh, hi. The door was locked.'

'Yes ma'am. It's always locked. You just have to ring the bell there on the side.'

'Oh,' Pea said, her face going hot as she saw the little sign over the doorbell that read PLEASE RING FOR ENTRANCE. 'I brought Griffin these to thank him for getting my dog out of the tree,' she blurted out and lifted the plate.

'Hey, you're the lady with the tree-climbing Scottie!' He laughed.

'Yep. That's me.'

'Come on in. I'll get the captain.'

He held the door for her and then motioned for her to sit on a bench that rested against the little lobbylike foyer. Pea sat and tried not to be too obvious about gawking around the fire station. About ten feet or so in front of her there was an arched doorway that led to the garage area where the fire trucks were kept. She could see the smooth cement floor and the front bumper of the nearest truck. To her right there was a counter that wrapped around to form what looked like a little communications area, complete with multipleline phone equipment and complex radio stuff. The man who was sitting there nodded briefly to her and then went back to his book, which Pea recognized as Christopher Moore's latest.

'I love Chris Moore's books,' she said conversationally.

He glanced over the top of the trade paperback and grunted.

'I think he's hilarious,' she said.

'Yeah,' he said, this time without looking at her.

'*Bloodsucking Fiends* is my favorite, but I love *Lamb*, too,' Pea said. By now she knew the drill. She'd try to make polite conversation, and he would make noises like he was pretending to listen to her. Men did it all the time. She had a theory that men only attempted to listen to really beautiful women – and then they were mostly only attempting to listen because it might get them into the beauty's panties. With women who were average – like her – they didn't even pretend to attempt to listen.

'Yeah,' he said absently, proving her theory correct. Again.

Pea sighed and started to chew her lip again – and then stopped. She looked at the fireman. Actually he was only an averagely attractive guy himself. Kinda youngish, like in his late twenties – he was probably only a year or two younger than her. He had nondescript brownish hair and an ordinary face and body. Of course, he had on the fireman's casual uniform – navy blue T-shirt, with the Tulsa Fire Department's logo in gold, and navy blue pants – so that probably made him more interesting looking. But still. The guy was *average*. Like Pea. And suddenly, just like that, it started to piss her off that he thought it was okay to ignore her. That everyone thought it was okay to ignore her.

'Uh huh, Chris Moore is a great storyteller,' Pea said. 'Whenever I read his books I laugh so hard that I give birth to a whole litter of those flying monkeys from *The Wizard of Oz*,' she said sweetly.

'Yeah,' the guy said.

'Wonder if there's something you can take to cure that.'

Pea made a strangled yelping noise that probably made her sound like Chloe. Her gaze shot from the clueless average guy to the doorway of the garage, where Griffin was standing, arms folded, grinning at her.

'Cure what?' the guy behind the counter said.

'Nothin', Honeyman. Don't worry about it,' Griffin said, still smiling at Pea.

Pea swallowed and wished frantically that her face didn't feel so hot. Again. It meant that she was blushing a bright, painful pink color that there was no way to pass off as attractively flushed cheeks.

'I was just, um . . .' Pea trailed off. What could she say she had just been doing? *I was just being a total smartass because your coworker was rudely ignoring me*. No, that wouldn't do. She raised the plate of brownies like she was making an offering at the shrine of the Forget-the-Stupid-Thing-I-Just-Said God. 'I brought you some brownies. As a thank you.'

Griffin wrinkled his brow and Pea realized he didn't remember who she was. A-freaking-gin! It had been three and a half hours since he'd rescued Chloe from the tree, and he'd forgotten her. For the fourth time. Great. How totally and typically embarrassing. Pea stood up and quickly placed the plate on the counter – thinking that's what she should have done in the first place. Just left the damn plate there with the stupid note and gone on to dance class before—

'Oh, that's right,' Griffin said, recognition clearing the confusion from his expression. 'You're my neighbor. Chloe the Scottie cat's mom.' He paused a beat and then chuckled before adding, 'Pea.'

'Yeah, Chloe and I just wanted to say thanks.' Pea pointed at the aluminum foil-wrapped plate, trying not to blush again, this time in pleasure, because he'd finally remembered her. 'We baked brownies. Well, actually, I baked them. She and Max begged for a taste.'

'Max, the real cat in the family?'

Pea felt another ridiculous rush of pleasure that he'd remembered. 'That's right. The one who's as good a climber downer as a climber upper.' Oh, no. Had she really just said climber downer again? She smiled gaily, hoping somehow he wouldn't notice that she was the biggest dork in the known universe. 'You won't ever have to rescue Max.'

'That wouldn't be a problem, ma'am,' he said, pretending to tip an imaginary hat. 'It's all part of the job.'

'We just wanted to say thanks,' Pea said, feeling herself getting caught in the blue depths of his eyes.

'Thank you, that was nice of you, and we always appreciate food around here,' Griffin said.

'Thank you,' Pea said, and then realized she had thanked him several times and had now begun thanking him for thanking her for thanking him. Well, hell. 'Okey-dokey then. I'll just leave the brownies. Don't worry about the plate. It's old. You can just throw it away when you're done. Or keep it. Or whatever.' Oh, God. She was babbling. 'Well, thanks again. And you guys stay safe out there.' Pea gave Griffin a jaunty little salute and then bolted out the door.

Her limited edition Thunderbird was a cream-colored sanctuary, which she decided was a perfect analogy since she had about as much social couth as Quasimodo. Pea closed the door and leaned her forehead against the steering wheel.

'I saluted him,' she said miserably. 'I really shouldn't be allowed out in public without supervision.'

◆ ◆ ◆

Dance class, which had been Pea's weekly escape from the annoyances and disappointments of the world for twenty-five of her almost thirty years, didn't work its magic that day. She felt sluggish and Madam Ringwater, her ancient but timelessly competent ballet instructor, had to reprimand her sharply for missing basic movements. Twice.

Pea couldn't stop thinking about Griffin.

She knew it was silly and childish and unrealistic, but she was smitten. Her year-long crush-from-a-distance had morphed into a full-blown close-encounter crush.

She was an idiot.

'Dorreth! Concentration, *merci*. I clearly asked for *battement tendu jeté* and not the *battement dégagé* you so sloppily performed.' Madam Ringwater stamped her practice stick against the smooth wood floor of the studio and spoke sharply in her thick French accent. '*Faites-l'encore!* Do it again!'

Pea gritted her teeth and began the delicate lift of her toe from the floor, trying to focus and move in time with the classical music.

Griffin had smiled at her and met her eyes. Twice. Stacy had even said she thought he was interested in her, and Stacy should know. She was happily married to Ken-doll looking Matt, and men still showed way too much interest in her.

Maybe she was right. Maybe he had been interested in her.

Then Pea remembered how Griffin hadn't even really recognized her, for the fourth time, when he'd first seen her at the fire station, and her stomach sank. No. He was just being nice and polite like a fireman should be. What was it he'd said? *It's all part of the job.*

But if she were gorgeous ... or somehow memorable ... maybe then his little almost-interest would change into real interest. And how was that supposed to happen? How was she supposed to become memorable?

Didn't she remember how disastrous it was to try to pretend to be something she wasn't? All she had to do was to think back to her freshman year in high school, and like it was yesterday instead of a decade or more ago, she remembered all too well that humiliation ... embarrassment ... failure. ...

No. The past was the past. She was a grown-assed woman now. She shouldn't let that childish stuff still mess with her. But she did.

With a huge effort, Pea pushed the memories from her mind and focused on her reflection in the wall-sized studio mirrors. She saw what she always saw. Plain, ordinary Pea. She had on her gray dance sweats, which were rolled down around her hips (which really weren't hips at all – she was too damn little to have those fabulous curvy, luscious hips she'd always envied in other

31

women). Her *ballet IS the pointe* long-sleeved T-shirt was tied up just under her ribcage, exposing way more of her skin than Pea was normally comfortable showing. But this was dance class, and dance class was somehow on a different standard when it came to showing skin and such. She wished she had great boobs to fill out the top of the shirt, but she didn't. She had what Stacy's daughter had once called bumps. Little bumps. Her hair was, as usual, crazily escaping from scrunchie bondage, and brown tendrils of it were plastered against her flushed and sweaty face. She hated her hair. Truly hated it.

Okay, but at least she wasn't all fat and saggy and out of shape. Truthfully she'd probably never sag. Her internal editor whispered nastily that was because she didn't have anything to sag, but Pea forced herself to ignore the voice in her head that was always so negative. It didn't really matter why she wouldn't sag – it just mattered that she wouldn't. Right? She didn't give herself time to answer the question; instead she took her mind down a path she rarely ventured.

Maybe she did have something that could be worked into unique or memorable. Or at least maybe she could have something attractive about her, like Stacy kept saying. Maybe she just needed some direction so she could develop her self-confidence. She wasn't in high school anymore, and there were no hateful girls on the dance squad to humiliate her and call her names. She was a successful adult. Actually she had managed to attain self-confidence about several things: ballet, cooking, her job as program director of Tulsa Community College. She even had self-confidence about her ability to create a great home.

She stared at herself in the mirror as she manically *battement tendu jeté*-ed. Why was it so hard for her to transfer the self-confidence that permeated the rest of her life to her personal style and appearance? Was it just her past that was holding her back? Her fear that if she tried and this time, as an adult, failed, she would truly be forever doomed to the ranks of wallflower and undesirable dork?

'Enough! We are *fini* for today, Dorreth,' Madam Ringwater said, with a look of disgust. 'You cannot *concentré sur le ballet* when your mind is on the boudoir.'

Pea gasped and froze mid-toe lift. 'But Madam Ringwater, I'm not—'

The ancient dance instructor lifted her well manicured hand, silencing Pea. '*L'amour fait des imbéciles de nous tous.* Now go. Next time you will work twice as hard, *oui?*'

'Okay. Yes. I'm sorry, Madam, I just . . .' Pea shrugged, not really knowing if she felt embarrassed or pleased. Impulsively she hugged the old woman before she grabbed her towel and hurried out of the studio. No one had ever said anything like that to her before! No one had ever even implied that *she* might be preoccupied with what went on in her bedroom. Maybe her life was changing.

Well, she was willing – she was! She would . . . she would . . . Pea chewed her lip as she got in her car and backed out of the studio parking lot. She would not let this . . . whatever it was that had suddenly grabbed hold of her go. Pea drove aimlessly for a while, and then her eyes widened when she saw the big red-and-white Borders sign for the Twenty-first Street store. That was it! She'd go into the bookstore and research how to get some style – some sense of nonordinaryness. She could figure out how to cook a gourmet meal, change her oil, tear down old wallpaper and make a room look magnificent. She could even plan classes for the entire continuing education department at her college. Surely she could teach herself how to be less . . . less . . . dorky.

Why had she not thought of it like that before? She knew the answer all too well. She had let the past rule her present. Pea wanted to slap herself on the forehead. Well, she wasn't going to let it control her future! Personal style wasn't some kind of dark, mysterious, unknown woman's territory that was off limits to her. It was just something she needed to learn. And this damn sure wasn't high school anymore. Post-high school and college she'd learned how to do all sorts of hard things. Successfully. Style had to be just another learnable skill. Sure, it was too embarrassing to ask someone like perfect, Barbie-like Stacy to teach her personal style, but couldn't she just read about it? Man, oh man! She'd been such an idiot! She'd already maybe kinda attracted an incredibly handsome man's attention who she'd been crushing on for a year. Didn't that mean she at least had potential to work with? Pea was going to make herself believe it did. She parked right in front of Borders and, like a woman with a mission, marched into the store.

Chapter Three

It wasn't until she'd seen the matron sobbing semi-hysterically in the women's self-help aisle that she thought about the English translation to the French sentence Madam Ringwater had said to her. *L'amour fait des imbéciles de nous tous*, Pea suddenly realized, meant *Love makes fools of us all.* She tried not to stare at the weeping woman who was holding a copy of a book titled *Why Men Love Bitches*.

Pea decided that maybe she was in the wrong section and left women's self-help to cross through the gay and lesbian studies section. No point in stopping there. Not unless she wanted to change teams. She paused and considered whether she'd be interested in having sex with a woman. No. Well at least she was sure about that. Pea left that section and moved to the adjoining shelves labeled New Age, where the brightly colored spines snagged her attention.

The first pretty book she pulled off the shelf was titled *Magick & Rituals of the Moon.* Curious, Pea thumbed through it. Chapter titles like 'The Full Moon Esbat' and 'Waxing and Waning Moon Magick' were as foreign to Pea as they were intriguing. She put the book back and let her eyes roam over the other titles. *Earth Power, Powerful Protection Magic*, and *Magical Rites from the Crystal Well* continued to pique her interest. Wow! She'd never heard of any of these books – or any of these ideas. Was this witchcraft? She noticed a book titled *Wicca Demystified* by Bryan

Lankford. Huh. Guess some of it was witchcraft. Pea shrugged, literally and figuratively. At least there were no sobbing women in this aisle. Then something flickered at the edge of her vision. Something like the flutter of butterfly wings or maybe the faint sputter of a candle in a breeze. Pea turned and she felt a little catch in her breath, as if someone had just whispered a cool secret to her. The hardback book's spine was the color of heavy cream and it beckoned with its richness. In silver script the title appeared to shine: *Discover the Goddess Within – Unleash Venus and Open Your Life to Love*. Her hand reached out, almost hesitantly, even though her full attention had been captured by the book. With a subdued *shush* sound it slid free from between the two books pressed against it.

Pea ran her fingers over the cover. The title was there in raised silver embossed script, along with the author's name, Juno Panhellenius, which should have seemed weird, but Pea thought instead it felt right that the author's name evoked a sense of ancient magic and mystery. The only decoration on the cover was the silver outline of a timeless (and very curvy) goddess figure. Her arms were upraised with the full moon resting between her hands. The goddess looked sexy and mysterious and desirable. Pea thought how odd it was that the book felt cool beneath the balls of her fingertips. She opened it and glanced down the table of contents: 'Know Venus and Know Confidence,' 'Know Venus and Know Beauty,' 'Know Venus and Know Sexual Confidence' ... and on and on until, finally, 'Know Venus – Evoke the Goddess!'

A trickle of excitement skittered through Pea's body. That was it! If she could teach herself to have the confidence of a goddess then surely she'd no longer be invisible! And what better goddess than the Goddess of Love, Venus herself? Who could ignore

Venus? If a woman had the allure of a goddess, what couldn't she do? (Or *who* couldn't she do?) Giggling softly, Pea clutched the book to her chest and hurried toward the checkout line.

Pea felt light and happy and hopeful as she pulled out of the Borders parking lot and, on impulse, headed downtown. She checked the time – five thirty-five. Yes! Her favorite restaurant, Lola's at the Bowery, would be open, but it was still early enough that it wouldn't be too crowded. She'd grab the corner table, which was perfect for reading, and order her favorite appetizer, the Italian antipasto platter. Oooh! She might even treat herself to one of Lola's specialty martinis; it'd be like she was on holiday!

What better way to turn a new page in her life?

'Admit it, Venus. I was right,' Persephone said.

'You were, and I don't mind admitting it. Tulsa is simply marvelous! I can't believe you've been keeping the secret of this modern kingdom to yourself,' Venus said.

'I'm not keeping it a secret! I told you about it.'

'Ha! Only after I saw those divine boots.'

'Of which you now own a pair, too.'

'Along with these adorable earrings!' Venus shook her head so that the long, hand-beaded dangles danced around her graceful throat. 'What was that wonderful bead place called again?'

'The Bead Gallery. The modern woman I'm friends with, Lina Santoro, introduced me to Donna Prigmore's gallery during one of my early trips here. As Lina says, she makes jewelry fit for a goddess.'

'So true, and such a lovely surprise. I'll also admit you were right about these drinks.' Venus sipped from the frosty martini glass and moaned dramatically in almost sexual pleasure. 'What did you call this inspired creation?'

'It's one of Lola's specialty martinis. You're drinking the Nuptial, a mixture of Skyy vanilla vodka and butterscotch schnapps. It says on the menu that you'll love it so much it'll be till death do you part!'

'Very appropriate for the Goddess of Love,' Venus said, laughing, and then she lowered her voice. 'Oops! By Hera's freezing tits it's hard to remember that no one knows who I am here, so I really should be careful about what I say.'

'Venus. Honey. Calling yourself a goddess won't make modern mortals believe you're *really* a goddess, but using that archaic curse will get you some weird looks from them. Not to mention you'd make Hera mad if she heard you.' Persephone grinned. 'And, anyway, how do you know her tits are freezing?'

'Well, they must be. She's always all' – the Goddess of Love paused and searched for the right word – 'nippley. You know it's true. And she always wears those see-through white chitons. Who could miss her *arousal?* They're so puckered and erect. It makes me think Zeus might not be taking care of her needs. As Goddess of Love, perhaps I should speak to him—'

Persephone choked on her martini, and then sputtered. 'Now that is something I want to see! You questioning the almighty Zeus about whether he's an adequate lover or not!'

'It's perfectly my right to question even Zeus.' Venus sniffed haughtily. 'Love is always my business.' Then her eyes widened and she grinned mischievously. 'Which is exactly why I bought . . .' The goddess reached down and pulled a long, cylinder-shaped box from one of the shopping bags by her feet. 'This!' She raised the box with a flourish.

Persephone shook her head and tried, unsuccessfully, to stifle a giggle. 'I can't believe you actually bought that thing.'

'How could I not after reading its name?' She pointed to the shiny black box that had the words *Venus D'My Lay* written in bright scarlet letters across it. 'How do you get in this thing?'

'You're going to open it? Right here?'

Venus glanced up at her, violet eyes bemused. 'Why not?'

'Well, it looks like a . . .'

Venus managed to wrestle open the lid and slide out its contents. Holding it up, she finished for Persephone, 'A big black phallus!'

'It certainly does.' Persephone stared. 'Actually it's disturbingly real. What does it feel like?'

Venus caressed the long, black shaft, running her slender fingers knowingly over its rounded head and fleshlike ridges and veins. 'It feels nice. Much more realistic than the phalli the ancients carve. I mean, really. Not even a god's penis truly gets as hard as marble, no matter what Apollo may boast. How does it work?' Venus enthusiastically shook the huge dildo with a jerking-it-off motion, getting several interesting looks from men sitting at the bar, which she chose, for the moment, not to acknowledge. 'It says it vibrates, but it's not vibrating.' She frowned.

'Give me that thing. You have to put in the batteries.'

'Batteries?'

'Modern magic that makes it work.'

'Oooh.' Venus sipped her martini while she watched Persephone insert batteries into the shaft of the phallus. 'So those things will really cause it to vibrate?'

'That's what the girl at Pricilla's Toy Box said.'

'She was oddly pierced. Did she remind you of an Amazon warrior, too?' Venus asked.

'Now that you mention it, there was something wild and warriorlike about her. She might not quite be an Amazon, but

I think Artemis would approve of her,' Persephone said. 'Here. Try turning it on now.' She passed the penis across the table and pointed to the hidden switch in its base. Venus stroked it on. The huge member came alive, humming happily.

Venus gasped. 'By Zeus's swinging testicles! It is magic!'

'Okay.' Persephone looked quickly around the chic restaurant, frowning severely at the men at the bar who were clearly being very entertained by Venus's uninhibited show. She took the vibrator from the goddess, flipped it off and put it back in its box. 'You really might want to rethink the divine genitalia cursing.'

'What?'

'The tits and testicles of the Olympians just aren't used as curses here.' She dropped the Venus D'My Lay in the shopping bag and unobtrusively kicked the bag under their table.

'Persephone. I am Goddess of Love.' Venus kept her voice low but firm. 'It's always appropriate for me to curse using references to genitals. Anyone's genitals.'

'Do you want to fit in here?'

'Of course! I adore modern mortals. I can already tell that the men are appreciative without being sycophants. And the women move with such a delicious sense of freedom and power. I plan on spending many happy days exploring this wonderful kingdom.'

'Then leave the genitals of the gods and goddesses out of it.'

Venus frowned, looking unusually pensive. 'I'm not sure I can. You know I prefer to refer to love whenever I can.'

Persephone raised one delicate eyebrow. 'Love?'

'Naturally. Genitals equal love – love equals genitals. Persephone, darling, do we need to have a more private talk? How have your orgasms been lately? Are you experiencing multiple releases? And when you don't have a partner, have you been pleasuring yourself adequately?'

Persephone raised her hands, palms out. 'Stop. You win. Use whatever curses please you most. Just be prepared to be questioned about them.'

'I'm always prepared to answer questions about love.' Venus smiled sweetly. 'But first I want . . .' She caught the young waitress's eye and waggled her fingers at their two almost-empty martini glasses.

'Did you ladies want another round?'

'Darling, you said your name was Jenny, didn't you?' Venus asked.

'That's right.' The waitress smiled. 'Two more martinis?'

'Yes, but this time let's try the Wake,' Persephone said.

'Excellent! You'll love it. I'll bring those right out.'

'The Wake?' Venus asked Persephone after Jenny hurried off.

'It's yummy – chocolate liqueur, espresso, vodka, ice crystals . . .' She licked her lips and shivered in delight. 'Trust me on this.'

'Oh, I do! It sounds decadent. I'm certain I'll love it. I've loved everything else in this kingdom.'

'Okay, you're really going to have to quit calling it that. There's no such thing as a kingdom of Tulsa. It's just Tulsa. Like Rome is just Rome, not the kingdom of Rome.'

Venus scoffed. 'Try telling those obsessively patriotic ancient Romans they're not a kingdom.'

'Point taken. I used a bad example. Here's the thing – you can be eccentric and different here – that's fine. You're incredibly beautiful—'

'Why thank you darling!' Venus interrupted.

'I'm just stating the truth. Anyway, you can get away with being . . . well . . . what modern mortals will consider weird because of your beauty.'

'Weird? I am not weird.'

'By Athena's widening ass you certainly are!' Persephone said, mimicking her friend's voice and using one of her all-time favorite curses.

Venus's violet eyes sparkled. 'Athena's ass is getting big. Come on. Admit it. She's become far too serious! All, "Look at me! I'm the gray-eyed Goddess of War, Wisdom and the Arts." ' She exaggerated a yawn. 'She needs to loosen up and in more ways than one. A few stretching exercises and a good jog would help her out as much as taking a lover or two.'

'You're incorrigible.' Persephone laughed. 'And you're not going to get me off the subject that easily. You can use your genital curses. You can even get way too personal about other people's love lives. But you can't go around calling Tulsa a kingdom.'

'Fine, fine, fine. It's not a kingdom. It's a city. I've got it. I'll remember. It's just that I'm having so much fun! I adore Tulsa and its mixture of cheeky modern men and confident modern women, especially because none of them have any idea who I am.'

'I told you it would be a freeing experience to visit the modern world.'

'Well I am Love, and I can officially say that Love is in love with Tulsa!'

The waitress put two fresh martinis on their table, along with two slender white slices of an exquisitely decorated cake. 'Here are your Wakes, ladies. And the owner, Lola, is testing out a new dessert – personal wedding cake. Please sample it with her blessing.'

'Wedding cake!' Venus laughed and clapped her hands together in a spontaneous show of girlish pleasure. 'How perfectly appropriate.'

'Are you getting married?' the young waitress asked.

'Me? No! I've been married forever. That's not why it's appropriate. It's just that I am Love. Naturally wedding cake should be a favorite of mine.'

The waitress continued to smile politely, but her face had turned into a question mark.

'She means she's fixed up a lot of her friends. Sometimes we just call her Love,' Persephone explained.

'She's good at fixing up people? That's cool.'

'You have no idea,' Venus mumbled through a big bite of wedding cake. 'Paris and Helen, Pygmalion and—'

'Thanks for the cake!' Persephone interrupted smoothly. 'And keep an eye on our martinis; we'll want at least one more round.'

'Will do.'

When she was gone Persephone bit into her own slice of cake while she shook her head at Venus.

'What? You don't like the cake. I think it's wonderful.'

'The cake is excellent. You, on the other hand, are a mess.'

Venus took a sip of the new martini and moaned softly in pleasure. 'By Apollo's golden phallus this is delicious!'

'Venus, could you please, please, please try to remember that to the modern mortals Troy existed thousands of years ago? And to them Pygmalion carving Galatea out of marble was just a myth.'

'Pygmalion? A myth? Impossible. He was a dreadful woman hater before I played matchmaker.' She grinned mischievously. 'Matchmaking with a statue. I must say that I outdid myself that time. How could people believe that love story was a myth?'

'You knew them!' Persephone hissed. 'And you're used to magic, unlike modern mortals.'

Venus cocked her head to the side and studied Persephone. 'You seem very tense. When was the last time you orgasmed?'

'That has nothing to do with it.'

'Of course it does. When was the last time?'

'Five days ago.'

'See there!' Venus nodded vigorously as if she'd just proved an excellent point to an attentive audience. 'That's your problem.'

'I don't have a problem.'

'Well you won't if we get you properly laid.' Venus looked around the restaurant, clearly checking out the men at the bar.

'No. Really. I'm fine. And if I'm not I do have a rather long list of mortal men I can call on,' she said smugly.

'Excellent. Then do so. Five days without a proper orgasm is entirely too long. But are you sure you don't want me to work a little love magic for you?' She waggled her long, shapely fingers and diamondlike glitter began to form in the air around them.

'No!' Persephone yelped, grabbing Venus's hand and causing the love dust to fall in a small, sparkling heap on their table. She quickly blew on the powdery substance and then went into a sneezing fit when it danced in the air around them before disappearing back into the Goddess of Love's fingertips.

'Be careful,' Venus said as she finished the last of her cake. 'That stuff isn't good for your lungs.'

'Thanks for reminding me,' Persephone said sardonically while she sniffed delicately. 'Just never mind on the love magic stuff. I'm doing fine on my own. Plus you know what happens when you get too involved in the love lives of the gods.'

'What are you talking about? I have made uncounted matches – *happy* matches.'

'Yes, you have. Happy matches between mortals. When you mess with our love lives, as in the immortals, of which I am one, things tend to go wrong. Drastically wrong.'

'You exaggerate.'

'Exhibit A – Athena and Odysseus. You decided Athena needed to love a mortal. Look me in the eye and tell me your meddling didn't cause the man to be absent from his wife and family for twenty years.'

Venus shrugged and looked uncomfortable. 'If Athena hadn't been so obsessive that little affair wouldn't have been such a bad thing.'

'So you're admitting it was a bad thing?'

'Maybe.'

'Fine. Exhibit B – the Scylla/Glaucus/Circe debacle.'

'That's not fair. I had no idea that Circe was so attached to Glaucus. I thought he and Scylla made a lovely match. You know I did think he was just scrumptious after he became a water deity. How was I to know that Scylla rejecting him would make Circe so jealous?' Venus pouted. 'I really don't know how you can hold that against me.'

'Okay. How about Exhibit C – Zeus and—'

'I get the point. Although how you could blame me for any of Zeus's silly affairs I'll never know,' she muttered. 'Anyway I won't meddle in your love life. Right now,' she added under her breath. 'But I do have the urge to, I don't know, *arrange* something for these fabulous mortals. Kind of as a payback for having such a lovely time in their *city*.' She enunciated the word distinctly, getting a grin from Persephone.

'Hey, meddle away with the mortals. It's fine with me. Whether they are aware of it or not, they're lucky to have the Goddess of Love be so interested.'

'Really!' Venus brightened. 'Matchmaking always gets my womanly juices flowing.'

'Venus. Please. TMI.'

'TMI?'

'Too much information. Keep your woman's juices to yourself.'

'You know, for Spring, you really are a prude.' She narrowed her eyes at Persephone. 'When was the last time you gazed at the beauty of your sacred lotus blossom with a mirror?'

Persephone choked on her martini.

'Just as I thought. You need to spend more private time with the core of your womanhood.'

'Mortals. Focus on the mortals, Venus,' Persephone said between coughs.

'If you insist . . .' Venus said, turning her attention to the mortals surrounding them even while she filed away in her mind that she'd have Persephone sent a special mirror when she got back to Mount Olympus.

Then all thoughts of Persephone and mirrors fled her mind as a group of laughing men entered the restaurant. They took seats at the gleaming oak bar and began a good-natured flirtation with Lola herself, who had emerged from the kitchen and was one of those timelessly attractive women who could have been anywhere from thirty-five to fifty-five and who would still be confident and sexy at sixty-five and seventy-five. Obviously the group of men were regulars as well as favorites with Lola and her waitstaff.

'Who are they?' Venus asked Persephone.

'*Firemen* . . .' Persephone purred the word.

Chapter Four

Highlighter in hand, Pea was poring over her new book. *Discover the Goddess Within – Unleash Venus and Open Your Life to Love* was propped open with two butter knives so that she could nibble on the delicious antipasto platter and keep reading at the same time. She'd breezed through the chapters on confidence and beauty and good sex, highlighting sections she needed to go back and study more thoroughly.

Wow! The book was such an eye-opener! She'd heard all her life about self-fulfilling prophecies and how envisioning things could make them happen, and she totally believed in that kind of stuff working for career advancement. That's one reason she just got a fabulous promotion from assistant program director of Tulsa Community College's Continuing Education Department to honest-to-god director. She was now her own boss, answering only to the president of the college and her board. And she was the youngest director at the college. But she had always believed in her management skills and knew beyond any doubt she was savvy in choosing teachers and classes that appealed to the adults in the community. Under her influence the adult ed department had become a popular, successful addition to the college curriculum.

She'd just never thought she could use the same logic and positive thought process to fix the lacks in her personal life. No. It was more than that. As she read the book and really thought about self-fulfilling prophecies she realized that she'd been self-fulfilling her personal ineptness that had started in high school. And boy did that seem silly. Basically hateful teenagers were still influencing her – a grown-ass woman. But this book was going to help her change all of that; it was going to give her a whole new viewpoint. The more she read, the more intrigued she became. It was filled with matriarchal beliefs all centering around the value of today's women and what was, apparently, an ancient belief in the divinity of the feminine. What a magical thought! That she was special and worthy of love, just because she held a piece of the Divine Feminine within her! It was heady, really, and more intoxicating than the wonderful pomegranate martini she was savoring.

She devoured the book and even ordered a second pomegranate martini. Why not splurge a little? She was, after all, a fabulous woman who deserved to be touched by the strong, sexy spark of the Divine Feminine! Pea turned eagerly to the final chapter, 'Know Venus – Evoke the Goddess!' Her eyes scanned the relatively short chapter, widening in surprise. It said that she had to memorize the invocation prayer to Venus, and then as she was pleasuring herself to orgasm, she was supposed to recite the invocation aloud. The Goddess of Love would then hear her and bless her with the power of love and beauty, confidence and desire. In other words, all the things Pea so desperately desired.

Okay, sure, it sounded bizarre – to masturbate while she was reciting a goddess invocation, and the old Pea would never had done such a thing. Actually the old Pea had never been very comfortable with the whole masturbation issue. Sure, she did it, but not very often and she always felt, well, *embarrassed* afterward. But that was the old Pea, and the old Pea was an insecure dork. The new Pea turned the page and began memorizing the invocation.

> Pleasure, joy, delight and bliss,
> Oh dear Venus, grant me this.
> With love and hope I call to thee,
> Work your magic just for me.
> Beautiful Venus, blessed be,
> Happiness and ecstasy
> Are the gifts I ask from thee!

And then she was supposed to orgasm. Pea sighed. It was going to take some serious memorization to get all of that right. So she got to work, taking the invocation line by line while she gnawed on the raw veggies left on the antipasto tray and tried not to gulp her second martini. A sudden vibrating sound and a gale of musical laughter totally interrupted her concentration. Pea looked up from the book and had to stifle her own giggles. Two utterly gorgeous women were sipping martinis while they passed back and forth a humongous black dildo, which was now vibrating for all it was worth. Pea couldn't believe she hadn't noticed them there before. They were the kind of women even women stared at. From her little tucked away corner table it was easy for Pea to watch them without being obvious. How in the world could two women have such totally perfect hair? One woman, who looked like she might be the younger of the two, although neither of them looked a day older than thirty, had long, thick brunette hair that was the color of rich earth or expensive mahogany furniture. The other woman's hair was long, too, lapping down well past her shoulder blades in bountiful, sun-filled waves. No, that wasn't right. Her hair was more

silver/white than gold — more like moonlight than sunlight —
but it did shimmer and shine like a precious metal.

Automatically Pea's hand went to her own hair. Even
though it was still pulled severely back in a ponytail from
ballet class, she could feel the brown frizzies that habitu-
ally escaped from it. Her hair was long, too. Really long. Of
course no one could tell that except when it was wet. After
it dried it kinked up into a puffy brown fuzz-balled mess.
No matter how much brushing she did it never straightened
out and acted right. Never. She'd even tried going to one of
those cool ethnic salons filled with brown-skinned beauties
with incredible hair and asking for straightening help. The
stylist had been nice, but the stuff she'd put in her hair had
just made it greasy, as well as frizzy. She really was the same
hopeless mess she'd been forever.

No! Pea shook herself mentally and stuck her nose back in
the goddess book. She was done with that defeatist attitude.
There was no way the Divine Feminine knowledge of Venus
could thrive in such a negative space.

But memorizing was difficult when the drop-dead gorgeous
women were having such a fun, animated conversation. Pea
couldn't exactly hear what they were saying, but she loved watching them. She chewed a piece of raw broccoli, wishing she hadn't
eaten all of the imported cheese and prosciutto. Maybe she
should go nuts and order another appetizer.

Male voices pulled her attention from the two women and
she felt a little zap of shock as she recognized the first man in the
door. It was Griffin! Actually it was all of the firemen who had
answered the call about Chloe. They were still in their casual
navy blue uniforms with Tulsa Fire Department printed in
faded gold across their chests and backs. They filled up the long

bar, joking and flirting with the chic lady Pea recognized as Lola, the owner of the restaurant.

Reluctantly Pea turned her attention from the firemen – Griffin in particular – back to the beautiful women. Rocklike, her heart sank into her stomach. Of course the two of them had noticed the entrance of one entire shift of firemen. And it was only a matter of time before the firemen, in turn, noticed the gorgeous women. Then what would happen next was more than predictable. The women would join the men and flirt and talk and laugh and probably get dates. The blonde was the most stunning of the stunning, and Griffin was her equal in masculine beauty. Of course they'd notice each other. How could they not? Beautiful people like that were made to be together. They'd probably fall in love, get married and have a litter of totally beautiful children. How depressing.

In the meantime, no damn body would notice her.

'Pea, can I get you anything else?'

The waitress's question made her jump and Pea could feel her cheeks heating at being caught staring at the two women. It made her feel like she was a kid up past her bedtime stealing a peek at the adult world. Nervously she stood up and grabbed her purse. She'd cover her ridiculous embarrassment by going to the ladies' room. Pea opened her mouth to tell the waitress that no thanks, she was finished and she'd just take the check, when, to her eternal mortification, what came out instead of words was the biggest, loudest, stinkiest burp in the history of the known universe. It seemed to echo against the glass liquor-filled cabinets that covered the wall behind the bar and hang in an odoriferous broccoli cloud around her. For a change, instead of being invisible, the entire restaurant turned to stare at Pea.

'Damn, girl! That one sounded ripe,' said a fireman who had graying hair and the beginnings of a pot belly. He slapped his thick thigh and chortled.

Pea wanted to die. She wanted to melt into the floor and slither under the door so that she could re-form outside in the parking lot far away from everyone who was still staring at her and then quietly and privately die. Naturally instead of doing something calm and cool and collected, like putting a couple of twenties on the table and sauntering out the door, Pea blurted, 'Excuse me. Sorry. Raw veggies always give me gas.' She heard the hysterical giggle and realized that it was coming from her mouth. Why couldn't she make it stop? Finally she was able to say with a gasp, 'I'll take my check after I go to the ladies' room.'

Keeping her head down, she practically sprinted past the men at the bar and the two gorgeous women. She could feel their eyes on her and she knew her face was, ironically, bright, shining, fire truck red. Escaping to the ladies' room she darted into a stall and buried her hot face in her hands. It was going to take a lot more studying before she was ready to be undorked by Venus or anyone else.

As Hera silently watched Vulcan study the images in his sacred fire, she reminded herself that she should always follow her intuition. Her instincts had told her to check on her son. Quietly. And here he was, seeming to be enchanted by the scene being played out before him. Hera, too, felt herself becoming intrigued as she watched the vision in the fire. The magical thread Vulcan had sent after Venus and Persephone was functioning much as an oracle. It was an opening to another time or place – and in this case – another world. Persephone and Venus could clearly be seen sitting at a table in an opulent eating establishment. As was typical of the goddesses, they were laughing and generally making merry.

Then, unexpectedly, the focus of the magic thread shifted. Hera decided the girl's shy giggle must have been what first caught her son's attention. Then she had to cover her mouth with her hand and stifle her own surprised laughter, which would probably have not been heard over Vulcan's snort of amusement, as both mother and son noticed the title of the book the mortal was reading.

'*Discover the Goddess Within – Unleash Venus and Open Your Life to Love*. Indeed,' Vulcan muttered, voice thick with sarcasm. 'It's always Venus – always she who gets credit for creating love.'

Hera stayed very still. She'd never heard her son speak of Venus except in terms of kindness and respect, even though all of Olympus knew that their marriage had been a sham from its inception. Rumor said, though she'd not heard the words directly from her son, that Venus and Vulcan had agreed upon a marriage of convenience because joining with the Goddess of Love should have made Vulcan appear more powerful – more Olympian – more accepted by the rest of the gods. And, in turn, joining with the God of Fire gave Venus the excuse she needed when she wanted to absent herself from the constant pursuits of those who longed to possess Love. Hera had always thought the arrangement served Venus much better than it did her son. The Goddess of Love did escape to her husband's realm in the bowels of Olympus when she was weary, and she reemerged refreshed and invigorated. But being married to Love had not made Vulcan more accepted. That it had been clear from the beginning that it was a marriage of convenience had actually worked against Vulcan. The general opinion of the immortals was haughty disbelief. How could one be married to Love, but remain untouched by her?

'Pea?' Vulcan said, and then actually laughed. 'What type of name is Pea?'

Hera just stood there and shook her head silently, continuing to be amazed at her son's show of interest in the small, ordinary-looking mortal.

A horrid sound emanating from the oracle flame brought Hera's attention back to the scene from the modern world. The shy young mortal named Pea had expressed gas! Noisily and messily and in front of everyone! The goddess watched as she fled from the room. How unfortunate for her.

'They should leave her be! She's humiliated enough without others making it worse,' Vulcan said with a growl.

Indeed? Hera thought how interesting it was that her son was showing such interest. The invisible thread of fire followed Pea, so that Hera could see her embarrassment. Vulcan watched, too, and made another angry sound low in his throat. Hmm . . . he was clearly identifying with the mortal woman. A sudden thought struck Hera. Perhaps that was it! Perhaps Vulcan had seemed unable to love because he had long been surrounded by the perfection of Olympus, and perfection had always rejected him. Perhaps he simply needed someone with whom he could identify – someone who might actually need him. She studied the mortal woman with the odd name more closely. It certainly looked like she needed something. Could that something be the love of the God of Fire?

'What is she doing?' Vulcan continued to mutter at the scene within the flames. Hera saw Pea standing at a sink, staring at herself in a mirror while she almost manically recited a—

Hera smiled. The child was a careful reader. She was reciting, over and over, an invocation spell that could only have come from the book that still lay open on the table where Pea had left it. Now wasn't this becoming a lovely twist on an already interesting situation? Hera's mind whirred with ideas ... schemes ... Wouldn't it be deliciously and ironically just if the invocation actually bound Venus's aid, which would in turn assure that Vulcan would continue to watch the mortal woman who had so unexpectedly captured his attention? It was, after all, Venus who Vulcan's magic thread was following. Yes, this was working out perfectly!

When the mortal began reciting the invocation again, Hera was ready to finish putting into motion that which she'd already helped to begin. From the shadows behind Vulcan she concentrated, calling to her the power of the Queen of Gods.

The child said, 'Pleasure, joy, delight and bliss, oh dear Venus, grant me this.'

Hera raised one hand and felt her divine warmth build on her palm as she whispered, *'Hearth and home I call on you. With my divine magic make this rite binding and true.'*

Pea said, 'With love and hope I call to thee, work your magic just for me.'

Hera continued, calling forth more and more of the power that was her birthright. *'Open Vulcan's eyes – let his heart be new, so that Love can finally pay her debt, which I now call due.'*

Closing her eyes, Pea earnestly spoke the final words of the invocation. 'Beautiful Venus, blessed be, happiness and ecstasy are the gifts I ask from thee!'

Almost at the same moment Hera concluded the binding, casting invisible power directly into the thread so that only she was aware of the weight of it as it sizzled from Olympus to Tulsa. *'By my command, hearken to Pea. Bind Venus's aid so that trapped in Tulsa she shall be, until true love sets our mortal free!'*

Instantly Hera felt the drain of such an immense use of power that she stumbled. Vulcan glanced over his shoulder and the image in the fire wavered, then disappeared.

'Mother? I did not hear you come in.'

Smoothly Hera covered her unaccustomed weakness and her eavesdropping by frowning down at the bottom of her silky white robes. 'I believe I've stepped on and torn the hem of my new gown. Vulcan, dear, can you not make the stairs down to your realm a tiny bit little less barbaric and not so steep?'

Vulcan smiled indulgently at his mother as he guided her from the flame room and into his rarely used reception chamber. 'Mother, the descent is steep. You should have just had a nymph summon me.' He poured her a glass of wine and was too busy soothing her to notice that her robe was not torn at all, and her smile was smug.

Chapter Five

'That poor mortal! I feel just awful for her,' Venus said, gazing after the woman who had let out the tremendous belch.

'She has extraordinarily bad hair,' Persephone said.

'It's not that bad. It's just thick and curly and she hasn't managed it properly.'

'Please. It's frizzy and awful. And what about those clothes?' Persephone shuddered. 'Why any woman would wear baggy sweatpants and that horried appliquéd shirt I'll never know.'

'She just needs some help.' Venus sipped her martini, then her eyes widened. 'You know, I could help her!'

'What are you talking about?'

'That poor mortal with the bad hair. I could help her.' Venus nodded enthusiastically, talking quickly over Persephone's protestations. 'I adore this realm, I mean *city*,' she corrected herself. 'It's so much less depressing and banal than say, Troy.' She rolled her violet eyes. 'I believe it would be exhilarating to make a mortal my own special project.'

'That's called community service here, and I can put you in touch with the downtown YWCA if you want to help the general populace—' Persephone began, but Venus cut her off.

'No, no, no. That's not personal enough. Think about it. To be advised, helped, coached, by the Goddess of Love herself! What a lucky mortal that would be.'

'Except no one here knows to ask for your aid. That's part of the beauty of the modern world. Remember?'

'Don't be so negative.'

'I'm not being negative. I'm being honest,' Persephone explained patiently. 'Here you're not a goddess. You're a beautiful, desirable woman. You would only offend a plain little nothing like that unfortunate girl if you began offering unasked for advice.'

Venus sighed. 'Fine. I understand that.' Then she brightened again. 'But if someone did ask for my advice I'd be overjoyed to help. It would be fun. Much more fun than dealing with hard-hearted Anaxarete, or that wretchedly annoying Psyche.'

Persephone shrugged. 'If someone here asks for your advice I don't see any harm in you giving it.'

'Then we are in complete agreement. As if Love would ever butt in where she's not wanted.'

Persephone rolled her eyes.

'Did I notice a ladies' room somewhere in that direction?' Venus asked innocently, pointing vaguely past the bar.

'It's over there through that velvet curtain. But hurry, we need to get going. I just remembered that I promised Mother I would make an appearance in Eleusis tonight. You know, mustn't miss the great festival of Eleusinian Mysteries.' She mimicked Demeter's regal tone and then drained her martini and signaled for Jenny to bring their check.

'I know.' Venus shared an understanding look with Persephone. 'Demeter does get so terribly serious about her festivals. Don't worry. I'll hurry. Oh, don't want to forget this.' She grabbed the Pricilla's Toy Box shopping bag and carried it with her as she walked quickly past the bar, almost ignoring the beautiful men who definitely weren't ignoring her. Even distracted as she was she spared them a small smile and automatically slowed her pace so that her hips moved with a beckoning, seductive roll, causing the firemen to fall silent, hypnotized by her beauty. Venus almost didn't notice. Almost.

She ducked through the curtain and followed the sign that pointed her to the left. The ladies' room wasn't big, but it was neat and very clean. Velvet curtained stalls lined the wall in front of her. She was admiring the way the burgundy fabric seemed to glitter in the light from the vintage chandelier that dangled overhead when she heard the oddest thing.

Someone was speaking her name. No, it was more than that. Someone was invoking her aid! How extraordinary. Quietly she moved forward. The poor belching mortal with the unkempt hair was standing before one of the antique sinks. Staring into the mirror, she was reciting an ancient invocation spell. The words wrapped around Venus like a lovely silken robe, caressing her skin and filling her with what felt suddenly like magical warmth.

'Pleasure, joy, delight and bliss, oh dear Venus, grant me this. With love and hope I call to thee, work your magic just for me. Beautiful Venus, blessed be, happiness and ecstasy are the gifts I ask from thee!'

As the invocation concluded Venus felt a tremendous tug within her, as if something was compelling her very soul to listen to this mortal's cry. She rushed forward, and still holding the Pricilla's Toy Box bag, she spread her arms dramatically.

'Of course I shall aid you!' Venus cried.

Pea gasped and whirled around, her hand going to her throat. 'Oh, shit! You scared me. I thought I was alone in here.'

Venus frowned mildly. 'Not quite the reception I usually receive when I personally answer an invocation.'

'What do you mean? Who are you?'

'Venus, of course. And your name is?'

'Pea,' she said automatically.

'Pea? What an odd name. Are you quite certain?'

'Of course I'm certain. It's *my* name. Well, actually it's my nickname but it's what everyone calls me.' Then Pea blinked, shaking her head like she was trying to clear it while her mind caught up with her words. 'Who did you say you were?'

'Venus, the Goddess of Sensual Love, Beauty and the Erotic Arts,' she replied a little smugly, using the most formal of her titles.

Pea's mouth flopped open.

'You besought my aid, and gladly I offer it to you!' Venus proclaimed with a flourish that made the tissue paper in her shopping bag rustle.

Pea closed her mouth, opened it and then closed it again.

'I understand. You must be overwhelmed with delight.' She walked around Pea, clucking her tongue softly. 'We do have considerable work to do.' Venus reached out and touched her appliquéd *ballet IS the pointe* shirt as if it were a rare insect she had the misfortune to discover. Then she shifted her attention to Pea's hair. Shaking her head she said, 'By Aeolus's gaseous anus, we must do something about this first.'

'What?'

'Your hair, of course. You don't *brush* it, do you?'

'Of course I brush it. What else am I supposed to—' Pea broke off, passing a hand across her forehead and looking utterly confused. 'Look. I don't want to be rude, but how is my hair your business?'

'You invoked my aid. I remember exactly what you asked for – you said, 'Happiness and ecstasy are the gifts I ask from thee.'

I already told you that I'm answering your plea. I'm here to help you find happiness and ecstasy. Clearly you can't find either with such misbehaving hair.'

'Okay. Well. Hmm. That's nice of you. I guess. And I appreciate your, uh, interest, but I'm fine. Really.' She started to move carefully around Venus like she was afraid the woman might suddenly explode.

'I saw you run in here because you were embarrassed,' Venus said gently. 'I don't think you are truly fine.'

Pea's cheeks flushed, but she put on a gay smile. 'Oh, that's just me. I embarrass myself all the time. I'm used to it.'

'If that were true, why does your smile not reach your eyes?'

'It does. I just . . . I'm . . .' Pea floundered. 'I have to go.' She rushed toward the door.

'If you would wash it and then apply a small amount of coconut oil, comb it only with your fingers and let it dry naturally I believe you could begin to tame your hair.'

Pea stopped short of the door. Turning, she met Venus's kind gaze. 'Coconut oil?'

She nodded. 'Pure coconut oil of the highest quality you can acquire. And it is of the utmost importance that you stop combing your hair. Do only this.' Venus ran her fingers gently through her own thick, silver-blonde tresses, starting at her scalp. 'And you must do this, too, to help encourage the curls to be round and full instead of . . .' She paused, searching for the right words. 'Instead of wilful and unruly like the wild mane of a lioness.' Venus reached up and scrunched handfuls of her hair, pretending to have errant curls instead of glistening waves.

'That works?' Pea said hesitantly. 'Really?'

'Would Love lie to one who has invoked her aid?' Venus smiled benevolently.

Pea chewed the side of her lip, her expression telegraphing that she was torn between being intrigued and being certain she was talking with a crazy person. 'Thank you,' she finally said, good manners winning out over all other considerations. 'I'll try it.'

Venus cocked her head to the side thoughtfully. 'Now, before we begin to repair your rather unfortunate manner of dress, I need to know if you are pleasuring yourself regularly.'

'Ohmygod! You did not just ask me that!'

'Of course I did, darling.' Wrinkling her brow, Venus tried not to show her frustration at the mortal's apparent lack of intelligence. 'It's a completely natural question. If you're not pleasuring yourself properly, how can you expect—'

'Stop! After the day I've had I can't take any more.'

'I'm just trying to help.'

'Weirdly, I almost believe you.'

With sudden inspiration, Venus pressed the Pricilla's bag into Pea's hands. 'Consider this a gift from your goddess.'

Awkwardly, Pea took the package and began backing toward the curtained door, obviously deciding it was easier to go along with the woman and escape than to argue with her about gifts and masturbation. 'Okay, well, again, I say thanks and I'll definitely take your hair care advice, if you will take a piece of advice from me in return.'

'How unusual – a mortal giving a goddess advice. Tulsa is such a refreshing place.' Venus looked curious and eager. 'Please, enlighten me.'

'From now on go easy on the martinis.' Pea smiled nervously and ducked back through the curtain.

'That certainly didn't go as expected,' Venus said to herself. Still trying to understand how a mortal could ask for and then reject her aid, she walked through the thick curtain and reentered the bar area of the restaurant just in time to see Pea trip up the little bar step and drop the Pricilla's bag – right in front of the row of firemen. The huge phallus rolled out of the bag to land, vibrating cheerfully, at the feet of a man who was so exceptionally handsome that Venus wondered that she hadn't noticed him earlier. He bent to retrieve it. Holding it carefully, he offered it back to poor, embarrassed Pea.

'Ma'am, I believe you dropped this.'

Speechless, Pea stared in horror back and forth from the vibrating penis to the handsome fireman.

'Ma'am?' The men around him were chuckling, but valiantly he managed to keep a sober expression. Then his eyes widened in recognition. 'Aren't you Pea? My neighbor with the Scottie who thinks she's a cat? The brownies you left at the station were good.'

Pea took the phallus from him, turned it off and dropped it back into the shopping bag. Venus noticed that her face was flaming red and she looked ready to cry, but when she finally spoke her voice was filled with self-effacing cheerfulness. 'That's me – Pea! Your neighbor, the Scottie cat's mom, loud burper, owner of a humongous vibrating penis and excellent brownie baker. I'd love to stay and talk with you, Griffin, but I'm off to embarrass myself fully somewhere else. I just reached my limit here.' Then, with the men's laughter following her out the door, Pea dropped some money on her table, picked up her book and fled.

'Pathetic. Truly pathetic,' Persephone said.

'I should zap them into silence,' Venus said. Her fingers twitched as she narrowed her eyes dangerously at the still laughing row of virile men.

'Venus, no, don't . . .'

She ignored Persephone and continued to glare at the men. The most handsome of them, the one who had been somewhat polite to Pea, met her eyes and Venus was caught by the blueness of his darklashed gaze. He nodded at her with a faint smile lifting his lips. The goddess reminded herself sternly that, no matter how chivalrous he had appeared, he was still part of the group of men who had laughed at Pea, so she should ignore him. But there was something about the sparkle in his eyes . . . the handsome tilt of his full lips . . . and especially about the way he looked at her – confident and openly appreciative, which was so different from the way even the most warriorlike of the ancient mortals ever dared look at her – that Venus didn't look away . . . couldn't look away. And that's when it happened. That *spark*. That lovely, inexplicable sizzle that sometimes happens between people that not even Love herself can always predict.

'Venus, would you please pay attention! I said don't do anything to them. You really shouldn't punish them. The mortal is obviously a ridiculous young woman.'

'She is not!' Venus reluctantly pulled her gaze hastily away from the intriguing man and snapped at Persephone with an unusual show of temper. Her head was oddly fuzzy and she was suddenly feeling like she might cry. 'She just needs some help. She's actually sweet. Confused, perhaps, but sweet.'

'Venus, what have you been up to?' Persephone asked as she took the love goddess's arm and propelled her from the restaurant.

'I only did what you said I should do.'

'What does that mean?'

'You were the one who said if a modern mortal asked for my aid that I should grant it.'

'I didn't say that.'

'Yes, you did.'

'No, I didn't.'

'Yes, you did.'

'Venus!' Persephone rounded on her. 'What – did – you – do?'

'I walked in the ladies' room and Pea was—'

'Pea?'

'The mortal you think is pathetic. Stop interrupting.'

'Sorry. Go ahead.'

'Pea was reciting an invocation.' Venus gave her a 'so there' look. When Persephone didn't say anything, she added, 'One of *my* invocations. She was actually asking for my aid. By name. Me. And you know the poor girl definitely needs my aid.'

'Are you telling me that you told her who you are?'

'Well, of course. She was calling me.'

'You said you're Venus, Goddess of Love.'

'Of course I did. That is who I am.'

Persephone began rubbing her right temple. 'And this Pea person said what in response to your proclamation?'

'She was surprised and seemed perhaps a little slow in her ability to understand.'

'You mean she didn't believe you.'

'You could put it that way.'

'Good. Then there was little harm done. Come on. Let's get you home before you're on the evening news.'

'The what?'

'Forget it. I'll explain all of this to you later. Let's get back. Demeter is going to be unbearable if I'm late again.' They left the restaurant and Persephone looked up at the prematurely darkening sky. 'And our timing is excellent. No one, mortal or immortal,

65

likes to get caught out in a nasty Oklahoma rainstorm, and it definitely looks like one is almost here.'

Venus sighed and didn't say anything else, quickening her pace to keep up with Persephone. She felt so odd – definitely out of sorts, like part of her was sad and embarrassed and very, very tired. Persephone linked arms with her and silently Venus hurried down the sidewalk with her while rain clouds roiled across the bruised-looking sky. They crossed the street in front of the renovated Tribune Lofts and followed the pedestrian bridge over the railroad tracks. They came to the spot in the heart of the bridge that locals had taken to calling the Center of the Universe because of the weird acoustical phenomenon they experienced when they stood dead center of the swirling brick-and-concrete pattern, which was actually a byproduct of having a portal to Olympus operating in the modern world.

Persephone glanced around them. 'Well, the storm is definitely making things easier for us. No one's out here.' She waved her hand at the space in front of them and the air rippled. A spherical area about as big as an ordinary door materialized, and without hesitation the Goddess of Spring walked into it, instantly disappearing. Venus sighed again and stepped forward, only to run face first into something so hard and impenetrable that, with a little yelp, she jumped back, rubbing her nose.

Persephone's disembodied head appeared from the middle of the sphere, like she was peeking out of a curtained alcove. 'What is taking you so long?'

'I don't know. I . . .' Hesitantly Venus moved forward, holding one hand out in front of her. When she came to the area of the shining orb near Persephone's face the air suddenly solidified, barring her from entering it. 'I can't get through,' she said faintly.

'Don't be ridiculous. Of course you can you just—' But Persephone's words broke off when she grabbed her friend's hand and attempted to pull her through the portal, but found that, although her own arm slid easily back and forth from one world to the other, Venus's encountered unmovable resistance.

'Has something happened and I've lost my powers?' Venus asked as Persephone reentered the modern world.

'That shouldn't matter. Even a modern mortal would be able to pass through Demeter's portal, which is why I'm so careful about no one seeing me come or go,' Persephone said.

While the Goddess of Spring was talking, Venus had turned to face a lovely tree that grew not far from them. She flicked her slender fingers at its winter naked branches and suddenly it burst into the delicate white blossoms of a Bradford pear in the middle of spring.

'My powers are fine,' she said.

'Let's try it again. Maybe it's the portal and it's corrected itself now. We'll go through together.' Persephone linked arms with her again. 'Ready? One – two – three!' The goddesses walked to the glowing sphere. Persephone moved through it easily, but Venus's arm was wrenched from hers as the Goddess of Love, once again, seemed to have walked into a glass wall.

'Fornicating satyrs and their furry balls!' Venus cried in frustration. 'What by all the levels of the Underworld is wrong with this goddess-be-damned thing?' But even as she cursed and paced a thought tickled at her mind . . . a thought that took her back to Lola's restaurant and the ladies' room and a simple invocation that had unexpectedly pulled at her soul—

'The invocation! I answered the invocation and agreed to give Pea my aid,' she told Persephone as the goddess reappeared from the portal.

'So? We've been answering invocations for eons. That never stopped us from returning to Olympus.'

'I know, but there's something different at work here. I don't know what for sure yet, but the invocation touched me in a way I've not been touched before.' Venus paused, concentrating. 'I'm bound to her!'

'Her?'

'Pea. That's why I've been feeling so odd – they're not my feelings. I've become linked to the mortal!'

'Oh no. Venus, what exactly did the mortal's invocation ask of you?'

'Pea asked that I give her happiness and ecstasy,' Venus said miserably.

'And you agreed? Aloud?'

Venus nodded. 'And I remember that I felt something during her invocation – something tugging within me that was compelling me to answer her.' The goddess closed her eyes and shook her head. 'I thought I was just experiencing the effects of our lovely martinis, but that wasn't it. It was the invocation itself; it was literal and binding.'

Persephone gasped. 'Which means you won't be able to leave this world until you've brought that pathetic mortal happiness and ecstasy.'

Chapter Six

'Don't call her pathetic. She just needs some help,' Venus said automatically.

'Well, she certainly has it now.'

'Yes, she does.' Venus drew herself up, straightening her elegant spine and lifting her perfect chin. 'I am Goddess of Love. I can certainly bring happiness and ecstasy to a mortal – modern or not.'

'Venus, you don't know anything about modern mortals.'

'What possible difference does that make? I know love, and love is timeless.'

'What are you going to do?'

'Go to Pea, of course.' Thinking, Venus began to brighten. 'She'll need a complete makeover – new clothes, hair, attitude, everything. Actually, it'll be fun *and* I'll be performing a good deed.'

Persephone looked doubtful.

'Once I've made her over I'll take her out and give her a few simple lessons on how to seduce men, and she'll be able to experience all the happiness and ecstasy she desires.'

'And how are you going to find her?'

Venus stopped and thought for a moment, then smiled. 'We're bound together, remember? I know where she is right now.' The goddess pointed toward Midtown Tulsa. 'Pea is there.'

Persephone let out a very ungoddessly snort. 'Of course she's there. *There* is a big area.'

'Don't be so droll. I meant that I can feel exactly where she is. I can will myself to her doorstep if I wish.' Venus laughed lightly. 'It's not like I'm here with no powers.'

'No, but if I don't give you these it'll be worse than having no powers – you'll have no money.' Persephone dug into her purse and pulled out a thick wallet. She flipped it open. 'Okay, remember how I paid for things today? These' – she ran a manicured nail down a row of neatly placed plastic – 'are credit cards. Think of them as you would bars of gold, only these won't run out – they have no limit. Remember to sign the slip of paper the clerk gives you and be sure to get the card back after you've made the purchase. Oh, wait. Let me fix them first.' Persephone clicked her fingers and the name on the cards changed from Persephone Santoro to Venus Smith.

'Why do I have to have such an average-sounding name?'

Persephone rolled her eyes. 'How's this?' She clicked her fingers again, and the embossed name changed to Venus Pontia, which means 'born of the sea.'

'Much better.'

'Now please pay attention and stop complaining. This' – she opened a compartment, exposing a thick wad of neatly placed bills – 'is cash.'

'I know how to use coins,' Venus said.

Thunder rumbled overhead and the goddesses glanced up.

'Zeus?' Venus asked.

'No, you really don't have to worry about him here. What you're hearing is an authentic Oklahoma thunderstorm, which really shouldn't be happening in February, but with Oklahoma weather you never really know what to expect.'

'You should go before it begins raining,' Venus said.

'I don't know . . . I don't like leaving you here.'

'I'll be perfectly fine. I've traversed the ancient world. I can certainly navigate my way around the Kingdom of Tulsa.'

'It's not a kingdom.'

'I was just testing to be certain you're listening.'

Persephone rolled her eyes again. 'Don't tell anyone besides Pea who you really are. Oh, and you'll have to perform some magic to convince Pea that you're not a raving madwoman.'

Venus frowned.

'You're not in the ancient world anymore. No one believes in us here. That's usually a good thing. For you, stuck here, it could be a very bad thing if you act too eccentric.'

'By Hera's freezing tits I am not eccentric!' At Persephone's knowing expression Venus held her hands up in mock surrender. 'What? The curses? Do you mean the curses?'

'You really should try to stop using them.'

'I don't see why,' she muttered.

'Would you please just trust me on this one? You need to fit in because you can't fulfill the invocation oath from the psychiatric ward of a hospital.'

Venus's smooth brow wrinkled in confusion.

'Just try to keep a low profile. Follow Pea's lead. She'll help you.'

'I'll be perfectly fine,' Venus repeated, giving her a gentle push toward the portal. 'Go on. You don't want to make Demeter angry.'

'All right.' Persephone moved reluctantly to the portal.

'If anyone asks after me I prefer you tell them I'm vacationing in the modern world.'

'Don't worry. This is no one's business but yours.' Before Persephone stepped through the glowing sphere she said, 'Oh, and go easy on questioning people about how often they masturbate and whether they look at their genitals. Modern mortals don't usually share that information with strangers.'

As Persephone and the glowing orb disappeared, Venus muttered, 'They don't talk about masturbation and their genitals? No wonder this world needs my aid.'

At that moment the sky opened and belched cold February rain upon the Goddess of Love.

Venus materialized in the shadow of the large oak in Pea's front yard. She'd been right when she told Persephone she'd have no problem finding Pea. It was like the little mortal was drawing her with an unbreakable chain, which was a good thing because it saved Venus from searching all over Tulsa in a nasty storm to find her. As it was, she was thoroughly miserable: shivering, wet and totally disgruntled. In retrospect Venus realized that she could have commanded the raindrops not to touch her, but wouldn't that be engaging in the kind of eccentric behavior Persephone had warned her against? Or did that just apply to genital issues? It was all so confusing. What she knew for sure was that Pea's little house looked warm and inviting with its wide front porch and its lights blazing cheerfully. *Well*, she reminded herself, *this is my mortal. The woman who invoked my aid. There's no need for me to be hesitant. She should be overjoyed to welcome me as her guest.* Holding that thought, Venus ran through the mud puddles to Pea's porch, thankful the generous roof held off the horrid cold rain. She took a moment to toss her hair back, knowing that even though it was wet, it still looked slick and sexy. She did grimace briefly when she glanced down at the silk knit sweater that was peppered with unattractive rain spots and her exquisite new black crocodile boots that were muddy and wet. At least the clothing Persephone had called jeans held up well in the torrential downpour. The Goddess of Love pinched her cheeks, chasing away the cold paleness that had lodged there, and put a brilliant smile on her face. Then she knocked on Pea's door.

Maniacal barking practically vibrated the walls. What type of beast did Pea own? Cerberus? One could only imagine. The door cracked and Venus recognized the frizzy tufts of Pea's out-of-control hair. Had the girl not taken her advice and purchased the coconut oil?

'Yes? Who is it?'

'It is I!' Venus proclaimed. When the mortal didn't respond she added, 'Venus, Goddess of Love.' When she still didn't respond she said, 'Your goddess. Remember? You invoked me at the restaurant.'

'I have my phone in my hand and my finger on the quick dial nine-one-one button, which I can push any second.'

Venus's brows drew together. 'That sounds lovely, darling. Could you do that while I'm inside, too? It's rather wet out here.'

'What do you want?'

Venus stifled a frustrated sigh. 'To fulfill your desire for happiness and ecstasy, of course. Didn't we already discuss this?'

'How did you find me?'

'Well, that's an interesting story. I believe that your invocation and my acceptance of it has somehow bound us together. You drew me here – so here I am.'

'I'm really sorry, but I think you should go away.'

Venus suddenly felt very near tears again and her words broke on an unexpected sob. 'But it's cold out here and I don't know where else to go.'

The crack in the door got bigger. Venus could see that Pea's hair was down and in wild disarray all around her shoulders.

And, worse, she was wearing some kind of nightwear that was a sweet pink color, but was also one piece and had feet attached to it. The Goddess of Love decided it made the mortal look prepubescent.

'Don't cry,' Pea said.

'I'm not.' Venus sniffed and wiped her eyes. 'It's just that nothing has gone the way I planned today, including you.'

'Okay. You can come in. If you say you won't mug and kill me.'

'I don't know what "mug" means, but it doesn't sound polite. And I certainly don't want to harm you, let alone kill you.'

'Well, then you can come in,' Pea said reluctantly. Standing aside Pea ushered her into the foyer of the neat little bungalow.

Relieved, Venus stepped into warmth that smelled like baking ambrosia. Then an angry ball of rather chubby black fur growled furiously at her.

'Manners, Chloe!' Pea said sternly.

Chloe growled again and barked a warning.

Venus laughed. 'With all that voice you must be as mighty as Cerberus!'

At the sound of the goddess's musical laughter, Chloe stopped growling.

'What a passionate girl!' She squatted down in front of the dog and then glanced up at Pea. 'Did you say her name is Chloe?'

'Yes, but be careful. She doesn't like strangers.'

'Well, that's just fine because Love is never a stranger. Am I right, Chloe my darling?' Venus cooed, stretching out her hand to the dog. Chloe sniffed delicately at her, and her tail started to thump. Just then a large gray tabby padded delicately into the room. 'Oh, and what a handsome beast you are!' Venus said.

'That's Max,' Pea said as the cat began twining his body around her unexpected houseguest. 'He loves everyone.'

'You needn't explain that to me,' Venus said happily, running one hand down the cat's body in a long caress while she scratched Chloe's ears with the other. 'Love recognizes one of her own.' When she finally stood up to face Pea, both animals curled contentedly at her feet. 'Good evening, Pea. Thank you for welcoming me into your home.'

'Are you lost? Can I call someone for you?'

'No, but that is a kind offer. You're really a very compassionate young woman, aren't you?'

'But if you're not lost then—'

'I'm not lost, Pea. I am trapped here.'

'Trapped? Here? You mean in my house?'

'No, I mean in your world.' At Pea's blank look Venus tried to explain. 'The world of modern mortals. I used to call it the Kingdom of Tulsa, but Persephone explained to me that this isn't literally a kingdom – it's a city.'

'Persephone? The goddess?'

'Of course.'

'And is she outside in the rain, too?'

'Oh, no. She was able to return to Olympus. It's only me who was unable to go back through the portal.'

'So you don't live here?'

Venus frowned. 'Of course not, darling. I have a perfectly lovely temple on Mount Olympus. I was here visiting. I bought these fabulous boots.' She pointed a toe so Pea could admire her new acquisition. 'They did look better before they got wet and muddy.'

Pea clutched on the one normal thing the woman had said. 'Why don't you take your boots off and let them dry? I'll get you a towel and something warm to drink and then we can figure out what to . . .' She paused, obviously struggling to find the right thing to say. 'To do to help you.'

'But that's just it! It's not what you can do to help me, but what I can do to help you – *then* I'll be able to return to Olympus and the ancient world of the gods.'

'How about we start with a towel and some hot chocolate?'

'Sounds divine.'

Venus pulled off her boots while Chloe and Max watched with open adoration and Pea brought her a thick pink towel that smelled delightfully of lavender. Then she led Venus into a cozy kitchen that was brightly lit and immaculate. Venus sat at the little antique breakfast table that was hand painted with wildflowers.

'I was just making myself some hot chocolate. It'll only take me a second to add to it so there'll be enough for both of us.'

Venus towel dried her hair while she watched Pea move confidently around the room. 'You are an excellent cook, aren't you?'

Surprised at the observation, Pea smiled at Venus over her shoulder while she continued to stir the milk and dark chocolate mixture. 'Yes, I am a good cook.'

'And your home is so lovely and comfortable. I can already see that you use colors wisely to make it feel open and welcoming.'

'Thank you.' Pea blushed a little.

'Which makes your personal appearance all the more confusing.' Pea's spine straightened and she stopped filling her mug midpour. Venus hurried on. 'I don't mean to insult you – just the opposite actually. What I mean is that it seems to me that you shouldn't have had to invoke my aid at all. You seem to understand style and aesthetics very well.'

'Only when it has to do with my home or even my work. When it's me, well, that's like a whole other world, or at least it's seemed like that since high school.'

'Very interesting,' Venus mused. Then she smiled brightly. 'But now I'm here and Love herself will aid you in attaining your dreams!'

Pea joined Venus at the table, handing her the buttercup-colored mug and a vintage blue linen napkin that was hand embroidered. As an automatic afterthought Pea reached for a tin on the nearby granite-topped counter that was decorated with pictures of Scottie dogs. She opened it and offered Venus one of the imported sourdough cookies she always kept inside. Venus took one and chewed daintily, then sipped her hot chocolate. 'Pea, this is delicious.'

'Thank you,' Pea said.

They ate and drank in silence. Venus looked around her with obvious curiosity at the lovely little home, and Pea tried not to stare too openly at her beautiful, but mysterious and mentally unsound, guest.

'The yellow of the walls is the same color as that of the cups from which we're drinking. That's an especially pleasing touch,' Venus said.

'Okay. Who are you? Really.'

Venus blinked in surprise. 'But I already told you.'

'It's impossible that you're Venus.'

'If you really believe that then why did you so earnestly invoke my aid?'

Pea fidgeted with a cookie. She looked up into the woman's unusual violet eyes and saw only kindness there. 'I was tired of being invisible.'

Venus didn't have to be bound to Pea by an oath to recognize the pain and honesty in her words. She took her hand. 'Tell me.'

'I'm worse than plain and ordinary. Where men are concerned' – she paused, thinking about the nerdy guys who did ask her out and grimaced – 'or at least men I might find attractive, it's like I don't exist.'

Venus squeezed her hand. 'Go on.'

'As you've already noticed, I have no style. My hair and clothes are never right.' Pea moved her shoulders restlessly. 'It started when I was about fourteen. I made this great dance squad at school – one that was tough to get on. I never really thought about how I looked or dressed or whatever before then.' She smiled sheepishly. 'I guess I was dorky, but too busy getting good grades and taking zillions of dance classes to know it. Anyway I thought I fit in with the rest of the girls.' Pea hesitated and pain flashed through her eyes. 'I was wrong. I was a good dancer. I made good grades. I tried to be nice to everyone, but I wasn't good enough.'

'Oh, darling, of course you're good enough!' Venus felt very close to tears again.

Pea smiled bravely. 'Well, I am smart. So I taught myself how to keep a nice home, how to cook like a gourmet, how to excel at my job. And today I decided that maybe, with, uh, your help and a how-to book, I could learn to be a better woman.'

'Oh, child. I can already tell that you are a wonderful woman. You don't need to learn to be a better one. All you need to learn to do is to show the world the truth of what you already are and to leave the past in the past.'

'I wish that were possible.'

'Of course it is possible!'

Pea smiled. 'With the aid of Venus, Goddess of Love.'

'So you do believe I'm Venus.'

Pea blushed again. 'Well, no. But I think you're beautiful enough to be the Goddess of Love.'

'Actually, I'm Goddess of Sensual Love, Beauty and the Erotic Arts,' Venus corrected her, and then sighed. 'What shall I do to convince you? Do you have something you would like me to gild in gold? Have you a tree you would like coaxed into bearing fruit?' She tapped her chin thoughtfully. 'Winter is still upon us, not that that matters, although I'm sure Persephone would say making a tree fruitful in winter is imprudent behavior.'

In spite of the crazy circumstances, Pea had to smile. 'Why not make Chloe a cat? She's been around Max since she was a puppy, and she's grown up believing she's a Scottie cat, rather than a Scottie dog.'

Venus glanced down at Chloe, who sat by Pea's feet. 'So you think you're a cat?' Chloe thumped her tail happily against the floor, and the Goddess grinned at the precocious black dog. 'Well, then I suppose you should be a cat.' With a small, simple gesture Venus flicked her fingers at Chloe. The air surrounding the dog suddenly began to shimmer with diamond-colored glitter, and with a popping sound, the Scottie disappeared and in her place sat a big black cat with over-large ears and odd-looking tufts of fur around her face that made her look like she had a beard.

Every bit of color drained from Pea's face. 'Chloe?' She choked out the word.

The cat's tail beat happily against the kitchen floor.

With a trembling hand, Pea reached down and touched what used to be her dog. Chloe purred riotously and her tail thumped harder. Pea's wide-eyed gaze shot to Venus.

'You *are* Venus, Goddess of Love.' She put her hand to her head. 'I think I may be sick.'

Concerned by her sudden pallor, Venus fanned her with a linen napkin. 'Should I get you something? I could conjure a lovely goblet of ambrosia. It's really very refreshing.'

'No! I just need to breathe.' Pea gulped air. Max sauntered into the room, took one look at Chloe, hissed and backed out

79

of the room so fast that his claws slid and paws skittered like he was on ice instead of tile. Chloe just tilted her head to the side and meowed questioningly.

'Could you please change her back?' Pea asked faintly.

The goddess shrugged. 'Of course.' With a flick of her wrist and more glitter, Chloe was once again a Scottie dog. As if she'd just come in out of the rain, Chloe shook herself and then sneezed violently before padding out of the room to find Max. 'There! She's good as new,' Venus said. Pea was still staring at her. 'What?'

'Well, uh, ma'am. I mean Your Highness – no that's a queen, not a goddess,' Pea murmured nervously before blurting, 'I don't know what to call you!'

The goddess smiled. 'Darling, Venus will do.'

Chapter Seven

'Tell me about your love life,' Venus said.

'It's nonexistent,' Pea said.

'You're a virgin?'

'Oh, god no!' Pea's hand flew to her mouth. 'I mean goddess no. I think.'

'You think you should say, "goddess," or you think you're not a virgin?'

'Venus, talking to an actual goddess is nerve-wracking enough without adding expletive confusion into the mix.'

Venus grinned, glad the little mortal had begun to relax. 'When in doubt, feel free to use the genitals of the gods as expletives. I certainly do.'

'Thank you. I think.'

'So you're not a virgin?'

'No.'

'But you're also not very experienced sexually.'

'No.'

'Do you masturbate frequently?'

Pea blushed. 'Do we really have to talk about this?'

'Do you really want to change?'

Pea drew a deep breath. 'I don't masturbate very often.'

'Why not?'

'For the same reason I don't like talking about it. It makes me feel uncomfortable, embarrassed and kinda guilty.'

'What a shocking attitude!' Venus snorted her disbelief. 'Before we change your hair, clothes or your makeup' – the goddess squinted at Pea's face – 'or rather your lack thereof, we must change your attitude about pleasure.'

'Okay . . .' Pea said doubtfully.

'Do you feel guilty and embarrassed when you prepare a sumptuous meal?'

'Of course not.'

'Even if you are the only one eating it?'

'No, that's silly. Just because I'm alone doesn't mean I can't—' Understanding brightened Pea's face. 'Oh! I see what you mean.'

'Pleasure, like this excellent hot chocolate, is meant to be savored and enjoyed, not denied.'

'Okay.' This time Pea said it with more certainty.

'If you don't know your own body and what pleases it, how can you expect a man to know how to give you pleasure.'

'That's logical.'

'Of course it is. Love isn't always illogical, no matter what Persephone says.' In response to Pea's questioning look, she said, 'The Goddess of Spring can be remarkably unromantic. I'll have to remember to work on that little issue in the future.' Venus shook herself and refocused on Pea. 'But one problem at a time. So – first I want you to begin pleasuring yourself regularly. Be uninhibited.' With a mischievous smile Venus made a graceful gesture with her hand and a crystal bottle of sun-colored wine appeared on the table in a wave of glitter, causing Pea to yelp in surprise. 'Do you have wine glasses, or shall I conjure some of those, too.'

'No! I have glasses.' Still staring at the sparkling golden liquid, Pea backed to a cabinet and pulled out two white wine glasses, and then brought them to the table. 'Can you make anything appear like that?'

'Of course I can. I am a goddess.' Venus poured the wine. 'This will help with your inhibitions.' She raised her glass and Pea did the same. 'To pleasure,' Venus said with a purr.

'To pleasure.' Pea took a hesitant sip. She swallowed, and her entire face became suffused with joy. 'This wine is amazing! I've never tasted anything like it.'

'It's ambrosia – the nectar of the gods.' Venus took a long, luxurious drink. 'Harvested by nymphs from rare flower blossoms found only in the Elysian Fields. It is simply divine.' The goddess took another drink. 'So, my plan to bring happiness and ecstasy to your life is really rather simple. First, you learn to accept pleasure.' Her shapely brows drew together. 'What do you think of while you masturbate?'

'I–I don't know. Not much of anything I guess.'

Venus shook her head slowly. 'Sad. Terribly sad. That must change, too. The next time you bring yourself pleasure – which should be tonight – I want you to fantasize.'

'About what?'

'Oh, darling! How tragic that you have to ask. Although I am, of course, the perfect goddess to ask.' She patted the mortal's hand. 'Pea, fantasies are personal. Let your mind roam free *without* guilty retribution. For instance, is there a particular man you find especially attractive?'

Pea's cheeks flushed with more than the potent wine.

Venus smiled knowingly. 'I see there is. Tell me about him.' She poured Pea more ambrosia.

'His name is Griffin. I guess you could say I've had a crush on him for awhile, but we sort of formally met just today. Actually he's what prompted me to get your book. He's the most gorgeous man I've ever seen, and he seems really nice, too.' Pea's slightly woozy grin faded. 'But he barely knows I'm alive. Wait, no. He probably does know I'm alive now. On the way out of the restaurant I tripped and dropped the bag you gave me. The dildo fell out and rolled, vibrating, to his feet. I'm sure he thinks of me as "that girl with the penis."'

Venus sipped her ambrosia, remembering the exquisitely handsome man who had retrieved Pea's phallus, and at the same time ordered herself to forget the spark that had passed between them. Pea was the focus here, not her own pleasure, and that beautiful man could definitely help bring Pea happiness and ecstasy.

'Then we'll just have to change the way he thinks of you,' Venus said with finality.

'Too bad it's not that simple.'

'Darling, with Love on your side, everything becomes much simpler.'

'And you' – Pea's hand was wobbly when she pointed at the goddess – 'are Love!'

'And you' – Venus laughed lightly – 'are finished with the ambrosia.' She scooted the bottle out of Pea's reach, reminding herself that mortals were highly susceptible to the rich wine of the gods. 'Now, this is what I want you to do—'

'Homework?'

'Well, you're at home, but I scarcely think pleasuring yourself would qualify as work.'

Pea giggled.

'Pay attention. When you pleasure yourself tonight I want you to think about Griffin.'

'Okay, I can do that.'

'Good. I want you to fantasize.'

84

Pea frowned.

Venus sighed. 'Imagine how it would feel to have his hard, masterful hands on your body, and his clever tongue exploring the wet cleft between your legs, licking and teasing your pleasure center until you can bear it no longer, and then imagine him impaling you with his throbbing phallus and stroking and stroking until you're both shuddering with the force of your mutual orgasms.'

'I can do that,' Pea said breathlessly. 'Well, good night!' She started to hurry a little unsteadily out of the room.

'Darling?'

Pea stopped and smiled back at her goddess.

'While this room is, indeed, comfortable and lovely, it doesn't appear to have a bed.'

'Oopsie!' Pea giggled. 'Come right this way.' She tried to gesture grandly, but ended up looking so unsteady that Venus had to grasp her arm to keep her completely upright.

'I need to remember to water the ambrosia next time,' she said under her breath as she supported a still giggling Pea down a short hallway.

'This is the guest room,' Pea said, managing to draw herself up and slur only slightly. 'The bathroom is through the other door. Make yourself at home. There's a bathrobe in the armoire. We'll take care of your clothes and stuff tomorrow.'

Venus gazed around the tidy, comfortable room decorated in different shades of white, eggshell and champagne, with antique-looking, lacy white dresses adorning one wall like three dimensional art, and a large framed picture of a wildflower-filled meadow decorating the other. The bed was white wrought iron and heaped with a thick comforter and pillows made of cream-colored vintage lace.

'Thank you, Pea. This is another lovely room.'

'Okey-dokey then. I'm off to do my homework.' And, giggling, she tottered away.

Smiling, Venus watched her go. She really was a delightful young woman. Fulfilling her desire for happiness and ecstasy couldn't be that complicated.

Vulcan told himself that he was checking on Venus. He knew she hadn't returned to Olympus, even though Persephone had. And he was, after all, supposed to be paying attention to the men she met – keeping in mind that perhaps one of them would have the potential to take his place. He was curious about the little mortal he'd watched in the restaurant, and yes, he'd been thinking of her. But that certainly wasn't the only reason he called open the thread of fire and gazed into his window to the modern world.

'I don't masturbate very often.'

Vulcan felt the jolt of Pea's unexpected comment down through his loins. Venus was there – in Pea's home – and, as usual, she was preoccupied with someone else's sex life! But why was she there? He continued to listen, intrigued by the sweet, shy mortal. Apparently, the Goddess of Love was there to give Pea guidance and help her find happiness and ecstasy.

'It's just like Venus to meddle in a mortal's personal life,' he said with a growl.

But the more Vulcan listened, the more he understood that Pea had asked for Venus's aid – that the little mortal wanted to change who she was – to become *more*, which was something the Fire God understood perfectly. He studied Pea. Yes, she was rather plain and dressed in an unflattering manner, but Vulcan could see through the dowdy charade to the compassionate woman beneath. He could also see that most people wouldn't bother to look below her surface – just as the immortals didn't look below his surface.

Pea spoke of a handsome man from the restaurant. Vulcan glowered, remembering how the mortals had laughed at her embarrassment. A man like that didn't deserve a rare creature like Pea! It wasn't that he was jealous. (How could he be?) It was just that he was concerned. He, too, was compassionate, though no one seemed to understand that about him.

His fierce expression changed to unaccustomed laughter as the ambrosia worked its magic on Pea. Surprised, he saw that Venus was going to stay the night in Pea's home. How odd! And then his surprise multiplied tenfold when the thread, which should have stayed with Venus, split, allowing him to move invisibly with Pea as she swayed happily down the hall to her bedroom.

His vision followed Pea into her comfortable bedroom, and he watched, filled with curiosity as she turned on soft, slow music and then began to light the candles that rested on her nightstand. Humming to herself, she pulled down her thick bed linens, and turned out the bright overhead light, leaving only the candles to illuminate the room. Obviously she was getting ready for sleep, but she didn't appear to be tired. Then Vulcan's eyes widened as Pea began to dance. Slowly, sensuously, she raised her arms over her head, rounding them gracefully as she moved to the music. Vulcan was amazed. Until then she'd given no evidence of such exquisite grace or, he admitted, such beauty. When she danced it seemed she cast off the skin of her awkward shyness and became an entirely new person. Hypnotized, he hardly breathed when she peeled out of the shapeless, one piece sleepwear and continued her dance, turning, dipping and stretching elegantly in only a pair of snug fitting, unadorned panties.

The thought passed through his heated mind that he shouldn't be watching her – that it was not entirely honorable to spy on so intimate a scene. But he could not stop his compulsion to watch her. Vulcan ignored his mind and, for once in his life, allowed his desire and his heart to rule him instead.

Pea's body was another surprise. She'd seemed so small and even fragile in the overly large clothes she wore. Now he could see that her body was sleek without being thin and lithely muscled without being bulky. Her breasts teased him. They weren't large, but they were exquisitely formed – no, they were more than exquisite. They were pouty globes that puckered invitingly. Her buttocks . . . Vulcan was mesmerized by the sight of her well-rounded, womanly bottom moving so seductively. It seemed to cry out for his touch – for him to cup her sweetness in his hands and lift her to him and . . .

He couldn't bear it any longer; she was like a drug invading his body. Vulcan succumbed to the overwhelming urge to touch her. Just for an instant he sent a single strand of his divine essence through the fiery thread and let it lick her body.

Pea writhed.

Shifting, he loosened the tie of the short linen wrap he wore slung low about his hips and his erection lifted, full and hard, against his belly. As if she could sense his desire, Pea concluded her dance and, skin glistening with a fine sheen of sweat in the flickering candlelight, she lay back on the bed. She closed her eyes and let her hands glide over her body. Hesitantly at first, and then with growing passion, she cupped her breasts. As her thumbs rubbed over her nipples her head fell back against the pillows. Vulcan saw her mouth open with a moan and watched as her caresses went from unsure to heated.

The god's breathing deepened with hers. His heartbeat increased. Mirroring her moan he wrapped his hand around his phallus and began to slowly pump while he continued to watch her.

Pea slid her hands from her breasts down her stomach, pulling off her panties in one smooth movement. Then she lifted her knees and let her fingertips play over the silken skin of her parted thighs.

Languidly her legs fell open as she moaned again. Her naked body was exposed to him now and he could see her luscious pink center and the dampness of the dark triangle of curls there. The fingertips of both of her hands glided over those curls, rubbing slowly, erotically, before she moved two fingers deeper into her core.

Vulcan gasped and allowed himself another indulgence. Following the fiery thread of his being, his essence covered her mound, caressing her with his heat and magic while he inhaled her scent and taste. Vulcan increased the speed of his strokes. With an intensity he'd never before felt, Vulcan longed to bury himself between her legs – to stroke her over and over and over – to feel her soft, wet heat and to claim her as his own.

Eyes still closed, Pea began to move her fingers faster, deeper within her folds – teasing and rubbing until her hips caught the rhythm, moving and thrusting. Vulcan's hand stroked faster, too. His whole world had become the alluring Siren in the fiery vision. His lust was white hot, drifting across her body like a living thing of its own. When she tensed and then cried out in ecstasy his own orgasm sped through his body, pulling him to his knees where he shuddered, helpless to a desire that left him physically spent, but still wanting more . . . still wanting her . . .

Vulcan watched until Pea fell into a satiated sleep, and still he continued to watch, and to dream. If only . . .

Chapter Eight

A delicious aroma tickled Venus awake. She glanced at the sky outside her bedroom window. Thankfully the rain had stopped. It was a clear, beautiful day and, judging from the position of the sun, almost midmorning.

Definitely time for the Goddess of Love to go to work.

She showered and dressed quickly, appreciating Pea's well-stocked guest bathroom with its generous selection of scented soaps and lotions. Then, humming an ancient fertility song, she followed the wonderful smells that had awakened her into the kitchen where she was instantly bombarded by Scottie and cat love. Cooing good mornings to Chole and Max, she fondled the adorable animals.

'Good morning, Goddess of Love!' Pea practically sang. 'I don't know how you like your coffee, but there's cream and sugar on the table, and if you have a seat I'll have our omelets ready in a jiff.'

Venus gave Pea a contemplative look and then smiled knowingly. 'I told you pleasuring yourself properly is a good thing.'

Pea glanced over her shoulder at the goddess. Her cheeks flushed, but her eyes sparkled. 'It must have been the ambrosia. I swear I felt like I was on fire. You were definitely right.'

'Of course I was. You must learn to trust me in these matters. I don't just know love; I *am* love.' She poured herself some of the dark liquid Pea called coffee, and then added a little cream and sugar. She sipped and her violet eyes widened. 'By Ares's stone-like buttocks, this is a delightful drink!'

'Ares?' Pea asked, flipping their omelets and adding a healthy sprinkling of shredded cheese.

'The God of War. He's tedious, always preoccupied with weapons and battle strategy and exercise, but I must admit his buttocks are perfect.' Venus drank her coffee and nibbled at a piece of jam-covered toast. 'Which reminds me – what type of men do you find most attractive? Muscular or lean? Tall or short? What is your preference?'

Pea slid one omelet on Venus's plate and one on her own, thinking carefully before she answered the goddess. 'Would it be stupid and clichéd to say that I like tall, muscular men?'

Venus's smile was like a cat lapping cream. 'Darling, there is nothing stupid or clichéd about enjoying a tall, well-built man.'

'I don't mean that he has to be all ridiculously bulked up, so that he spends all his time obsessively working out.'

'Like Ares.' Venus nodded agreement.

'I want a man with more depth than that. Like Griffin,' she added shyly.

'Of course you do, and we shall get you one – perhaps even this Griffin you admire so,' Venus said matter-of-factly, and she silently congratulated herself on not being the slightest bit interested in Griffin anymore. 'But first we have to do something about all of this.' She waved her fork at Pea.

'Okay. I'm ready.' Pea looked around the room nervously. 'But if you're going to start making things suddenly appear I'd appreciate it if you'd wait until I'm done eating. I know it sounds silly to you, but stuff popping out of the air makes my stomach hurt.'

'Naturally I could conjure whatever I desire, but that would only be a temporary fix to your problems. I return to Olympus and you're back where you were before I began making things pop out of the air.' Venus paused and gave Pea's footie pajamas a disdainful look. 'Darling, where do you shop for your clothing?'

Pea shrugged. 'Discount stores. Wherever there's a sale.'

'Good. Now I know where we will *not* be shopping. So tell me where you would never shop because you believe only the very beautiful and chic go there.'

'Saks Fifth Avenue at Utica Square,' Pea said through a bite of omelet.

'Then it is to Saks Fifth Avenue at Utica Square that we shall go. But first – your hair.'

Pea sighed. 'I think it's hopeless.'

'Darling, nothing is hopeless when Love takes charge.'

Pea parked her Thunderbird in front of Saks and couldn't resist looking in the mirror at herself one more time.

'I told you the coconut oil would work,' Venus said smugly.

'It's amazing. I didn't realize I had these great curls. All I thought I had was frizz. Lots and lots of frizz.'

'That's because you were brushing it and not using the correct product.'

'I'll never brush it again. Promise.'

'And you'll only wash it . . .' Venus prompted.

'Every third day at the soonest. And I'll use mild shampoo and extra rich conditioner.'

Venus nodded. 'Excellent. But I'm not finished with your hair.'

'Huh?'

'Trust me. Now, we shop.'

Pea sighed and reluctantly got out of the car. Venus glanced down at her sneakers. 'Our first stop will be the shoe department.'

Pea sighed again.

*　　*　　*

'Darling, you're a natural in those stilettos!' Venus lounged gracefully on a cushioned bench and watched Pea walk the length of the department in the utterly chic, very sexy silver leather peekaboo pumps with the fabulous three-and-a-half inch black heels.

'Clearly she's a dancer,' gushed the effeminate salesman who had introduced himself as Fabio.

'Are you, darling?' Venus asked.

'Well, yes. I've been taking ballet since I was about five.'

'No wonder your body has such suppleness and natural grace. You know, the forest nymphs could learn a thing or two from you. I've noticed that their frolicking has become rather wooden lately.'

'It's so hard to find a good nymph anymore. Even the queen show down at the Holiday Inn doesn't have a decent one,' Fabio said, with a great fluttering of his well-manicured hands.

'Fabio, darling, wherever did you get that perfect shade of lip gloss?' Venus asked.

Fabio blushed becomingly. 'At the Bobbi Brown counter. I love how natural it looks.'

'Pea, we'll have to remember to get you some before we leave.' Venus turned her divine smile on Fabio. 'And we'll take the shoes she has on and the four other pairs I have selected here.'

Pea made a faint squeaking sound.

'And how will you be paying for this, madam?'

Venus pulled the gold card from her clutch purse and winked at Pea. 'With this.'

Fabio glanced at the card and smiled, lip gloss sparkling merrily in the light from the department's crystal chandelier. 'Venus Pontia – I knew you were a goddess the moment I saw that fabulous hair!' he gushed.

'Of course you did, darling. Be a dear and box up the shoes.' Then she hesitated, taking in Fabio's perfect grooming and clearly impeccable taste in clothing. 'Do you think you could carry the shoes to the clothing department with us? I would love to get your help outfitting my friend.'

'Goddess.' Fabio lowered his voice and motioned for Venus to lean close. 'Just exactly how much shopping do you plan to do in our humble establishment today? A large amount or a truly obscene amount?'

Venus's smile was sly. 'Truly and utterly obscene. This' – she raised the credit card as if it was the key to paradise – 'has no limit.'

'Oh!' Fabio and Pea gasped together. Then he bowed dramatically to the goddess and said, 'Lead on, divine one. I am yours to command.'

Venus's smile widened. 'Of course you are, darling.'

'So what are the two things you're going to always remember when purchasing clothes?' Fabio drilled Pea, sounding disturbingly like a PE teacher.

'Color and cut,' Pea said automatically, still unable to stop staring at herself in the dressing-room mirror.

'See what a difference paying attention to those two makes?' Fabio said, clearly pleased with himself.

'I do.' Pea nodded enthusiastically.

'And do you approve, my lady?' He stepped back dramatically so that Venus could have a full view of Pea.

The goddess approached Pea, studying her carefully. She stroked the sleeve of Pea's cashmere sweater, which stopped just above the waistline of her slacks to show the faintest hint of skin when she moved. 'You must wear this blush color often. It makes your skin radiant. And remember, you've worked hard for that lovely curved waist – stop being afraid to show it.' Pea pulled self-consciously at the sweater. 'I know,' Venus said, with sudden inspiration. 'Think of it as you do that wonderful car you drive.'

'Huh?'

'You said it was quite costly.'

'Yeah, but worth every penny.'

'And you worked very hard for each of those pennies?'

'Definitely.'

'After working so hard and attaining something so beautiful you wouldn't hide it away in the car house, would you?'

'Garage,' Pea said, with a hasty look at Fabio, but he was rummaging through the blouses.

'Whatever,' Venus said. 'The point is you wouldn't hide it.'

'No, I wouldn't even think of it.'

'Then think of your body like your car. You worked hard for both. Both are beautiful. Neither should be hidden.'

'I never thought of it that way before.'

'Like pleasure, beauty should be savored and enjoyed.'

'Brilliant!' Fabio gushed, finally pulling himself away from the waiting blouses. 'Like pleasure, beauty should be savored and enjoyed.' He sighed dramatically and then impulsively went to Venus and squeezed one of her hands. 'My God! You have put my entire life's philosophy into one exquisite sentence. I have to tell you how much I have enjoyed assisting the two of you this afternoon. It has—' Fabio hesitated. Obviously moved, he had to dab at his eyes and draw in a deep, cleansing breath. 'It has been a life changing experience.'

'Oh, darling.' Venus patted his cheek kindly. 'Love and beauty were created to change lives.' She cocked her head and studied

95

Fabio carefully before she continued. 'And, yes, you should open that business you've been considering.'

Fabio gasped and clutched his pearls. 'Ohmygod! How ever did you know I was thinking of opening my own boutique?'

Venus waved her hands dismissively. 'Let's just call it woman's intuition, shall we? And I also sense that your boutique will be a very popular place.'

'Fit for a goddess?' Fabio asked breathlessly.

'Absolutely, darling.' Then, while Fabio was redabbing his eyes and reapplying his lip gloss, Venus turned her attention back to Pea. Her eyes traveled down the length of the fitted gray tweed slacks that were cropped cleverly so that Pea's shapely calves were visible. 'Exquisite. A perfect fit. Now add that black leather jacket and you will be conservative enough for daywear at your job, *and* you'll look appropriately alluring.' Venus smiled at Pea's reflection in the mirror. 'Because looking alluring is always appropriate.'

'So says the Goddess of Love.' Pea grinned back at her.

The short, stout saleslady whose gilded name tag read *Donna Vivian* stuck her head into the large dressing suite. 'Fabio, how are your ladies doing?'

Fabio, recovering from his burst of emotion, gestured grandly at Pea. 'Perfection! We have attained perfection.'

'Excellent. If there is anything else your ladies need, I'll be tidying the Marc Jacobs collection.' Donna Vivian began to discreetly disappear, but Venus motioned for her to join them in the dressing suite. 'Darling, your hair is impeccable.'

Donna Vivian inclined her head slightly, accepting the compliment with the special grace of those who cater to the very rich. 'Thank you, madam.'

Venus continued to study her hair. 'Fabio, don't you agree that the color is perfection itself.'

Fabio nodded. 'Of course. Donna Vivian is known for her impeccable taste.' He sniffed and added, 'She and I use the same colorist.'

Venus smiled brightly at Fabio and Donna Vivian. 'Then may I ask who does your hair?'

'But of course, madam. The cut and color are done by Farah, the master hair stylist and colorist at Cypress Avenue Salon,' Donna Vivian said.

'The cute little place on South Utica?' Pea asked.

'Exactly,' Fabio said.

'Good. We'll go there next,' Venus said.

'Oh, dear.' Fabio looked flustered and Donna Vivian shook her head sadly back and forth. 'I'm afraid it takes weeks to get an appointment with Farah. And it's Sunday. Cypress Avenue is one of the few upscale salons in Tulsa actually open on Sunday, which makes *them* incredibly busy today, but it makes *me* totally distraught to tell you this. There is no possible way you can get in. The best I can do is to give you her card so you may call for an appointment.' Fabio squeezed Venus's arm apologetically. 'I am ever so sorry.'

Venus smiled sweetly. 'Her card would be perfect, and don't you worry yourself about us not being able to get in. Oh, and we will take them,' Venus said.

'Them?' Donna Vivian and Fabio asked together.

'All of them.' Venus's grand gesture included all of the clothes hanging from the half-dozen ivory hooks. 'And she'll wear the outfit she has on. Oh, Fabio, darling, don't you think those adorable silver pumps we just purchased will go perfectly with what Pea is wearing?'

'Too divine for words,' Fabio agreed.

He and Donna Vivian bustled about, collecting the mounds of clothing that lay like resting butterflies all about the suite.

When they left, Pea turned to Venus, tears making her honey brown eyes bright.

'I don't know how to thank you for all of this.'

Venus touched her cheek gently. 'Happiness and ecstasy are the gifts I give to thee.'

On impulse, Pea hugged her. 'You really are a wonderful goddess!'

Sniffing and wiping her eyes delicately, Venus said, 'Of course I am, darling. Now let's finish by seeing about your hair, and then I do believe it's time for a lovely and leisurely meal.'

'Do you think you could conjure some more ambrosia?'

Venus lifted her brows. 'Only if I conjure some water, too.'

'My friend would like Farah to color and trim her hair,' Venus said. 'I think some lovely dark honey lowlights to bring out the color of her eyes and a quick shaping without taking off too much length.'

The extremely young and extraordinarily blonde receptionist frowned. 'I'm sorry, but Farah is booked until . . .'. She checked her computer log book. 'Until the end of next month. And then she only has one opening.'

'No, I'm afraid that won't do,' Venus said pleasantly.

The receptionist's frown deepened, but before she could respond the phone on her trim white workstation rang.

'Cypress Avenue Salon, how may I be of service to you?' She paused. 'Oh, I'm sorry to hear about that Mrs. Rowland.' The blonde blanched. 'No, I had no idea Dobermans could make such a mess with feather pillows. Of course I'll tell Farah your cancellation is an emergency and will reschedule you for your regular time next month. Good-bye, Mrs. Rowland.'

'Seems Farah has an opening,' Venus said.

'Well, she does, but I have to call the first person on the list of our clients who are waiting for a Farah cancellation. I'm sorry, ma'am. There's just no way I can work you in without an appointment,' she said firmly, and began clicking through her computer waiting list.

'Really?' Venus said breathily.

'Maybe we should go,' Pea said softly.

Venus just smiled and shook her head slightly.

The cell phone in Pea's purse rang. 'Hello?'

The receptionist said, 'Hello, may I speak with Pea Chamberlain, please? This is Mindi at Cypress Avenue.'

Pea smiled, and instead of talking into her phone, she caught the receptionist's eye. 'Uh, Mindi, I'm Pea Chamberlain.'

Mindi blinked. 'Oh, well then. It appears you're next on our list of clients waiting to see Farah. I'm sorry, ma'am. I didn't recognize you as one of our regulars.'

'She's had a recent makeover,' Venus said.

'Well, she looks wonderful.'

'She does indeed. Speaking of wonderful, while I'm waiting for Pea's trim and color, I'd very much enjoy a pedicure.'

The blonde's frown returned. I'm sorry, ma'am, Cheryl is completely—'

'Mindi, my three o'clock just called and cancelled her pedicure.'

Mindi began to look a little shell-shocked. 'Cheryl, this lady just requested a pedicure.'

'Then I can fit her right in.' Cheryl smiled.

'What a lovely coincidence,' Venus said. 'Oh, and I'd very much like a glass of that special champagne you keep chilled in the back room.'

'Of course, ma'am.'

'How did you know they have champagne?' Pea whispered as they were led back to the bowels of the salon.

'Darling, Love can always sense the presence of champagne.'

Chapter Nine

'Farah is a genius!' Stopping at the red light on Utica Street, Pea turned her head this way and that so her new lowlights could catch the rays of the fading sun in the car's rearview mirror.

'She did a wonderful job, but you need to remember that you had amazing hair even before Farah worked her magic, just like you had an amazing body even before our visit to Saks.'

A tap on the window of their car caused both women to jump in surprise. Pea looked up and gasped. 'Oh. My. God! It's Griffin!'

'Open your window!' Venus hissed, her stomach fluttering involuntarily at the sight of the handsome fireman. *He's for Pea!*

Pea pressed the button to lower her window.

'Evening, ladies. Would you be interested in donating your change to the fire department's drive to help Jerry's kids?' Then his look went from Pea to Venus and his smile changed from polite to sexy. 'Good to see you again, ma'am.'

Venus tried to mutter a dismissive, 'Oh, hello,' but was mortified when her words came out sounding more purr-ish than perfunctory.

'Hi, Griffin,' Pea said brightly. 'Sure, I'll donate.' Her hand shook only a little as she dug through her purse for change.

Griffin held the boot up and pulled his appreciative gaze from Venus long enough to smile at her. 'Have we met, ma'am?'

'Yeah, I'm your neighbor. Remember? You got my Scottie

from the tree and then later you returned my penis to me,' Pea blurted, blushing scarlet.

Venus sighed and rolled her eyes.

Griffin looked like someone had hit him over the head. 'Pea?'

'That's me!' The light changed and someone behind them honked. 'Well, see ya.' Pea sped away.

'Perhaps next time you shouldn't mention the penis. Men – mortals and gods – tend to be intimidated by women who own larger penises than they have.'

'I'm a moron,' Pea said with a moan.

'Of course you're not. You were just nervous. Let me tell you a little something about men that will make speaking with them much easier for you. They desire us even more than we desire them.'

'How can that be true?'

'It goes back to the whole penis thing.'

'But I've known women who chase man after man. They seem way more interested in the men than the men seem in them.'

'That's not desire – that's neediness, and you're not a needy woman. I'm talking about real desire. Something that's raw and hot and passionate.'

'Are you being serious?'

'Absolutely.'

Pea shook her head. 'That can't be true, at least not true for me before today. No way would Griffin want me more than I would want him. And, anyway, he was definitely more interested in you.'

The resentment in Pea's voice was none the less obvious for its hesitancy.

'Darling, I'm sure that was your imagination,' Venus said smoothly, refusing to acknowledge the instant connection that had, once again, sizzled between Griffin and her. Instead she continued, 'Did you notice how obviously pleased he was when he realized you're you?'

Pea chewed her lip. 'Well, I supposed he was, but still I can't believe he could want me more than I want him. He just doesn't seem that interested.'

'He would be if he had touched you, stroked the softness of your skin, felt the wet heat of your passion. You would make him burn even before your own body began to simmer.'

'You think so?'

'Trust me.' Venus pointed at a parking space they were coming up on. 'Park there.'

'But the restaurant is way over on the other side of Utica Square. We'll have to walk almost a block to get to it.'

'Exactly,' Venus said.

'That man just whistled at us!' Pea whispered excitedly to Venus.

'Yes, he certainly did. Look around darling, every man with a pulse is looking at us.' She leaned close to Pea's ear and added with a throaty laugh, 'And I do mean *us*. You're sexy and confident and beautiful, and they all know it.'

Pea looked at Venus with eyes that were huge and stunned. Then she glanced around them. 'By Ares's perfect ass you're right!' she said with a gasp.

Venus's laughter called even more eyes their way. 'Oh, no! You mustn't pick up my habit of cursing. Persephone will say I'm a horrid influence on you.' But the Goddess of Love said it with a smile. She was so proud of Pea. The two of them didn't just walk across the upscale shopping area – they strutted. *Pea* strutted. Venus could literally see her confidence growing by the moment. The little mortal was actually tossing that lovely, curly mane of hair back and holding her chin high as she strode by Venus's

103

side, matching her measure for measure. Venus couldn't have been more delighted. And dinner did nothing but reinforce Pea's newfound confidence. The waiter was young and terribly handsome. He fawned over them – both of them – and one man at the bar sent them a delightful bottle of very good wine. Overall, the whole afternoon was an excellent boost to the mortal's ego.

And now they were back at Pea's cozy kitchen table, indulging in what Venus thought happily was feeling like a wonderful new tradition – drinking Pea's excellent hot chocolate and talking like old friends, only tonight Pea wasn't wearing that wretched contraption she called footie pajamas. Tonight she was wearing the blush-colored silk nightdress Venus had insisted she purchase from the luxurious lingerie department at Saks and its matching rose-colored robe. With her hair all tumbling around her shoulders in big, glossy curls and her face flushed with excitement and the wine from dinner, Venus thought Pea could easily have been mistaken for a goddess herself. Kindness, Venus decided. Pea could be the Goddess of Kindness.

'Do you think he'll be there tomorrow?' Pea asked, pulling Venus out of her reverie.

'He?'

'Griffin.'

Venus felt a ridiculous jolt at the sound of his name, which she carefully hid. 'There?'

'The street corner. You're not paying attention.'

Venus smiled at her. 'Sorry, I was thinking about how absolutely beautiful you look.'

Pea grinned happily back at her.

'And I have no idea if he'll be there tomorrow or not. Pea, darling, the corner of a busy street is not the most opportune place for you to seduce him.'

'I'm not going to seduce him!' Pea practically squeaked.

'Of course you are. You're just not going to do it on a street corner.' Venus ignored the strange sense of excitement just hearing the man's name gave her. It was ridiculous anyway. Even had Pea not been besotted with him, it had been ages since she had dallied with a mortal. Actually, it had been ages since she'd dallied with anyone.

'Venus?'

'I'm sorry, Pea. My mind was wandering. What were you saying?'

'I said, how am I going to have even a shot at seducing . . .' Pea stopped and giggled at the word seducing as if shocked that *she* was thinking of seducing a man. '. . . Griffin if I don't see him?'

'Leave that to me,' Venus said.

'You're not going to do anything like start a fire, are you?'

Venus wiggled her brows. 'Love, start a fire?'

'Promise me you won't burn down my house.'

'I wouldn't think of burning down this delightful home!'

'Or any of my neighbors' houses.'

Venus pouted prettily. 'It was a logical idea, but I suppose I can think of something else.'

'I'll count on it.' Pea yawned and glanced at the clock. 'Oh, jeesh! It's almost midnight. I have to get up and go to work tomorrow.' Worry furrowed her forehead. 'What are you going to do while I'm gone?'

'Research,' Venus said without hesitation.

'Research?'

Venus nodded. 'You have a computer, don't you?'

'Of course, but how—'

Venus waved away her question. 'Persephone explained it all to me. Computers are like magic. She said anything you want to know about the modern mortal world can be discovered through them, especially if you use a particular magic called Google.'

Pea laughed. 'Okay, no problem. I'll give you a quick lesson before I go to work tomorrow.'

'What type of work do you do, Pea?'

'Actually, I just got a major promotion. I'm the youngest director at Tulsa Community College. I'm in charge of curriculum for our continuing education department.' Pea thought for a second and then added, 'I guess you could say that I decide what types of classes we offer adults so that they can learn new things and expand their minds.'

'That sounds like a great responsibility.'

'It is, and tomorrow is going to be a long day. I'm interviewing instructors for several new classes we're going to offer this summer.'

'Then you must get your rest.'

The two women wished each other warm good nights and went off to bed. Pea considered pleasuring herself again, but decided she was just too tired, and fell into a contented sleep almost as soon as her head hit the pillow.

Ironically Venus didn't even consider pleasuring herself. Instead she lay awake a long time, and when she finally fell into a restless sleep she dreamed of fire and a blue-eyed, dark-haired mortal.

Vulcan tried to stay away from the thread that opened a window to the mortal world – a window to Pea – and he succeeded for most of the day. Finally, his mind was so filled with thoughts of and questions about the little mortal that he could bear it no longer. Vulcan conjured the thread to him and gazed into the fiery pillar. His breath caught and he felt the thrill of long dormant emotions surge through him.

She was radiant! He watched her walk across a shopping park at Venus's side, proud and graceful and confident. She looked like the woman she had changed into the night before when she began to dance. And her clothes, her hair! She was different, yet not. She was still Pea. Still the sweet, exquisite creature he desired so passionately and so unexpectedly. Now she was just *more*. Venus had accomplished it; she had worked her magic on Pea.

Vulcan studied Pea carefully. No, his first impression had been wrong. He could detect no dusting of goddess magic on the mortal. What Venus had accomplished she had done without the use of her divine powers. She had made what had been hidden on the inside of Pea become visible. Vulcan swallowed hard and felt his chest tighten. He would not be the only man – mortal or immortal – who noticed her beauty.

It was a torment to watch the men watch Pea all through dinner. He especially wanted to blast into ash the young waiter who smiled too much and paid too many compliments to her. And the man at the bar! Vulcan wanted to reach through the thread and give him a burning reason to leave the restaurant and leave it in a hurry. But that wasn't the worst of it. She'd spoken about that gods-be-damned Griffin again! And now Venus had agreed to put her mind to getting the two of them together.

No! He wanted to yell through the thread. *He isn't good enough for you!* But he didn't yell, of course. After all, what could he do about Pea seducing Griffin? He was in Olympus and the mortal was in the modern world.

And so what if they were in different worlds? Vulcan stood up straighter and stopped rubbing his hand through his thick hair in frustration.

Persephone visited the modern world of mortals.

Venus visited the modern world of mortals.

He, too, was one of the Olympian gods. He had the power of immortals at his fingertips, as well as the magic of fire, if he chose to use it. Well, it was about time he chose to use it. There was nothing but himself stopping him from pursuing his heart's desire.

Yes. It was definitely time the God of Fire paid a visit to the modern world of mortals.

Venus was thoroughly entranced by the magic of the Internet. After Pea gave her a brief lesson and left for work (wearing her chic new black slacks, russet-colored silk blouse and fabulous black stiletto boots), the first thing Venus did was to Google herself.

'91,000,000 entries!' The goddess practically squealed. And then, just out of curiosity, she Googled Persephone. '3,920,000 entries. How interesting.' She couldn't wait to tell Persephone. And *she* thought she was such an expert on the modern world. Well, maybe she was, but clearly the modern world was more interested in love than spring.

Venus played for a while. Actually more than a while. She was fascinated by all of the different artistic renditions she found when she narrowed her Google search from Venus to Venus art. She, of course, was familiar with Botticelli, and although she could appreciate the beauty of the paintings, she had never really liked them. He made her look too empty headed and nymphlike. The *Venus de Milo* appealed to her aesthetic senses more, but it didn't look anything like her. She found a lovely sculpture in green alabaster of herself by a modern artist named Kelly Borsheim which she liked very much, and then she discovered the fantasy art of Michael

Parkes and was so enamored with it that she ordered five limited-edition prints.

'I'll just take them back with me. I mean, it's not like I can't get Persephone to help me carry them,' Venus told Chloe, who was curled contentedly by her feet.

Then she began surfing using random words and phrases, like 'romance' and 'love' and 'sex' and 'erotica,' quickly discovering a fabulous site called Smart Bitches Trashy Books dot com that had her laughing and reading the archives for hours. She especially appreciated the women's intelligent insight into how men so often underestimate and discount things labeled as 'for women only.' Of course she also appreciated the Smart Bitches creative cursing, and promptly decided to add several of their favorites, like asshat, ass-burger, man-titty and 'Bitch, please!' to her already formidable selection of genital curses.

And, finally, she settled down to the more serious task of figuring out a way to finish helping Pea. Googling 'Tulsa Community College,' she educated herself on Pea's employer before typing in her job title and reading exactly what it was she did for a living.

Fully informed, as well as impressed by Pea's responsibilities, Venus Googled 'Tulsa firemen,' and settled in with her cup of coffee to go through the 113,000 entries.

She almost choked on her sourdough cookie when she clicked into the firemen's calendar entry and beheld a half-naked Griffin on the cover of the latest edition.

'Bitch, please!' She breathed heavily as she tested out one of her new curses and fanned herself with the half-eaten cookie.

Griffin was, without a doubt, edible. She would like to eat him. Actually she would like him to eat her—

'No! Pea wants him. So Pea will get him.'

She clicked out of the dangerous calendar site – after ordering a copy. For Pea, of course. Then three sites later she cheered aloud, waking Chloe abruptly and sending her into a barking frenzy. Venus grabbed the little Scottie and hugged her. 'That's it, Chloe! That is exactly how I'm going to get Griffin and Pea together, and it's happening tonight!'

Then, realizing how much preparation there was to be done in the three hours she had left before Pea got home from work, Venus got busy.

Chapter Ten

'Honey, I'm home!' Pea joked as she hurried in the front door. Chloe rushed to her, *harrumphing* happily while Max rubbed around her legs.

'Finally! You simply must hurry. Being fashionably late is usually in good taste, but tonight I don't want you to miss one moment with Griffin.' Venus spoke quickly, motioning for Pea to follow her back to her room. When she didn't move, the goddess turned back and placed her hands on her hips in annoyance. 'Pea. Stop staring and start moving. I said we are going to be late.'

'You're . . . you're . . .' Pea swallowed, eyes huge. 'Wow! Look at you.'

Venus's annoyance faded. 'You like my regalia?' She turned slowly so Pea could get the full effect.

'It's incredible. I mean, you're beautiful anyway, but in that . . . uh . . . whatever it is, you're breathtaking.'

'This' – Venus gestured grandly at the almost transparent mixture of fabrics that draped seductively around her body, clinging and molding perfectly to the goddess's exquisite body – 'is what a Roman goddess is expected to wear when seen in her full glory. Tunica.' She pointed to the short cream-colored underdress that left much of her lovely legs bare. 'Stola.' She held out part of the draped fabric that crossed from one side of her body to the other and was a silver-white color that complemented her hair. 'And, finally, the palla.' With a flourish Venus spun gracefully around causing the piece of violet silk (the exact shade of her eyes) that was attached to the back of her silver shoulder clasps to flutter in the goddess-made breeze like a diaphanous cape.

'Absolutely beautiful,' Pea said. 'Are you dressed like this because you're going back to Olympus? Is the portal open to you again?' She smiled, but it didn't stop her face from looking sad. 'I didn't think you'd be leaving so soon. Can't you at least stay for dinner and maybe one more night?'

'Darling, are you filled with happiness and ecstasy?'

Pea's brow wrinkled as she thought about Venus's question. 'Well, I'm happy, I mean work was great today – you should have seen the way everyone looked at me. Everyone looked at *me*. Like I'm not invisible anymore! And I can't tell you how many compliments I got on my hair.'

Venus smiled at Pea's exuberance. 'Yes, you're happy. But are you filled with delicious, seductive, passionate ecstasy?'

'I really don't think so.'

'Neither do I, and until you are, I'm not leaving.'

'Then why are you dressed like that?'

Venus rolled her eyes. 'All this talk has made me forget. Follow me back here and I'll tell you while you get changed.'

'Changed? What am I changing into?'

'Your own goddess regalia,' Venus said.

'Me? Why?' she asked, but followed Venus eagerly.

'Pea, my darling, we are going to a masquerade party.'

Pea stopped in the hall outside her room. 'Venus, what are you talking about?'

'I found out about it while I was on the Internet today. Which, by the way, is a simply marvelous type of magic. Did you know there are ninety-one million sites about me? Ninety-one million! And not even four million about Persephone – and she's always so smug about – oh, never mind. I'm getting completely off the subject. While I was looking up pertinent information about your fireman, I happened to find an advertisement for a masquerade gala event being hosted at that fabulous restaurant where you and I met.'

'Lola's?'

'Exactly. The announcement said that they are trying to raise money for new equipment or some such for the Tulsa Midtown Fire Station, which is the exact station your Griffin is from.'

'Defibrillators,' Pea said.

Venus raised an eyebrow.

Pea shrugged. 'It was on the news. The fire station wants two new defibrillators for their paramedic units. So the masquerade is a fundraiser.'

'You already knew about it?'

'I suppose. I didn't really think about it. It isn't exactly something I would go to.'

'It is exactly something you *are* going to go to – actually, we're going to go to.'

'But we have to have costumes . . .' Pea's voice ran out as her eyes widened in understanding.

'Yes, darling, we do have to have costumes.' She took Pea's arm and pulled her into the bedroom. 'Hurry! I spent all afternoon conjuring things from Olympus; I can't wait to show you how to truly dress like a goddess!'

'Are you sure I shouldn't be wearing panties?' Pea nervously smoothed her hands down the front of her robes as if she was afraid a wind might spring up and lift them above her head.

'Of course I'm sure. Nothing should bind your delicate woman's lily under the silks of a goddess's robes. Besides, going without underclothing is a freeing experience. You'll see. And stop fidgeting.' Venus gave Pea's curls one more scrunch. 'It would have been much easier to prepare with the aid of a score of nymphs, but I am pleased with our end result.' She stepped back to survey her work. 'Okay, you can turn around and look at yourself now.' Together they gazed at the goddess in the mirror.

Pea's tunica was the same seductive cream color as Venus's, and it left exposed more of her legs. Venus examined them critically and nodded in silent approval at how long and strong and shapely they looked. Her stola was a sweet, blushing pink. A color that should have seemed innocent, but draped silkily around Pea's body, tucked and folded cunningly here and there to accentuate the indentation of her waist and the perfect roundness of her breasts, the maidenly shade of pink became alluring and seductive, conjuring images of hidden parts of her body. Her palla was liquid gold and it glistened with even the slightest of Pea's movements.

'Simply lovely. I knew the stola would complement your—' Venus broke off when she saw the tears pooling in Pea's eyes. 'What is it, darling?'

Pea shook her head back and forth as she began to cry. 'It's a beautiful outfit, and, yes, it's fit for a goddess. But in it I look like a sparrow trying to wear the feathers of a peacock.'

Venus blinked in surprise. 'That is simply not true, Pea.'

'Yes, it is.' She sobbed. 'I know it is. It's always been true.'

Venus took Pea's hand and led her to the bed. 'Sit,' she told her as she turned to retrieve the box of tissues from the bathroom and hand them to Pea. 'Blow.'

Hiccupping, Pea did as she was told. Then Venus sat beside her and took her hand.

'Now, tell me what happened to make you have such a distorted view of your appearance.'

Pea sniffed. 'It—it wasn't just one thing.'

'Tell me,' Venus repeated gently.

'Remember I told you about the dance squad I was on in high school, and how I thought I fit in, but that I really didn't?'

Venus nodded.

'Well.' Pea sighed. 'There was more to it than just not fitting in. I know it sounds silly, but I used to not realize that I was so dorky looking. Really. I thought I was normal. Like everyone else. I mean, I had friends – not on the dance squad, but friends. I just didn't think it would be a problem making friends with a new group.'

'What happened?'

Pea blew out a shaky breath. 'I made the squad with no problem. I've taken dance since I was five, so I really knew what I was doing. Anyway, I made the squad the first year I tried out. I was the only freshman who made it.' Venus noted that she didn't seem to have any pride in the fact that she'd accomplished something so difficult. 'So I was going to the very first meeting of the new squad. I was really excited and unbelievably happy – basically just looking forward to making new friends and doing a lot of cool dancing. As usual, I dorkishly spilled a bunch of stuff out of my purse right outside the girl's locker room door, and while I was picking it up I heard them.' Pea swallowed, fighting back more tears. 'They were talking about me, making fun of me really. They said that no matter how much dancing I did, I'd never dance away from all of my ugly. And—and they called me broccoli head, because of my hair.'

Venus shook her head. 'Young women can be so pointlessly cruel, especially when intimidated by another's talent.'

'They weren't intimidated by me!' Pea said quickly.

'Weren't they? How long ago did this happen?'

'It started a little over ten years ago, but it went on for all four years of high school. I know it's stupid to still let something bother me that happened so long ago, but—'

Venus's raised hand cut off Pea's words. 'It isn't stupid that something that happened during your formative years still affects you. That isn't why I asked how long ago it was. I asked because I want you to realize that you are now an adult, a successful, independent adult, looking *back* on events that happened to a child. You can now see them through an adult's eyes – a viewpoint that should make issues like the other girls' jealousy and insecurity clearer.'

Pea chewed her lip. 'I guess I never really thought about it like that.'

Venus pulled on Pea's hand and led her back to the mirror. 'Think about it.'

'I'll try,' Pea said doubtfully.

Venus sighed. 'I do wish you could see yourself as others see you.' Then the goddess's eyes widened. 'That's it!'

Pea frowned. 'What?'

'I shall simply give you the ability to see yourself as others see you.'

Pea took a step back from the goddess's already glittering fingers. 'I'm really not okay with that zapping stuff you do.'

'Oh, darling, I'm not going to zap *stuff* this time. I'm going to zap you.' Then while Pea stared wide-eyed at her, Venus said, '*Allow her mind to believe the beauty in her others perceive!*' Then the goddess flicked the glittering dust of her magic on Pea.

The little mortal sneezed tremendously. Venus sighed and handed her another tissue. Then she took Pea by the shoulders and turned her so that she was looking at herself head-on in the mirror.

'Oh, my . . .' Pea breathed deeply, lifting a hand as if to touch the girl in the mirror. 'I–I never imagined I could look so beautiful,' Pea said. 'It's magic. It'll disappear.'

'Of course it's not.'

'But you just—' Pea waggled her fingers, imitating Venus.

'Darling, I didn't make you look different. I just allowed you to see yourself as others see you. This' – she pointed at Pea's reflection – 'is utterly real.'

'Are you positive you didn't use magic to make me look like this?'

'This is exactly what I've been trying to tell you. Pea, darling, you have your own magic. Your beauty and kindness and intelligence are enough to enslave any man.'

'But I don't want to enslave Griffin.'

'Don't you?'

Pea blushed. 'Well, maybe a little. I guess what I really mean is that I don't want magic to be the reason he wants me.'

'Don't worry, darling. The only magic you'll use tonight is the eternal magic all confident women have access to. Simply believe in yourself. Then relax and allow your inhibitions to be freed. Give yourself over to passion and ecstasy, at least for this one night.'

'Okay. I'll try, but it might take one or two of Lola's pomegranate martinis.'

'Whatever works for you. I'm bringing the lovely credit card.'

'Whoever said you can't live off love was absolutely wrong.'

Venus sniffed daintily. 'I would certainly never say anything so blasphemous.'

'Me, either. Or at least not after the last couple days.' She grinned at her amazing reflection. 'I'm ready. Let's go before I forget I look like this.'

'Wait, I almost forgot.' Venus riffled through the piles of discarded fabric on Pea's bed. 'Here – this one is for you, and this is for me.' She handed Pea a spectacular half mask. It was covered with tiny slivers of gold crystals and it tied on with a pink velvet ribbon. The one she kept for herself was much like Pea's, except it was covered with what looked like tiny glittering diamonds and tied on with a silver ribbon. 'The Internet announcement said that all costumes were welcome, and the only requirement was that everyone wear some kind of mask.' They tied on each other's masks and then took one more look in the mirror.

Slowly, Pea reached out and took Venus's hand. 'You've made me into a goddess.'

Venus squeezed her hand and smiled. 'No, my little mortal friend. All I did was show you how to release the goddess that had been within you all along. Now let's get in that fabulous car of yours, drive to Lola's masquerade, and commit some goddess-like debauchery.'

Laughing, Pea said, 'Hey, who am I supposed to be? I mean, you're obviously Venus. Which goddess am I pretending to be?'

'You're my Greek incarnation, Aphrodite. People tend to describe me as shorter and more petite when they call me Aphrodite, so you fit the part perfectly.'

'So you and Aphrodite are actually the same goddess?'

Venus sighed. 'I can't tell you how annoying this is for me, especially after finding so many irritating references on the Internet that made it seem like we're two different deities.'

'I guess I thought you were, too. If I'd ever really thought about it.'

'Pea, if you moved to Europe and the people there began to call you by another name because it fit better with their culture, would that make you two different people?'

'Of course not.'

'Exactly. In Italy they call me Venus. In Greece they call me Aphrodite. Either place I'm still me.'

'But tonight I'm going to be you, too.'

'Yes, you are. Make me proud. Debauch like a true Goddess of Love.'

'I'm ready for it if you are,' Pea said.

'Darling, Love is always ready.'

Giggling together, they hurried from the house.

A masquerade ... Vulcan stroked his chin thoughtfully. Everyone must wear a mask. Venus had said it was a gala event. It would probably be crowded with mortals, all in costumes, ranging from the ordinary to the outrageous. Not that he'd been to many mortal parties – or many parties of the Olympians. But he wasn't entirely ignorant of the way the world worked, mortal or immortal. He had simply chosen to observe, rather than participate.

Until now.

Venus was going to the masquerade as herself. He, too, would go as himself. He'd simply wear a mask and be careful to stay away from Venus. He would be the last person, mortal or immortal, she would expect to see. As long as he didn't draw attention to his limp, there was really no way she would recognize him at all. He'd just stay in the background ... blend with the crowd ... and perhaps find a way to spirit Pea away.

'I feel like a damn fool,' Griffin said to his friend and station lieutenant, Robert Thomas.

'Hey, come on. Ya look fine.'

'That's easy for you to say. Your costume isn't so short it's showing your ass.'

Robert laughed. 'This is one of the times being short works for me.' He adjusted a section of his toga. 'I don't know why the chief decided we had to be dressed in a theme.'

'Yeah, ancient Rome. He's been watching way too much History Channel. But even that wouldn't have been so bad if he hadn't gotten the bright idea that I needed to be God of Fire.' Looking down at his name tag, which read, *Hello, my name is: THE GOD OF FIRE*, Griffin snorted and shook his head. 'What the hell was he thinking?'

'He was thinking that as our captain, and fearless leader, it makes sense that you get the best costume.'

'Hey, you can have it.' Griffin gestured at the breastplate with built-in muscles and the short, pleated tunic that ended a couple inches above his knees. 'If I go outside to get away from this crowd, I'll freeze my ass off.'

'Nah, Lola has those propane heaters set up all down the side-walk. People are dancing their asses off out there, not freezing them off. You'll be fine, Captain.'

Griffin snorted again and reminded himself not to spread his legs as he leaned back in his barstool. He hated this kind of crap. Not that fundraising for the station was crap, but the schmoozing and politicking that went with it was absolute bullshit. It was the only thing he didn't like about his promotion to captain. He wished the Powers-That-Be would just leave him the hell alone and let him do his job. And his job was not dressing up in a skirt and being paraded around in public. He'd had enough of that with that stupid calendar cover shoot. He would have never done it if it hadn't been for his sisters' excitement. They loved the thought of their big brother being on the cover of the national firefighter's calendar. Women . . . His sigh was deep and long suffering. They drove him crazy. Sure, he liked them, and because he'd been raised with four sisters he even kinda understood them. Sometimes. Hell, being raised with four sisters was the biggest reason he was still single, although he'd never tell Alicia, Kathy, Stephanie or Sherry that. They'd go nuts and bug him even more than they did now about settling down and getting married. No thanks. He'd watched three of the four of them go through hellish divorces, and he secretly thought it was only a matter of time before Alicia, the youngest and newly married, dumped Mike. The guy was a controlling dickhead. Nope. Until he saw more evidence of at least a decent statistical probability of love lasting, he was just fine being single.

'Well, slap me and call me Santa Claus. I do believe I'm in love.' Robert thumped him on his breastplate, almost causing him to spill his beer.

'What the hell's wrong with you?'

Robert pointed at the crowded entrance to the restaurant and Griffin felt his mouth go dry.

'Fucking goddesses!' Robert sputtered.

Two women had stopped to pay the cover charge for the fundraiser and were filling out their name tags. Robert had been right. They were goddesses. Familiar goddesses. Not that it was really possible to tell who anyone was for sure in the damn masks they all had on. But . . . His eyes were automatically drawn to the taller of the two women, and he felt the jolt of recognition all the way down in his groin. It was the woman from the bar – the woman who had been in that little Pea girl's car the day before. He couldn't see her violet eyes through the mask from across the room, but that hair! No way could he mistake that hair. It was an unusually light shade of blonde, long and thick, hanging well past her shoulders. God, he loved her hair. It made him want to fist his hands in it and move it out of the way so that he could taste that soft, sweet place where her shoulder met neck and then—

His cell phone rang, jarring him out of his fantasy.

'What?' he growled.

'Griffin, don't sound so grumpy.'

'Alicia, I'm kinda busy here at the fundraiser.'

'I know, but I wanted to remind you that you promised to change the oil in my car,' his sister said.

'Alicia, can't your husband take over this little chore? I mean, you've been married for a year now.'

'You know Michael is totally useless when it comes to cars. And I didn't think you minded all that much.'

Griffin wanted to say that Michael was totally useless when it came to just about anything, and he definitely wasn't good enough for his baby sister. Instead the hurt tone in her voice had him saying, 'I don't mind, Alicia. How about I come over right after my next shift? I'll bring the pizza.'

'Cool! I'll have the beer. You won't forget?'

'Only if you keep bugging the crap outta me.'

'Okay, Mr. Grump. I'll see you in a couple days. Bye bye.'

Griffin grunted in the phone and snapped it shut.

'One of your sisters?' Robert asked.

Griffin nodded.

'Stephanie?'

'No. Alicia.'

'Alicia, huh? Hey, she's single again, ain't she?'

'Not yet, but I'm hoping she'll come to her senses soon. Anyway, forget about it.'

'What? What's wrong with me?'

'What about what's her name, uh, Melissa? I thought you were seeing her,' Griffin said.

Robert shrugged. 'I am. Kinda. But it's no big thing.'

'And that's what's wrong with you.' Griffin slapped him on the shoulder and started to get off his barstool – carefully, so that his damn skirt didn't fly up too damn far.

'Hey! With your sister I'd be different,' Robert protested.

'Like I said before, forget about it.'

Griffin left Robert still grumbling to himself at the bar and started to weave his way through the crowd of masked partygoers, keeping his eye trained on the silver blonde fall of hair and the almost see-through costume of the woman who looked every bit the part of a goddess. He'd buy her a drink. Or two. What harm could a drink or two do? It wasn't like he was going to fall in love or anything stupid like that.

Chapter Eleven

'What do you want on your name tag?'

The woman looked up at him expectantly. Vulcan stared silently down at her.

'You know, who you're pretending to be tonight,' she prompted.

'I am Vulcan,' he said.

'Let's see.' She tapped the capped end of the Sharpie against the table. 'Vulcan was supposed to be God of Fire, right?'

'Correct.'

'Yeah, I kicked ass in my mythology class last semester. Hey – I think there's another God of Fire here, too. You'd think y'all would've called each other to make sure you don't have the same costumes.' She giggled a little. 'Anyway, careful you don't clash. You could burn the place down, and that would be embarrassing with all you firemen here.'

She grinned at her own joke and handed him a name tag with *Hello, my name is GOD OF FIRE* printed boldly in black marker. Following what the others had done, Vulcan put it on his chest and then he moved slowly into the large, crowded restaurant, already feeling relieved that the lighting was low enough that if he was careful no one would notice his limp – or at least Venus wouldn't. He'd waited until she and Pea had found a table near the dance floor in the main room before he entered, though it had been hard to keep his eye on them through the press of costumed people. Normally he would have hated a crowd like this, but tonight was markedly different. He kept reminding himself no one knew who he was. It seemed true; no one stared and pointed at him. There were no gods or goddesses silently laughing at him, and no mortals cowering away from him in fear. For at least this one night he was accepted; no different than any other mortal man. It was, as Venus and Persephone had already observed, an amazingly freeing experience.

Unconsciously he relaxed his usually too-rigid posture, allowing his arms to swing free and his body to move with an ease he rarely experienced outside his personal realm. His limp became less awkward. Had he been able to observe himself, he would have been shocked to see a tall, broad shouldered man who exuded power. His thick, dark hair, which he wore short because of the heat in his realm, usually evoked disdainful looks from the golden-maned Olympians. Here he fit in perfectly amongst the firemen and their military hair cuts. He wore a half mask that was the warm color of a candle's flame, and only the blue of his eyes, his lips and the firm, square line of jaw were left visible.

'Hey handsome,' purred a woman who ran a quick finger down his bronze breastplate. She was dressed in a short black skirt and matching black sweater that sparkled with tiny threads of glittering silver. Her sweater was unbuttoned low enough that the red of her bra was exposed, along with her generous breasts. Her mask was also red, as were the horns on her head and her wild, shoulder length hair. Her name tag read, Hello, *my name is SATAN.*

Vulcan had to force himself not to jump back in surprise at her touch.

'God of Fire, huh? You can light my fire anytime, baby.' She moaned breathily.

'I'll keep that in mind, Satan,' he surprised himself by saying with a smile.

The woman licked her reddened lips and smiled coquettishly before allowing the crowd to wash her from his side as the tide of people headed to the dance floor.

The mortal woman had flirted with him! *No one knew who he was.* Logically he'd realized it before then; he'd even repeated the fact to himself as he moved through the restaurant. But he hadn't really *known* it until the moment the woman had spoken to him.

It was enough to make him throw back his head and shout with happiness for the first time in his long life!

With growing confidence, he met several of the other mortal women's eyes. Not one of them turned away from him in disgust. Not one of them cringed in fear. One of them actually winked at him. The others smiled invitations. Even through their masks he could easily read their interest. His heart thudded with newly discovered excitement. If those women – those indiscriminate mortals who he had never spoken to, but who clearly were showing interest in him – if those women could find him desirable, then did it not stand to reason that Pea might desire him, too?

Vulcan moved to stand against the wall, just another in a long line of costumed, virile men. When the harried waitress took his order he repeated what the man standing nearest to him had asked for, a Boulevard Wheat Beer. As he sipped the brew, which was actually rather tasty, a little like satyr winter ale only less sweet, he focused his attention on Pea and Venus. Using the invisible thread of fire to amplify his already divine hearing, he listened and waited.

*　　*　　*

'Oh. My. God! This is so much fun!' Pea sipped her pomegranate martini and nibbled at the sweet chili roasted pecans their waitress, Jenny, had brought them.

'Oh. My. Goddess would be so much more appropriate,' Venus corrected.

'Sorry, you're right. We're goddesses. I should get the words right.'

Venus smiled indulgently at her little mortal friend. 'Don't be too hard on yourself. I've had an eternity to get used to it. You're doing very well for your first night as a deity. To us – goddesses inside and out!' Venus and Pea tapped their frosted martini glasses together. 'And what is this divine music? I've never heard anything like it.'

'The band is the Full Flava Kings. They specialize in oldies. Right now they're singing something called classic Motown. Totally danceable and utterly fantastic.' Automatically, Pea's body moved to the sounds of 'The Way You Do the Things You Do,' and she sang along with the chorus.

'You should dance,' Venus said, smiling appreciatively at the sinuous way Pea's lithe body swayed to the music.

'Oh, no. I don't dance.'

Venus laughed. 'Of course you do. You said you've been taking lessons since you were a child.'

'That's different.' Pea lowered her voice and looked around nervously. 'That's dance class.'

'So you don't really like to dance?'

'I love to dance,' Pea said quickly. 'But *that* kind of dancing.' She jerked her chin at the crowded dance floor. 'Is different.'

'You need to relax and trust your body. Believe me. Love is an expert on bodies. *That* kind of dancing is exactly what you need.'

Pea opened her mouth to argue with Venus, but a male voice interrupted her.

'Beautiful Goddess, would you honor me with a dance?'

Pea and Venus looked from each other to the masked man who stood in front of their table. He was dressed all in black – black leather pants, black silk shirt, black cape and mask. And he appeared to have a rapier in a sheath at his hip. His name tag read: *Hello, my name is ZORRO.*

Venus arched a brow, a movement that was lost behind her mask, but the slight upward curve of her full lips was unmistakable. He was certainly tall and well formed. His jaw line was firm. His manners appeared to be passable. Yes, he might do for a start.

'Hi, Zorro,' Pea said brightly.

The man hardly glanced in her direction. He had eyes only for Venus.

The goddess frowned.

'Dance with me, lovely Venus,' he said.

No, this wouldn't do at all. She wanted Pea to dance. She had been frolicking with men for centuries. It was second nature to her. Tonight it was Pea's turn.

'Go ahead,' Pea said, with a little too much enthusiasm. 'I'll be fine waiting right here.'

Venus looked at Pea, easily seeing through her masks – the physical one she wore tonight and the emotional one she'd worn for too much of her life. Pea was used to waiting in the shadows while others danced . . . loved . . . lived. *Not tonight*, Venus promised herself. And with a sudden inspiration the Goddess of Love opened her mouth and belched like a Greek sailor.

The masked man drew back half a step.

Venus waved her hand in front of her mouth. 'Whew! I think I've had too much to drink! And those pecans were certainly better going down.' While Pea and the costumed man were

128

averting their eyes in embarrassment, Venus surreptitiously wiggled her fingers at Zorro. She didn't bespell him – she wouldn't do that to Pea. The mortal had been right about not catching a man with magic. Pea deserved to capture a man who was truly attracted to her on her own, by her own merit. All Venus did was to divinely erase any interest he had in her, thereby allowing his attention to shift to an alternative 'goddess.'

He blinked, for a moment clearly disconcerted, but quickly recovered. With a flourish of his cape he bowed to Pea.

'Aphrodite, your sister goddess is not interested in the dance. Don't break my heart by saying you aren't, either.'

'She wouldn't think of it,' Venus said, giving Pea a sly shove under the table.

'But I . . .' Pea began.

'You are a goddess,' Venus said. 'And goddesses dance.' She met Pea's eyes within the sparkling mask. 'Trust me,' she said softly. 'And trust yourself.'

'Okay. Well. I'd love to dance. Thank you.' Pea took the masked man's offered hand and let him lead her to the crowded dance floor.

Venus smiled happily as she watched Pea begin to move with the beat of the music. The little mortal really was very graceful. And, of course, she had been right. As soon as Pea started to dance her natural ability and years of training took over. Even from her table Venus could see that Pea was singing to the music and having a wonderful time. The song changed to something called 'Brick House,' and even more people surged onto the dance floor. Venus saw Pea begin to swim through the crowd back to her, and she quickly blew a dusting of desire onto one of the toga-dressed men who lined the wall behind her. Instantly he intercepted Pea. Venus met Pea's gaze and nodded an enthusiastic *yes* for her to keep dancing, but even while Pea moved back onto the floor and began gyrating to the new song, Venus could feel her reticence. And she realized the problem. Pea was worried about her! She knew what it felt like to be left behind – to be the one not asked. Pea would probably only dance once more, and then she'd insist that she return to the table and sit with Venus.

The solution seemed simple. Venus should just dance. All she had to do was to meet the gaze of any of the many men who had been throwing her appreciative looks and he would rush over and beg to be allowed to escort her to the dance floor.

The goddess sighed. If she did she knew what would happen. It had happened for countless ages. She would draw the desire of the men in the crowd like candlelight beckons moths. The other women in the room – including Pea – would seem pale and lacking when compared to love incarnate, and then where would they be? Back to Pea not getting enough attention.

She supposed she could scatter around some of her divine magic, directing it to dim her allure, but she knew how difficult it was to camouflage love. And if she left, went back to Pea's home, the child would certainly follow her. She tapped her finger against her martini glass. What, by the moon-colored globes of Diana's firm buttocks, was she supposed to do?

'That was a nice thing you did for your friend.'

The deep voice instantly refocused Venus's attention. The man was dressed in what she was pretty sure was supposed to be a facsimile of an ancient Roman officer's uniform. Of course the modern mortal had missed the mark. What he wore was entirely too pretty, but even as she observed the unauthentic details she was taking in his long, strong legs, wide shoulders, and the sensuous lips that quirked with just the right touch of self-humor beneath the mask. Then she read his name tag and she couldn't contain her smile.

'I'm sorry, God of Fire, I have no idea to what you're referring.'

'The belch. You did that on purpose so the Zorro guy would ask your friend to dance instead of you, didn't you?'

Venus pulled her gaze from his beautiful lips and looked up to meet blue eyes in a red mask that was tied over thick, dark hair. Those eyes . . .

The Goddess of Love felt the jolt of recognition all the way through her suddenly flushing body. It was Griffin!

She glanced out at the dance floor before speaking. Thankfully Pea's back was to her. She should order him away before Pea recognized him. Venus looked up at Griffin. He was watching her with a simmering heat in those brilliant blue eyes that turned the red mask predatory, and it was clear that she was his prey.

Men simply did not look at the Goddess of Love like that. They showed more respect, more fear, more worship. It was inappropriate of him. It was also terribly exciting.

Purposefully she didn't speak. Instead she flipped her long hair back over her shoulder. Then she took a sip of her martini. She expected him to do the male equivalent of a woman's fidget – to fill the silence between them with the ceaseless, self-involved monologues so many men used to cover any hint of masculine embarrassment. That would certainly lessen his appeal.

But he didn't babble self-indulgently. He continued to trap her with his unwavering gaze and his patient, confident silence.

'You're very perceptive,' she finally said.

'It comes from having four sisters. And you didn't answer my question.'

'No, I didn't. Four sisters and how many brothers?'

'None. Just the sisters.'

Venus smiled. 'Are you the eldest?'

'Unfortunately.'

His tone made her laugh and, as if her amusement had directed it, 'Brick House' moved smoothly into an alluring song about a place called 'Baker Street.' Over Griffin's shoulder, Venus could see Pea, with a look of determination on her attractively flushed face, beginning to make her way through the dance floor back to the table, even though the man with whom she had been dancing was clearly trying to coax her into staying.

'Come on, my goddess. You need some air.' Griffin tucked her hand into his elbow, and before she could make any kind of protest at being manhandled or at the presumptuous way he had called her *my* goddess, he began guiding her from the room.

Venus looked back and caught Pea's surprised gaze, quickly pantomiming that she was going outside, and fanned herself like she was overly hot. With a shooing motion, she made it very clear to Pea that she should keep dancing. Pea's partner saw the exchange and seized the opportunity, taking her hand and pulling her back onto the dance floor as Griffin maneuvered Venus through the restaurant's front door.

Outside the night was calm and cool, the moon beautiful and full. Tall, iron trees pumped pools of warmth around the wrought iron tables and chairs that were placed up and down the sidewalk in front of Lola's. A large outdoor oven perfumed the air with the scent of pinion smoke. Small white lights decorated the ornamental trees, casting a magical glow from their winter branches. The band's music could easily be heard outside, and a few costumed couples were dancing on the sidewalk. It was a lovely, romantic scene, and Venus was very aware of the tall man who still had her hand trapped. True, she hadn't tried very hard to disengage herself, which was (she told herself firmly) more at surprise at being touched without her permission than because of the attraction she felt for Griffin.

Of course, she should pull her hand from his arm. His warm, muscular arm.

'Over here,' he said. Not giving her a chance to move away, Griffin guided her to an empty table, pulled a chair back for her, and only then released her hand so that she could sit.

'So, tell me. Why did you want Pea to dance instead of you?' he said as he sat across from her.

'You recognize Pea?' Venus hated the sliver of jealousy she felt. Ridiculous. After all, her intent that night had been to bring Pea to this very man's notice.

'Of course. As soon as I saw you I realized she must be with you. You two were at Lola's the other day, and then day before yesterday you were in the T-Bird together.'

'Again, you're very observant.' She made herself add, with a lie, 'And you're clearly interested in my good friend, Pea.' He hadn't been looking at Pea on the dance floor. His attention had been clearly, predatorily, focused on her. 'So, we should go back inside so you and Pea can—'

His touch broke off her words as his hand covered hers. 'I am not interested in your little friend.'

'You're not?' Venus's mouth felt dry.

'No.' His thumb made a lazy circle on the soft skin of her hand. 'And I'm glad you sent Zorro packing. Cutting in on a crowded dance floor like that can cause an ugly scene, and I definitely would have cut in. Scene or no scene.'

Venus's hand tingled where he was touching her. Her stomach clenched. She pulled her hand away from him. 'I'm not dancing tonight,' she said abruptly.

133

'Why not?' He was totally unruffled that she'd pulled away from him. Instead he gave her another slow, steady smile.

Venus opened her mouth to make a flippant remark and found herself thrown off by the way he kept looking at her. Then it hit her, right in the gut. *He really has no idea that I'm the Goddess of Love. He's truly seducing me as he would a mortal woman.* The thought was so profound that she blurted the truth.

'It's important that my friend bask in attention tonight. When I dance I tend to call attention to myself, especially male attention, so I thought it would be best if I left the dancing to her.'

Even through the mask, she saw his expression shift to surprise. 'That's unusually generous of you.'

'You believe that I'm not usually generous?'

As before, he took his time answering her. 'Experience has taught me that women who are very beautiful can be callous about others' feelings.'

'That's a cynical point of view.'

He shrugged. 'I think it's realistic.'

'Are your sisters very beautiful?'

His lips quirked. 'They are.'

'And callous?'

He held up his hands, as if in surrender, and laughed, a sensuous sound Venus felt tickle up and down her spine. 'I'll never say that. Instead I'd just say that my beautiful sisters are like all women – complex.'

Venus smiled. 'An excellent answer. And you should know that I am Goddess of Love.' She pointed at her name tag, loving the freedom of being able to proclaim it, and at the same time remain unrecognized. 'So I speak with authority when I say that Love may seem callous, but usually only to those untouched by her.'

'I recognized you right away, Goddess. Venus is actually my favorite goddess.'

One of her slim brows arched up. 'Is she?'

Griffin lifted a shoulder. 'Okay, she's the only goddess I know anything about.'

Intrigued, Venus asked, 'And what do you know about her?'

'Just the normal stuff. You know, born of the ocean, Goddess of Love and Beauty. That's about it. Anyway I'm interested in what you were saying before. Did you mean that true love is generous, versus the pretenses of love, like lust and infatuation?'

Her smiled was delighted. Not only did he know about her birth, but he'd managed to keep up with her conversation. Too often men, mortal and immortal, did nothing but stare into her eyes, or at her breasts, and let their minds sink down between their legs when they spoke to her. This man was sexy and confident and intelligent – definitely a lethal combination. 'Yes, that's exactly what I meant. True love can be differentiated from its imposters by its generosity. Are you always this perceptive about women and love?'

'I think there are a lot of people who would say that I don't usually pay much attention to either.'

'I don't believe that. Not from the brother of four beautiful sisters.'

'Generous and wise,' he said, with a smile, enjoying her insight. 'But then, I am in the presence of a goddess.'

'You are, indeed.' Venus inclined her head graciously, enjoying their banter almost as much as she liked the easy way he talked with her, and the predatory way he looked at her. There was nothing submissive or worshipful about Griffin, and she found that refreshing as well as alluring.

A tattooed waiter cleared his throat and asked for their order.

'I'll have another lovely pomegranate martini, darling,' Venus said.

'Macallan scotch, straight up.'

The waiter nodded and hurried off, and the music changed again. Venus couldn't stop her body from moving with the rhythmic beat of a song that proclaimed, 'It's raining men.' She laughed as all the women on the sidewalk began to dance together, raising their arms and singing loudly to the chorus.

'Go on, dance with them.'

Glancing through the plate-glass restaurant window, Venus found Pea, still buried on the dance floor.

'Pea's fine. Dance for me, Goddess of Love. I'll protect you if anyone can't handle himself.'

Griffin's tone was a clear challenge. Perhaps he should experience a little of the passion Love could evoke.

'I'll remind you later that I warned you.'

He grinned mischievously. 'Why not see what Love can do?'

'Yes, darling,' she said with a purr. 'Why not?'

Feeling sexy and deliciously decadent, Venus joined the other women. The music entered her body, as it always did, and the goddess let herself go. She danced for Griffin, forgetting Pea's infatuation, forgetting the other people on the sidewalk, forgetting everything except the beat of the music, the glorious magic of the night, and *him*. Tossing her hair and moving in perfect harmony with the modern music she was graceful and seductive – alluring and adept. The women who danced around her tried to emulate the silk-swathed vision in the blazing mask, drawn by her laughter and beauty. The men stared hungrily at her, especially Griffin. She could feel the heat of his gaze as if his hands were on her, and it made her flush with excitement and anticipation.

Venus danced, and for the first time in her eons of existence she reveled in the fact that no one knew she was anything but a beautiful, frolicking mortal. She didn't have to consider what Love loosened would mean to Griffin. He wasn't worshipping a deity. He was simply ogling a beautiful, mortal woman. When the song ended, Venus collapsed against the other women, and they all laughed breathlessly.

The tempo of the music changed. The lead singer of the band began to croon, 'Thanks for the times that you've given me. The memories are all in my mind . . .'

'Dance with me.'

Venus looked up, and Griffin was there. His blue eyes seemed to blaze with the intensity of his fiery mask. He didn't wait for her answer. Without another word he pulled her roughly into his arms. One hand took hers – the other pressed firmly against the small of her back, holding her body against his.

Venus let him claim her. She had never allowed herself to be led by any man, but Griffin masterfully guided her away from the others, melding her body to his and moving them in seductive time to the music until they were dancing alone under a tree in a mixed pool of twinkling light and shadows.

No one had ever taken her in his arms without her permission or by her express command. No one. Neither man nor god, in all the eons of her existence, had touched her without her approval. Until now. Venus couldn't believe how incredibly seductive it was. She met his eyes and let the crackling intensity of sexual chemistry sizzle between them.

She wanted him.

The thought surprised her. Then she was shocked by her surprise. By the overused phallus of Neptune! Why shouldn't she allow herself the indulgence of this delicious man? Why not give in to this seductive game of pretending to be mortal?

Because Pea desires him drifted through her mind. But Griffin had made it clear that he didn't desire Pea. So why deny herself such a virile lover? It didn't make sense. And, surely, Pea would understand. Pea wouldn't continue to be interested in a man who so clearly wasn't interested in her. Besides, how long had it been since she truly paid attention to her own desires?

Venus knew the answer. For centuries she had fallen into the habit of seeing to the needs of others – of answering the heartfelt prayers of others – of ignoring her own desires. She even knew when the habit had started. It had begun with her marriage to poor, solitary Vulcan. What an abysmal mistake that had been.

And the thought struck her that perhaps Pea wasn't the only one whose life needed a makeover.

Chapter Twelve

From the instant she began to dance, Griffin felt as if someone had punched him in the gut. He had never seen anything so beautiful.

No, that wasn't right. She wasn't just beautiful – that was too simple a word. If love could be made physical, this woman whose name tag so appropriately read Venus, Goddess of Love, would be his choice for the personification. And it wasn't just about sex – although he was goddamned sure every man out there, including himself, had hard-ons from watching her move. It was about her uninhibited laughter. The joyous way she tossed back her hair and embraced the music as if she actually were an ancient pagan goddess they should fall to their knees and worship.

He sure as hell understood why she hadn't wanted to dance inside. After watching her, how could a man be interested in any other woman?

'Fucking weird,' he muttered to himself, never taking his eyes off her. He couldn't remember the last time a woman had gotten under his skin like this. Shit, women had been chasing him around since he'd outgrown his teenage zits and gawkiness. He'd been happy to return their interest, but he'd never had the desire to settle down with one. Two of his sisters said he was commitmentphobic. The other two said he had high standards and refused to settle. He thought the truth was probably somewhere in between.

Then this blonde walked into his life.

The dance ended and Griffin was on his feet heading toward her without consciously telling himself to move. Several of the other men had the same idea and he heard himself literally growling at them. He wanted her. He wanted her worse than he'd ever wanted anyone.

'Dance with me.'

He hadn't waited for a response, but had taken her in his arms and begun maneuvering her away from the eyes of the other men. She felt soft and warm and she smelled like an exotic spice he couldn't place. They danced slowly under the tree, still not speaking, and he started to worry that he'd done something wrong. Or had he just imagined that she was as kind and smart as she was beautiful? Maybe she wasn't saying anything because she didn't have shit to say. He tried to look through her mask to the woman beneath, but all he could see were those violet eyes and those luscious lips that smiled so easily before, but were now set in a line that managed to look both aloof and sad.

'You were right,' he said, falling back on what always worked with his sisters. Make them right and everything got instantly better.

'About?'

'About not dancing inside the restaurant.'

'Yes,' she said absently.

'Once, twice, three times a lady . . .' was all that filled the silence between them, and Griffin was beginning to feel desperate. At a total loss, he blurted the truth.

'You look sad.'

She seemed to shake herself and refocused on him. 'Not sad, just thoughtful.'

'Anything I can help with?'

'Are you taking care of me as you would one of your sisters?'

He splayed the fingers of his hand intimately against the small of her back, very aware that all that separated his flesh from hers was a couple layers of flimsy silk. He held her gaze with his. 'I don't feel brotherly toward you at all.'

'Good.' She sounded breathless.

He pulled her closer. He felt the slow, steady heaviness in his loins tightening and heating in response to her.

'I don't even know your name,' he said huskily.

Her smile was teasing. 'You should. You're dancing with your wife.'

Her words took him completely off guard.

Venus laughed and the sound was so compelling that his desire to see her laugh and smile more was suddenly as great as his physical desire for her.

'Don't look so shocked,' she said, still laughing. 'You're Vulcan, God of Fire. I'm Venus, Goddess of Love. Vulcan and Venus are married.'

He let his hand trace a lazy circle around the small of her back. 'Sorry, *Venus*, my mythology is rusty. Are you sure the God of Fire is Vulcan? I thought that was Ares.' Then he was ferociously glad that he was semi-clueless about mythology when his comment made her toss back her head and laugh again.

'Oh, I'm sure!'

He grinned. 'So we're married.'

'Definitely.' She lowered her voice to a conspiratorial whisper and leaned even closer to him. 'But rumors have it that it's just a marriage of convenience and strictly platonic.'

'Bullshit!' he said, pretending offense – which he found damn easy to do. Just imagining being in a platonic marriage with this woman was enough to set his teeth to grinding. 'No wonder I never got into those myths. Too damn hard to believe.'

'You don't believe our marriage is platonic?'

'No, I don't.'

She shrugged, eyes still sparkling playfully. 'Who am I to argue with my husband?'

It was his turn to laugh. 'I don't believe the Goddess of Love would be a submissive wife any more than I believe she'd be a passionless one.'

'Well, husband, I'm glad to see we understand each other.' She paused, and added in a voice that was suddenly hesitant and a little shy, 'You might be surprised, though. Even a goddess can make mistakes. Who knew love could be intimate with loneliness?'

'You've been lonely, wife?' He meant it to be a teasing question, but the unexpected sincerity in her expression turned his tone serious.

She looked into his eyes and Griffin felt his heart contract. What had made this incredible woman so sad? He didn't know, but he did know that if the guy was here he'd make him sorry he ever drew breath.

'I have,' she said softly. 'We should have never married. We've both been unbearably sad. Friendship can only be an addition to, not a substitute for, true love.'

Griffin felt her words move through him. Like they had parted a curtain, he realized just how alone his loveless life had become. 'And neither is waiting and searching.' He drew a deep breath, not sure where this was leading them, but not wanting to break the spell of intimacy. He leaned closer to her and whispered. 'Is there any way we can reconcile? How can we make this better for both of us?'

She turned her violet gaze up to him, as if she was searching his face. 'Maybe for just this one night we could become two different people.'

'Anything for you, my goddess.'

'I've been meaning to speak to you about calling me *your* goddess like that. It's very presumptuous, you know.' Her expression had cleared, and her full lips tilted up. Griffin felt himself being drawn down to the inviting softness of her mouth.

'Well, since I'm your husband, newly reconciled at that, I think I'm entitled to a little presumption.' He bent, and before she could say anything more, kissed her.

She stiffened for only a moment. Griffin kept the kiss soft, allowing her plenty of time to break it and step away from him. But she didn't. Instead she relaxed and melted into his mouth. What started as a sweet, teasing question of a kiss deepened, and when he felt her arms glide up and around his shoulders Griffin became utterly lost in her. She opened her mouth to him, allowing him to drink her in. She tasted of spice and woman and sex. His response to her was primal and fierce. The thought passed through his lust-fogged brain that she made him feel so ablaze that he could actually be the God of Fire. Then he couldn't think at all. The only thing he could do was touch, taste and desire her.

He pulled her deeper into the shadow of the tree so that its trunk obscured most of their bodies from the view of people outside the restaurant, and he positioned himself so that his body was between her and the street. Then, in their small pocket of privacy, he devoured her. She leaned into him, molding her thighs against his. She moaned into his mouth and he cupped her sweet, soft ass in his hands, lifting her so that he could rub his erection against her.

'Is it good? Do you like it?'

143

'Yes,' she whispered against his lips.

He reached up and pulled her silken shoulder strap down, baring her breast. Her pink nipple was puckered and ready for his mouth. He bent to lave the bud, circling it with his tongue before he sucked it into his mouth, hard and fast. Her gasp made him lift his head. She was panting, her lips parted and wet.

'You taste so damn sweet,' he managed to say.

Spreading her legs, she moved her hips so that he had access to more of her.

He pulsed against her. 'Let me feel you.'

She moaned and whispered, 'Yes.'

Blood rushed through his body, filling him so that he felt engorged, unbearably hard and tight. He reached between them and easily found a slit in her silky dress.

'Ah, god! You have nothing on under there.' His voice sounded strange to him, deep and almost sobbing with lust as his fingers glided over her wet heat.

She didn't speak. Instead she lifted one leg, wrapping it high on his hip. Then she moved her own hips, lifting so that the tip of his penis joined his fingers and both were sliding against her slickness without actually penetrating her.

'If you don't want this, you have to tell me to stop now.' He gasped the words, knowing that soon he would be unable to think rationally. 'And please don't tell me to stop.'

'Don't stop,' she whispered.

With a growl, he took her ass in both of his hands and backed her against the tree. She braced herself with her hands on his shoulders, and then he moved forward, sliding into her tight heat with unbearable slowness as both her legs came up around him and he held her firmly.

'Christ, you feel incredible!'

Through the roaring of his pounding blood he heard her gasp and he covered her mouth again, drinking in her moans and muffling her cries and his own as he tunneled deeper. When he felt her spasm rhythmically around him, he tilted her pelvis even more so that he could sink himself fully inside her, his own orgasm building and building.

'Hey Captain, that you over there?'

Griffin had no fucking idea how his lieutenant's voice managed to penetrate the raw passion that was filling his brain, but later he thought how grateful he was that it had. No damn way he would ever have forgiven himself if anyone had seen what was going on between them.

'Captain! Hey!'

Griffin lifted his head from her and looked around the tree to see Robert waving and coming toward him.

'What is it?' Griffin roared. Slipping out of her, he angled his body so that she was even more covered as she hastily straightened her costume and tried to regain her footing.

Robert froze where he was, clearly surprised by his friend's angry tone.

'Uh, the chief is asking for you. He wants you to explain to the mayor that plan you have for training the community on the use of the mini-defibrillators. Seems the mayor might have some funding you could use.'

Griffin fought to make his brain work while he got his breathing under control.

'Go.'

He glanced down at her. She was still straightening her costume and she wasn't looking at him.

'Just go,' she repeated.

She tried to move out of the cage of his arms, but he only tightened them around her and threw Robert a quick, 'Tell the chief I'll be right there.'

Robert nodded, gave Griffin one more curious look, and then disappeared back into the restaurant.

'It's okay. He's gone now,' Griffin told her.

'You should go, too.'

Griffin felt an awful wave of frustration, mixed with a terrible sinking. It couldn't end like this. It wouldn't end like this. He reached out and pulled the silk ribbon that still held her mask into place, and it fluttered away like a freed bird, leaving her face naked to him. She was so incredibly beautiful the words he'd been planning to say wouldn't come to him. The silence between them grew, and in a gesture that was both proud and vulnerable, she lifted her chin and met his eyes.

'I said, you should go, too.'

'Don't do that,' he whispered roughly, finally finding his voice again.

She looked away from him, clearly trying to hide the hurt in her eyes. He cupped her face in his hands, forcing her gaze back to his.

'You don't know me, so you're going to have to take my word for this till I can prove it to you. I'm not the kind of man who uses a woman and then walks away. This' – he gestured at the tree – 'has never happened to me before. I should apologize to you, but I'd be lying if I said I was sorry it happened, and I won't lie to you.' He paused, rubbing his thumbs up and down the smoothness of her cheeks. 'What I will apologize for is leaving.'

She stared at him for a long time with those expressive violet eyes. Finally she said, so softly that he had to strain to hear her,

146

'This has never happened to me before, either. I'm usually the one in control.'

'Let me take care of this business with the mayor. I'll try to make it short and be right back. Say you'll wait for me at our table.'

'I'll wait for you,' she said.

'Good.' His kiss was rough and thorough, and then he reluctantly followed Robert's path into the restaurant.

Chapter Thirteen

What, in all the sexless levels of the Underworld, had just happened to her? Everything had seemed fine. She'd been playing at being a mortal, and she'd been having a wonderful time, especially enjoying the titillation of Griffin's possession of her. She'd definitely enjoyed dancing for him, and the way he'd taken her in his arms, again without her permission, and danced her away from the crowd. Then they'd fallen into that weird conversation about Vulcan. By the flabby thighs of Bacchus! Why had she opened up that Pandora's box? Or, more precisely, why had she admitted such intimate things to a man who was practically a complete stranger – and a mortal one at that? Then, he'd kissed her, and that's when it had happened. She'd lost control.

With shaking hands she retied the mask on her face, grateful for the camouflage, and walked quickly back to their table where her pomegranate martini waited. She took a long drink, letting its coolness soothe the heat that was still pulsing through her body.

The mortal had brought her to orgasm!

Not that she wasn't capable of orgasm. Please – she was Goddess of Love – an orgasm was as natural as breathing to her. What had shocked her beyond words was the fact that the orgasm had been uncontrolled. She hadn't planned it. *He* had made it happen. Then another thought hit her and she cursed aloud. Pea was obsessed with him! So she'd just fornicated against a tree with the mortal her friend, and charge, desired above all others.

She should follow him inside the restaurant and smite him with a swift blast of her divine power. She could do it quickly. None of the other mortals would even have to know. She could reprimand him. Put him in his place. And then wipe his memory clean of their encounter and plant within it a desire for Pea.

But she didn't move.

For one thing, Griffin had said he had no interest in Pea. And Pea had already made it clear that she didn't want magic to be the reason Griffin desired her. So if Venus meddled with his mind, filling it with passion for Pea, she would actually be creating something her friend didn't want. Wouldn't she?

For another thing, it was hypocritical for her to smite him for manhandling her when it was that very thing – the blasphemous way he treated her – that she found so exciting. Venus scoffed and took another long drink from her martini. She could hardly believe that her knees felt weak and she was still flushed and breathing entirely too hard. Clearly it had been too long since she had sipped from passion's cup and her own lust had become an insistent burning heat simmering dangerously within her, until the least little touch of a man had caused her to ignite. Really! She should be ashamed of herself. Venus tapped her martini stem and tried to remember the last time she'd masturbated.

It certainly hadn't been anything like getting ravished beneath that tree by that delectably irreverent man, her errant thoughts whispered.

'Waiter!' She lifted her arm and the young, tattooed man hurried over to her. 'I'd like another martini and something sweet. Something sweet and very chocolate.'

149

'Lola has an excellent chocolate mousse on the menu tonight.'

'I'll take it. Actually bring me two.' At the waiter's surprised look, she added absently, 'I'm meeting someone.' He nodded and rushed off.

'Well, it's true,' she muttered at her half empty martini. Or at least it was supposed to be true. He'd asked her to wait for him. He said he would return. But if he didn't . . . if he didn't . . .

If he didn't she didn't know what she would do. The Goddess of Love had no experience with rejection.

Pea was having the time of her life! She'd never danced so much (except in ballet class), and she certainly had never felt this beautiful. She was actually flirting. So far there hadn't been one man who stood out from the others. Unfortunately she hadn't found Griffin. And it wasn't as if she hadn't been looking for him – she definitely had! But between dancing song after song and trying to peer through the masks everyone was wearing . . . well . . . Griffin could practically be standing right beside her and she might not know it.

Full Flava Kings belted out the conclusion of 'Do You Love Me' and, laughing breathlessly, Pea thanked the Roman soldier with whom she'd danced the last two songs.

'How about the next one?' he asked, grabbing her hand and trying to keep her on the dance floor as Full Flava's female lead began singing, 'You Can't Hurry Love.'

'Thanks, but I need a break. I'm dying of thirst.'

He still didn't let go of her hand. 'Come on, just one more.'

'Thanks, but no.' Pea repeated as she tried to pull her hand from his, not liking his too tight, too insistent grip.

'You can't just walk out on a guy like that. Not after the way you dance.'

'Sorry, I don't know what you mean. It was just a dance,' Pea said, frowning at him and trying not to let him mess up her good mood.

His voice lowered and through the eyeholes in his mask his gaze looked narrow and pissed off. 'Not the way you move, it's not just a dance. Don't even try to pretend something else.'

Pea stared at him, not sure if she should laugh or scream. Having a man too interested in her wasn't a problem she was used to. Maybe she should belch on him.

'A goddess is only touched when she gives her permission, otherwise you will invoke her wrath, and the wrath of a goddess is a terrible thing to behold. Even the gods themselves tremble at the thought.'

The deep voice rumbled from somewhere behind and above her. Pea started to turn around to see who was speaking, but she found herself mesmerized by the look on her ex-partner's face. Under his beige mask his face had blanched white, and through the eyeholes she could see that fear had replaced the anger in his gaze.

'Hey, man. I didn't mean anything.'

'Then you should apologize,' Pea said, feeling the need to stand up for herself – by herself. 'But not because I'm a goddess. You should apologize because you were rude and pushy. Hello – when a woman says no, she means no.'

'I'm sorry,' he said hastily, and then he retreated into the dance floor crowd.

Still frowning, Pea watched the terrified man scuttle away. Then she started to turn to confront whoever it was who thought he was her savior. 'I appreciate you being a gentleman and step-ping in, but it was really no big deal. I could have handled it my—' Pea's words choked in her throat. The man standing behind her was magnificent! It wasn't his size that took her breath, although he was tall, probably at least six foot four. It wasn't his thick black hair that was somehow utterly untamed by his short, military-looking haircut. It wasn't the great costume he was wearing with the molded breastplate that looked so authentic and the leather-pleated tunic that left much of his long legs bare. No, it was none of those things that struck her speechless. It was the look in his dark, expressive blue eyes. His gaze seemed to shine through his flaming gold mask, touching her with such incredible longing that it made her tremble.

Neither of them said anything for a long, intimate moment, and then he spoke. His deep voice was so gentle that she could hardly believe this was the same man who sounded so harsh and dangerous just moments ago.

'You said you were thirsty. I would be honored if you would allow me to buy you something with which to quench your thirst.'

Pea realized her mouth was hanging open and she quickly closed it. 'O-o-okay,' she stuttered, while her inside voice was shrieking, *Now is not the time to sound like a dork!* She drew a long breath and ordered her mouth to stop its ridiculous babbling. She. Was. A. Goddess! And goddesses were totally capable of conversing in a rational manner with handsome men. And, anyway, she needed to practice on someone who took her breath away so that she would be ready to be coherent if she got another chance to talk to Griffin. 'Okay,' she repeated in a more reasonable tone, pulling herself together. 'It's only right that I let you buy me a drink. You did come to my rescue, even though I could have handled him just fine myself.'

'Of course you could have . . .' He glanced at her name tag and his lips turned up just slightly. '. . . Aphrodite, Goddess of Love.'

'Yeah,' she said and then realized she sounded about sixteen, and added, 'Still, I do owe you a favor for your honorable display of chivalry.'

'Let there be no talk of debts between us, Goddess,' he said. 'I only want you to drink with me if you truly wish it.'

Pea felt her stomach flutter. His voice worked on her like a slow, sexy ballad. 'Well, I did say I was thirsty.'

His half smile instantly changed into a lovely, full-on grin that made Pea's stomach butterfly. He led her back to her table, and she noticed that he limped, which didn't stop him from holding out her chair and, just like a knight of old, bowing her into it.

'Thanks,' she said. Luckily her waitress was just passing by and she ordered a pomegranate martini and a large bottle of Pellegrino – to help keep her head clear. There was something about this man that was intoxicating enough without boozing it up. He said he'd have the same. 'Well, so, um, you're' – Pea squinted at his name tag – 'the God of Fire. Wow. That's a big job.'

He shrugged and looked surprisingly uncomfortable. 'It's something that must be done.'

'I'd say so. I mean, without you how would we light and heat the earth?' Pea said, proud of herself for her pithy comment.

Unfortunately he looked even more uncomfortable. His broad shoulders moved restlessly.

'Sorry,' she said quickly, wanting to put him at ease. 'I imagine you firemen guys might feel silly dressing up as gods and such tonight. I mean, truth be known, I'm not a real goddess. I'm just me.'

His chocolate brown eyes darkened even more, and he leaned forward. 'I know what you are. You're something better than the gilded, perfect Goddess of Love.'

Pea smiled, thinking of Venus's beauty. 'What could be better than the Goddess of Love?'

'You, Pea,' he said earnestly. 'You don't need the magic of the immortals. You're unique and honest and real. That outshines the cold perfection of the gods.'

His words made her heartbeat speed up. 'How do you know my name?'

'I've seen you here before. Saturday. You—'

'Oh, great!' Pea put her masked face in her hands. 'You saw the Great Belch and Penis Drop.'

'That's not what I saw.'

His voice was so gentle that she lifted her face from her hands. Their eyes met.

'What did you see?'

'Myself.'

Pea blinked. She couldn't have heard him right. 'Yourself? I don't understand.'

His smile was shy. He seemed to almost have to struggle with himself to keep talking. 'It sounds unbelievable, I know. But Saturday when I watched you all I could think was that I knew exactly how you felt. I knew . . .' He paused and then began again. 'I *know* what it's like to be the one who doesn't fit in.'

'You?' she said incredulously.

'Appearances can be deceptive.'

'Don't I know it! I mean, you saw me Saturday. Clearly, you can tell I've had a big change since then. This' – she made a sweeping gesture at herself – 'isn't really what I've looked like for the whole rest of my life. I've had some . . . um . . . help recently. But since you saw me Saturday, which was before my makeover, you already know I'm usually not this put together.'

Slowly he reached out and covered her hand with his own. 'I saw how real and kind you are, and that is something I find very beautiful.'

His hand was warm and big and strong. She could feel the roughness of his calluses against her smooth skin, and it excited her to imagine that he'd earned those calluses by fighting fires and saving lives. It did something else, too. Something that totally shocked her. It conjured images of the night before last when the ambrosia loosened her inhibitions and she'd touched herself and brought herself to an earthshaking climax. It had felt so good, so decadent, so sexy and . . .

'What are you thinking about?' His voice caressed her.

'Me?' She pulled her thoughts back to the present, trying to ignore the way her face flushed. She felt hot and wet, a sensation that was all the more obvious because of her lack of underwear. 'I don't know . . . I was just daydreaming, I guess. Sorry.'

'Don't be sorry. Tell me what you were daydreaming about.'

'I can't!' she blurted, then cleared her throat and tried to laugh nonchalantly, as if it was just some kind of silly girl thought that had made her blush and blurt.

Instead of accepting her glib response, his hand tightened over hers and he said earnestly, 'You feel it, too, don't you?'

She started to conjure up a laugh and a flippant remark, but something in his dark, intense gaze caught her, and it was as if she could see through his public layers to his private heart. Suddenly, inexplicably, she knew exactly what he meant.

'You mean our connection, don't you?' She said it so softly that he had to lean closer to her to hear. Their shoulders brushed, sending another tingle through Pea's body.

'I do. There's something between us. I felt it Saturday, and I came here tonight hoping to see you again – to talk with you.'

155

Pea thought how ironic it was that she'd come tonight hoping to see Griffin, and this gorgeous man had come tonight hoping to see her. Huh!

He shifted restlessly in his seat. 'I'm not good at this. I've never been good at talking to women, but you conjured me here – you compelled me here. Forgive me if I'm not more practiced at the arts of love.'

'I think you're doing just fine,' Pea said.

Chapter Fourteen

There was a pause in their conversation while the waitress brought them their drinks, and Pea was pleased to note that he didn't take his hand from hers. They sipped their martinis silently while they just looked at each other – at first shyly, and then Pea felt the temperature of his gaze change and it seemed his eyes devoured her.

The Full Flava King's female lead singer handed the microphone over to the male lead. The music slowed and the lights dimmed, and he began crooning the old seventies love song, 'Always and Forever.' Pea swayed slightly to the music.

'Dance with me,' she said.

His body jerked as if she'd hit him.

'I don't dance. I can't.'

But she saw something else in his eyes. She had no idea why he was so easy for her to read, but as odd and impossible as it seemed, she knew deep in her soul it wasn't that he didn't want to dance with her – she knew he was afraid to dance with her. His transparency gave her the courage to speak, to say words she'd never even considered saying to any man before.

'It's not really dancing.' Her voice was gentle and persuasive. 'It's just holding me in your arms and moving to the music.'

He closed his eyes. 'My leg . . .'

'Does it hurt?'

'Not enough to speak of,' he said automatically, then with more honesty he added, 'It . . . it just makes me move awkwardly, so I've never danced.'

'Ever?'

'Ever.'

'Then let me teach you.' She stood and held out her hand to him. 'Trust me. I promise it'll be okay.'

Slowly, as if he were swimming against a great tide of the past, he stood and put his hand in hers, allowing her to lead him to the dance floor.

Pea guided him into position – his left hand holding her right, his right at the small of her back. Then she looked up at him and whispered, 'Now just move slowly with the music. I'll follow you.'

At first he didn't budge. They just stood there on the crowded dance floor, like a tableau, frozen in time. Then, hesitantly, he began to sway in time to the tempo. Pea followed him. Now that she was standing so close to him, she was impressed anew by his height and the breadth of his shoulders. He didn't look at her. Instead he stared somewhere over her shoulders, his entire body tense. She thought it was a little like dancing with a mountain.

'Relax, you're doing just fine,' she said.

His gaze whipped down to meet hers and she was touched by his startled, unsure look. How could any man who was so big and muscular and *handsome* be unsure of himself? Men were so funny sometimes. A simple slow dance could completely throw even a macho fireman off guard.

She squeezed his hand and smiled up at him. 'Loosen up your shoulders before you break something.'

'Am I holding you too tightly?' he said, quickly slacking his grip on her and taking half a step back.

'No, it's okay to hold me tightly. It's a slow dance.' She closed the space between them. 'When I said you were going to break something I meant something inside you.'

'Oh,' he said. 'Oh, I see.' He gave her a quick, nervous smile and settled her back into his arms, but he also stared over her shoulder as if the answers to the most complex questions in the universe were printed behind her.

'Hey,' she said.

He glanced down.

'This would work better if you looked at me. Just forget about being nervous and concentrate on the song.' *And me*, she wanted to add, *concentrate on me*, but she couldn't quite get the words out.

As if he'd been reading her mind, he said, 'And you? Can I concentrate on you?'

She smiled. 'Absolutely.'

'That I can do.' He pulled her even closer, and this time his gaze didn't leave hers.

'Every day love me your own special way . . .'

She heard the first part of the chorus of the love song, but the longer she met his eyes, and the closer her body moved to his, the more he blotted out everything – the song, the people around them, the world. How could she read so much in a face that was partially masked? It was like he was a code, but she'd been given the key to understanding him. And understand him she did. Overwhelmed, she saw desire and fear and loneliness and longing in his eyes. And love . . . incredibly, inexplicably, impossibly, she saw love.

'Yes,' she whispered, even though he'd said nothing aloud. 'Yes, I want . . . I want . . .'

Then she noticed that the music had changed from the slow ballad to an enthusiastically sung version of Rick James's 'Super

Freak,' and they were the only two people not gyrating to the funk.

'You want?' he asked.

She wanted him. Pea almost blurted it, that she wanted to taste him and know him and love him. What the hell had gotten into her? Totally disconcerted, Pea stuttered, 'I . . . um . . . want to . . . to . . . to go to the ladies' room,' she finished in a rush. 'Will you wait for me?'

'Always.' He lifted her hand, which he was already holding, turned it over, closed his eyes and pressed his lips against her skin.

The touch of his lips made a sweet, slick sensation tingle all the way from her palm to her crotch.

A couple dressed as sixties flower children, complete with masks painted in psychedelic peace signs, did the bump right into them, shattering the bubble of intimacy Pea felt. Reluctantly she pulled her hand from his.

'I'll be right back.'

Feeling a little lightheaded, Pea maneuvered her way through the crowd to the burgundy curtained entrance to the ladies' room. There were two parts to the restaurant's ladies' restroom area. A series of stalls were found down a short hall, directly to the right of the entrance to the lounge. In front of the entrance there was a room that was more of a makeup check and hair rearrange area. It was a twenties' style powder room, with a marble counter and sink and a great mirror. Pea dashed into the room and closed the door. She leaned against the counter, staring at herself in the gilt-framed mirror. A beautiful stranger looked back at her from beneath a sparkling mask.

'Who am I becoming?'

The knob on the door jangled and she turned the water on hastily, pulling one of the towelettes from the dispenser.

'I'll be out in a second,' she said, turning off the water and trying not to sound as breathless and out of sorts as she felt.

The door continued to open, and she turned to give the intruding woman a disapproving frown.

He stepped into the room and closed the door behind him, locking it.

They stared at each other.

'I wanted to be alone with you,' he said. Then he shook his head in obvious frustration. 'No, that's not right. I *needed* to be alone with you.'

Pea knew she should ask him to leave. Or shove past him. Or threaten to scream. But when she regained the ability to speak, her traitorous voice didn't demand that he do any of those things. Instead she heard herself saying, 'Would you do something for me?'

'Anything within my power.'

'Take off your mask.'

He untied the black velvet ribbon that held the half mask to his face and let it fall to the floor. Pea didn't speak. She simply reached up and untied her own mask, letting it, too, flutter out of her fingers. Then she studied his face.

He wasn't traditionally handsome, like Griffin, which didn't mean that he wouldn't turn heads and cause women to send him inviting, lingering looks. His face was strong and well made. His cheekbones were high and his jaw square. His nose was almost hawkish and that mixed with his thick, black hair and dark eyes gave him a definite bad boy look. And his mouth ... Pea's eyes got caught there ... his mouth was full and sensual. Then she lifted her eyes to meet his again, and in the way he was looking at her she saw a whole new world waiting for her there – with this man who was such a familiar stranger.

161

'If I don't touch you again soon I think I may go mad,' he said.

Pea didn't think; she just responded. 'Then touch me.'

He closed the space between them so quickly her breath caught in her throat and she automatically jerked back from him a little.

He froze, his hands already lifted as if to pull her close.

'Please, don't ever fear me. I couldn't bear it if you feared me.'

Those eyes again . . . they captured her and she could see the pain and the honesty in his words.

'I'm not afraid of you. It's just that you're so big.' Nervously she laughed a little.

'I'm sorry I'm not smaller.'

She lifted one hand and let it rest on his chest. 'Don't be sorry. I didn't say I didn't like it.' Surprised, she felt him tremble under her touch, and that small reaction sent an answering spark of hot desire through her body. Staring into his bottomless black eyes she whispered, 'Kiss me.'

He bent and possessed her with his mouth. There was nothing hesitant or tender about his kiss. It was all heat and desire and heady, overwhelming passion. Her arms went up around him and she answered his need with her own. His heat and his taste engulfed her, calling to mind leaping flames and the slow burn of a fire being fed and fed and fed.

They strained against each other. To Pea it felt like he was trying to press himself into her skin. 'Yes,' she said against his questing mouth. 'Yes, closer.'

He moaned and lifted her off her feet to set her on top of the marble counter. Then his moan turned into a rumbling growl when she slid her long bare legs around his hips and pulled his hard cock against her wet core.

'Closer,' she repeated, and gasped as his rough hands skimmed up the outside of her thighs, lifting the thin silk of her draping robes around the top of her hips. His hands slid between her and the cool marble of the counter to cup her butt.

'Ah, gods! I think you've bespelled me. You're so sweet and soft. Let me taste you, Pea. I want to taste you.' He finished with a moan.

Before her mind could catch up with her hormones, he'd dropped to his knees in front of her and pulled her toward him, cocking her hips up so that her legs opened and she was completely exposed to him.

She couldn't believe what was happening! The thought flashed through her mind that it was probably something exactly like this that Venus had had in mind when she insisted Pea not wear panties tonight. But Pea wasn't the Goddess of Love. Her first instinct was to pull away and close her legs, but at that instant he looked up at her.

'Don't turn away from me. Let me pleasure you.'

Mesmerized by the fire in his eyes and the heat of his touch, she nodded and, once again, told him, 'Closer . . .'

He kissed the inside of first one thigh and then the other, his tongue circling her skin, drawing ever nearer to her core. Then his hands tightened on her and his mouth moved to her labia, beginning a slow, steady glide of his tongue the length of her sex. At first he just tasted her, teasing the bud of her clit as he explored her wet folds.

Pea moved restlessly, wanting more. She spread her legs wider. His response was instant. With a moan he plunged his tongue inside her. Pea gasped.

'You taste like ambrosia, only slick and hot.' His words vibrated against her mound. His tongue snaked out, gliding

163

slowly over her sex, rhythmically circling her clit and then gliding away again.

'Oh, god! What are you doing to me?' She gasped.

'Making you my own,' he murmured.

'Yes.' She panted. 'Yes, closer!' She wound her fingers in his
thick hair and pulled him more firmly against her.

With a snarl the tempo of his teasing changed. Now he
focused on her sensitive nub, circling it with his tongue and then
suckling it . . . circling it and suckling . . .

Pea felt the world spiral down. Her back bowed and all she
knew was his mouth against her and the hot, insistent vibration
of his tongue. She lifted her thighs and began to move with him,
showing him the speed of her pleasure.

'Yes,' he whispered against her. 'Give yourself to me.'

He moved one hand to spread her sex open to him, and then he
covered her with his mouth. His tempo changed again, this time
to a steady, rhythmic pulsing against her clit. She ground herself
against him. Faster and faster his tongue flicked against her and
she heard her own incoherent cries for more echo around them,
mixing with his guttural moans of pleasure, creating a cacophony of sex and sound. Then, when she thought she could bear
no more he pushed even harder into her. Opening his mouth he
began sucking her clit until the pressure was incredible. Then
fire exploded over her body as her orgasm cascaded through her.
Pea threw back her head and screamed her pleasure.

The knock at the door was hard and insistent.

'Everything okay in there?' a male voice demanded.

Pea could barely think. She felt like her body had dissolved.
Then his strong arms were anchoring her back in the real world.
He kissed her gently. 'Answer him, little one, or I will be forced
to get rid of him myself.'

Pea cleared her throat and looked over his shoulder at the closed door. 'Yeah,' she called, trying not to sound entirely breathless. 'Everything's great.' She grinned mischievously up at him.

'Good,' the voice responded. 'Oh, it's last call. The bar's closing. And, just in case you have a fireman hidden in there with you, you should know they're loading up the trucks from the Midtown Station. Time to go!'

'Ohmygod, you have to get out of here!' Pea blushed at the thought of everyone seeing him leave and knowing that she'd just been serviced in the ladies' lounge.

He looked down at her, and she saw understanding in his eyes. He touched her cheek with his fingertip. 'No one will know about this. What happened here belongs to us alone.'

'You won't go back and tell the rest of the guys at the fire station?' Pea knew she sounded like a little girl, but she was feeling vulnerable and overwhelmed by what had just happened between them.

'Your honor will always be safe with me.' He kissed her again. 'Now go out first. I will follow.'

She wrapped her arms around his neck. 'Find me in front of the restaurant. There's someone I want you to meet.'

'I will find you, little one,' he assured her. He lifted her off the counter, and watched with proprietary eyes as she straightened her robes. He helped her tie on her mask, and then brushed the thick curls of her hair aside so that he could kiss the soft spot where her neck met her shoulder. Pea shivered and leaned back into him so that his still engorged cock pressed into the valley between the round globes of her ass. He whispered huskily against her skin, 'If you don't leave right now I may keep you here with me for an eternity.'

She turned and smiled up at him. 'That doesn't sound so awful.'

He touched her cheek again. 'Go, little one.'

They kissed and she hurried out the door, glad of the mask that hid most of her flushed face. Pea joined the crowd making its way to the restaurant's front door. With a shaking hand, she tried to pat at her mussed hair and tug her costume more firmly into place. What in the hell had she just done? Now that she wasn't with him, Pea was filled with questions and second thoughts. Who was he anyway? And her next thought brought her to a complete halt. My god. She didn't even know his name!

The man behind her bumped against her. 'Hey, ya gotta keep moving in this crowd.'

'Oh, sorry,' she muttered and forced her legs to move again. Mortified, Pea ducked her head and kept plowing toward the front door, hoping Venus was still outside, and not because she wanted to introduce the goddess to a man whose name she didn't even know, but who she had just let bring her to orgasm in the ladies' lounge. What had she been thinking?

She definitely needed the advice (or the absolution) of a goddess.

Chapter Fifteen

The door to the lounge closed and Vulcan began to pace back and forth across the small space. Emotions he'd never experienced before had unexpectedly been awakened within him. When the dried flower arrangement on the little vanity table began to smolder he drew several deep, calming breaths in and out . . . in and out. It wouldn't do to set the place afire. But oh how he'd like to burn – to show outwardly the wildfire that was raging inside him.

He had shocked himself. His intention that night had simply been to be near her, to perhaps speak with her. Never in his wildest dreams and imaginings had he thought to ravish her! Yet something had happened within him just before the arrogant fool tried to force Pea to stay with him on the dance floor. Suddenly all of the need and desire and passion that had been simmering within him for eons had bubbled over into a full heated boil. He had wanted her before, but tonight he had found the will to act on his desire.

And it had worked! He had actually touched her and tasted her and brought her pleasure. His cock was still engorged with the memory of the sounds of her satisfaction. Would he ever get enough of her? He wanted more and more. He wanted to bring her back with him to Olympus and show her . . .

He stopped pacing. Show her what? How he was shunned and outcast amongst the glory that was Olympus? Then what would she feel for him? Pity? Contempt?

No. He would not take her to Olympus. He would woo her here, in the modern world of mortals, as a man would. Resolutely he retied his mask and walked to the door. She said to meet her outside the restaurant, and she would introduce him—

'Gods! What was I thinking!' He growled. There could only be one person to whom she wanted to introduce him. Venus! Had his mind stopped working entirely? He could only imagine the goddess's shock and surprise at having Pea present him to her. Not that the Goddess of Love would be angry at his infidelity – on the contrary. From the very beginning there had been no pretense of anything more than respect and a rather tenuous friendship between them. Their marriage had been an arrangement, intended to be mutually beneficial. They weren't in love. In actuality their passionless marriage had been the butt of many Olympian jokes. If she discovered he was Pea's lover, would Venus laugh at him? Just the thought made him shudder. No, the Goddess of Love was not cruel. She wouldn't laugh, but she would be shocked. There was little doubt that she would betray his true identity to Pea. Then he would no longer be her passionate mortal lover. He would be the pitiable God of Fire, who had been rejected by Love herself.

'No!' he cried. Their relationship was too new. Perhaps later, after they had had time to build a foundation between them, then he could tell her his secret. Now the only thing he could do was to return to Olympus and make plans to come back to her another day.

He would also pray that she would forgive him for leaving her tonight.

With a deep sigh of despair, the God of Fire closed his eyes and willed himself back to the portal, leaving only a shimmer in the air and the heat of his passing as evidence that he had ever been there.

Griffin hadn't returned to her.

Venus couldn't believe it. It was ludicrous, really. Who stood up Love? Again she considered following him and confronting him and blasting the goddess-be-damned, insolent, arrogant fool into nothingness.

But she couldn't. It was humiliating enough that she was sitting out there, drinking alone (and eating both orders of chocolate dessert). If she went into the restaurant after him it would be an outward acknowledgment of what he had done, and the inner shame of it was enough.

When the bright red trucks pulled up to the curb, Venus ignored them and the costumed, masked men pouring out of the restaurant. If he came up to her she would pretend not to know him. Then she'd blast him with—

'Venus! There you are! I'm so glad I found you.' Pea hurried up to Venus's table.

'Hello, darling.' Venus smiled absently at Pea, trying to refocus her mind from thoughts of revenge. 'I hope you've been having a lovely time.'

'Well . . .'

Pea's odd tone finally got the goddess's full attention. Venus frowned and really looked at the little mortal. Yes, all the signs were there: flushed face, rosy, bruised looking lips . . . 'Pea.' She gasped. 'Have you just orgasmed?'

'Wow, you're really good at figuring out love stuff, aren't you?' Pea flushed an even brighter pink and looked like she was on the verge of tears. 'Yes,' she whispered, and then mouthed the words *oral sex*.

'I'm such an idiot.' Pea hid her masked face in her hands.

'Darling,' Venus began reasonably, completely confused at why Pea should appear so upset by such good news. 'There's nothing for you to hide your face and be ashamed of – it's lovely that you had a delicious sexual encounter.' What in the ancient world was wrong with the girl? Then realization hit Venus. There was nothing wrong with having a delicious sexual encounter unless the man behaved in a boorish or unsuitable manner, as Venus could, unfortunately, attest to knowing entirely too much about. Venus pulled Pea's hands from her face and forced the mortal to meet her eyes. 'Pea, with whom did you have sex?'

Pea sniffed. 'His name tag said God of Fire.'

Venus felt a sickening jolt. 'By Cupid's bright pink ass, that does it!' The curse exploded from the goddess. 'Griffin performed cunnilingus on you?'

'Griffin? No, I said his name tag said God of Fire, not Griffin. I only wish it had been Griffin. At least I know him.'

'Darling, I'm confused. You're telling me that you allowed a man, whose name tag read God of Fire, but whom you don't know, not even his name, to perform oral sex upon you?'

Pea bit her lip, nodded, and started to cry, all the while throwing furtive looks over her back at the crowd still streaming out of Lola's. With a sob, she said, 'I told him to meet me out here, and now I don't know what I was thinking. I imagined this big connection between the two of us.' Pea paused, pulled off her mask and wiped at her face. 'But I don't even know his name, so how "connected" could we have been? And he was definitely a fireman. What if Griffin finds out I let a stranger do *that* to me in the ladies' room? He'll never, ever even look at me,' Pea said with a wail.

Venus blanched. It was more likely that Pea would never ever speak to her again if she found out that while she'd been having sex with a stranger, her friend and mentor had been fornicating under a tree with the man with whom Pea was obsessed. By the genitalia of all the gods, how had she made such a total mess out of this night?

'Let's get out of here,' Venus said, grabbing Pea's arm and beginning to steer her toward the parking lot.

Neither of them saw Griffin rush out of the restaurant and stand, hands on hips, scanning the crowd until he, too, was finally pulled reluctantly aboard one of the fire engines just moments before it drove away.

'Darling, drink your hot chocolate,' Venus told Pea. 'And wipe your face. You're done crying now.'

'That's right, sluts probably don't ever cry over their ... their ...' Pea struggled with the vocabulary. '... their numerous nasty illicit encounters.'

Venus tried unsuccessfully to hide her smile. 'Pea, having *one* sexual encounter with a stranger does not make you promiscuous. And besides that, it's worse than archaic to believe that women can't take their pleasure as they will. It's restrictive and smacks of double standards. Doesn't the modern world allow women more freedom than that?'

'I suppose,' Pea muttered into her mug. Then she glanced up at Venus. 'I just feel like a fool.'

'Why?'

Pea sighed. 'I imagined this huge connection between him and me, and I got really, really intimate with him. But the truth is I don't know him at all. I mean, I was there to try to connect with Griffin, the man I've been thinking about for over a year, but I end up with another man's face between my legs.'

171

'Tell me why you felt you had such a connection with the man,' Venus said hastily, purposefully sliding the conversation away from Pea's Griffin infatuation.

'It's going to sound silly and romantic,' Pea said.

'Which means I'll be able to understand perfectly. Tell me,' Venus coaxed.

'Well, I just felt this incredible connection with him. It was like I could look into those amazing dark eyes of his and see his soul. And, somehow, it seemed like he and I were the same. It sounds stupid now, but then it felt like we had things in common – important things like not usually fitting in.'

Venus raised a brow at that. 'Really? How did you two meet?'

'He just appeared all of a sudden. It really was sweet. He thought he needed to rescue me from this jerk who didn't want to take no for an answer.' Pea smiled for the first time since she'd left the restaurant. 'He asked if he could buy me a drink, and I said okay. Then we talked and talked. He was sensitive and romantic and sexy. One thing led to another, and we were suddenly alone, and all I could think about was how amazing he felt and how much I wanted him.' Pea finished in a rush, blushing furiously.

'Darling, you did nothing wrong. Well, except not learning his name,' Venus said.

'But what about Griffin and—'

'Griffin wasn't the one who pursued you, this man was,' Venus said slowly, studying Pea. Was now the right time to tell her that her supposed beloved Griffin had fornicated with and then discarded the Goddess of Love herself?

'I know, and I know it's probably wrong, but I can't help but still feel this *thing* for Griffin.' Pea's eyes started to shimmer with tears again, and Venus realized that now was definitely not the right time to tell her.

'Is this *thing* you feel actually for Griffin or for the idea of what Griffin represents to you?' Venus asked gently.

'I don't know,' Pea said.

'You are interested in the man you met tonight, aren't you?' Venus redirected the conversation again.

Pea nodded. 'But I don't even know who he is.'

The goddess smiled. 'Of course you do. You said he's a fireman.'

'Yeah, but there are like a zillion firemen in Tulsa.'

'Well, darling, then we had better get to work.' Venus sat up straighter, the seeds of a plan beginning to grow. Perhaps all Pea needed was to see this mystery man again, especially if she could compare his obvious interest in her with Griffin's obvious disinterest. Unless the rogue pretended interest in Pea so that he could use her and cast her aside, too. Then Venus knew what she'd do with him, and it wouldn't be pretty.

'Get to work? How?'

'I've been considering that.' Venus tapped her fingernail against the mug. 'In battle it is often best to engage one's enemy on one's own territory.'

'Huh?'

'You need to see your fireman again.'

'Griffin?' Pea perked up.

Venus frowned. 'I meant your *other* fireman, but it certainly wouldn't hurt to see them both again.' She lightened her tone. 'It's always good for a woman to have choices.'

'That does sound good.' Pea nodded. 'But how?'

'Your job.'

'My job?'

'Exactly. Your job. You are in charge of educational and recreational instruction for the community. Am I correct?'

'Yeah.'

'The firemen who were at the masquerade were all from the Midtown Fire Station. Correct?'

'Yeah.'

'Then consider this – what if all of the men from the Midtown Fire Station were commanded to take instruction from your university.'

'It's really just a community college,' Pea said.

Venus waved her hand dismissively. 'That is inconsequential. What is of consequence is that the firemen must come to your place of instruction – your place of power. And *there* you can learn more about both men and choose between them. Here's what I have in mind . . .'

Joe Daniels, training deputy chief for the Tulsa Fire Department, thought he'd died and gone straight to heaven when the blonde beauty walked into his office the next morning. He shot to his feet, fiddling with his tie and sucking in his stomach.

'Deputy Chief Daniels, my name is Venus Pontia.'

When he held out his hand for her to shake, she simply bowed her head slightly. He cleared his throat and wiped his sweaty, unshaken palm on his slacks.

'P-please, have a seat.'

'Thank you, Chief Daniels.'

She sat in the leather chair situated in front of his desk and crossed her incredibly long legs. He tried not to stare or stutter.

'Please call me Joe.'

Her smile illuminated the room. 'And you may call me Venus.'

He thought no one had ever been better named.

'What can I do for you, Venus?'

'I know you're a very busy and important man, Joe, so I'll get right to the point. I'm working with Ms. Chamberlain at Tulsa

Community College in the Continuing Education Department. It has come to our attention that some of your men, specifically the men at your Midtown Station, have been under quite a bit of stress lately.'

Joe frowned, wondering what she knew that he didn't. He hadn't been aware the Midtown guys were having any problems at all. Hell, that group had just had a successful benefit last night. But before he could say anything her smile and the uncrossing and then recrossing of those incredible legs distracted him.

'Because of this stress, Ms. Chamberlain has created a series of classes for the Midtown firemen that will focus on teaching them relaxation techniques.'

Joe opened and closed his mouth. What was she talking about?

'Oh, no need to thank us, darling. The outcome of the classes will be thanks enough.' She handed him a paper. 'Here are all the details. Be sure the first class reports to the Metro campus tomorrow morning at nine sharp.'

'But, ma'am,' he sputtered. 'I can't possibly—'

Abruptly he lost his train of thought. It happened the same instant the extremely hot Venus waved her fingers at him, a little like she was saying a funny hello. Weird . . . really weird.

'I'm sorry, Joe, what were you saying?'

'Saying?' He couldn't seem to stop smiling at her. Good lord he felt fabulous!

'Yes, about the classes for the Midtown firemen.'

He blinked and then his thoughts arranged themselves and he knew exactly what he'd been about to say.

'Damn good idea! Damn good. I'll have the men there first thing in the morning. I've heard reports that the Midtown Station was under stress, and this is the perfect answer to the problem.'

'Well, Joe, it really was your idea. After all, you called Ms. Chamberlain's office and asked her to create the class. I'm just following up on your instincts, which are truly commendable.' The beautiful Venus beamed and then wiggled her fingers at him again.

God, he couldn't remember the last time he'd felt so good! And it *had* been his idea, now that he really thought about it.

'Excellent, Venus! Excellent!'

'Thank you, Joe. Please call us again any time our college can come to the aid of the fire department.' She stood, smiled at him, and then sauntered from his office.

'Now that is one fine looking woman,' he muttered, and then whistled low to himself. But he didn't have time to sit there gathering wool. He had work to do. Every one of those Midtown boys not on duty in the morning had to be at that college destressing class, and he was just the man to make it happen. He lifted his phone and started dialing.

Chapter Sixteen

'You didn't say anything about me teaching the class!' Pea said.

'Of course you must teach the class. I can not bespell the entire college.' Venus paused, considering for a moment. 'Well, perhaps I could, but it would certainly be dreadfully complicated and who could say how it would affect the general populace?' She shook her head. 'No, it's simply easier if I tweak things here and there, as I did with the deputy chief, and we keep this as much to ourselves as possible.'

'Venus, I've never taught a class before.'

'Oh, you have nothing whatsoever to worry about. Just teach what you know.'

'Cooking? For stress relief?'

'Actually, darling, I was thinking more of your dancing.'

Pea's eyes got big and round. 'Ballet for firemen?'

Venus shrugged. 'Why not?'

Pea giggled. 'You've got to be kidding.'

'Not at all. Dance is an excellent stress reliever, and you're an experienced dancer. Besides that, it will provide a good opportunity for all those delicious men to see you at your best.'

'I don't know . . . What if *they're* really there, Griffin and *him*. No way will I be able to teach with them . . . you know . . . looking at me. Not after what I did with *him*.'

'Darling, please remember that the reason we've manipulated events so that the men come to you is because they will be on your territory – your place of power. You're in control this time. You do the choosing. Plus I'll be your behind-the-scenes assistant. If you get in trouble, I'll simply . . .' Venus waggled her fingers.

Pea looked only a tiny bit less worried. 'Oh yeah.'

'Then it's all decided. Let's have one more cup of this luscious coffee and then we'll be off to the college. We wouldn't want to be late for class.'

Pea glanced at her watch and frowned.

'What is it, darling?'

'Well, if you'd told me yesterday that I was going to have to teach a ballet class I could have bought something a little nicer to wear than the sweats and T-shirts I usually wear to ballet.'

Venus's smile was slow and knowing. 'I've already taken care of that little detail. There's a lovely new Coach bag in your closet. Inside it you'll find what you need for your first day as a dance instructor.'

'You think of everything, Venus!' Pea hugged her.

Venus patted her arm. 'Not everything, darling. Just everything important.' With an effort she pushed the thought out of her mind that if she *really* thought of everything and if she *really* was as together as Pea believed her to be she wouldn't have let that man dupe her, nor would she be hiding the fact from Pea.

No matter, she thought as she blew on her coffee and watched Pea hurry down the hall to her room to retrieve her new dance bag. *Somehow I'll make him sorry he ever trifled with Love, and I'll figure out how to fix Pea's infatuation with the cad.*

The goddess ignored the sick feeling in her stomach. It wasn't possible that Griffin had hurt her. He'd just surprised her when he'd left her sitting there and not returned. That's all it was. She'd help Pea connect with her mystery man, or if he wasn't suitable, she'd simply find her friend a man who had honesty and integrity, as well as sex appeal. *Then* she'd return to her normal life on Olympus. Perhaps she'd plan a lovely orgy with satyrs and forest nymphs. That's it. An orgy would fix her right up.

After all, it was completely, utterly impossible for the Goddess of Love to be lonely.

'You look beautiful, darling! Simply beautiful.' Venus brushed a nonexistent piece of lint from Pea's shoulder. 'I knew the blushing pink leotard and wispy skirt would complement your figure and your complexion perfectly. And don't worry. There's nothing at all for you to be nervous about.'

'I may puke.'

'No, you may not.'

'Okay, tell me again. You're sure you . . . zapped everyone in my office so that they'll think this is normal?'

'What they see will appear normal to them today. Tomorrow they won't remember a thing. The firemen will all think of this little class as just something they were directed to do – nothing out of the ordinary at all. Except they will particularly remember the alluring beauty named Pea who conducted the class.' Venus paused, considering. 'Do let me know if you're interested in any of them at all. I can have him "remember" asking you for your phone number.'

'Wow. You can do all that?'

'Darling, Love can do anything.'

'Oh yeah. Sometimes I forget. I don't have much experience with real love.'

'Well, we'll fix that very soon.' Venus patted her arm. 'So, if you're ready, let's go.'

They walked down the hall a short way from Pea's office to a large classroom. Both women stopped and peered through the small glass rectangle in the closed door.

'I can't do this!' Pea leaned against the wall, looking scarily pale.

'Of course you can. I'll be right here and—'

'No! I can't walk in there without knowing what to expect.'

Thinking fast, Venus said, 'Fine. I'll go in first and . . . and . . .' The goddess hesitated. And she'd what?

'Take attendance?' Pea offered.

'Exactly,' Venus said with relief. 'I'll simply take attendance and check to see if everyone is there and ready. While I do that, you watch from out here. Then you'll know if Griffin and/or your mystery fireman are here, and *then* you'll know what to expect.'

'O-okay,' Pea stammered doubtfully.

'Okay,' Venus said firmly. She straightened her exquisite violet suit, running her hand down the front of the black silk shell that was just low enough to expose the tops of her creamy breasts. She waggled her fingers. A pen and a professional looking clipboard appeared with a list of names on it.

'I really wish you wouldn't make things suddenly appear without warning me first.'

'Sorry, darling. I keep forgetting how sensitive you are.' She checked her lipstick in the semi-reflective glass of the door. 'Ready for battle?'

'Well . . .'

'Of course you are. I'll be right back. Just think of what I'm doing as reconnoitering.'

Venus ignored Pea's groan and put her hand on the doorknob of the classroom she'd 'tweaked' earlier, zapping away the desks and what she considered unneeded paraphernalia. She was glad Pea was nervous. It forced her to set a good example and seem confident and collected. Truth be known, the Goddess of Love's insides felt unusually jittery. She didn't allow herself to hesitate further, but swept into the room, putting on her most officious air. As was only right, the men gathered in the middle of the room fell silent, instantly giving her their appreciative attention. They were attentive but casual, dressed in jeans and Tulsa Fire Department T-shirts.

'Good morning, gentlemen.' Venus was all business. 'When I call your name please acknowledge that you are present.' She began going through the alphabetical list, looking carefully at each man as he responded.

'Allen, James.'

'Yes, ma'am.'

'Barber, Joshua.'

'Present, ma'am.'

'Bennett, Kevin.'

'Here, ma'am.'

'Carter, Corey.'

She was pleased that she said the next name without so much as a hint of hesitation. 'DeAngelo, Griffin.' The group of men stirred to allow him to move forward from near the rear of the room.

'Good to see you again, ma'am.' His unmistakable blue eyes met her steely violet gaze, and he tipped an imaginary hat and gave the confident, sexy smile she recognized all too well.

Venus blushed. The Goddess of Love actually flushed a sweet, soft pink that lifted up her long neck into her high cheeks. Then she realized she was blushing and she stopped it instantly. She was here for battle, not for love.

'Griffin?' Venus made her tone purposefully clueless.

'Yes, ma'am, Griffin DeAngelo.' He stepped forward and held out his hand like a perfect gentleman – the expression in his knowing eyes the only evidence that there was anything more between them than passing acquaintances. 'I don't think we had a chance to be *formally* introduced the other night.'

Venus looked from his hand to his eyes. For the first time in her existence, she didn't know what to say. By all the hairy scrotal sacs of the gods he was arrogant! He'd ravished her and left her, and now here he was smiling and playing the gentleman?

'I can't tell you how glad I am to see you again, my goddess,' he said under his breath for her ears alone.

She realized she was still staring at him and his hand was still stuck out in front of him. Drawing herself up, the goddess put her hand in his.

'Well met, Griffin DeAngelo,' she said.

Still holding her hand he smiled slowly. 'And your name is?'

'Venus,' she said. 'Venus Pontia.'

His smile widened. 'So you really are a goddess.'

'Of course I am, darling,' she said automatically, and pulled her hand from his. Then she went back to methodically calling off names from her list.

But her mind was in tumult. Venus ignored the fact that she could feel those brilliant blue eyes staring at her with that possessive, predatory gaze that had entrapped her so easily before. He was clearly acting as if he'd done nothing wrong, but he'd left her, the Goddess of Love, sitting out there in front of the restaurant waiting for him – and he hadn't returned.

One does not stand up the Goddess of Love.

She finished the list and, without another look at Griffin

DeAngelo, left the room. Venus leaned her back against the closed door.

'Griffin's in there! I saw him.' Pea peered up at Venus. 'Are you okay?'

'Yes, of course I am.' Venus took a deep breath and tried to pull herself together. Why did she allow that mortal man to affect her so much? And that, she feared, was the point. She didn't *allow* Griffin anything. For the first time in her experience, a man didn't wait on her permission to touch and taste and possess her.

'Venus?'

The goddess mentally shook herself. 'Griffin is in there, but is your mystery man there, too?'

'No.' Pea sighed.

'Are you quite sure?'

'Yeah. I mean, I'd definitely recognize him after what we did.' Pea's blush perfectly matched her leotard.

'Oh.' Venus drew another deep breath. 'Well, at least that's settled. He's not here, but Griffin is. So you just go on in there and teach the class. You'll be the center of attention for a full hour. If Griffin doesn't show interest in you after that, then I can promise you he's not worthy of your attention.'

'I really can't.'

Venus sighed. 'We've been all through this. Of course you can. You're good at dancing. Just go in there and do what you're good at.'

Pea grabbed Venus's hand. 'Please don't make me!'

'Darling, I'm not going to *make* you. This is something you should be confident enough to do.'

'I'll make a fool out of myself.' Her eyes filled with tears. 'It's not about confidence. It's about being comfortable in front of groups of people. I know you zapped me and let me see myself as others see me.' With her free hand Pea gestured down at her body. 'So I know I'm actually pretty and not the gawky dork I was in high school. But that doesn't mean that I'm good in front of crowds – that I'll ever be good in front of crowds.'

'But, Pea, you—'

Pea didn't let her continue. 'Is changing who I am the only way I can be good enough?'

'Of course it's not! I never meant for you to feel like that.' She hugged Pea hard. 'You're good enough exactly as you are. I just wanted this for you.'

'I know, but . . .' Pea hesitated.

Venus pulled back and looked into the mortal's eyes. 'But you didn't want it for yourself. Not this part of it?'

'Seeing myself clearly and being confident in my beauty is one thing. Getting a man by pretending to be something I'm not is another. I've been standing out here thinking about that, and I've decided that I don't even want Griffin if I have to do that.'

'You know, Dorreth Pea Chamberlain, you are very wise for a mortal.'

Pea grinned. 'So you'll teach the class for me?'

'Well, I'm not dressed for ballet.'

'Please. Like you couldn't zap yourself a leotard?'

'I don't really know ballet.'

'Then teach what you know.'

'Hmm . . . teach what I know. Now *that* might be interesting,' Venus said thoughtfully. 'Pea, I believe you may be right about this, and I will take your advice.' The goddess raised her hand and then glanced at Pea. 'Prepare yourself. I'm going to zap.'

Pea closed her eyes. Venus waggled her fingers and a very large, very full tote bag appeared. She hefted it over her arm.

'You can open your eyes now.'

'What are you going to teach?'

Venus's smile was dazzling. 'What I know, of course, darling.' And, she added silently to herself, *I'm also going to teach that mortal man a lesson.*

Chapter Seventeen

'Good morning again. You may call me Venus. I will be your stress relief instructor for this class. You may sit anywhere.' She wiggled her fingers at the shadowy rear of the large classroom and chairs appeared. 'Pull those out here, please, they are much too far away.' She spoke matter-of-factly, not giving any of them time to remember that there were no chairs in the rear of the classroom when they'd first entered it. While the men were dragging out the chairs and taking their seats, Venus dug into her bag and pulled out sheets of thick parchment paper. Each was covered with an intricate diagram. Ignoring Griffin, who of course chose to sit in the front and center of the class, she began passing out the papers. The men stared at the diagram, stunned and speechless.

'We are going to talk about how to bring a woman pleasure. I will be referring to your diagram of the feminine lotus flower during our discussion. Please feel free to ask questions.' She paused and let her words soak through the men. Not surprisingly, she noticed many stunned looks. 'Gentlemen, are you confused? Do you have questions already?' she asked.

One of the older men hesitantly raised his hand, and Venus nodded for him to speak.

'Well, ma'am, I think we're wondering what girl flowers have to do with stress relief.'

'Darling, I'm using the term "feminine lotus flower" as a representative term.' Venus paused and saw that the men still looked confused. She sighed. 'As a representative term for the vagina,' she clarified.

Several men sent her shocked looks. She tried not to notice that Griffin was smiling.

'Uh, ma'am?' The same man had his hand up again.

'Yes,' she said cheerfully, trying her best to be patient with the mortal dolt.

'Uh, I still don't understand what the . . . ur . . . vagina blossom has to do with our stress relief.'

'*Lotus* blossom,' she automatically corrected. 'What is your name?'

'J. D. Maples.'

'Are you married J. D.?'

'Yes, ma'am.'

'Would it not relieve an innumerable amount of stress in your life if you knew how to bring your wife such pleasure that she eagerly welcomed you to her bed and searched for excuses to ask you to press your naked body against hers?'

J. D.'s mouth opened, then closed. 'I see your point, ma'am.'

The group of men made noises of agreement.

'I thought you would.' Venus smiled. 'Now women have several different types of orgasms, but to avoid confusion today we shall concentrate on only two of them, the clitoral and the vaginal orgasms. In addition we will also talk about discovering each woman's deep pleasure zone.' Venus thought for a moment before she recalled the name she'd learned during her many Google searches. 'The G-spot. You should know that women do tend to have preferences about which orgasm they enjoy most, but—'

Griffin's hand went up. Venus forced herself not to frown. 'Yes, um, did you say your name was Mr. DeAngelo?'

'Griffin,' he said, his confident half smile never wavering. 'Please call me Griffin.'

'Very well. Did you have a question already, Griffin?'

'Yes, ma'am. I was wondering about the orgasms. How do we know which one our lover prefers?'

'You ask her,' Venus said coolly. 'But I believe I can answer part of this question for all women without having to ask even one of them besides myself, of course. All women prefer the type of orgasm that is followed by a man of integrity keeping his word and not suddenly disappearing.' She met his gaze steadily, though she took little pleasure in the fact that his smile had vanished. Another hand went up on the left side of the room. 'Yes, another question?'

'Ma'am,' said a very young fireman. 'There's something wrong with my diagram.'

Venus walked quickly to him and glanced over his shoulder. 'Darling, your lotus blossom is upside down.'

'Oh, sorry,' he mumbled, blushing a bright, painful looking scarlet.

'Please don't apologize. You are here to learn. And it is well acknowledged that, though the phallus is delightful, the feminine lotus, the heart of a woman's sexuality, is more complicated.'

'Sometimes there are circumstances that can't be helped,' Griffin suddenly said, causing the men to send him curious glances.

Venus blinked innocently at him. 'No, Griffin, the circumstances don't matter. Vaginas are always more complicated than penises.'

She tried not to let the humorous crinkle around his eyes and the fact that he was grinning widely in response to her wit affect her. But she had to admit – at least to herself – that he was awfully cute.

'I have no doubt whatsoever that lotus blossoms are as complex as they are intriguing. I just wondered what a man should do when the, um, *complexity* of a situation has been confused with circumstances beyond the man's control and orgasm interrupted – for either party. What would you recommend then?'

'Communication,' Venus said.

'Is that all?' He did smile then.

'That and groveling,' yelled a man from the back of the room, which caused everyone to laugh.

'I see I have at least one advanced student,' Venus quipped, grinning at the class and meeting Griffin's eyes, but only briefly.

'Well, ma'am,' Griffin said, sending her a warm, intimate smile, 'I'm ready to learn.'

There was a general murmur of good-humored agreement.

'I do appreciate attentive men,' Venus said, not able to keep herself from meeting Griffin's sparkling blue eyes again.

Then she walked quickly to the blackboard and pulled out a set of colored chalk from her tote bag. Locating the pink chalk, she said, 'Please follow along on your own diagrams as I sketch a rather simplistic version of the one I gave each of you.'

Another hand shot up. 'Excuse me, ma'am. Should we take notes?'

'Only if you truly wish to pleasure a woman.'

Returning to her sketch, Venus heard Griffin chuckle as he and the rest of the men scrambled for pens and pencils.

Perhaps she should listen to what Griffin had to say about why he didn't return to her. It could hardly hurt to hear his side of things. After all, Love was supposed to be kind and fair and patient. Yes, she'd hear him out, and then she'd sit Pea down and tell her everything. If he had some horrid, lame excuse she'd explain to Pea what a cad he was and how better off she would be without him. If he truly had a viable reason he hadn't returned to her . . . well . . . then she'd simply tell her friend the truth. Pea was smart and compassionate. She'd understand. Feeling suddenly lighter and happier than she'd felt in days, she finished the sketch with a flourish and turned back to the class.

'Now can anyone tell me where the clitoris is located?'

She smiled at the flurry of raising hands.

Vulcan couldn't concentrate. Yes, he methodically stoked the great furnace that heated the core of the ancient earth. Of course he kept check on various volcanoes, both on land and under the oceans. The last thing he needed was an eruption today, especially with his already tumultuous emotions. As always he was mindful of the many cleansing wildfires burning supposedly out of control. But all these things he did automatically. His thoughts were on Pea.

With a growl he gave up and strode through the gleaming rooms of his subterranean palace to the central pillar of ever-burning flame. Vulcan reached into the inferno and found the thread that bound him to Venus, the modern world and Pea.

As usual, the thread led him first to Venus. His brow furrowed. What in all the levels of the Underworld was she doing? Drawing an enormous vagina on a board with colored chalk? Disbelieving, he watched as a room full of virile men questioned her about the female orgasm. The Goddess of Love was teaching a class in the art of stimulating a woman! Vulcan motioned for a chair to materialize and settled down to pay attention. Their marriage hadn't been a success, but there was absolutely no doubt that Venus was beyond compare when it came to understanding the intricacies of pleasure. He knew he wasn't particularly experienced in the ways of lovemaking. The other goddesses shunned him because they knew love had, essentially, rejected him. And, ironically, no mortal woman wanted to chance offending the Goddess of Love by coveting her husband. Over the eons he'd grown weary of trying to explain that Venus hadn't truly rejected him, that theirs was a marriage of convenience – however misconceived. It had simply become easier to be alone. Until recently.

With Pea he was experiencing something completely new – a chance to be loved for who he was, not for who people perceived him to be. Clearly he could use all the help he could get on the subject of seduction, so Vulcan settled in to pay attention to the goddess's discussion of something she mysteriously called a woman's G-spot, but found even then he couldn't keep his mind from roving to Pea.

And when the invisible thread followed his thoughts, leaving the classroom and snaking restlessly down the hall, he had no will to stop it. Quickly and silently it followed his desire. Pea was sitting at her desk in the tidy office he'd observed her working in the other times he'd watched her. There was a rather rumpled-looking man sitting across from her. She was holding a file of papers and asking him questions. It didn't take long for Vulcan to ascertain that there was a professorial position open at Pea's college in the field of history, and the man was applying for it. Pea didn't appear impressed with him. She actually sighed and chewed on her pencil after he left.

'Boring . . . dry . . . nope. He won't do. He'd put them all to sleep,' she muttered to herself. Then she glanced at her watch. 'Half an hour till the next interview . . .' She sighed again and started to click around on a contraption Vulcan knew was called a computer – a thing that held so much knowledge it was the modern world's version of magic.

Her next interview . . .

Why couldn't her next interview be him? Venus was masquerading as a teacher at Pea's college; why couldn't he? Vulcan sat up straighter, shocked by his own thought. Yes, why not? He wanted to see her again. He wanted to woo her and make her his own. He'd already decided he would never bring her to Olympus, so that meant he was going to have to come to her eventually. Why not now? Why wait any longer? The God of Fire was ready to act – and act he would. He'd just need to stay out of Venus's way, at least until after Pea was in love with him. Well he'd already observed that Venus was being kept busy. Now was an excellent time to make another foray into the modern mortal world and hopefully into Pea's heart. He'd worry about the rest of the details later. What was important right now was being with Pea again.

So . . . he'd need the correct clothes. Something like the other man had worn only less disheveled looking. His rumpled appearance certainly hadn't impressed Pea. And he didn't have much time. He needed to get there before the next man arrived in order to redirect the mortal – an easy thing to do – then take his place in Pea's office and begin winning her heart.

Because that was, indeed, what he wanted. Damn Olympus and the gods and their intrigues and prejudices. He wanted someone of his own. Someone untouched by *them*. He also wanted a life of his own, and by all the dark levels of Tartarus, he would do anything it took to get it.

Chapter Eighteen

'Come on in,' Pea said in response to the quick knock on her office door. She glanced at the clock. Her next interview was five minutes early. *Well*, she thought as she shuffled the papers on her desk and put Robertson Brown's file at the top of the heap, *at least that means Mr. Brown is eager. Let's hope he's also more interesting than that last—*

When he stepped into her office all of the air left her body. Literally. Just like the one time she'd made the mistake of riding a horse. She'd fallen off and had not been able to breathe for several very uncomfortable seconds. This was the same sensation. All she could do was sit and stare and struggle for air.

'Hello,' he said, with a warm smile that seemed to reach inside her body and turn her to liquid.

She sucked in a breath and said in a rush, 'You're Robertson Brown? My next interview?'

'No. Yes.' He stopped and drew a deep breath. 'I'm sorry. Seems I'm more nervous than I thought I would be. I am not Robertson Brown, but I would like to be your next interview.'

'I thought you were a fireman.'

He nodded as if he expected her to say that. 'Yes, fire has been my job for a long time. But recently I've decided I want to make a change.'

'To teaching history in our Continuing Education Department?' She felt flushed and out of sorts and had to fold her hands together to keep them from fidgeting.

'Yes. Yes, I would like that.'

Pea just stared at him. She couldn't believe he was standing there in front of her in a suit that was a little outdated, but fit well and was neatly pressed. He seemed to fill her office. She hadn't remembered him being so tall and muscular and imposing. But his mouth . . . his mouth she did remember . . .

'Do you mind my intrusion?'

She jumped a little. 'No, no. Not at all. But if Mr. Brown shows up I'll have to interrupt our interview. He did have an appointment.'

'Agreed.' Vulcan nodded.

'Okay, so, well, have a seat.'

But instead of sitting in the leather chair in front of her desk he walked directly up to her, his distinctive limp in no way overshadowing the sense of strength and power he carried with him. He reached down and coaxed one of her hands away from clutching the other, then he lifted it to that incredible mouth of his and pressed his lips against her skin. The heat of his touch thrummed through her body. Their eyes met and Pea felt the jolt of his gaze as if it, too, were a physical thing.

She hadn't imagined their connection. It was here in the room with them, alive and pulsing and real.

'Forgive me for having to leave you that night.'

'I didn't think I'd see you again,' she said.

Still holding her hand he shook his head. 'I could not stay away from you, little one.'

'Who are you?'

'I am the man you have bewitched.'

She smiled and pulled her hand reluctantly from his. 'I don't think I can put that on your paperwork.' Trying to regain some semblance of professionalism, she continued. 'I meant what is your name?'

Pea's simple question had him looking totally out of sorts, which actually made her feel better. He wasn't exaggerating about her making him nervous if he had forgotten his name.

'V,' he finally blurted. 'Can.'

'V. Cannes? Like C-a-n-n-e-s?'

Looking shell-shocked, he nodded.

'What does the *V* stand for, Victor, or something awful like Vlad?'

'Victor,' he said quickly, and seeming to recollect himself, he sat down.

'Well, Victor, you're not my next interview, so how did you find out about this job opening?' *And how the hell did you find me? Or was this just a weird coincidence?*

He sat very still for a moment, frowning, and then his face cleared and he pointed at her computer. 'I found out about the job through the computer, but that's not the only reason I'm here. The truth is I had to see you again.'

'You're not really interviewing for a job?' Pea tried to sound severe, but she couldn't keep the smile from tilting her lips. It hadn't been a coincidence!

'I'll admit that my first thought had been to simply see you. The job was a far secondary consideration.'

'So you're not here because you want to teach history?'

'I'm here because of you, but I believe I would enjoy teaching history. Ancient history.'

'Really? What kind of ancient history?' She should stop. It wasn't like this was a real interview, but he was interesting and sexy and . . .

His smile was slow, and more than a little mischievous. 'I'm well acquainted with the ancient myths.'

Pea grinned back at him. 'Lately I've become pretty well acquainted with mythology myself.'

He leaned forward, his expression going suddenly from playful to serious. 'And what do you think of the ancient myths – the stories of a time when gods and goddesses walked the earth?'

Thinking of Venus, she smiled warmly. 'I like what I've found out so far.'

'Do you?' He covered her hand with his.

And it happened again. She wanted to drown in him. Just like that magical night his eyes had captured her. But no – it was more than that, more than just his eyes. It seemed she knew his soul. How could that be? It felt real, but surely she had to be making all this up in her overly romantic imagination.

'You're not imagining things,' he said, speaking quietly and earnestly.

'How do you know what I'm thinking?'

'I know *you*. We're connected. I don't know how, but I do think I know why. I think we're the same, you and I. Until I met you I only knew how to be an outlander. I had resigned myself to being alone. Then I saw you and I felt that I had finally come home.' He gave a little laugh and rubbed a hand down his face as if he thought he might be dreaming and needed to wake himself up. 'It does sound unbelievable, though, doesn't it?'

'Yes. It sounds unbelievable.' Then when disappointment started to fill his expressive eyes, she continued. 'It *sounds* unbelievable, but that's not how it feels.'

'So it's not just me? I'm not in this alone?'

Pea knew she should make a joke or laugh or say something to water down what Victor was saying and to lighten up what was happening between the two of them. She should remind him that they weren't in a romantic movie with a guaranteed happily ever after. Love at first sight was only possible in movies and books – total fiction. In the real world it fell apart, leaving behind the flotsam of divorce and broken hearts.

And then there was Griffin. But was there really Griffin? Or was her infatuation with him more like the impossibility of the movies, and was what was happening with this man more like the real thing?

Then she met his eyes again and she couldn't say any of those things because what she saw there was too raw, too possible, and she suddenly wanted him with a ferocity that surprised her. She wanted *them* and this sparkling new possibility of a future that wasn't a life crammed full of pets and work so that the lonely nights and the solitary meals and the dreaming about a man she couldn't ever have while she watched everyone else couple off was bearable.

'You're not in this alone,' she said, even though it made her stomach clench and her breath catch. 'But I'm afraid. This is all—'

'Don't say it's all happening too fast,' he interrupted. 'After eons of not believing it could ever happen, how can we not want to embrace this magic between us, no matter how quickly it seems to be happening? Can we not just give it a chance and see where this new path leads us?'

Pea's brows drew together as she considered what he was saying. His seemed to take her feelings and refract them back to her.

'Please don't say no.'

Pea continued to study him silently, and all of a sudden it felt like a key turned within her, unlocking a secret room in her soul where all the love she'd been keeping to give to a man, *her* man, had been stored. Instead of feeling unsure and afraid and hesitant, Pea was filled with an incredible sense of rightness.

'Victor, I'm going to take a chance on you – on us actually. But you have to promise me something.'

'Anything within my power.'

'No more disappearing.'

'You have my oath.' His smile was wide with relief. He kissed her hand again and caught her gaze with his own hope-filled one. 'You won't be sorry for this. If it is within my power, you won't ever be sorry.'

'I believe you.' Pea felt like giggling.

He stood abruptly. 'Come! Let's leave this place. I'll take you anywhere you wish – just make the request and I will make your desire come true.'

Pea did giggle then. 'I have to admit that's the best date offer I've ever had, but I'm not off work for' – she glanced at the clock – 'about six hours.'

'Six hours?'

She nodded. 'Yes, but I don't have any plans this evening.'

He smiled. 'Then may I see you this evening?'

'Yes, you may.' They grinned foolishly at each other until the time *really* registered in Pea's mind. 'Oh, jeesh! What am I thinking? My friend should be done teaching her class in just a few minutes. I have to meet her and . . .' Pea scrambled around, discarding comments like *See if she somehow fixed me up with Griffin* or *Make sure she didn't zap stuff from nowhere and freak out her class*. Instead she settled for, '. . . and make sure her class went okay. It's her first day of teaching.'

'Then I will leave you to your work and see you again in six hours.'

'Could you make it more like seven hours? I want to have time to get home and, you know . . .' She gestured down at her clothes.

'Ah, of course. In seven hours then.' He turned to leave.

'Uh, Victor? Would you like my phone number and address so you know where to pick me up tonight?'

Looking chagrined, he returned to her desk and took the paper she'd scribbled her information on.

'I'm not very good at this,' he said. 'I'm sorry. You deserve someone who is more . . .' He moved his broad shoulders restlessly. 'More practiced in the ways of love.'

Her teasing smile faded. She knew too well what it was to feel awkward and not good enough. 'Don't say that. I like how you are. I don't want a suave playboy. I want someone I connect with – someone who understands me and someone I can count on.'

'I give you my word that you may trust me. Always,' he said.

'I'll hold you to that, Victor.'

He took her hand, and when he bent, she thought he was going to kiss it again. But this time he surprised her by leaning forward farther and kissing her on her lips. It was a kiss filled more with promise than passion, but his scent enfolded her along with the heat of his body. He reminded her of a warm fire on a cold night, and she felt an answering heat within her. When his lips left hers, she wanted to pull him down to her and sink into his mouth.

Instead she found her voice and said, 'I'll see you in seven hours.'

'Until tonight, little one.'

Before he returned to Olympus, Vulcan followed the signs to the college's research center. It took a little magical nudging sprinkled judiciously on a few mortals here and there, but soon he was seated in front of a computer with a rudimentary knowledge of search engines. It wouldn't do for him to be blundering about the modern world without at least a basic understanding of the times and people. He cracked his knuckles and began pointing and clicking the intriguing little device they called a mouse.

Chapter Nineteen

'Thank you, ma'am. That was a great class!'

Venus smiled beatifically at the young fireman who had, at the beginning of the class, been holding his diagram upside down. 'Thank you, darling. I'm pleased you enjoyed it.'

'More than that, ma'am!' he gushed. 'I can't wait to . . .' He broke off, blushing. 'Well, I mean thanks. I learned a lot.'

'You are most welcome.' Venus stood by the classroom door, saying good-bye to her class. It really had gone well. They had been attentive and enthusiastic. She had thoroughly enjoyed herself, which she had to admit to herself, had a lot to do with the fact that the most attentive, enthusiastic and handsome member of the class had been Griffin, who was currently hanging back, very obviously waiting for the rest of the men to say their good-byes and leave.

The last grateful fireman finally left, and the goddess's stomach fluttered as Griffin approached her.

His eyes smiled at her. 'I didn't know you were a teacher.'

'I'm really not. At least I'm usually not, though I suppose you could say that I have done my share of instruction about love.' She paused, struggling to get the modern words right.

'So you're a therapist?'

Relieved that he'd provided her a viable profession, Venus nodded and smiled innocently. 'Yes. A sex therapist. I taught class today as a favor for a friend who works here at the college.'

'Then I will have to remember to thank your friend for causing you to be here today.'

'Really? Why is that?' She felt better with the conversation leaving the technical whys and hows of her being there.

'I went back to find you, but you weren't there.'

He was being blunt, so she decided to match him in honesty. 'I waited until it was clear you were in no hurry to return to me. Then I left.'

He blew out a long, frustrated breath. 'I didn't mean to be gone so long. I didn't *want* to be gone so long. The mayor and the chief wouldn't let me get away until I explained every aspect of the community education plan I have proposed for the Midtown Station to them. I'm sorry if it seemed like I stood you up.'

Venus felt herself bristling. 'Actually I never considered that you might have stood me up,' she lied. 'I simply wearied of waiting, so I left.'

Griffin frowned in response to her haughty tone.

'Well, it was lovely to see you again, and I do hope you enjoyed my class.' Venus turned from him and started stuffing chalk and vagina diagrams back into her bag. Why was she being so short and rude to him? She'd wanted him to talk to her – wanted him to apologize to her. And here he was doing both and she was suddenly cutting him off. Venus silently considered her emotions.

She was hurt! By Hercules's scraggly scrotum, Griffin had hurt her when he hadn't returned, and the reminder of believing he'd stood her up still hurt!

'Oh, gosh! Hi, Griffin.' Pea's sweet voice broke the silence.

Venus turned back to Griffin to see Pea looking flustered, but holding out her hand for him to shake. The goddess's heart plummeted into her stomach.

Griffin's smile was genuine as he took her hand. 'Hello, neighbor. Nice to see you again, Pea. I should have realized you were the friend Venus was helping out here at the college.'

'You should have?' Pea asked, with a confused little smile.

'Yeah, at the masquerade party Venus said you two were close. Actually maybe you could help me out here. I'm trying to make up for the fact that I got pulled away by business that night and left her outside by herself too long.'

'At Lola's masquerade?'

'Yeah, and now she's pissed.' He glanced at Venus, and what he saw made him add, 'Not that I blame her. But I can make it up to her. Tonight. With dinner. How about you act as my reference and convince her that I'm just an ordinary guy and not an axe murderer.'

'Or a liar?' Pea asked, only she wasn't looking at Griffin. She was staring at Venus.

'Definitely not a liar,' Griffin said. 'That's what I want to prove to her.'

'Pea, I can—'

Pea's blank expression didn't change, but she interrupted the goddess with a smooth, 'Venus will let you make up for your mistake.' Venus opened her mouth, but Pea talked right over her. 'I have a date tonight, so it's only right she should have one, too.'

Venus blinked in shock. 'A date? Tonight? With . . .'

Pea's blank mask cracked just a little. 'With *him*, Victor. He came to my office while you were teaching class.'

'And all is well between the two of you?' Venus asked.

'Yes, everything's okay,' Pea said coolly. Then she cut her eyes at Griffin. 'So there's no reason you shouldn't go out with him. None at all.' Pea gave her a tight smile before walking quickly away.

Griffin stepped closer to her and Venus felt her stomach flutter again.

'Say you'll go out with me tonight.' His gaze caught hers, pulling it away from Pea's retreating back. They stared at one another. Griffin was so close Venus could easily imagine his body against hers, and even through her worry for Pea, she found herself wondering what it would feel like if she and Griffin were naked and able to take their time pleasuring each other. Would it be as good as the rush of lust she had experienced during their hasty coupling under the tree . . . ?

'Yes, I will,' Venus heard herself say.

He stepped even closer to her and Venus could smell his unique scent and feel the heat of his body. 'You won't regret it,' he said.

'I—I have to go talk to Pea,' Venus said abruptly. 'I'll see you tonight.' She started to walk away, but his voice made her pause.

'When and where tonight?'

'Six o'clock.' She picked the time randomly, her mind already trying to figure out what she was going to say to her friend. 'Oh, and right now I live with Pea.' At least Venus hoped she still did.

Griffin smiled and nodded. 'I'll be there at six sharp, my goddess.'

Pea was sitting at her desk staring at the wall when Venus entered her office. The goddess couldn't remember when she'd ever felt so terrible.

'Forgive me, Pea,' she said, without any preamble. 'I should have told you that I'd been with Griffin that night.'

Pea shrugged and wouldn't meet her eyes. 'Whatever. You're a goddess, and goddesses can do whatever they want.'

'No, that's not ture.' Venus sat heavily in Pea's interview chair. 'Actually you are partially right. As a goddess I can literally do whatever I want to do, but as your friend there are things I wouldn't do.'

'You mean like go after the guy I have a major crush on while you're making it look like you're helping me catch him?'

'That's not how it happened.'

Pea finally looked at her and Venus hated the hurt that so obviously filled the mortal woman's eyes. 'Then explain it to me, because from where I'm sitting it looks exactly like that's what happened. And worse than that, it looks like you're one of those terrible girls who made me so miserable in high school.'

'Oh, Pea, no!' Venus felt her eyes fill with tears. 'Please don't think that! What happened was an accident, and the biggest mistake I made was not telling you about it.'

Pea lifted her chin and finally met Venus's gaze. 'I just want to know one thing. Was it all a lie? All that stuff you told me about myself?'

Tears spilled down Venus's cheeks. 'No! I didn't lie to you, not even about Griffin. I just didn't tell you everything I should have. I wanted to. I even started to. But I didn't want to hurt you. And,' Venus added as she wiped at her face with the back of her hand, 'I didn't want to lose your friendship.'

'Tell me what happened.'

Venus drew a deep breath and told Pea everything – from the instant connection she'd felt – and tried her best to ignore – with Griffin to how he approached her at the masquerade. By the time Venus got to the part about him ravishing her under the tree, Pea was listening wide-eyed. Then she explained how she believed Griffin had stood her up.

Pea had stayed silent until then, but she blurted, 'You thought he stood you up! That's why you looked so strange and sad when I found you outside.'

Venus opened her mouth to assure Pea that it hadn't been that big of a deal. The Goddess of Love is, after all, always in control, always fine. But before she could say the words she realized how false they were, and she realized something else. She wanted to talk to Pea about all of this – she *needed* to talk to Pea because the mortal had truly become her friend.

'I've never been stood up before, and I – I didn't know what to do or how to act,' the goddess admitted. 'I just sat there and hurt. I should have told you what happened, but I didn't even know how to say it. Then when you told me about the other man I thought that if I could just get them together, you'd see how much better your new guy was than Griffin, and even then if you didn't see what a cad Griffin was, I give you my word, I wouldn't have let him use you and hurt you.'

'Like you thought he used and hurt you,' Pea said.

'Yes, like that.'

'It feels awful, doesn't it, to think you've been rejected and lied to, especially by someone you care about?' Pea said quietly.

Venus couldn't find her voice; she only nodded and wiped fresh tears from her face with the tissue Pea handed her.

'You do care about Griffin, don't you?' Pea said.

'Yes, I do,' Venus managed to choke out. 'But not as much as I care about you. If it hurts you, I won't ever see him again. I give you my solemn oath.'

Pea smiled at her friend, and Venus was relieved beyond words to see the love and trust return to her eyes. 'You know, you were right about Griffin.'

'He's a terrible cad?' Venus sniffled.

Pea laughed. 'Well, maybe. But I was talking about what you said about him yesterday – or really what you said about how I felt about him. It wasn't Griffin I wanted. It was what he represented to me: the perfect man I could never find, never have as my own.'

'You're wrong about that. You can find the man who will be perfect for you, and you can make him yours.'

Pea's smile was more than a little naughty. 'Oh, I know that.'

'I think it's your turn to talk now. I want to hear about Victor.'

'I want to tell you about him, but first I think I'm going to knock off for the rest of the day. You and I have dates to get ready for.' Pea grabbed her purse and stood up, looking questioningly at the goddess when she didn't move.

'Do you forgive me, Dorreth?' Venus asked solemnly.

'Of course I do, Goddess. That's what friends do, forgive each other's mistakes.'

Venus studied Pea with newfound respect. 'Thank you, Dorreth Pea Chamberlain. You are a truly good person.'

Pea flushed and grinned. 'I like to look on the positive side of life.'

'An excellent attitude to practice.'

'Yeah, I got it from Oprah. As she would say, being strong and positive is one way of being a powerful, modern woman.'

'Oprah?'

'Think of her as a sister goddess.'

'Really? A modern woman who's a sister goddess? I want to hear all about her, too,' Venus said, as she stood and linked arms with Pea.

'So little time . . . so many goddesses . . .' Pea laughed as the two of them went arm in arm from her office.

*　　　*　　　*

'You know, there's really no reason for you to be so nervous,' Pea told Venus for the zillionth time.

'Of course there is. I've never been on a date.'

Pea giggled. 'Do you know how unbelievable that is? I mean, you're the Goddess of Love!'

Venus frowned severely at Pea. 'Of course I am. What does that have to do with this?'

'How is it that you've never been on a date before? You're the most beautiful woman I've ever seen. Men must fall all over you.'

Venus's expression lightened. 'Thank you, darling. And of course men fall all over me.'

'Then why no date until now?'

Venus sighed and joined Pea sitting on the end of her bed. 'It's different with the immortals. We don't date. We have delicious passion-filled torrid affairs. Unions that blaze across the heavens and cause wars to be fought and civilizations to thrive.'

'Jeesh, then why bother with Griffin at all?'

'Because he treated me like a mortal woman. *He* seduced *me*. And not because I'm the Goddess of Love, but because he desired the woman he believed me to be.' Venus's voice was so faint Pea leaned closer to hear her. 'Until that night at Lola's, I've always been in control. If I want a god – he succumbs to me. If I desire the attentions of a mortal – he gratefully worships me. I've always been the seducer, never the seduced. I've always been so in control that I even decided on a marriage of convenience.'

'You're married!'

Venus nodded her head but shrugged her shoulders. 'In name only. He's not physically perfect, so he's an outcast in Olympus. He thought by marrying me he could gain acceptance. I thought by marrying him I could gain . . .' She paused. She was getting ready to say her normal line – that by marrying Vulcan she thought she'd gain a shield to retreat behind. That even Love grew weary and looked for a quiet place to rest, and stoic, outcast Vulcan and his fiery realm could provide her with that. But recently she'd begun questioning her motives in marrying Vulcan. Aloud she heard herself admitting, 'No. That's not true. I pretended that I needed him for one thing, while I was really using him as an excuse. I hid behind the marriage so that I didn't have to look at the emptiness in my own life.' She smiled sadly at Pea, violet eyes brimming with tears. By the Titans' enormous manhoods, she hadn't cried so much in centuries. 'Ridiculous, isn't it?' Venus said miserably. 'That Love could be lonely.'

'I don't think there's anything at all ridiculous about you.' Pea put her arm around the goddess. 'I think you're beautiful and kind and amazing. And I also think that one very important point has been made clear today. You didn't come here just for me. You came here for you.'

'For me?'

'Maybe the Goddess of Love came to Tulsa to find herself.'

'But I know who I am. I am Love.'

'How long has it been since you've known love?' Pea asked gently.

Venus studied the mortal sitting beside her whose arm was draped so casually and comfortingly around her. Ancient mortals weren't ever so relaxed in her presence. They were forever seeking ... searching ... beseeching her to fulfill their fantasies. But Pea wasn't like that. Although her heart's desire had been what bound Venus to this world, Pea had, from the beginning, seemed more concerned for Venus's welfare than her own. Even today, when Venus had hurt the little mortal, and it had appeared she'd betrayed her, Pea remained open to her and even offered the goddess comfort.

Then Venus did something she hadn't done for eons. She answered Pea's question with complete honesty, thereby admitting the truth to herself.

'I can't remember the last time I allowed myself to love. It's hard to believe. I've been loved, evoked love, fought for love and caused love, but it is quite possible I have never actually known love.'

'It's time that changed, don't you think?'

'I'm not sure that I know how to go about it.'

'Well, I'm not an expert or anything, but I think the key to knowing love might be in letting go.'

'Letting go?' Venus asked, feeling incredibly out of her element. *She* was taking advice about love from a mortal who until a couple days ago didn't know how to control her own hair? But as Venus looked into Pea's eyes and saw wisdom and compassion there, the goddess remembered something she should have never forgotten. True love wasn't found in good hair or the right clothes, make-up or shoes. True love was found in the soul – as was wisdom and compassion.

'Yeah, letting go. Think about it. It makes sense. You can't know love unless you're willing to let go of a bunch of things like fear and selfishness and *control*.'

'Control?'

'Control.'

'Are you sure about that?'

'I'm afraid so.'

'How did you get to be so wise, Pea?'

Pea grinned. 'I've been hanging around a goddess. She's rubbed off on me. Now stop procrastinating and zap yourself a pair of black slacks and a violet cashmere sweater. Something the exact color of your eyes that will hug your curves and show off those great boobs. Zap up a black jacket to match the slacks while you're at it. And wear your hair up tonight so that he can see your beautiful neck. Then if Griffin's really a good boy you can take your hair down for him. Later,' she finished mischievously.

Venus gave her a quick hug and then stood up. 'Do I need to remind you to close your eyes?'

'Nope.' Pea closed her eyes. 'Oh, wait.' She opened one eye and peered at Venus. 'Forget the jacket.'

'But what if it gets cold tonight?'

'Well, it just might. Then there you'll be, all nipply and jacket-less.' Pea exaggerated a sigh. 'Whatever will you do?'

'I don't think I taught you that,' Venus said.

'You taught me the attitude. I made up the words to go with it.'

'Close your eyes.' Venus conjured up the outfit Pea had recommended and decided leaving out the jacket was, indeed, a stroke of brilliance. She studied herself in the mirror, pleased at what she saw in her reflection. The goddess glanced back at the bed. Pea was still sitting there with her eyes screwed tightly shut and an up-tilted curve to her lips. She did absolutely adore this little mortal. 'Open your eyes now darling, and let's be sure you're ready for your own date.'

Pea opened her eyes. 'Oh, mine is easy. I've decided that I'm going to fix him dinner – here. I'm just going to wear those fabulous jeans you picked out for me and that silk knit sweater. Um, and my new lacy white lingerie.' She blushed, but only a little.

Venus raised her brows. 'Planning on letting him see your new lingerie?'

'Oh, gosh I hope so!' she said in a breathy voice, and then her soft blush flamed a deeper color. 'Is that wrong? It is, isn't it? I should be going slower. I mean, no matter what I see when I look into his eyes, I don't really know him.'

'Darling, there's one thing my eons of experience have taught me. Love has no timetable. I've seen couples be slow and careful and wise about love, only to have it sift through their hands like sand in a sieve. I've also seen couples whose love flares the moment they first look in one another's eyes and never ceases to flame for one lifetime after another. It's the lovers, not the time.'

'How do I know if it's real?'

'The same way lovers have known throughout eternity. Trust yourself and listen to your heart.'

'Okay. I will if you will.'

'Agreed,' Venus said. 'Now help me pile my hair up and I'll scrunch some more coconut oil into your lovely curls.'

Chapter Twenty

'Okay, remember. This dating stuff is really not that big of a deal. Well, I mean it's not that big of a deal until he introduces you to his family, then you really should get nervous for all sorts of reasons.'

Venus gave Pea a panicked look.

'No, no, no. You don't have to worry about that tonight. Sorry, I shouldn't have even mentioned it. Here's what you do tonight – you let go of that famous control of yours and see what he has planned for you two. All you have to concentrate on is relaxing and having a good time.'

'Relaxing and having a good time,' Venus repeated. Were her palms moist? Impossible. The Goddess of Love simply did not get sweaty palms. She rubbed them down the thighs of her slacks just to be safe.

The doorbell rang and Venus felt her nervous heartbeat flutter in her throat. Pea winked at her, yelled at Chloe to quit her barking and opened the door.

By Hermes's flamingly gay gonads, he looked delicious! He had on black slacks, a black sweater and a camel-colored cashmere jacket. He was freshly shaven. Venus knew if she leaned into him she'd be able to smell the scent of warm man mixed with just a hint of the soap he used. And she very much wanted to lean into him.

'Hi again, Griffin,' Pea said.

'Hello, Pea.' Griffin squatted down and held his hand out to the grumbling Chloe. 'Remember me, Scottie cat? Remember me, kitty-kitty-kitty?' Apparently Chloe did because her grumbles turned to a tail-wagging wiggle and she allowed Griffin to scratch her on the head. When he stood up his eyes met hers. 'Good evening, Venus.'

'Griffin.' She just said his name, but it came out as an audible caress and she watched his lips curve up in response.

'Where are you two kids going tonight?' Pea asked cheekily.

Griffin laughed. 'It's a surprise.'

Venus started to frown, but before she could tell him she didn't like surprises, especially from mortal men, Pea was already chattering happily away.

'A surprise! That's perfect. Venus *loves* a good surprise – it's so *out of control*. Isn't that right, Venus?'

'Yes, that's right,' Venus said reluctantly, getting the message Pea was telegraphing perfectly.

'Good,' Griffin said. 'Then are you ready to go? I'm cutting it kinda close as it is.'

'Yes, ready,' Venus said, thinking, *No, not ready*.

As she walked past him to the door, he said, 'Do you want to grab a coat?'

Venus threw Pea a look over her shoulder. 'No, I'm fine. I am warm natured.'

Pea grinned back at her as she closed the door.

Venus walked confidently to the vehicle in Pea's driveway – until it registered on her mind what her eyes were seeing.

'Why is it so big?'

'Well, I need it to haul my . . . ur . . . things around.'

'What is it?'

'A Dodge Ram Dooley,' he said, opening the passenger's door for her. 'Sorry about the step up.'

Venus looked at the inside of the huge black truck, which was a ridiculous height off the ground. 'By Hermes's flaming ass . . . hat.' Remembering Persephone's comment about modern mortals not appreciating her divine genitalia curses, Venus faltered, mixing the ancient with one of the modern profanities she remembered from the Smart Bitches Trashy Books site. 'How am I supposed to climb up into that creature?'

Griffin laughed. 'By Hermes's flaming asshat?'

'Everyone knows how gay he is and that he wears that winged hat all the time as his own personal fashion statement.'

'Everyone knows this?'

Venus's eyes shifted from the truck to Griffin. 'My hobby is mythology,' she said quickly.

'Your name is Venus, you're a sex therapist, and your hobby is mythology. Are you sure you're not really a goddess?' he teased.

'If I was I could just zap myself up into that thing,' she muttered.

He laughed again and held out his hand to her. 'Come on. I'll help you.'

As his strong hands steadied her, and the jolt of reconnecting with his warm flesh tingled teasingly through her body, Venus was suddenly grateful for the huge truck and the need for his assistance. 'Thank you,' she said.

'My pleasure, ma'am.' He reached up and pulled her seat belt down and across her, securing it in its holder. His face was very near hers and she could smell the scent of warm man and soap she had fantasied about earlier. He looked into her eyes and gave her his slow, sexy smile. 'I want to be sure you stay safe,' he murmured, his breath warm and sweet against her cheek.

Unfortunately he didn't kiss her. Instead he climbed down out of the truck and hurried around to his own side.

Venus was surprised by how smooth the big truck drove, and she decided she liked the feeling of sitting up above just about everyone else on the roadway. Griffin pressed some buttons and soft music floated between them, which called to mind the slow dance they'd shared, which in turn brought back her nerves. She blurted, 'Where are we going?' in a voice that sounded much too abrupt. She drew a calming breath. 'I mean, you said it was a surprise, but can't you give me some hint or clue?'

'Sorry, didn't mean to sound so mysterious. I was really just kidding around with Pea.' He glanced sideways at her and she thought that he, too, suddenly looked a little nervous. 'We're going to an art opening. If you don't mind.'

Venus's brows lifted. 'You're taking me to an art opening?'

He looked at her silently before turning his eyes back to the road. 'Sounds like you find it hard to believe I appreciate art.'

She took her time answering him. His voice had sounded neutral, but something in the tense set of his shoulders told her that she had inadvertently offended him. 'The truth is you seem more warrior than artist to me.'

'Can't a man be both? You're the mythology buff. If I remember correctly weren't several of the gods artists, or at least musicians, as well as warriors?'

Venus felt a little shock of surprise. He was right, though. Apollo was a gifted musician as well as a skilled warrior and God of Light. Ares was God of War, but he was also a poet – though in her opinion a rather dry one. Athena, who was Goddess of War and Wisdom, had also long been recognized as Goddess of the Arts, too. And even Vulcan was an accomplished metal sculptor, as well as God of Fire. 'Yes, the gods and goddesses were known for the duality of their natures. But unless the true surprise you're going to reveal to me tonight is that you are one of the gods, it has been my experience mortal men tend to be one or the other, either artist or warrior. But—' She paused and he glanced over at her. She smiled warmly at him. 'I suppose an exceptional mortal man could be both.'

'So you'd think I was exceptional if you found out I was both?'

'Did I say exceptional?' she teased. 'I meant unusual . . . abnormal . . . aberrant . . . or maybe simply peculiar.'

He laughed and she was glad to see the tension leave his shoulders.

A building outside the truck caught her eye. 'Isn't that Lola's restaurant we just passed?'

'Yeah, the art show is down the street at one of the renovated Brady Street warehouses. I hope you don't mind a little walk. The weather's great tonight, and it's hard to find a good spot for this truck on the street, so I thought I'd park at the lot across from the Tribune Lofts, and we could walk from there.'

'I don't mind a brisk walk,' she said, but his mention of the Tribune Lofts had distracted her. They were near the portal. Odd that she'd forgotten all about it, and the fact that she was literally stranded in the modern mortal world. Funny, she hadn't really felt stranded, not since Pea had opened her home and her life to her. Pea seemed to be happy and well, and after her date tonight with the sexy Victor who was, apparently, an expert in cunnilingus, her life would quite probably be filled with ecstasy. That would fulfill the oath that had bound her to this world. So it was a very real possibility that she could walk down the street tonight and be allowed to disappear back to the ancient world – her world.

'Ready, Venus?'

She mentally shook herself. Griffin had parked the truck and was holding her door open, with his hand outstretched, ready to help her climb down from her passenger's side perch. She unclicked her seat belt and slid her hand into his.

She'd think about Olympus later.

The renovated warehouse was an excellent place for the art show. Venus was impressed by the lighting and the tall, smooth walls that were painted a pure white reminiscent of new snow and winter nights. They would showcase paintings well, she decided. But tonight the art being exhibited was of a different medium. Tonight they were exhibiting sculptures made of different types of metals welded together in an astonishing array of shapes and sizes. Venus studied the artist's work. She didn't need to look at the nameplates or the studio's flyer to recognize that all of the pieces had been created by the same artist.

'Grace,' she said abruptly.

'What?'

She looked from the sculpture she'd been studying to Griffin. The tension was back in his shoulders and he seemed to carry with him a strange nervousness, almost as if he had a wire within him that was strung too tightly. He'd started acting oddly ever since they'd entered the gallery. Yes, he'd been attentive and charming, and there was definitely a sexual tension that brewed steadily between them, but he'd also been on edge.

'I just realized what it is all of the sculptures have in common. It's a gracefulness. Even though each sculpture is different, they have a similar feel, as if they had been molded by the same heart.' She had his full attention now, which she definitely liked. 'I don't have to read the nameplates to know that all of these were created by the same man.'

'What makes you think the artist is a man?'

Venus smiled knowingly. 'I know a man's touch when I see it. For instance—' She motioned for Griffin to follow her over to a sculpture of which she was particularly fond. It was a large piece, titled *Phoenix*. The metal was copper. The sculpture was of the outline of a naked winged woman flying up from a nest of jagged copper flames. 'Look at the full, curving lines of this woman, especially her hips and breasts, and also look how he has given us the illusion of long, flowing hair that mingles with the flames so that the two, hair and flames, eventually become one. This was created by a man who loves the female form and who has an excellent eye for beauty.'

'Couldn't a woman love the female form, too?'

'Of course, but it has the sensuality and masculine energy of a man's hands.'

'Do you like it?'

'Yes, very much. I like them all actually. Do you know the artist?'

A cacophony of female voices interrupted his reply, and Griffin turned his head toward the entrance to the gallery as an excited group of four attractive young women burst into the warehouse.

'They did come.' He wasn't looking at Venus and his voice sounded strained.

'They?' Venus frowned at the gaggle of noisy young women. Why was Griffin interested in them while he was on a date with her?

'*They* are my sisters.' Then he did look at her. 'I hope you don't mind meeting my family.'

'Your family?' Venus realized she sounded squeaky, but she couldn't seem to help it. Pea had said meeting the family happened later!

He smiled and nodded apologetically. 'Yeah, I guess I should have warned you sooner, but I didn't want to scare you off.'

'Oh. Well. Oh,' was all Venus could manage.

'And one other thing,' he said quickly as the group of girls caught sight of him and began to move in a single rush toward them. 'I'm the sculptor.'

'You're the ...' Venus began and then simply stopped and stared at him as the truth hit her. The name on the plates had been D. Angel. DeAngelo. Of course he was the artist, which explained why he'd been so tense and silent. This was *his* art opening. 'How extraordinary,' she murmured.

Chapter Twenty-one

Griffin's sisters were enchanting female whirlwinds. They reminded Venus of forest nymphs. They also reminded Venus of why she could only spend a limited amount of time with forest nymphs. The little creatures were exhausting.

'Yep! We've been tellin' Griff for *years* that he shouldn't be so hush-hush about his art. It's cool, really. And it doesn't make him less macho. It's not like he's an interior designer or somethin' like that. He's a *fireman*. You don't get much more macho than that,' said Alicia, rolling her eyes in the direction her brother had disappeared with the gallery owner. Alicia was the youngest of the group, and Venus thought she was cute in a spaniel-like way, even though she was clearly the most scatterbrained of the sisters.

'You wouldn't believe how hard it was to get this show together,' said Sherry, the oldest and also the prettiest. She looked a lot like her brother with her thick, dark hair and her amazing blue eyes.

'Yeah, Sherry took the slides of Griff's work on the sly, and then snuck with them to the gallery owner, pretending to be his publicist,' said Kathy. Venus loved her short, spiky haircut and thought it made her neck look incredibly swanlike. She also liked the sparkle in her blue eyes, which definitely reminded her of Griffin. And Kathy's job fascinated Venus, too. She was a radio personality on something called a soft rock station. Venus would love to question her about what that meant, especially because that would mean she could listen to her talk more – Kathy's voice was a smoky mixture of woman and sex appeal, and it was truly a sensual experience just to hear her speak.

'I wasn't pretending,' Sherry said, tossing her long hair back over her shoulder. She grinned at Venus. 'I am a publicist. I just usually promote bands and not artists.'

'And Griffin's not paying you,' Stephanie said. She, too, had Griffin's dark hair, but her eyes were more green than blue. She'd explained that she was working on an advanced degree at the University of Tulsa. Venus wasn't sure what a jurisprudence was, but it sounded important, and she liked Stephanie's intensity.

Sherry laughed. 'No, he's not paying me. But he is going to change the oil in my car for the next fifty thousand miles.'

'Hey! He's going to change the oil in *my* car,' Alicia whined.

'You girls fighting over me again?' Griffin grinned at his sisters, then handed Venus a fresh glass of champagne. 'Here ya go, my goddess. Thought you might need a drink after spending time with this group.'

'*Your* goddess? That sounds awfully presumptuous of you,' Sherry said.

'Yeah, don't you need a goddess's permission before making her your own personal deity?' Kathy practically purred.

Venus smiled and caught Griffin's eye teasingly. 'Your brother is the kind of man who lays claim to what he wants. I suppose it's a good thing Venus is Goddess of Love and not war. Love has a more docile temper.'

'Docile? You?' Griffin's lips tilted up.

'She didn't say she was docile, doofus. She said she was *more* docile than the freaking Goddess of War, which still means you should watch yourself,' Alicia said.

'Exactly,' Venus said.

'I've already decided that she's more naughty than nice.'

'Is he insulting me?' Venus asked Sherry.

'I don't think so. In his own way I think our Griff means it as a compliment.'

'Hey. I'm right here.'

In perfect unison all four sisters rolled their eyes at him.

'You're driving her away from me and dooming me to a passionless, lonely existence where I'll be known as the crazy old fireman/artist who spends all his time changing the oil in his sisters' cars and never has a moment to himself.'

'And the problem with that would be what?' Sherry said sweetly.

'Hey, would you get all hunched over and put on a French accent like Kevin Kline in *French Kiss*, and mutter stuff like, *Those girls make my ass hurt*, while you suck on a disgusting cigarette and drink little glasses of red wine?' asked Kathy.

'Kat, you've got to give up that Netflix subscription. You're spending way too much time watching and rewatching movies,' Sherry said.

'I like movies.' Kathy pouted.

'Are you feeling the need to run screaming from this place?' Griffin asked Venus.

She laughed. 'I like getting to know your sisters.' It was clear from the way his sisters doted on Griffin that they adored him as much as he obviously adored them. What a multilayered man he was: fireman and warrior, artist and loving brother. The sisters continued to argue about the oil-changing schedule and Griffin. Venus sipped her champagne and glanced up over the lip of her glass, catching his gaze. While he watched her she took the strawberry that garnished the rim of the glass and licked the tip of it. She saw Griffin's breath catch. Yes, he certainly was multidimensional, which included the healthy dose of passion she knew all too well was simmering just beneath his surface. A passion she would love to sample again and again and . . .

'Yoo-hoo! Love birds! Jeesh, get a room.' Alicia giggled.

Griffin laughed good-naturedly. Then he held out his hand to Venus. 'Well, my goddess, are you hungry? I could take you home and feed you.'

Venus smiled at his use of her nickname and realized, now that she didn't feel so nervous about their date, she was actually hungry, and she'd definitely like him to take her home. 'Yes, I am.' She took his hand, liking the way he wrapped it through his arm, as if he were a gentleman warrior, escorting his lady love who belonged to him and only him. And she thought again how much she enjoyed being treated like a woman and not like a deity. Then she remembered exactly why they were there and added, 'But you can't leave your own art show.'

'Why not? My publicist is here. She's better than I am at this kind of stuff anyway,' he said, grinning at his sister. 'See you girls later,' he called over his shoulder as he pulled Venus with him toward the warehouse door.

'Good-bye girls,' Venus called over her shoulder.

The sisters waved at her while they blew kisses at their big brother.

Outside the sidewalk was busy with people going to and from the art show and the other little shops that had purposefully stayed open late to capitalize on the gallery opening. It was a beautiful, clear night, but the wind had whipped up, making it a little cool, and Venus snuggled closer to Griffin.

'Here, take this.' He slipped off his jacket and put it around her shoulders. 'And let me walk on the street side of the sidewalk. You never know when some idiot will drink and drive and jump the damn curb.' Then he threaded her arm back through his, and tucked her on his left side, keeping her close to him. She was enveloped by his warmth and she felt protected and cared for – two feelings that were foreign to the Goddess of Love. She usually made certain such things were brought to others' lives. Had anyone, god or mortal, ever worried about anything as simple as whether she was too hot or cold or whether she was protected? She knew the answer too well. She'd been worshipped for eons. People made pilgrimages to ask boons of her and to be granted the blessing of love in their lives. But people didn't care for and protect her. She was a great goddess – they wouldn't believe she needed or desired their care.

Well, they were wrong.

'Thanks for being patient with my sisters. I know the four of them together can be a little overwhelming.' His words broke into her internal reverie.

She smiled at him. 'They're going to be mad at you for leaving early.'

'Nah, I'll just be changing a lot of oil. And here's the secret.' He bent down and whispered into her ear. 'I don't really mind doing it. The girls are always grateful, and I like knowing that they're taken care of. I still change my mom's oil every three thousand miles.'

Venus wasn't exactly sure why oil needed to be changed so much, or from what into what it needed to be changed, but she liked the fact that Griffin did it for the women in his life almost as much as she loved the way his breath tickled her ear and sent sensuous shivers down her neck.

'Too bad you didn't get to meet my mom tonight. She's on a cruise with two of her girlfriends. She'll be pissed when she gets back and finds out she missed the art opening.'

'What about your father?'

Griffin's open, warm expression faltered. 'He left us when I was a teenager. Found a younger wife and made a new family.'

'I'm sorry,' Venus said. So he'd been father as well as brother to his sisters and the man his mother depended upon. Little wonder he understood women so well.

Griffin shrugged. 'Don't be sorry. It happened a long time ago.'

'It was his loss,' Venus said.

'That's what I used to tell the girls when they'd get down about it.'

They'd stopped at the passenger's side of Griffin's huge truck. On impulse, Venus said, 'You're a good brother, Griffin DeAngelo. May you be richly blessed for your kindness to your family.' Then she kissed him softly on the cheek, purposefully sending just a hint of her magic through him with her blessing – not enough for him to notice, but enough to bring him unusually good luck for the next several days.

When she pulled back she thought he would smile, open the door for her, and help her into the truck's maw. Instead he surprised her by taking her in his arms and lowering his mouth onto hers. Over his shoulder she saw the fullness of the winter moon and it seemed to be shining a beam of silver light down on them. *An omen*, she thought as her eyes closed and she opened her mouth to Griffin's possession. *A lover's moon shining for us alone is an excellent omen. It's saying I should allow myself a lover who isn't a suppliant or an immortal. It's saying I should allow myself to love.* And then she wasn't able to think about anything except Griffin's mouth and the perfect way they fit together as she slid her arms up around his neck and molded herself to him.

226

'Come home with me,' Griffin murmured roughly against her lips.

'Yes,' she whispered.

Griffin's two-storey stucco house was just down the street from Pea's snug little home. He unlocked the door and ushered her into a dimly lit, spacious room. Instantly a huge long-haired calico cat began winding around his legs, purring a welcome. Griffin scratched the top of her head.

'Venus, meet Cali Alley Cat. She's not really an alley cat, or at least she's not since she adopted me, but the name stuck to her. I'll get her saucer of milk. If I don't she'll never leave me alone. Make yourself at home.' He hurried toward a room at the rear of the house, and then called over his shoulder. 'Oh, the real lights are there by the door. Sorry, I should have flipped them on for you.'

He disappeared into what Venus assumed must be the kitchen, and she reached behind her and flipped up the light switch. She turned back to study Griffin's home, and felt herself freeze with shock as she stared with disbelief at the huge iron sculpture that predominated the room. Though he had borrowed the subject from another artist, she knew the work was Griffin's. It had the same graceful, sensuous lines as did all of his sculptures. It was exquisite, and it made her feel breathless and humbled and more surprised than she had been in centuries.

'This piece is my favorite. I didn't exhibit it tonight because it'll never be for sale,' he said softly, handing Venus a glass of white wine.

'It's Botticelli's *The Birth of Venus*.' She was amazed her voice sounded so normal. 'Only it's not.'

'His painting inspired it, but Botticelli's *Venus* never felt right to me. So I fixed her.' His laugh was a little nervous. 'Or at least I tried.'

227

'You fixed her,' Venus said, still staring at the sculpture. The seashell had been hammered from what appeared to be a single huge sheet of copper, and Griffin had aged and tarnished it, so that it had a green mossy tint that reminded her of the sea. The Venus that was rising from the ocean was created by more of the copper, only this metal had been polished until it glittered like faceted gems. His lines were sweeping and erotic. He'd fashioned her hair from tiny pieces of metal that lay over one another, giving the effect of a mermaid's tail as it wrapped around the generous curves of her body. She was no longer nymphlike. Instead she had the alluring sensuality of a more adult woman who was ripe and experienced and intriguing.

Venus moved closer to the sculpture. 'It's hard to believe you did this all of metal. It looks too warm – too realistic.'

'Kind of a switch on what women are, don't you think? They look soft, but are really stronger than men usually give them credit for being.'

She glanced over her shoulder at him and caught his cocky smile. But she found it sexy and endearing rather than overly arrogant. The man certainly did know women. Smiling, she asked, 'Why Venus?'

He grinned back at her. 'Don't you remember? When we met I said she's my favorite goddess.'

Venus nodded faintly. She hadn't remembered. She hadn't really even thought about it.

'Yeah, I'm intrigued by her,' he said, staring at the sculpture. 'The Goddess of Love, born from the sea – not even needing a man to come into being.' He shook his head. 'I suppose it's always seemed a little sad.'

'Sad? What do you mean?' Venus felt her mind fluttering about like it was suddenly filled with confused butterflies.

'Well, think about it. The Goddess of Love doesn't need a man. It makes me think that the goddess carries love around with her, creates it for other people, but doesn't keep any of it for herself. It makes her seem untouched and untouchable.' He raised his glass to her and his playful grin was back. 'But your hobby is mythology. What do you think of your namesake?'

She waited a long time before answering. Then she said the most honest thing she could. 'I think she would love your sculpture of her.'

He walked over to her and fingered the escaping wisps of her silver-blonde hair. 'So, my goddess, have you decided what I am yet?'

'What you are?' His nearness was making her breath come faster.

'Before we got to the gallery you said a man who is an artist and a warrior had to be either exceptional . . . unusual . . .' He paused, twining a strand of hair gently around his finger. 'What else was it you said?'

Venus raised one brow at him. 'I said a man who is an artist must be either exceptional, unusual, abnormal, aberrant, or maybe simply peculiar.'

'And, my goddess, what is your decision about me?' His blue eyes were boyishly mischievous.

'I'm leaning toward exceptional or peculiar.'

Griffin moved even closer to her. 'Let me see if I can shift the vote in favor of exceptional.'

He didn't give her time to respond. He simply cupped her face in his hand and bent to possess her mouth. She let him take her in a kiss that blazed through her skin. Venus reveled in the fact that this man took her, without hesitation, without making his touch a game of worship that ended in his begging a boon off her. She'd heard it so many times for century after century: *Accept this offering of my body to you, Great Goddess of Love, and please grant my request to have the maiden I desire love me.* Even the immortals weren't above asking for her to help them. Vulcan had even married her, ironically, because his desire had been to hide from love. She was well and truly sick of it. Tonight she wouldn't be Venus the Goddess. Tonight she would be a mortal woman who was being loved by a mortal man, which meant she would relinquish her famous control to Griffin.

Without a word, Griffin put her glass of wine next to his on a low metal coffee table. Then he took her hand and led her to the wide stairs to the second floor and the loftlike bedroom that opened to below. His bed was large, with an iron frame and covered with a thick dark comforter and king-sized pillows. He didn't turn on any more lights, but let the illumination from the room below spill softly over them, creating an effect much like candlelight. Griffin sat on his bed and pulled her close to him so that she stood between his legs. Then he tunneled his hands into her hair, causing the precarious updo to come undone and fall down her back and around her shoulders.

'I wanted to do that from the moment I saw you tonight,' he said.

She shook her head so that all of her hair came free. His hands moved from her hair, down her neck, and then slowly, slowly, they continued down, outlining her body as if he wanted to memorize her shape and form. She shivered, thinking how his hands had the ability to create such beautiful, sensuous works of art – how they had somehow been able to create a perfect rendition of her without his even knowing it.

'Are you cold?' he whispered. His hands moved from the back of her thighs up and around, until his thumbs caressed the core of her womanhood. Venus's breath caught on a moan of pleasure. 'I can warm you up,' he said, his voice going all rough, like speaking had suddenly gotten difficult. She rocked forward against his firm touch, thoroughly aroused by the sensation of his hand stroking her through the layers of soft panty and rough slacks.

'I remember everything about how you felt that night. I haven't been able to get you out of my mind. You're like a drug that won't clear my blood.' His voice was deep and his breathing had increased. 'I remember how hot and wet you were, how I slid into you and how I could feel you come.'

She met his passion-glazed eyes and the heat and desire she saw there had lust thrumming through her already sensitized body. 'Did you think about me when you masturbated afterwards?'

'Over and over again.' He moaned. 'I thought I'd lost you.'

'I thought you'd used me and then cast me aside,' she admitted.

'Never!' His eyes were bright with passion. 'I would never do that to you. Come here, Venus.'

He reached up and pulled her mouth down to his. She opened her lips and accepted the heated thrust of his tongue, so that Griffin devoured her. Still kissing her, he turned and swept her off her feet so that she was lying across his bed. His hands moved down to unzip her slacks and she lifted her hips so that he could skim them from her body, pulling her stiletto pumps off at the same time and tossing them to the floor with the slacks. His fingers splayed low across her stomach, then they slid seductively down over the silky wisp of black panty she was still wearing to circle her clit with his thumb, and down still farther to gently stroke the folds of her vagina in the same caress he'd been teasing her with before he'd taken off her slacks.

'You're so wet your panties are soaked,' he said.

And then she groaned in frustration as his hand left her clit so he could pull off his own clothes in several impatient movements.

He was truly a beautifully built man. Darker and more masculine than Adonis, taller and stronger than Achilles. She wanted him to claim her as his own with a desire so fierce and so overpowering that it made her dizzy. When he lay back down beside her she found the hard length of his phallus, and she let her hand stroke him while she met his teasing tongue. He chuckled deep in his throat and grabbed her wrist.

'No, I don't want it to be over too soon. Tonight we take our time with each other.'

'I don't know if I can wait,' she said, with a rush of breath.

He smiled. 'I can. I can wait. And so can you. This time I'll be the teacher.' Then he began unbuttoning her sweater, following the trail his fingers were making with his lips and tongue. When her black silk bra was finally uncovered he flicked his tongue along the top of it until he found the hard nub of her aroused nipple. He licked and sucked it through the thin layer of silk, causing her breath to pant hard and fast. His talented artist's hand caressed a path down her body, sliding off her panties. Then he cupped her ass and brought her firmly against his erection. But instead of plunging into her wetness, he positioned the head of his cock so that it could slide back and forth, from her clit down and then back up. He rocked her body against his and she gasped, grinding herself closer to him.

'You're making my cock all wet,' he whispered against the nipple he was still teasing with his tongue and teeth.

'Enter me!' She moaned. 'Please . . .'

'Not yet, my goddess, I want you to come first.'

'Yes,' she cried. 'Oh, Griffin, yes!' She rubbed her soft slickness against his engorged head faster and faster until she felt the delicious explosion build between her legs and cascade out through her body.

But instead of stopping at her orgasm, Griffin pulled off her bra and cupped her breasts in his hand, kneading and caressing while he repositioned himself against her wet heat. This time the head of his cock was pressed lower, so that it slid back and forth the length of her velvet slit, teasing her opening but never entering it.

'I remember what you taught us in class today.' His voice was rough with lust. 'How, if a man truly cares about a woman's pleasure, she can have one orgasm after another. He just has to keep her aroused and then he can bring her to climax over and over.' He thrust against her, his hard phallus gliding against her soft wetness. 'Is this the right place?'

'Yes.' She moaned. He slid himself over her, back and forth. One of his hands firmly cupped her ass and kept her grinding rhythmically against him, and the other teased her breast, holding it up to his hot mouth. When she came again she couldn't help crying his name.

'Now,' he said, pressing her against the bed and holding himself up so that he could look into her eyes. 'Now I have to be inside you.' And he plunged into her, impaling her already engorged vagina with a ferocity that made her moan her pleasure aloud. The feeling of fullness was almost too much for her to bear. The sound of his heavy breathing mixed in perfect harmony with her own pants, and she could smell the musty scent of their mingled sex. He captured her mouth, and Venus immersed herself in the salty, sexy taste of him. Everything combined to heighten her desire for him. She reached between them and cupped him with one hand, squeezing gently and teasingly. With the other she stroked his hardness as he thrust in and out of her, loving that the cream that covered his phallus was her own wetness.

'You're mine,' he said with a growl, moving his mouth from hers to trail down the slope of her neck, where his teeth teased and nipped, as if he actually was a virile male animal marking her as his own. Intensely aroused by his possession of her, Venus lifted her hips, meeting him with equal passion. She was still stroking him when his shaft began to spasm, and he pounded against her so deeply that he found the pleasure center within her, finally releasing a gush of overwhelming sensation as her cries of ecstasy mirrored Griffin's.

Chapter Twenty-two

A couple days earlier Pea would have found it utterly bizarre that she wasn't feeling one hint of nerves while she puttered around the kitchen getting ready for a date that had the potential to be amazing.

'I've gained confidence,' she told Chloe, whose attention was focused solely on Pea, as if the Scottie could will her to drop something.

Chloe sighed, disgruntled at Pea's neatness.

'Well, it's true. And it's not just about the hair and the clothes and the makeup.' She chattered at the dog, ignoring Chloe's grumpiness as she tossed the salad. 'It's about the goddess I've found in here.' She pointed at herself with a long leaf of romaine lettuce.

Chloe woofed softly at her and Pea laughed, tossing her a dog biscuit.

'Try to behave yourself tonight. There's something special about this one. I can see it in his eyes.'

Pea carried the salad out to the deck, putting it on the little picnic table that was already set with a cheery red-and-white-checked tablecloth and matching napkins. Her good china looked strangely perfect mixed with the casual chic of the little Italian picnic she'd set up. The Chianti was open and breathing – the garlic bread was keeping warm in the oven, and the spaghetti sauce was ready. Pea lit the candles on the table and added more pinion wood to the large chimenea. Then she completed the finishing touch by plugging in the minilantern lights that she'd strung along the inside of the lattice woodwork of the sides of the deck. Pea smiled. Everything was perfect. Even the weather had cooperated and stayed as unseasonably warm as the Channel 6 news guy had predicted.

'How magical,' she whispered. 'To eat outside in February.'

Pea decided it had to be a good omen.

She was stirring the sauce when he knocked on the front door. Her stomach did get a little flip-floppy then, but it was more anticipation and excitement than nerves. Pea scrunched her curls one last time, quickly reapplied her lip gloss and opened the door. He was wearing a black cable knit sweater and a dark shirt under it, with a pair of jeans that fit him well enough to make Pea's mouth water for more than spaghetti.

'Hello,' he said.

'Hello,' she said.

Then they just stood there, staring at each other and smiling until Chloe's insistent barking registered on both of them.

'What do you call her?' he asked.

'Chloe. I'm sorry her manners aren't better. She doesn't really like men, but hopefully she'll get used to you and then be quiet.'

He crouched down and reached his hand slowly forward, palm down, offering Chloe a sniff.

'It is good that she is protective of you,' he said to Pea, and then turned his attention back to the disgruntled Scottie. 'You are a fierce advocate for your lady, aren't you?'

Pea watched him curiously. His tone was completely serious. He didn't sound coaxing or cajoling, as so many people did when confronted by a growling dog. Instead he sounded appreciative, something Chloe seemed to instinctively react to. She'd quit growling and was cocking her head attentively at the tall man.

'I would never allow harm to come to her. I give you my oath on that, little protectress.'

Chloe sniffed his hand and wagged her tail. Then she sneezed and went in search of her cat.

'Well, that's truly weird. Chloe doesn't usually like men.' Pea smiled at him. 'So you winning her over must mean it's safe to let you in.'

Victor stepped into her home and lifted her hand, pressing his lips to it in greeting while his eyes met hers.

'The hours passed slowly.' He let loose of her hand reluctantly.

'I thought they would for me, too, but I had to help my, uh . . . friend' – she floundered over what to call the goddess – 'get ready for her date tonight, so time passed really fast. I had a lot to do.'

He smiled and sniffed the air. 'Something smells delicious. Are we not going out for dinner this evening?'

'I thought it would be nice to eat in.' She almost added, *If you don't mind*, and then thought better of it. The old Pea would have worried and fussed and stressed about whether she was being too forward taking charge of their date. The new and goddess-improved Pea believed she had a right to choose the venue of their date – that her desires were important. She wanted to eat in, so they were going to eat in. If he didn't like it, and her fabulous food and her amazing home, then he wasn't the man for her. Period.

'I'm honored that you would cook for me.'

Pea beamed at him. Victor had given her the exact right answer. 'I like to cook.'

'You also like to make a comfortable home,' he said, glancing around her living room.

'Yes, it's important to me.' Pea was pleased that he'd noticed. She'd brought men home before. Not a lot of men, but a few. A couple of them had had 'eloquent' comments like, 'nice house' or 'great place – the value will definitely go up in this area' but none of them had understood that her gift was in making a 'nice house' a home.

And Chloe had hated every last one of them.

'Of course it is important to you.' He nodded like he actually did understand. 'Your home is your creation, so it should reflect you.'

'Then let me show you my favorite room – the kitchen.'

She motioned for him to follow her into the kitchen. She went straight to the stove and automatically stirred the sauce. Pea smiled over her shoulder at him. 'I hope you like spaghetti.'

'I will like anything you prepare.'

Her grin widened. 'Want to try it to make sure?'

'If you would like me to, I will. Tonight, Pea, your every desire is my command.'

Pea felt the thrill of the message behind his words begin to quiver deep within her core. She wanted this tall, powerful man whose limp made him somehow accessible and human. She wanted him and the promise of their future that she read in his eyes.

Pea lifted the spoon to him and blew on it gently, as if she were brushing his skin with her breath. 'Then taste, but be careful it's hot.'

His smile crinkled the corners of his eyes. 'I'm very comfortable with hot.'

He tasted the sauce and it seemed he was tasting her. Again.

'Delicious,' he said.

'Are you hungry?'

'For many things.'

Pea loved the rush of heat he caused within her body. Part of her wanted to drop the tasting spoon and have him take her right there on the kitchen table; the other part of her (the more sane part) wanted to prolong this sweet game of foreplay they'd just begun.

The sane part of her won, but only just barely.

'Good. Dinner's almost ready.' She turned up the water that was waiting for the angel hair pasta. 'Let me show you where we'll be eating.'

She took him out the back door to the patio. 'Perfect' was all he said, but it was enough. It was exactly what Pea thought of it, too.

'Why don't you pour us some wine, and I'll finish up the pasta.' At the door she turned back, about to ask him to feed the chimenea some more wood, but he'd apparently anticipated her request. He'd already gone to the outside fireplace and was stoking it, although with the sudden intensity with which it was burning she wasn't sure the thing needed any more encouragement.

Well, she thought as she added the pasta to the boiling water, *he's a fireman. He should know what he's doing with fire.*

It didn't take long to finish the last touches for dinner, but she was eager to get back to him and glad she'd chosen angel hair pasta, which cooked in a snap. Pea loved the way his eyes lit up when she returned, and then was ridiculously happy at the hearty way he dug into the meal, which complimented her even more than his words of praise.

When she looked back on the meal she was surprised to recall how easily they spoke of nothing – the warm weather, how the lanterns made the deck look fairylike, the recipe for the spaghetti she'd discovered in an old out-of-print Italian cookbook. Normal things. Mundane things. It was almost as if they had always been together.

'I'm glad you chose outside for us to eat,' he said, after he'd swallowed his last bite and poured them each another glass of Chianti.

'I was worried about it turning cold, but the night is beautiful and the chimenea helps.' She nodded at it, surprised to see it still burning merrily.

Victor smiled. 'A good fire always warms things.'

'I would think a fireman wouldn't be so fond of fire.'

'When you are intimate with fire it's hard not to appreciate it, and learn from it, as well as respect its destructive ability.'

'Appreciate and learn from it . . .' She paused, sipping her wine. 'Okay. What has it taught you?'

'Fire teaches about purification and renewal. For instance, a wildfire that rages across a forest is, at first, what appears like a disaster. In truth the forest grows back healthier because it has been cleansed of choking weeds and dead wood.'

'That makes sense. What else does it teach you?'

'I see stories in the fire.'

'Stories? What do you mean?'

He studied her solemnly before he answered, and Pea got the odd but distinct impression that he was weighing her . . . considering how much he could or could not say to her.

'Think of fire as you would an oracle. It's ever-changing and it really does have a life of its own. It breathes. It eats. It can die. Yet it's eternally old. So why can't it collect stories?'

Pea thought about it. It made a strange kind of sense. 'I suppose it could. I guess it just needs someone who knows how to hear the stories to translate them.'

Victor's smile was brilliant. 'Exactly.'

'Tell me some of them.'

Victor considered, glancing up at the sky as it seemed to Pea that he sifted through his thoughts and memories. 'Come with me and I will show you.' He stood and held out his hand to her. Pea took it without hesitating, and he led her to the far edge of the deck that had been built with a wide, waist-high ledge. During the spring and summer, Pea kept large pots of geraniums on the ledge so that her deck seemed to be in bloom.

Victor dropped her hand, and she had just begun to feel the loss of that physical contact with him when he rested both hands on her waist.

'May I?' he murmured.

She looked up into his dark eyes, and didn't care what he was asking. *Anything*, she thought. *Tonight I want to give him anything and everything.*

'Yes,' she said.

Surprising her, he lifted her so that she was sitting on the ledge, then he turned her, so that instead of facing him, Pea was leaning back against him, and his strong arms were braced on either side of her. When he spoke, his lips were beside her ear, his cheek resting softly against her hair.

'Fire tells stories of ancient times – ancient peoples – ancient beliefs.' He pointed up into the night sky. 'For instance did you know that the full moon for this month has been known for ages as the quickening moon?'

Pea looked up, following his direction. 'The quickening moon? Sounds beautiful.'

He brought his hand down and let it rest on her thigh, where he began to caress her softly, as if his touch was part of the story he was weaving for her. 'Generations ago it prodded people to look inside themselves for dormant possibilities as the creatures who slept deep in the womb of the earth felt the pull of being on the cusp of spring's awakening.'

'What else does it tell you?' Pea asked, as she gazed at the full February moon, mesmerized by his deep voice and the heat that radiated from his touch.

'The fire of this world calls to mind the brilliance of the constellations – those distant stars that have their own cold fire.'

He looked to the south and pointed just above the visible horizon. She turned her head and felt a delicious shiver of sensation as he swept back her hair and kissed the curve of her neck.

'Do you see the small constellation there?' His lips moved against her skin as he spoke. 'The one that has the double star?'

'Yes.' She breathed the word so that it sounded more like a moan than an acknowledgment. She could feel his lips turning up in a smile as the tip of his tongue flicked out to tease her skin.

'That is the constellation of the ram. The story goes that the king of Thessaly had two children, Phrixus and Helle, who were abused by their stepmother. The gods heard the children's cries, and Hermes sent a ram with a golden fleece to carry them to safety on its back. Helle fell off the ram as it was flying across the sea known as the Hellespont. Phrixus was heartbroken, but was carried to safety on the shores of the Black Sea at Colchis, where he lovingly sacrificed the ram to the gods in thanks, and its fleece was guarded by a terrible dragon. The gods honored the ram by sending its soul to the heavens.'

Pea gazed at the beauty of the stars as Victor kissed and caressed her, his strong hands sliding up her thighs while his deep voice painted images of an ancient past. She leaned back into him, reaching up to lace her hands together behind his neck, giving him complete access to her breasts.

'More,' she whispered. 'Tell me more.'

'I'll tell you the story of my favorite constellation.' One hand briefly left her body to point to a group of stars that was actually familiar to her.

'It's the Milky Way and the Southern Cross,' she said.

'Look deeper,' he said, sliding his clever hands up under her sweater and cupping her breasts. She couldn't suppress a moan and she felt him smile against her skin again. 'In the ancient world that group of stars is known as Centaurus. The stars are the soul of Chiron.' His thumbs grazed over her sensitive, puckered nipples. 'He was one of the most gifted teachers who ever lived, and in honor of him, the mighty Zeus placed the centaur's soul amongst the stars.'

Pea was entranced by Victor. It was as if he had created a mythical world for her, filled with the magic of his deep voice, and the passion of his warm touch. She felt languid and very, very sexy as she turned so that she was facing him. His eyes were shining with desire, and his hands still caressed her body intimately, as if he was memorizing each curve.

'Your stories are beautiful,' she said breathlessly.

'You make me want to share my world with you,' he said.

'I like the way you see the world.' Pea touched his face, and then brushed her thumb over his bottom lip, remembering how his mouth felt against her body. Then she moved her hand down, so that it lay flat on his chest, pressing against the place over his heart. She could feel it beating, strong and steady, as she leaned toward the warmth of his body.

'I want you to see my world. I want you to always be with me,' he said, then bent to cover her lips with his and desire chased all thoughts of the stars and eternity from her mind.

When they finally broke the kiss, it was to stare at each other. Pea touched Victor's cheek again.

'You said I could have anything I desire tonight?'

'Yes.'

'Then what I desire is you.'

Chapter Twenty-three

Pea's bedroom reminded Vulcan of her. It was soft and inviting – just as it had been the night he had watched through the thread of fire as she pleasured herself. The remembrance made his manhood grow even stiffer, and the blood that already drummed hot and thick through his body had his loins aching with need for her.

They hadn't spoken since she'd told him of her desire. He'd kissed her again hungrily. She'd broken the kiss, but only to take his hand and lead him to her bedroom. Now she was moving around the room lighting moon-colored candles that scented the air with the sweetness of gardenia. He watched her with a longing that had become a familiar, tangible thing.

Then she stood before him, soft hair curling around her face and down her shoulders. It caught the flickers from the small, perfect candle flames so she appeared to be gowned in a veil of her shimmering tresses. He longed to sink his hands in her hair and pull her to him. He must have made an involuntary move toward her, because her whispered words caused him to halt midstride.

'I want to undress you.'

Vulcan felt a terrible clutching in his stomach at the thought of Pea seeing him naked. Rationally he knew his leg was not grotesque. It simply twisted in, and was much more noticeable when he walked than when he was standing still. But many lifetimes had taught him that even this slight imperfection was cause for ridicule.

'Un-unless you don't want me to—'

He pressed a finger against her lips. His hesitation because of his own insecurities had caused the budding self-confidence she'd exhibited that night to falter, and he couldn't bear to see embarrassment and doubt shadow her eyes.

'I want you to undress me. But I'm afraid my leg will make me unattractive to you,' he said honestly.

She touched his cheek again, and caressed his lip with the softness of her thumb, as she had before when she had told him of her desire for him.

'Don't ever think that. I want you. Not some perfect version of you.'

No one had ever said such a thing to him. Unable to speak, he nodded his consent. First, she tugged at his sweater and then smiled up at him. 'You're too tall. You have to bend down or I can't get this off.'

Her easy, sweet smile almost undid him. He hugged her briefly and fiercely, and then bent so that she could pull off his sweater. Under it he wore a dark, long-sleeved shirt of a style that seemed to be popular in this world. She began working the line of buttons undone. He wanted to rip the shirt from his body and press her against his naked chest, but that was unlike him. Then Vulcan drew a deep, surprised breath. Everything he'd done tonight was unlike him! With one strong, sure motion, he ripped open the confining shirt and pulled Pea into his arms.

She groaned and returned his kiss, splaying her fingers across his back. Her touch made his skin feel ultrasensitive and he shivered under her caressing fingers.

Then her restless hands moved down, finding the closing of the pants the Internet had taught him were called jeans. He kissed her deeply as she brushed one hand over the swell of his erection while the other played with the button above the zipper. She looked up at him, meeting his eyes. Her lips tilted up, making her appear very nymphish. He smiled down at her, glad to see the teasing self-confidence had returned to her manner.

'I like it that you're already hard.' A blush bloomed over her cheeks at the wantonness of her words, making him smile down at her.

'It's you! Just thinking of you makes me desire you.'

'Good,' she said softly.

She unzipped his jeans, freeing his erection. Her gaze found his once more, only this time her eyes looked a little startled.

'Going commando? I'm glad I didn't know that while we were eating. I don't think we would have finished the meal, and then I would have missed out on the lovely stories you told.'

Commando was a new word to him, but Vulcan was spared having to answer her because she'd taken his phallus in her hand and began stroking the length of him. He strained beneath her touch, feeling so hard and engorged that his skin should split. She took her hand from him long enough to skim his pants down his body. He stepped out of them and his shoes, and stood completely naked – in body and soul – before her.

Her eyes traveled the length of his body. He knew she could clearly see how his left leg turned in, how the brand of his father's anger marred the line of his body. He had to force himself not to shout a command that would instantly extinguish the small flames of the candles and plunge them into concealing darkness.

'You're beautiful,' she said breathlessly.

Then, before he had time to recover from her words, she knelt before him. Her fingers caressed their way up his thighs – *both* of them. Her light touch caused his muscles to quiver and his phallus to throb with a bittersweet mixture of need and pleasure. She took her time, following her fingers with her mouth, licking and kissing a path up to his core. She took his sac in her hand, squeezing and teasing, and then both of her hands encircled him . . . stroking . . . pulling the length of him toward that beautiful moist pinkness that was her mouth.

He shuddered and moaned when her tongue flicked out and licked the clear drop of liquid his arousal had caused to seep from the head of his cock. Then her tongue was back, swirling around his engorged head. At his hissing exhalation of breath she paused and looked up at him.

'I want to take you in my mouth, to love you with my mouth, my body, my heart. Will you let me?'

'Yes, Pea, by all the gods, yes!' he rasped.

Without any hesitation she opened her pink lips and sucked as much of him as she could take into the wet heat of her mouth. He couldn't stop himself from burying his hands in her hair as she sucked and withdrew, sucked and withdrew, each time flicking her tongue against the sensitive underside of his shaft.

Having his hardess in her mouth was an erotic seduction that was both physical and visual. Watching his hard phallus slide in and out between her full pink lips as she moved her hand in a synchronized caress with her mouth was almost more than he could bear. He wanted to explode, but he didn't want the sucking and pulling and hot lick of her tongue to end.

Somewhere in the middle of one of her strokes he felt his orgasm begin as a sharp, sweet agony he couldn't contain. He meant to shout a warning to her – he might have pulled out of her mouth, but she wouldn't let him. As his body tightened and the heat of his seed began to pump from him in hot, sharp release, she stroked and sucked harder, until he was dry and replete.

When he was finally able to focus again, he was surprised to realize he was still standing. Hard to believe he hadn't collapsed. His hands were still trapped in Pea's curls and he caressingly untangled them. She looked up at him then, her eyes shining.

Victor's sensuous storytelling had excited her as no other foreplay had ever done. Leading him into her room, she'd already been wet and hot and ready. After bringing him to orgasm with her mouth, her desire for him throbbed through her body. She smiled up at him, enjoying every moment of his dazed, drained expression.

'My turn,' she said, purposefully dropping her voice to a sexy tease. She began to slowly strip off her clothes, loving the hot intensity with which he watched her every move. She realized, of course, that he couldn't get hard again so soon, but she couldn't wait to feel his naked skin against her . . . his strong arms around her . . . his mouth on hers . . .

Naked, she lay back on the bed. Inhibitions totally gone, she opened her legs to him. And then watched in amazement as his cock began to swell.

'Let me inside you. I have to have you. I have to make you mine,' he said huskily as he got on the bed and knelt between her open legs.

Disbelieving, she reached forward. Her hand closed around his stiff shaft, proving that she wasn't imagining his second erection. She stroked him, feeling herself liquefy with pleasure. He was simply amazing!

'You've already made me yours,' she said, meeting his gaze, trusting that he saw their future in her eyes as she had seen it in his.

'Yes.' He gasped. 'We belong to each other – for eternity. I love you, Dorreth Pea Chamberlain. I want to spend my eternity with you.'

Pea felt his words wash against her skin as if they carried a palpable shiver of sensation with them, even though her mind said that it was impossible for words to carry physical sensation. She knew it wasn't rational, but it was as if by speaking words of love to her, he had somehow actually bound them together for eternity.

'Yes,' she murmured. 'I belong to you – always.'

She guided him to her and groaned as he tunneled slowly within her wetness. Then all gentleness and hesitation fled before the heat and the passion that filled them, and Victor began pumping, thrusting, pounding into her. She met him thrust for thrust, lifting her hips from the bed and angling her pelvis so that she fully accepted each of his thrusts. He rode her in the ancient dance of lust until she could feel her body gathering for orgasm. She lifted her legs, moaning. With a sound that was very much like a growl, he took her leg and raised it high, anchoring it over his muscular shoulder that was slick with sweat. The new position opened her more fully to him, allowing him to plunge deeper into her, bringing her to the edge of her release. She wrapped her arms around him and exploded, gasping his name. Then he followed her over that sweet edge and groaned his pleasure. She held his shuddering body close . . .

. . . And something over his shoulder caught her eyes. She blinked, trying to focus and bring her breathing under control, and clearly saw that the flames of the little scented candles she'd lit earlier were shooting in a crackling *whoosh* all the way to her ceiling!

She cried out, but Victor was in the midst of his own ecstasy, and he must have mistaken her shouts for pleasure. She was tensing to push him off her so she could run for the fire extinguisher, but she realized that though the candle's flames were high and unnaturally bright, they didn't burn the room. They blazed with Victor's orgasm like benign flamethrowers absent of heat and made only of color. Pea continued to stare at the flames as Victor pumped his seed into her. And as his orgasm faded, so did the flames of the candles, until finally, when he collapsed against her, his face buried in the crook of her neck, their small, flickering fires had returned to normal. If she had had her eyes closed, she would have missed it.

But her eyes hadn't been closed.

She hadn't missed it.

The truth hit her hard. It all fitted. His sudden appearance coinciding with Venus's visit. His powerful aura. His odd, archaic speech patterns that could have been evidence of a good education and maybe a lot of foreign travel, but was really something else entirely. And, most telling, his knowledge of ancient mythology and storytelling.

Victor was nuzzling her neck and lightly kissing her while he whispered something sweet she could almost hear against her skin.

'Who are you?'

Her voice was flat and matter-of-fact. But postcoital Victor (or whatever the hell his real name was) didn't seem to notice. He kept nuzzling her and murmured, 'The man who loves you, little one.'

'Bullshit.'

That got through to him. He pulled back and saw her rigid body language. Frowning with obvious worry, he rolled slowly off her. Pea ignored the sexy, wet feeling of his body sliding from hers.

'Pea?'

'You're not mortal.' It took her saying it aloud, and the shocked look in his eyes – not shocked as in *What the fuck?* but shocked as in *How the fuck did she find out?* – for her to know for sure her instinct about him had been right. He wasn't like any other man, because he wasn't literally a man.

'Who are you?' she repeated, crossing her arms over her bare breasts – not that she wanted to hide from him. She didn't. She was, quite simply, thoroughly pissed at him.

'Why are you asking me that? Why would you believe that I'm not mortal?'

'Okay. Please. While you were coming the flames on the candles were shooting to the ceiling like miniature flamethrowers. That. Is. Not. Normal.' She spoke each word separately, enunciating carefully.

Clearly distressed, he sat up. 'The candles did that?'

'Oh, and did I mention that they flamed way up the side of my wall to my ceiling, but they didn't burn anything?'

He glanced surreptitiously over his shoulder at the candles, as if he didn't want her to see him looking.

'And that's not normal, either?'

'You know it's not.'

'I didn't know they were going to do that. This' – he gestured from her back to him – 'has never happened to me before.' Then he attempted a smile. 'But I'm glad they didn't burn anything.'

Pea ignored his attempt to lighten the tension between them. 'Do you think I'll believe that you've never had sex before?'

'Of course not. I didn't mean that. I meant that I've never been in love before, so I had no way of knowing that any fire in my presence would . . . ur . . . respond to the intensity of my emotions.'

'And just exactly why would fire respond to you?' Pea asked. Even through her anger at him, she was intrigued to discover who he really was.

He drew a deep breath. 'My name isn't Victor. I'm sorry I misled you to think so. I'm just not used to all this and I – stupidly – hadn't thought things out past seeing you again.' He wiped a hand across his face. 'I hadn't even thought about what I'd say when you asked me my name.'

'And your name is?' she asked impatiently.

'Vulcan,' he said.

'V. Cannes.'

'I'm not a very imaginative liar.'

She snorted. 'You could have fooled me.'

'But I didn't fool you. In truth, I didn't want to fool you.' He reached for her, and she jerked away from him.

'Please don't pull away from me,' he said.

'Don't you dare tell me what to do! I don't give a damn if you are a god. I won't be bullied.' Pea realized she was actually more confused than angry, but she couldn't seem to control her pissed-off reaction. She was in love with an ancient god. Just the thought caused a weird ringing sound in her ears, and she was afraid if she stopped being mad that she would start being sad – or worse, scared.

'I wouldn't bully you!'

'Ha! So you'd just lie to me? And badly at that. Why not bully me? Why not zap me into . . . into . . . into a tree or something if I make you mad!' Isn't that what the gods did who seduced mortal women? Why hadn't she paid closer attention to mythology in school? Didn't she have a copy of an old Edith Hamilton mythology text somewhere in one of her bookshelves? Jeesh, she hoped so. She had some serious reading to do.

'A tree? Why would I want you to be a tree?' He looked honestly shocked.

'How would I know! For that matter, how would I know anything about you? Hasn't it all been a lie?'

'No!' he shouted, and the flames in the candles flickered wildly in response.

'See there!' She pointed. 'You just made the flames act weird again.'

'I'm sorry. I won't let them harm anything.'

'Why do you have control over flames?'

'Because I'm Vulcan.'

She let out a big puff of frustrated breath. 'I've been out of school for a long time, and I didn't really pay much attention to mythology even then.'

His brow furrowed in confusion.

Pea rolled her eyes. 'I don't know which god Vulcan is.'

'Oh.' He didn't look offended, as she thought he might. He just shrugged and said, 'I'm God of Fire. My realm is deep within the bowels of Mount Olympus. At my forge I keep the fires of the ancient earth burning. I also work in metal – things you would normally associate with a forge.'

'Then it was a lie.' Pea felt sick.

'Stop saying that!' He glanced at the candles to make sure they were behaving before he continued. 'I misled you about my name, but nothing else. I do work with fire. I have been watching you. I do love you.'

Pea shook her head. 'I don't mean that. I mean you lied about being an outcast, about not belonging. You're a god! One of the immortals. I know Venus – I know how amazing you Olympians are.' She bit her lip, determined not to cry, and pulled the sheet up over her body. It was bad enough he was seeing her naked emotions. She wasn't good at covering them, but at least she could cover her naked body. 'It was mean of you to pretend to be like me.'

'But I am like you! I wasn't pretending. Look at me!' He stood up, naked beside her bed. 'Really look at me. My leg is twisted; I am lame. Compare my imperfections to Venus's blazing beauty. I am far from physically perfect. That makes me an eternal outcast amongst the golden immortals of Olympus.'

The buzzing was back in her ears. 'But that doesn't matter.' She reached out and touched his imperfect leg.

He took her hand and knelt beside the bed, burying his face in her palm. 'It matters to the immortals. I know how it feels not to belong, and now that I've found you, I know how it feels to be accepted and loved. I can't lose you, Pea. Not now. I couldn't bear it.'

And then Pea gasped as Venus's words rushed from her memory, all of a sudden making sense. *He's not physically perfect, so he's an outcast in Olympus. He thought by marrying me he could gain acceptance.*

'Oh, no . . . You're married to Venus,' she said faintly.

'Yes, but—'

The rest of his words were lost when Pea burst into tears.

Chapter Twenty-four

'Little one, don't cry! Everything will be well. You'll see.'

'Get – me – a – Kleenex!' Pea said between sobs, pointing to the bathroom that was attached to the master bedroom.

Vulcan pulled on his jeans and rushed into the bathroom.

Pea took a deep, calming breath and managed to shout, 'The little paper cloth things in the pink box!' Like the God of Fire would know a Kleenex if it jumped up and bit him.

Vulcan reemerged from the bathroom with the box. He handed it to her, and then he sat on the edge of her bed, watching her as if he expected her to combust at any moment. Pea blew her nose and wiped her eyes. She took another deep breath, which she was pleased to note, only had one little hiccupping sob in it. Then she leveled her gaze on Vict—She gritted her teeth and mentally corrected herself. She leveled her gaze on Vulcan, ancient God of Fire. Quietly, in what she considered a calm and reasonable tone of voice, she spoke.

'Okay. I don't know how you do things on Olympus or under Olympus or wherever. But here, in what Venus and I'm sure you, call the modern mortal world, girlfriends do *not* fall in love with each other's husbands. Not unless they're very, very stank and quite ho-ish.' She sighed at his confused expression. 'Just take my word that I'm not stank or ho-ish, nor would I ever want to be. Which means I cannot fall in love with my girlfriend's husband.'

Vulcan's smile was slow and sexy. 'You love me. You just said you love me.'

'Hello! Did you hear the rest of it?'

His grin stayed in place. 'Venus and I don't live together as husband and wife. Our marriage was a mutually agreed upon arrangement – one that hasn't worked out particularly as planned for either of us. She didn't lead you to believe she loves me, did she?'

Pea chewed her lip. 'No. She said she was married, but that it wasn't like a real marriage.'

Vulcan nodded, and didn't look in the least bit upset by his wife's description of their non-marriage. 'And isn't she with another man at this moment?'

'Maybe.' Weirdly, she felt like she might be telling on Venus if she said more.

Vulcan lifted one brow up. 'Maybe?'

'Okay, yes. She's out on a date.'

'Which is perfectly fine with me.'

'This feels wrong.'

Vulcan took her hand again. 'Would it feel better if Venus and I agreed to revoke our marriage?'

'I don't know.' Pea shook her head, feeling close to tears again. 'This is happening so fast.'

'But Pea, little one, we've already talked about that. The speed at which our love is happening is not important. It's the love itself – the connection we feel in our souls – that is important.' He leaned forward and cupped her face in his hands. 'Look into my eyes. See the truth there. I have existed alone for what you would consider an eternity. Until I glimpsed you through my thread of fire just days ago, I was convinced the only way I could have peace was to become as the ram and Chiron.'

Pea's eyes widened. 'You were going to die and become a constellation?'

'Yes.'

'But you can't! You're immortal.'

'So was Chiron, but as with the centaur, I can die if Zeus wills it.'

'No!'

Vulcan smiled and caressed her cheeks with his thumbs. 'Only now I can't die and retire to the constellations because I've found my home, and it is here with you. If you will have me.'

'But your realm – the forge . . .'

'All problems that can be conquered if you love me.'

Pea met his eyes. She knew he was an ancient god, yet somehow that knowledge changed nothing. She hadn't loved his supposed mortal shell. What she'd responded to from the first moment she'd looked into his eyes went beyond the physical and had less to do with mortality than eternity.

'I do love you,' she whispered.

'Then we'll figure out everything else. Together.'

'Together,' she repeated before his lips met hers and she lost herself in the taste and touch, magic and heat of him.

Griffin woke up like he always did – without an alarm clock. Something wasn't right. He glanced at the digital dial of his bedside clock. Five-thirty in the morning. He had to be at the fire station by seven. Plenty of time. Smiling, he turned over, automatically reaching for Venus. Her side of the bed was empty. That's what was wrong. She was gone. He pulled on his boxer shorts. She wasn't in the bathroom. He went to the edge of the loft's balcony and looked down. Relief washed through him when he saw her sitting on the couch staring at his sculpture. Cali Alley Cat was curled up beside her and Venus was absently stroking her. But his relief was short lived. Venus was crying. Silently tears were falling down her cheeks. The windows of his living room were just starting to be lightened with predawn, and Venus was framed in the muted, dovelike colors of early morning. The artist in him responded before the man. Her beauty was extraordinary, especially with the touch of sadness softening her features. She should be painted and sculpted. Poetry and songs should be written about her.

Then the man took over from the artist. She was crying. Had it been him? Had he somehow made her sad? Was she regretting their lovemaking? The thought made him feel sick. Venus was the most incredible woman he'd ever been with and he didn't want her to regret one moment with him. *He wanted her to spend the future with him.*

The thought shocked him. He'd never seriously considered a future with any of his lovers or girlfriends or whatever they called themselves. Venus was different. She made him feel different. And it wasn't just because she was incredibly beautiful and witty and intelligent and kind. She had that elusive *something*. Actually they had that elusive something – together. That extra spark that changed friendship to love and lovers to soul mates.

Soul mates? Was that what they were? The idea shook him, but he didn't back away from it. Everything within him was telling him insistently, *This is the one! She's mine! The one I've been waiting for!*

He grabbed his bathrobe and hurried down the stairs. She didn't notice him until he touched her shoulder, then she jumped and wiped at her eyes hastily. Cali meowed shortly at him, and jumped haughtily off the couch. *Little traitor*, he thought.

'I didn't mean to startle you.' She was wearing the sweater he'd had on last night. It was way too big for her, making her look young and very, very sexy.

'Do you have coffee?' she asked.

He frowned. Did he have coffee? He didn't want to talk about coffee. He wanted to take her in his arms and tell her he loved her and that he would fix whatever it was that was making her cry, but her tears threw him off, almost as much as his thoughts of soul mates and futures.

'Yeah, I have coffee,' was what he said instead.

'Would you make me some?'

'Yes.' Thoroughly confused, he went to the kitchen and started a pot of coffee. 'Do you want a muffin or something to eat?' he called.

'No,' she said. 'No, thank you.'

He ground his teeth together. She was being awfully damn polite. He waited impatiently for enough coffee to brew to fill two cups, and then hurriedly returned to Venus. She was still sitting on the couch, still staring at his sculpture, but she'd stopped crying.

'Is black okay? I have milk and sugar if you want it.'

'Thank you, it's fine like this.' She took the cup from him and sipped.

Griffin sat next to her and, on impulse, leaned over and kissed her softly. 'Good morning.' He was pleased that she leaned into him and accepted his kiss.

'Good morning,' she said.

They drank their coffee in silence until Griffin couldn't stand it any longer. Then he put his cup down and turned to her.

'What is it? What's wrong?'

She sighed. 'It's hard for me to put into words.'

'Is it me? Did I do something to upset you?'

'No. You've been perfect.'

260

Well, hell. She said it like it was a bad thing. He drew a deep breath and asked the question he dreaded. 'Are you sorry about last night?'

'No, of course not!' She finally looked at him. 'Last night was wonderful.'

He brushed his knuckles across her damp cheek. 'Then why are you sitting here crying?'

She looked back at his sculpture. 'You were right,' she said slowly.

'About?'

'About Venus.'

'And that makes you sad?'

She nodded. 'It makes me sad because recently I've realized that I have too much in common with her.'

'What do you mean?' For some reason her words, or maybe it was the resigned sound of them, made his stomach tense.

'You said that it seemed Venus didn't need a man, which made her untouched and untouchable, which is especially tragic because Venus *is* Love.'

It was his turn to nod.

'I've been like that.' She sounded introspective, almost as if she'd forgotten he was there and was simply talking aloud to herself. 'I've helped countless others find love. I've been asked over and over again to make their passions and obsessions and desires come true, but when it came to me having those things in my own life . . .' She moved her shoulders restlessly. 'Love has brushed by me, passed over me, gone around me, and sometimes even visited me briefly, but in the end Love moved on without me.'

Griffin took her hand, and she turned to face him. Never in his life had he wanted anything as badly as he wanted to make the sadness leave her eyes, and as he tried to figure out what to say to her to make her melancholy better, he realized that his well-guarded freedom from relationships and his avoidance of love in general had been nothing more than empty steps taken in a life only partially lived. He wondered, briefly, if the artist in him hadn't recognized his loneliness long before now – wondered if maybe that was why the subject of most of his art was women . . . even though commitment and relationships were what he'd avoided so diligently for most of his life.

Griffin realized that he was afraid to say what came next, but he was more afraid of not saying it.

'I've never been married. I've never even been engaged. The truth is I've avoided love as much as you have. After seeing my sisters' and my mother's troubles with it, I thought it was best to just live without the damn emotion.'

At the mention of his sisters, Venus's lips tilted up, lightening the sadness in her expression a little. Griffin forged ahead.

'Then I met you. And now I see a chance to have what's been missing in my life. I see the chance to have love.'

'Even if love comes with complications and troubles and . . . how did you put it . . . too much damn emotion?'

He smiled and caressed her cheek again. 'Even if.'

She looked away from him again. Instead of easing her sadness, it seemed his declaration of love had the opposite effect on her.

'Venus, am I misunderstanding what's happening between us? If you don't think you could love me—'

'I could love you,' she said quickly. 'I do love you,' she added softly.

He smiled, but again his relief was short-lived.

'But love isn't always enough. Things between us might be too complicated,' she said.

'I thought that was the point of love – to complicate things.' He tried for a light tone, but when she met his gaze her distraught expression made his teasing stop. 'What is it?' He pulled her into his arms. 'What could be so terrible?' The sick feeling in his stomach expanded to include his heart. 'Is there someone else?'

'No. There is no one else.' She shifted in his arms so that she could look up at him. 'Your life here is very important to you, isn't it?'

'Yes.' His brow furrowed. 'Is my job what's bothering you? It's dangerous, yes, but I'm careful.' He knew some firemen whose wives were terrified every time the alarm sounded. He would hate to think of Venus living in that kind of fear. Could he give it up? Could he just be an artist? He wasn't sure, and he definitely didn't like to think about the possibility that he might have to choose between the love he had for his job and the love he had for her.

'It's not your job. I respect what you do. And a warrior's life is never without risk; I understand that. I was thinking of your family – your sisters and mother. You wouldn't want to leave them.'

'No, I wouldn't.' Then he understood. 'You're not from Tulsa, are you?'

'No, I'm not. I'm only here temporarily, as a . . . favor for Pea at the college. When I'm finished helping her, then I really must go.'

'Where are you from?'

She stared up at him, and he thought she looked oddly lost. 'I'm from far away.'

He smiled and kissed her forehead. 'What? New York? Chicago? Or, God help us' – he chuckled – 'Los Angeles?'

'Rome. And I also spend quite a bit of time in Greece.'

His eyes widened in surprise. 'You're right. That is far away. So . . . would you consider relocating?'

'I can't. I have other obligations, too,' she said miserably.

'Then we can work out some kind of travel schedule and see what happens. A long-distance relationship isn't impossible. The world really isn't that big of a place anymore.'

She looked doubtful.

He held her tighter. 'You wouldn't let something like distance change how you feel about me. Would you?'

She touched his face, tracing his lips with her finger. 'I wouldn't, but I'm afraid that when you realize just what loving me entails, you will.'

'What can I do to make you believe I'm not so easily gotten rid of?'

She wrapped her arms around his shoulders. He loved how she felt pressed against his body. His hands slid down to the curve of her waist and she shivered in response to his caress.

'Just love me now, and let me hold to the fantasy of you a little while longer.'

'I'm not a fantasy. We're not a fantasy,' he said, before fiercely claiming her mouth. He wanted to say more, to assure her that he wouldn't let anything or anyone come between them, but her insistent mouth moved from his, down his chest, until she found the swell of his growing erection. When her mouth closed around him, words left his mind completely and he was only able to moan her name.

Chapter Twenty-five

'Oh, crap! Look at the time. It's after seven.' Pea disentangled herself from Vulcan's arms and dashed, naked, into the bathroom.

'Where are you going?' he called drowsily after her.

'To work. I have to be there by eight.' She stuck her head out of the bathroom while she piled up her curls and covered them with a plastic shower cap. 'I'd take the day off if I could, but I have interviews coming in – you know, for the job you pretended to want – and I really have to be there.'

'I didn't pretend. I believe I would like to be a history teacher.'

'You'd be a good one, too,' she said.

He grinned at her. 'Your hat is funny looking.'

She narrowed her eyes at him. 'It's a shower cap, not a hat. And I'm not funny looking.'

'Yes, you are, endearingly so.'

Pea decided that if it endeared her to him, then maybe the silly shower cap Venus had insisted she use to protect her now frizzless curls was worth it. Still she stuck her tongue out at him, which only made his smile grow.

'You could bring your clever tongue over here.'

Pea glanced down his naked body and saw that Vulcan's smile wasn't the only thing that was growing. She felt the answering heat inside her, and wished she had a little more time to . . .

'No! I can't. I really have to get to work.' She ducked back into the bathroom and tried to wash her face, brush her teeth and talk to Vulcan – all at the same time. 'And don't you have to go back to Olympus or wherever and do some God of Fire-ing or forging or whatnot?'

She could hear him laugh.

'So you will, once again, make me count the hours until I may see you?'

'Yep,' she called. 'Hey, while I'm taking a shower make yourself at home. I have lots of breakfast stuff in the kitchen, and the automatic coffeemaker should already be working its magic.'

She squealed around her toothbrush when he stuck his head in the bathroom.

'Are you quite certain you don't need my assistance, my lady?'

'Yes!' Pea ignored his sexy leer and pushed him out, shutting the door. She giggled and hummed all the way through her shower.

Pea was ready for work in record time. She checked her watch as she hurried from her bedroom. It was seven-thirty. She could have a short breakfast with Vulcan and still make it to work practically on time. And anyway she was never late for work. A few minutes this one time wouldn't hurt.

Vulcan was sitting at her kitchen table. Surprisingly his bulk didn't look awkward or out of place there. Instead he seemed to complement the room, filling it up and making it even homier. He was sipping a mug of coffee with his eyes closed, which made her smile.

'So you hadn't had coffee before, either?'

'Never,' he said, opening his eyes and grinning at her. 'Its smell is as divine as its taste.'

She poured herself a cup. 'Do you mean that literally, God of Fire?'

He hesitated, and then smiled like a little boy. 'I think I do.'

Pea laughed, but her laughter turned into a choking fit. When Vulcan wasn't blocking her view she could see that her table was filled with hand-etched silver platters brimming with hunks of aged cheese, exotic fruits, bread that smelled freshly baked and thinly sliced pieces of cold meat.

'What is all of this?' she sputtered.

He looked from the feast to Pea. 'Breakfast?'

'You zapped it here?'

Vulcan studied her for a moment. 'Zapped – as in I could have zapped you into a tree?'

'Which you wouldn't do, remember?' Pea said through partially clenched teeth.

'Which I absolutely would not do.'

'Then yes, that's what zapped means.'

'Then yes, I zapped the food here.'

'Vulcan,' she began, hesitated, and then bent to kiss him on the cheek and patted his back, too, for good measure. He did look scrumptious at her kitchen table, and he probably didn't know any better. 'I'm a little uncomfortable with zapping.' She sat in the chair closest to him so that their thighs brushed together intimately. 'Zapping isn't something that happens in Tulsa.' At Vulcan's disbelieving frown she added, 'Truthfully. Zapping would freak out most modern mortals.' After a pause she began to fill her plate.

'Freak out?' he said.

'Think of freak out as being uncomfortable multiplied times ten.'

'And this really makes you uncomfortable?'

'Really.'

'I had no idea.'

'Oh, I believe you. Venus was shocked to find out it was a problem, too.'

'Then I will refrain from zapping.'

'I would appreciate it.'

'Your request is this god's command, my lady.' He gave her a little seated bow with a flourish, which made her giggle and blush.

And it was in the middle of her blushing giggle that Venus burst into the room.

'Pea, darling, I have so much to—' She pulled up short when she saw Vulcan.

'Hello, Venus,' he said.

'Hello, Venus,' Pea said.

'What, by all of the flapping phalluses of the gods, is he doing here?' Venus asked.

Pea looked at Vulcan. 'I thought you said she wouldn't be upset.'

'Yes, but I didn't say she wouldn't be shocked.'

'*She* is right here!'

'Venus, please don't be mad,' Pea said, her face starting to crumble.

'I'm not mad!' Venus shouted. Then she closed her eyes, took a breath and started over. 'I'm not mad,' she said in a more sedate tone. 'Why should I be mad? I'm just wondering why Vulcan is sitting at your kitchen table having breakfast.' The goddess glanced at the laden table and her eyes widened. 'And a zapped breakfast from Olympus at that.'

'I told him to make himself at home while I was in the shower,' Pea said.

'Which I did,' Vulcan said.

'Yeah, and he didn't know how I felt about the zapping part so—'

Venus's upraised hand silenced Pea.

'The two of you are making no sense.'

'Sorry,' Pea muttered.

Vulcan shrugged.

Venus narrowed her eyes at him. He was certainly being uncharacteristically chatty. And he looked relaxed. And he was wearing jeans and a sweater. She studied him harder and felt a jolt of pure shock. Vulcan had had sex! Good sex, too, from the look of him. She opened her mouth to say that it was about time, and an insane thought crossed her mind. The Goddess of Love turned her sharp gaze on Pea, who wouldn't meet her eyes and who began to squirm in her chair. Literally.

'By Gaea's earthy vagina! You've had sex!' Venus gasped. 'With each other!'

'Please don't be mad,' Pea repeated.

'Stop saying that,' Venus said.

'Don't bully her!' Vulcan shouted.

'Don't yell at me!' Venus yelled.

Chloe rushed into the room, paws sliding on the tile floor, barking manically.

'Now see what you've done,' Pea said, with tears spilling down her cheeks while she bent to comfort the agitated Scottie.

Venus drew in a deep, calming breath. Then she cooed at the Scottie, 'Chloe, darling, I'm sorry for raising my voice at the horrid God of Fire. I didn't mean to upset you.' She walked over to Pea and the dog and ruffled Chloe's fur. Then she smiled at Pea and tugged on one of her curls. 'I didn't mean to upset you, either.'

Pea sniffed and gave her a watery smile.

'You shouldn't have made her cry,' Vulcan said. His tone was back to normal, but he was frowning sternly at the goddess.

269

Venus threw up her hands in irritation. 'Would you please tell me what in all the levels of the sexless Underworld you're doing here?'

'You might be interested to know that rumor has it there's sex going on in the Underworld or at least in the Elysian Fields part of it,' Vulcan said.

'Vulcan . . .' The goddess's voice dropped in warning.

'No zapping!' Pea shouted, causing Chloe to growl.

'Then he'd better—'

'He's Victor!' Pea blurted.

Venus blinked. 'Victor? As in the cunnilingus Victor?'

'You told her that?' Vulcan said.

'As if she had to tell me,' Venus said.

Vulcan snorted.

'Yes, that Victor,' Pea finally said.

'Explain this, Vulcan. And know that if you hurt this mortal child you will suffer my wrath, that I promise you.'

The God of Fire drew himself up and met the Goddess of Love's piercing gaze. 'I commend you for being protective of her, Venus, but you need not worry. I love her. I would never harm her.'

'How could you possibly love her?'

Pea turned to Venus. 'Don't you think I'm worth loving?'

'Darling, that's not what I meant at all. It's just that Vulcan and I are . . .' She hesitated, choosing her words more carefully. 'Vulcan and I have known each other for a long time, and love doesn't exactly come easily for him.'

'She knows we're married,' Vulcan said.

'Then she also knows it is a marriage in name alone.'

'Love didn't come easily for him because he hadn't met me yet,' Pea said.

Venus looked at her mortal friend. Her eyes were still bright with tears and her face was flushed, but Pea met her eyes steadily.

'You know me,' Pea said. 'And you know him. Can't you see how alike we are?' Pea's gaze moved from Venus to Vulcan, and she held out her hand to him. Vulcan took it and lifted it to his lips. Until that moment Venus could have never imagined him doing such a thing. Still looking at Vulcan, Pea continued, 'Can't you see that we belong together?'

'Yes, Goddess of Love,' Vulcan said, while he gazed adoringly into Pea's eyes. 'Really look at us and then tell us what you see.'

Venus looked at them – not with the eyes of a shocked friend or an in-name-only wife – she looked at them through Love's eyes, and what she saw had her drawing in a sharp breath. They were the same. They had the same sweet, displaced souls that had apparently finally found their way home.

'You belong together,' she said.

'Oh, Venus, I knew you'd understand!' Pea threw her arms around Venus and hugged her tightly while Chloe barked joyously until Max sauntered into the room, sniffed in disdain at all of them, then exited quickly with the Scottie hard on his heels.

'I'm going to need a cup of coffee,' Venus said, when Pea finally let loose of her.

'An excellent drink, almost as delicious as ambrosia,' Vulcan said.

'I'll get it for you.' Pea wiped her eyes and began puttering happily about her cupboards. Over her shoulder she said, 'And how was your date with Griffin?'

Venus wasn't sure where to look, especially when she realized her cheeks felt warm.

'Griffin? Isn't he the fireman who was so attentive in your class?'

'By the tits of—' she began sputtering, but Pea's steady hand squeezing her shoulder had her biting back the nasty reprimand and accepting the cup of excellent coffee.

'Yes, Vulcan has been observing the modern mortal world,' Pea said, in a calm, reasonable tone of voice.

'I watched a good part of your class. It was really quite interesting and informative,' Vulcan said.

'I'm pleased I could be of help,' Venus said, with only a hint of sarcasm.

'The date?' Pea prodded.

'It went well.'

'Well?' Pea said. '"Well" as in I was kinda bored but it was fine, or "well" as in he rocked my world?'

'Well as in . . .' Venus looked at Pea, and instead of saying something flip and clever, she had the sudden desire to tell her friend what was really in her heart. '. . . as in I think I'm in love.'

She ignored Vulcan's shocked look and returned Pea's hug as the little mortal threw her arms around her.

'Oh, Venus! I told you so! I told you that you were here for yourself as much as you were here for me.'

'You were right, darling.' Venus smoothed her hair back. 'I honestly believe you were right. But loving a modern mortal can be complicated.' She looked at Vulcan. 'For instance, how are you going to make this work with Pea?'

'I haven't decided yet.'

'We,' Pea corrected him. 'We haven't decided yet.' She gave Vulcan a stern look. 'Just because you're a god it doesn't mean you get to make all the decisions.' She pointed at her own chest. 'I have my own goddess inside me, too. You shouldn't forget that.'

'Well put, Pea,' Venus said, loving that Pea had quite obviously come into her own, complete with a healthy dose of self-confidence.

'I had a good teacher,' Pea said. 'Oh, speaking of that, we have to get to work!'

'We?' Venus and Vulcan said together.

Pea laughed. 'We meaning Venus and me.' She leaned over and kissed Vulcan soundly on the lips. 'And didn't you say you had some God of Fire stuff to do, too?'

'We?' Venus persisted.

'In all our rushing around yesterday I forgot to tell you. The Director of Training for the fire department called my office to say what a total success your stress-relief class was and that he was sending over the next shift this morning. So you have another class to teach today.'

'Satyr's balls! I forgot to zap myself out of the firemen's memories,' Venus muttered.

'You're going to have to fill out some paperwork, too. You know, taxes and such,' Pea said.

'Taxes?'

'Why don't you let me explain all of it to you on the way to work? We have to hurry or we'll be late.'

Venus frowned. 'I didn't get to finish my coffee.'

'I'll pour it into a travel cup,' Pea said.

'It's not the same,' Venus mumbled.

Vulcan stood and pulled Pea into his arms. Venus watched with interest. In all the eons she'd known him, the God of Fire had never shown even the slightest inkling toward being interested in romance, yet here he was, taking Pea gently in his arms and kissing her quite thoroughly. Odd. Truly odd. And this new depth to him did make him look strong and handsome and sexy. Well, good for Pea! And good for Vulcan, too. Venus was honestly happy for them.

'Tonight, little one,' he said.

'Tonight.' Pea stepped out of his arms and closed her eyes. Vulcan gave Venus a quick, friendly smile and then disappeared. With her eyes still closed, Pea said, 'Can I look now?'

'Yes.'

'Okay, let's go. You can tell me all about last night and Griffin, and I'll explain the loose ends with Vulcan,' Pea said as she hunted through the cupboard for her travel mug.

'You know, darling, I could save us quite a bit of time by zapping us to school.'

'No!' Pea's face blanched totally white.

Venus sighed. There were just some things about modern mortals she would never understand.

Chapter Twenty-six

'I can't believe vulcan has been watching us.' Venus paced around Pea's office.

'Well, actually, he was watching me,' Pea said.

'You know, this is very unlike him.'

Pea grinned at the goddess. 'Love does that to some people.'

Venus raised a brow. 'Indeed.'

'Yep. Speaking of – let's hear about Griffin. And don't scrimp on the details. I mean, you were gone *all night*, and you did say the *L* word.'

'Griffin is a spectacularly talented lover,' Venus said.

'Well, that's great. But I'm assuming it takes more than that for you to fall in love with a man . . . or god . . . or whatever.'

Venus studied her hands. She couldn't believe how difficult it was to talk of her innermost feelings. For eons she'd been encouraging couple after couple to do that very thing. Finally she understood why they'd looked so uncomfortable. The goddess sighed and tried to order her feelings into words.

'You know how it is with you and Vulcan – how the two of you seem so much alike that you have the almost innate ability to understand one another without many words?'

'Yes, that's how it is with Vulcan and me.'

Venus looked up from her hands to meet her friend's eyes. She felt unusually close to tears as she continued. 'That's how I feel with Griffin. It's ironic, really,' she said, on a little sob. 'He's an incredible man. He should have found love years ago. And me, I *am* Love, yet it seems I've not really known myself for ages. Not until I looked into that mortal man's eyes. Then suddenly I was found.' Venus wiped her eyes. 'Foolish of me, isn't it?'

'Of course not!' Pea took her hand. 'Why shouldn't you deserve a great love for yourself?'

'Pea, I've been so busy assuring that everyone else finds love that I haven't thought to save any for myself.'

'Then that changes now.'

'You think it can?'

'It already has. You've found him. You love him. He loves you, right?'

'He says he does.'

'Well then, what's the problem?'

'He doesn't know who I am.'

'Yes, he does. He knows you're beautiful and kind and intelligent and funny and sexy. That's who you are.'

'I am also an immortal goddess. One of the Twelve Olympians. My place for eternity must be on Mount Olympus. Pea, I can't leave my realm. How would the world survive without Love?'

Pea squeezed her hand. 'It wouldn't. Griffin has to move to Olympus. That's all there is to it.'

'I already kind of asked him that.'

'Kind of?'

Venus looked chagrined. 'I told him my work was in Rome and Greece and I couldn't leave it to move to Tulsa.'

'And?'

'And he doesn't want to leave his family. His sisters and his mother depend on him. He said we could have something called a long-distance relationship.'

Pea curled her lip. 'Ugh. Totally not acceptable.' Then she brightened. 'But it would be acceptable if he knew who you *really* are. I mean, you can zap yourself back and forth from Olympus to here, right?'

'Yes.'

'So can't you zap him, too?'

'Of course. But you hate zapping. Maybe he will, too.'

'Please,' Pea scoffed. 'He's a guy. He'll be fine with the zapping. And truthfully, if Vulcan has to zap me around so that he and I can be together, I'll take a Xanax and let him zap away.'

'Xanax?'

'Ambrosia in a pill.'

'Oh, good.' Venus nodded thoughtfully. 'So you believe I should tell Griffin the truth. All of it.'

'I do. Actually I think it's the only answer.'

'What if he doesn't like the idea of being loved by a goddess?'

'Come on, Venus! What man wouldn't like the idea of being loved by a goddess? Especially *the* Goddess of Love. He should be overjoyed.'

'Well, being overjoyed certainly sounds reasonable to me.'

'When are you seeing him again?'

'Later today. He's going to be on duty, but he said if I come by this afternoon we could have dinner together in the park beside the station. That is, if no one sets anything on fire that he has to put out.'

'Perfect. Tell him who you are then. He'll be at work for the next twenty-four hours or so. Isn't that how their shifts go?'

Venus nodded. 'He said they're usually on for a day, and then off for two.'

'So tell him today, and he'll have time to get used to it before he sees you again. Easy-peasy.'

'Do you really think so?'

'Absolutely. I mean, am I not the most mundane mortal you've ever met?'

Venus smiled at her friend. 'You might be.'

'So if I can get used to loving an immortal, anyone can.'

'You know, you're really very wise.'

'I know. Now, you have a class to teach, and I have interviews to conduct. This evening you'll figure things out with Griffin and I'll . . .' She paused and waggled her eyebrows. '. . . with Vulcan.'

Venus laughed. She turned to leave Pea's office to head to what she was quickly considering *her* classroom, but was brought up short by the little mortal's next words.

'You know you could return to Olympus at any time now, don't you?'

Venus glanced back at Pea. 'I–I haven't really given it much thought. I guess maybe I can.'

Pea's smile was warm and filled with the love she felt for the goddess. 'Of course you can. You were only trapped here until you fulfilled my wish for happiness and ecstasy. You've made sure I've been blessed with both in quantities I'd never imagined.'

'Oh, Pea. I didn't bring those things to you. I just helped you find the way to discover them yourself.'

'Thank you, Venus, Goddess of Love,' Pea said.

Venus tilted her head in regal acknowledgment. 'You are most welcome, darling.' Then the Goddess of Love took her bag of vagina diagrams and, smiling, hurried to the classroom in which she would hold court.

Vulcan stood in front of the pillar of fire, hands on his hips, and he threw back his head and laughed joyously. He had found her and she loved him! She knew who he was and she accepted him.

278

Never again would his life be a solitary pit of loneliness, where he'd simmer the eons away by himself. Instead he would be with Pea. He would love her and have children with her and watch her grow old and . . .

Vulcan came to an abrupt halt. He would watch his mortal love – the mate of his soul – grow old and *die*. Then he would be right back where he had been before he'd ever loved her. No! It would be worse. His centuries of loneliness had been bad enough before he knew her. Now they would be unbearable.

'No!' he shouted, and the fire flamed high and hot in response. 'I will not live without her.' But what choice did he have? He could turn her into something – an ever-flowing brook or a meadow of eternally blooming wildflowers. Vulcan shook his head. 'I cannot do that. Pea cannot abide zapping,' he muttered, disgusted with himself for even considering it. 'Plus, it wouldn't really be Pea, and we wouldn't actually be together.' No. Changing Pea wasn't the answer.

So the answer must be that he had to change himself. Not long ago he had been eager to become a cold constellation to escape his existence as an outlander, which was why he'd turned his attention to the modern mortal world to begin with. He'd meant to discover a mortal man who would be willing to take his place as God of Fire for eternity. Vulcan rubbed his chin thoughtfully.

'Who was it Venus said she loved?'

A name seemed to whisper from the pillar of fire: *Griffin*. Yes! That was his name, Griffin. The God of Fire raised his hands and shouted a command into the pillar of flame, 'Let me see the modern mortal Griffin!'

The order snaked from Olympus, sizzling down the invisible thread from one world to another, until it came to rest at Tulsa's

279

Midtown Fire Station. Vulcan called a chair over to him and settled in to observe the mortal man.

In the shadowy stairwell of Vulcan's domain, Hera smiled smugly and padded silently back up the stairs.

'Hey Capt! One of your sisters is here.'

Griffin looked up from the stack of inventory papers he was trying to make sense of. Why in the hell didn't the grocery money ever balance?

'What?' he barked. Had Robert said something about one of his sisters?

'Wait, scratch that. *All* of your sisters are here!'

'Shit!' Griffin cursed under his breath and pushed up from his dilapidated office chair. What were all of his sisters doing here? Like that wouldn't cause a damn stampede of testosterone-filled idiots. He checked the clock as he hurried from his office. Venus would be there in less than an hour. Plenty of time to get his sisters out of there, settle the men down to dinner and take a much-earned private break with her. But first things first.

He rounded the corner to see his four sisters sitting in Sherry's cherry red Mustang GT Convertible – *with* the top down (did it have to be so damned warm for the end of February?), *with* half of the damn station slumped around the car eyeing the giggling, flirting girls like prime rib.

Well, in theory he had plenty of time. Time and his sisters often existed at the opposite ends of the world.

'Griff! Hey! We thought we'd come by to remind you of our date tomorrow.' Sherry waved at him and smiled like she was Miss America.

'How about you and I have a date tomorrow, sugar?' said a young fireman in a brand new spotless uniform.

Griffin glared at the new recruit. Damn punk had ears that were still dripping wet. He'd never so much as sniffed a real fire, and here he was coming on to Sher?

'How about you finish cleaning the latrine and then you and I will have a talk about why you don't call my sister sugar,' Griffin said with a growl.

The new recruit shoved his hands in his pockets, muttered an apology to Sherry, a 'yes, sir' to Griffin and hurried back into the stationhouse.

'Okay gentlemen, the show's over. Go on about your business.'

Reluctantly the crowd around the Mustang broke up. The men called good-byes to the girls as they shuffled slowly back to the cards and *Sports Illustrated* magazines they hadn't really been interested in to begin with.

'Griff, you're just a big fat ball of no fun.' Alicia pouted.

'And just exactly why can't that adorable young thing call me sugar?' Sher asked.

'Because, as you have explained over and over to me during most of the thirty plus long years I've know you, terms like *sugar* and *honey* and *sweetie pie* are derogatory to women.'

'I said that?' Sher asked Stephanie.

'Constantly.' Stephanie nodded.

'Was I talking about adorable young firemen?'

'Apparently not,' Kathy said.

'I didn't think so, because I really don't feel degraded. So there must be exceptions to—'

'Why are you girls here?' Griffin interrupted before she built up any more steam.

'We were just passin' by, and like Sher said, we thought we'd stop in and remind you that you're supposed to change our oil tomorrow,' Alicia said with a chirp.

'*Our* oil? As in four cars?' Griffin scowled at his sisters.

'You said you would,' Alicia said.

'Not all in one day!'

'But, big brother, you can do *anything*!' Stephanie beamed at him.

'And I'm cooking,' Kathy said.

'Ribs?' Griffin felt his annoyance begin to fade.

'Ribs with garlic mashed potatoes,' Kathy said. 'I also managed to get my hands on some early sweet corn for corn on the cob.'

'And I'm bringing the beer,' Stephanie said.

'Import or that grocery store crap?'

Stephanie looked totally offended. 'Import, of course.'

'I'm making pineapple upside-down cake for dessert,' Sherry said.

Griffin couldn't stop the slow smile. His sisters annoyed the crap outta him sometimes. They could be a pain in the ass. But they sure as hell knew what he liked.

'So, let's say my place, tomorrow at five-ish?' Stephanie said.

'Yeah, all right. You bribed me into it.'

His sisters laughed and broke into enthusiastic applause.

'Now get out of here before you make some poor, unsuspecting fireman lose his mind.'

Sherry put the Mustang into reverse, and as it rolled backward she called, 'Hey! You can bring your new girlfriend.'

'Yeah!' Alicia yelled. 'We like the goddess.'

'I'll see what I can do,' he told them, and waved and shook his head as Sherry laid rubber on the street in front of the station.

Vulcan chuckled. Griffin's sisters were amusing nymphs, and they adored him. What would it be like to have a large, boisterous family where everyone cared for each other? Where sisters joked with their beloved brother and families ate together, loved together, raised children together and were there for each other as they grew old and passed on to the afterlife?

It would be wonderful.

Vulcan could see Pea fitting into a family like that seamlessly.

Griffin DeAngelo was only a man. He didn't have vast powers he could wield at will. He didn't have a realm of his own. He wasn't an immortal. But Vulcan envied him with an intensity that caused the pillar of fire to crackle and hiss.

He also realized that it would do no good for him to consider this mortal man as his replacement. There was no way Griffin would want to exchange lives with him. And why should he? The mortal's life was filled to brimming with happiness and the magic of family. Things Vulcan was afraid he could only observe and envy.

Chapter Twenty-seven

Pea pulled up in front of the fire station. 'Okay, if you don't want to zap yourself back to my place, just call me when Griffin's break is over and I'll come and get you.'

'I don't want to interrupt your time with Vulcan.'

'Oh, don't worry about it. He doesn't know I got off work early. He won't be over for another two hours or so, and if he is, so what? He said he was dying to ride in a car. He can just come along.'

'I'm nervous,' Venus said.

'Well, that's perfectly normal. If you can use the word "normal" in reference to telling the mortal man you love that you're a goddess,' Pea said brightly. 'Anyway, there's nothing wrong with being nervous. But my gut tells me everything's going to be okay.'

'I hope you're right.'

'I'm using my goddess intuition.' Pea grinned and tapped the side of her head. 'Oh, don't forget your picnic basket.' Pea handed Venus the basket of cold chicken and some of the leftover bread and cheese and fruit Vulcan had zapped up for breakfast.

'That's right. Silly that the Goddess of Love would forget that the way to a man's heart is through here.' She lifted the basket and pointed to her stomach.

'So the old saying really is true?'

'Darling, I made up that old saying.'

'Wow. I had no idea the saying was *that* old,' Pea said.

'Thankfully, I'm well preserved.' She could hear Pea giggling as she drove away.

Venus was smiling as she walked toward the front of the fire station. She had just figured out that she needed to press the little upraised button, when the door opened.

'I thought I saw you walk up! Come on in.'

Venus nodded gratefully at the fireman and then remembered his name. 'Thank you, J. D.'

J. D. yelled into the back of the station, 'Hey y'all! Our sex teacher is here!'

Venus braced herself for the inevitable stampede. It's true she was new to the modern world of mortals, but she certainly was not new to the world of male adoration. True to form, the guys crowded around her, all talking at once about how great the class had been and how much their wives/girlfriends/lovers had appreciated the increase in their education. The goddess smiled beatifically and thanked the men, whom she was beginning to think of as 'her boys.'

'Okay, okay, enough all ready. You're going to smother her.' Griffin growled at the men, who parted to let him through to her with only a few disgruntled looks. 'She's my date, which means I'm pleased to say I'll be taking her away from you knot heads.' Griffin folded her arm through his lovingly and gave Venus an intimate blue-eyed look that made her want to begin at his toes and lick him all the way up.

'Look at me like that in public and I might make a spectacle of myself,' he whispered, leaning close to her as he led her from the group of gawking firemen.

'I've been known to enjoy a good measure of pomp and spectacle,' Venus whispered back. 'But I do believe I'd prefer doing so in private.'

'I'll be in the park. I have my pager on,' Griffin called over his shoulder. 'If anything happens, beep me, but only if someone's bleeding or on fire.'

Venus thought she heard one of the boys mutter something about *No fire could be as hot as she is*, which made her smile contentedly. Men were men were men. It was just like Pea had said, all of this would work out.

They walked hand-in-hand to Fontana Park, which butted up to the backyard of the Midtown Fire Station. It was supposed to turn cold later that evening, but the sun still tinted the Oklahoma sky with a palette of brilliant colors, and the late February day felt balmy and unseasonably warm. But it was February, and an off-time for the park, so Venus was pleased to see that it was deserted. Griffin led her to a sweet little picnic table that was ringed with winter-naked trees.

'I like this place,' Venus said, looking around at the well-kept park. 'It feels nice here. Like it's somewhere families come and play.'

'It is. For most of the year this park is filled with families and children,' Griffin said. He tried to peek into the picnic basket, but she playfully slapped his hand.

'Let me set this out properly. Pea would be very upset if she knew you were grabbing at the food like a barbarian.' Venus pulled out the checkered tablecloth and the place settings Pea had so meticulously packed for them, and as she did so she thought about what it would be like to be a mortal woman, to come here with Griffin and their daughters and spend the day as a family.

The Goddess of Love stopped that indulgent fantasy. She could never be the mortal wife of an ordinary man, no matter how much she might secretly desire it. Her place for eternity was on Mount Olympus. The most she could hope for was that she would be allowed a brief respite of time with this man – this unexpected love of hers – before she had to return to the business of immortality. If only Griffin would understand that, accept that . . .

'Griffin, there is something I must tell you.'

'You didn't make this chicken,' he said, as he bit into a succulent leg.

Venus's forehead furrowed. 'No. I didn't.'

'I didn't think so. I'll bet Pea did.'

'Of course she did. Pea is an excellent cook, and she's very generous. It was her idea to fill this basket with food.'

'She's a great girl.' He popped a piece of Olympus's finest cheese into his mouth.

'Of course she is.' Venus shook her head refocusing her thoughts. 'Pea is not what I wanted to talk with you about. Nor did I want to talk about cooking.' She glanced at the food Griffin was busily tearing into. 'Or chicken or whatnot.'

'Sorry. I got distracted. I'm starved.' He wiped his mouth, grinned at her, and gave her a quick, but thorough kiss. She thought he looked boyish and happy and very much in love. 'What did you want to tell me?' But before she could reply, he said, 'Oh, by the way, my sisters came by and asked if you'd like to come to dinner tomorrow. I know they're a little much, and yes, all four of them will be there, but I can promise you the food will be good.' His eyes crinkled at the corners as he continued, 'And they did ask me to invite you. I believe their exact words were, "We like the goddess."'

Venus felt her throat close with the intensity of her emotions and she had to take a quick drink from one of the water bottles Pea had packed to cover the fact that she couldn't make her voice work. His sisters recognized her. Oh, not consciously. Somewhere in the depths of their feminine souls, they knew who she was and they accepted her. It moved her beyond words. Now if only their brother would accept her, too.

'I would like very much to be with your family tomorrow,' she finally managed to say.

'Good. I want you to be,' Griffin told her.

'Griffin. We must talk.'

'You already said that.' This time she seemed to have more of his attention, though. At least he was looking at her while he chewed. She drew a long, steadying breath.

'I want you to know who I really am.'

'Okay with me. I want to know everything about you.'

Stalling, she took another long drink of water.

'Hey, you're not going to tell me anything bizarre like you used to be a man, are you?' he joked.

'Of course I didn't used to be a man, but you might find what I have to tell you bizarre.'

'Okay, go ahead.' He wiped his mouth with a napkin. 'Tell me something bizarre.'

'I am Venus, ancient Goddess of Sensual Love, Beauty and the Erotic Arts.' She used her full and most formal title, deciding if she was going to tell him, she might as well be thorough. 'I visited the modern mortal world several days ago on a shopping spree with Persephone.' Venus frowned, remembering. 'Actually it's the Goddess of Spring who is really responsible for this whole incident. She took me to Lola's, and it just so happened that at the same time Pea was there. She invoked my aid using some kind of spell that bound me here until I helped her. You know Pea used to really be a mess – she was sweet, but had no idea what to do with her hair. And you should have seen the

288

shoes she used to wear . . . ugh. Anyway I've been helping her, which is why I've been staying with her. Not that I'm sorry I came here and met you and Pea,' she added hastily, then took a deep, calming breath, afraid the explanation was getting away from her. 'Persephone and that whole thing really isn't what's important. What's important is that you know I am an ancient goddess, one of the Twelve Olympians. I live in my temple on Mount Olympus.' Griffin didn't say anything. He was just looking at her with a very odd expression on his handsome face. He had quit eating, though, so she was sure she had all of his attention. 'My temple is actually quite nice. I'm sure you would like it. Of course you may come there.' She paused, frowning. 'Unless the zapping between worlds bothers you, then I'll come here. Either way, like you said this morning, a long-distance relationship is possible. And I do love you, Griffin, and want this to work between us,' she finished in a rush.

'Well, at least that explains why you were so moved by my sculpture.'

'Exactly!' she said, beginning to feel the stirrings of relief. He didn't seem shocked or upset. Perhaps this would be easier than she thought.

Griffin started to chuckle. He reached forward and kissed her again. 'One of the things I like best about you is your sense of humor. So what you're really telling me is that you expect me to treat you like a goddess. Okay. I can do that.'

Venus shook her head. 'No, that's not it at all. I actually like it that you treat me as if I'm a mortal woman. I don't want you to worship me or fear me or ask boons of me, which is really how a goddess is treated. I want things to go on between us as we have begun them. But you must know the truth about me.'

'That you're a goddess.'

She nodded. 'Venus. Or Aphrodite, if you want to address me by the name the Greeks use. I've always preferred Venus, though.'

'And you're being serious. You really believe you're Venus.'

She sighed. The look he was giving her clearly said he was afraid she was completely mad. 'Remember when we first met at the masquerade ball? The clothing I was wearing wasn't a costume. It was what I normally wear on Olympus. Well, minus the mask,' she added. 'I simply zapped the robes from my temple for Pea and me to wear.' Venus glanced around them. Good. The park was still deserted. 'Like this—' Venus passed her hand in front of her body, and her jeans, sweater and jacket began to shimmer until within moments she was standing before Griffin, dressed in the full, glorious regalia of a true goddess.

'Shit!' he cried, and took two quick steps away from her.

'I'm sorry,' she said hastily, walking toward him. 'Pea hates it when I zap things, too. But I needed to show you that I'm not insane.'

'I think I might be,' Griffin said, taking two more steps away from her.

Feeling foolish and a little worried, she stopped chasing him. 'No, no. Don't worry, you're not. This is all true. See, you can touch the robes, they're real.' She held out her silk-clad arm, but he made no motion to touch her. She sighed. 'Pea made the chicken you were eating, but the cheese and bread were zapped from Olympus. You don't have to be worried about touching things from there; they won't hurt you.'

'I need to sit down.' Griffin walked around her and sat on the picnic table bench. He was still staring at Venus and shaking his head.

'I suppose this might take a little getting used to,' Venus said. She walked back to the table, too, but was careful not to get too close to Griffin. She really didn't want him to move away from her again.

'A little?' he said incredulously.

'Well, it's not like it's changed who I am. I've always been Venus – from the first moment you spoke to me at the party until now. I'm no different. It doesn't really change anything.'

'Yes. It does.'

Venus felt a shiver of worry clench through her body, making her feel lightheaded. His voice had changed completely. He spoke in a cold, emotionless tone. His expressive eyes had flattened to those of a stranger.

'But it doesn't have to. I still love you. You still love me – *me*.'

'No, Goddess. This changes everything,' he said quietly.

She noticed he didn't comment at all on her declaration of love or on the reminder that he was supposed to love her in return. And all at once the worry that had been fluttering through her began to change to anger. Hadn't he meant what he said?

'Why?' Venus asked, her newly emotionless tone mirroring his. 'Why does who I am change things? Or were you lying about loving me?'

'You're calling *me* a liar!' He stood up. 'What about all that crap you gave me about not having love in your life until now? Christ! You *are* love! So what was I, just a mortal toy for you to play with? Some kind of rat in a maze experiment?'

'How dare you!' Her righteous anger caused the trees that ringed their bench to quiver as if the hand of a giant – or a goddess – had suddenly shaken them. Griffin glanced at the whipping branches, his eyes widening. 'When I spoke those words to you I was showing you my heart. I have been alone, for far longer than your mortal brain could even begin to comprehend.'

'The Goddess of Love? Alone? Because I'm a mortal man do you think that also makes me a fucking idiot?'

'Until this moment I didn't.' In some part of her mind, Venus knew that his harsh words were more a reflection of his shock and hurt at thinking that she had deceived him, than a reflection of his true feelings for her. But once the wrath of a goddess is roused, it is a force that is hard to quell . . . and Griffin had definitely aroused her wrath.

'The Venus I loved was like me. She'd avoided love until we met. Now she was willing to finally commit, to figure out a way to make a future together.'

'I am still that Venus!' Her shout caused the ground around them to shudder.

'How! How do you propose we make a future together? I may not know much about mythology, but I think I have the part right about you being immortal, don't I? Hell! Are we even the same damn species? Can we make children together? And what happens in ten, twenty, thirty years when I'm an old man and you're still young and beautiful and unchanged? Did you think about any of those things when you decided to play at loving a man?'

Venus stepped back. She felt as if he had slapped her. She drew around her the dignity and power of a great goddess. She felt the shimmer of her divinity caress her skin and the silver-blonde mass of her hair begin to lift and crackle with a life of its own. She knew her violet eyes were glowing with an unearthly light, just as she knew that the brilliance of her immortality unbridled would be difficult for any mortal to gaze upon. Venus didn't care. She wanted Griffin to see her magnificence. She wanted him to see what he had lost forever. When she spoke, her voice was magnified by the magic that was her birthright.

'No. I did not think of those things when I allowed myself to love you. I thought only of how our souls called to one another. I see now I must have been mistaken. Your soul is too tainted by mortal fear and selfishness. It is not courageous enough to love mine. I leave you now, Griffin DeAngelo, son of man, and return to Olympus where I belong. I could wipe your memory clean of me, as easily as I would wipe chalk from a slate, but I will not. I want you to remember always that you denied Love herself.' Then Venus, Goddess of Sensual Love and Beauty, lifted her arms and in a cascade of shooting sparks, disappeared.

Chapter Twenty-eight

When Venus rematerialized inside Pea's kitchen, her anger was already beginning to drain. Barking wildly, Chloe barreled into the room, but when she recognized Venus her snarls changed to welcome yips, and then worried whines when the goddess sat on the floor, scooped the Scottie up in her arms, and burst into tears.

'Venus! Ohmygod! What's wrong?' Pea rushed into the room and crouched beside her.

'He – hates – me!' she sobbed.

'Oh, sweetheart! He couldn't hate you. No one could hate you. Come on. Sit up here at the table. I'll pour us some coffee and we'll figure this out.' She pulled Chloe gently from the goddess's lap, and then helped Venus to her feet and hugged her hard.

'No–no.' Venus hiccupped, taking her usual place at Pea's table. 'It's not going to be figured out. Pea, he doesn't want me now that he knows I'm a goddess.'

Pea set mugs of steaming coffee before both of them. 'Tell me everything. And here, use the linen napkin as a Kleenex. It's an emergency.'

Pea listened while Venus replayed the scene with Griffin for her, only occasionally gasping and muttering under her breath about how stupid guys could be. When she was finished Venus blew her nose and wiped her eyes. Pea didn't say anything. Instead she got up and brought out of the freezer a long sleeve of something hard wrapped in aluminum paper.

'It's my special stash of Belgian dark chocolate. Eat it. It'll help.'

Venus nodded woodenly and broke off a piece of the chocolate and let the dark sweetness dissolve in her mouth as she sipped Pea's delicious coffee. 'You're right.' The goddess sniffled. 'It does help.'

'Okay. First, I'm really mad at Griffin, too. He behaved like an asshole.'

'I think Smart Bitches dot com would call him something worse. Something like ...' She paused, thinking and sucking on the chocolate. 'A goddamn stupid-ass cockhumping whoremonger or maybe an assburger.'

'You're right. Their curses are excellent. Let's call him a cockhumping assburger. It's way worse than an asshole.'

'I agree,' Venus said.

'So we're really mad at him, *but* I don't think you should give up on him.'

'I have to, Pea. I can't change who I am, and even if I could, I wouldn't.'

'I just think that he was shocked, and that's why he reacted so badly. After he has time to think about what a moron—' Venus raised a brow at Pea. 'I mean what a cockhumping assburger he's been, he'll be all sorry and apologetic and will grovel properly to get you back.'

'You didn't reject Vulcan when you found out he was a god.'

'Well, that's not really a fair comparison. I'd already become friends with you, so I was kinda used to the idea of immortals hanging out in Tulsa.'

Venus shook her head. 'He asked if we were even the same species. I don't know if I can forgive him for that.'

'Do you love him?'

'Yes,' Venus said softly.

'Then I think you can learn to forgive him.'

'I don't know. In a way he's right. There's always going to be this mortal/immortal issue between us. When he's old and stooped I'll still look like this. I will eternally look like this.'

Pea's face had gone pale and Venus realized the significance of what she had said. The goddess took Pea's hand. 'You should know that I would still love Griffin if he was old and stooped, and after he died I would eternally mourn his death and hold his memory as sacred. As will Vulcan with you.'

'I know. At least I think I know. But it is daunting and more than a little scary to know that you're in love with a being who will never age – will never die.'

'But you're courageous enough to continue loving Vulcan.'

'I don't think I'd call it courageous, but yes. I am going to continue loving Vulcan.'

'Griffin doesn't have your courage. Or perhaps it is closer to the truth for me to say that he doesn't have your love.' Venus blinked back the tears that threatened to well in her eyes again.

'Don't give up on him yet. Men aren't as good at adapting as women. Plus' – Pea shrugged, smiled and popped a piece of chocolate into her mouth – 'we have more sense.'

'You're definitely right about that.' Then all kidding left the goddess's voice. 'I don't know if I can do it, Pea. I don't know if I can open myself to him ever again. What if he rejects me again?'

'But, Venus, isn't that just part of love?' Pea asked gently. 'You have to be vulnerable to truly be loved.'

'Yes. If you're not vulnerable to love, you'll never really be open to experiencing it. I just don't know if I can be vulnerable again. Rejection hurts.'

'Who rejected what?' Vulcan's deep voice rumbled from between them as he materialized in the kitchen.

Pea squealed and clutched her heart. 'Okay, y'all have got to stop with the sudden materializations. Use. The. Door. Or you're going to give me a heart attack.'

'Sorry, little one.' Vulcan bent to kiss Pea. He smiled at Venus. 'Hello, Goddess.'

'Vulcan.' She nodded absently at him.

Then he sniffed in the direction of Pea's mug. 'Coffee . . .'

Pea laughed and swatted at him when he tried to take her cup from her. 'Who knew immortals would be so crazy about something as simple as coffee.' She pointed to the pot. 'Help yourself.'

Vulcan poured himself a cup and scooted his chair over so that he could sit with one arm around Pea. He glanced at Venus and then took a second look. 'You've been crying,' he said.

'Griffin didn't respond well to finding out Venus is Venus,' Pea said.

'He rejected you?'

Venus let out a long sigh. 'Please don't rub it in.'

'My friend, you know I would never do that.'

Venus smiled sadly. 'Yes, I know.'

'He hurt you,' Vulcan said.

'He did.'

'Shall I punish him for you? I could cause his blood to turn to lava and his brains to boil,' Vulcan said cheerfully.

Pea frowned at him and elbowed the God of Fire. 'I don't think that would be very nice.'

'It is a considerate offer, and I thank you. But I'm afraid I'll have to decline. It seems when you love someone the thought of them being tortured doesn't bring you the pleasure it should. Even though he definitely deserves to be tortured.'

'I could thrash him.' Vulcan glanced at Pea, who was still frowning at him, and added, 'But not severely enough to cause him permanent damage.'

Venus shook her head. 'No, thank you. I'm just going to return to Olympus and try to forget about Griffin DeAngelo. I hate to think about all the catching up I'll have to do. I really have been here ignoring my divine duties too long.' She stood up.

'Wait! You're going to leave? Just like that?' Pea said.

'Darling, you knew I couldn't stay with you forever.'

'But I didn't think you'd leave so soon. You'll come back, won't you? I mean, no matter what happens with Griffin, you'll come back and visit.'

Venus touched the little mortal's cheek. 'Yes, darling. I'll come back. How could I stay away? We'll go to Lola's for pomegranate martinis and dancing and then come back here for hot chocolate and girl talk. And I do believe you'll be visiting Olympus from time to time yourself.' Venus turned her attention to Vulcan. 'Which reminds me. My friend, it is past time you and I corrected a mistake we made eons ago. We meant well, you and I, but to marry for less than what you and Pea have is a sham and a lie.'

'I will always wish you well, Goddess of Love. You have been a friend to me when the other immortals shunned me. I won't ever forget that,' Vulcan said.

'I'll ask Zeus and Hera to hear our petition tomorrow evening. Join me in the Great Hall and together we will dissolve our union officially.'

'Thank you, Venus,' Pea said, blinking back tears.

Venus smiled. 'Just promise me one thing.'

'Anything,' Vulcan and Pea said together.

'Promise me that you will love and honor each other for as long as you both shall live.'

'I promise,' Pea said.

'You have my eternal oath,' Vulcan said.

'Good. I'll be watching. Don't make me have to come down here and smite either of you.' Venus tugged on one of Pea's curls, purposely lightening the mood before one of them started to cry. 'Now, Pea, you'll need to close your eyes so that my zapping doesn't scare you.'

'This one time I think I'll keep my eyes open. I love you, Venus,' Pea said.

'And I love you, too, darling.' The Goddess of Love lifted her arms and disappeared.

Vulcan put down his coffee mug and turned to Pea. With his arms open he said, 'Are you going to cry now, little one?'

'Yes!' she said on a sob, and burying her face in her true love's shoulder, Pea had a good cry.

Chapter Twenty-nine

'I'm a fucking idiot!'

The words exploded from Griffin as he tossed the unbalanced ledger across his desk. For hours he'd been locked up in his office by himself, fuming. Then when the fumes had fizzled, he had been left with the stark, cold truth. He'd rejected the woman he loved with all his heart and soul. And why had he done something so asinine? Because he found out she was a goddess. And not just any goddess. The woman he loved was *the* Goddess of Love. Venus. Aphrodite. The woman men had been immortalizing for thousands of years in song and poetry and art. But he had rejected her. Griffin cringed, remembering the look of hurt on her face when he'd let his shock and fear explode as rage and rejection.

He had to figure out some way to make it up to her – to apologize to her – to win her back. Then he'd be a man about it and deal with the fact that the woman he loved was a real goddess. That she wouldn't age or die – that she had unbelievable power.

'She should have blasted some sense into my thick head!' he muttered. Actually, on second thought, he was probably lucky she hadn't.

So now what? How did he start cleaning up the mess he'd made? She'd said she was returning to Olympus. He groaned and rubbed his temples where the same headache had throbbed for hours. It wasn't like he could call her.

Or could he?

She was a goddess. So she heard the prayers of mortals. Didn't she? It was at least worth a try. He cleared his throat.

'Venus?' he called to the air. 'Are you there? Can you hear me?' He swallowed and started again. 'Venus, Goddess of Sensual Love, Beauty and the Erotic Arts, I ask you to hear me.' Nothing happened. Okay, he'd try it another way. 'Venus, I'm sorry. I love you. Is there any way you could forgive me for being such a fucking idiot?' He paused. 'Could you shake something if you hear me?' Still nothing. Obviously he wasn't going about this in the right way. So how the hell did one go about summoning an ancient goddess? He didn't have a clue.

Then he sat up straighter. *He* didn't have a clue, but he knew someone who did! Venus had said that Pea had used a spell to evoke her aid. He'd get Pea to give him the spell! Griffin glanced at the wall clock. Shit! It was almost two in the morning. He'd have to wait. But as soon as his shift was over he'd go directly to Pea's house and camp out on her front porch if necessary until she agreed to help him contact Venus.

The goddess would forgive him. She'd have to. He wouldn't stop trying until she did.

Minutes later when the station's alarm shrieked Griffin was actually relieved. At least he'd be kept busy for the next few hours – it would make time seem to pass faster.

Like a well-oiled machine, he and his men flew into action. As Griffin pulled on his forty-plus pounds of equipment and moved quickly to the engine, his lieutenant handed him the rip of paper that had the address of the fire printed on it. Griffin climbed into the driver's seat, his mind working as smoothly as the big engine he drove. The fire was at the Twenty-first Street Borders Books and Music. The good: one, the store was close, so they'd be there in minutes; two, it was two o'clock in the morning, so it was closed and there should be no lives in jeopardy. The bad: one, it was one of those huge two-level stores, so the fire could be large; two, it was a store filled with books, which meant lots of fuel for a quick, hot fire. It could go up like a torch.

Before he sighted the store he knew he'd been at least partially right. It was a huge fire. By the time they pulled up in the big parking lot, the entire front of the store was engulfed in fire. Flames shot out of the windows, shattering the plate glass.

As always at the scene of a fire, everything began to happen in double-time. The men piled out of the engine. Griffin barked commands. The police that were already there started moving the watching civilians back while the hoses and ladders were quickly put into position.

'Captain!' Griffin looked up to see Robert running from the ladder truck over to him. 'Nine-one-one dispatch radioed. A cell phone call just came from inside the store. The night watchman is trapped near the rear offices.'

'Follow me around back!' Griffin snapped. The well-trained men knew exactly what to do. They grabbed the proper equipment and jogged after their captain.

'Break it down,' Griffin said.

Robert and J. D. went to work with the axes. The steel door folded like a flower under the strength of their blows.

The escaping ghosts of black smoke rushed out at them.

'Which office is he trapped by? Where?' Griffin asked Robert.

'Don't know. His phone cut out. Nine-one-one got the manager on the line and he says the whole rear of this thing is office and storage space.'

'So he could be anywhere,' Griffin said. It wasn't a question – there was no need for anyone to answer. 'All right, let's go in. J. D.,

Robert go right.' He glanced at the rookie, who looked pale, but who met his eyes calmly. 'Bennett, you come with me to the left. Keep your masks on – it's smoky in there. Let's go!'

Griffin always thought entering a burning building was like entering a living beast. It had a personality. It breathed and changed. It was as unpredictable as a wild animal.

This one was no different.

That the flames hadn't reached the rear of the store yet mattered little. The heat was there. The smoke was there. The danger was there.

Griffin moved to the left, ignoring the growl of the fire that was moving ever nearer. He kept visual contact with Bennett, and every few minutes had J. D. and Robert checking in.

The damn place was a maze of filled-to-overflowing book-shelves and cubicles. He was getting ready to check another office, when a cry down the hall ahead of them called his atten-tion forward. It sounded like someone was pounding on the far door.

'Capt, that door looks like it opens to the bookstore,' Bennett said.

'Yeah, stay close.' He took off jogging down the hall.

The heavy door was locked. Griffin used the handle of the axe to pound twice on it. Two desperate knocks instantly responded.

'We got him,' Griffin called. Then he put his face close to the door. 'Can you hear me?' he shouted.

'Yes! Help me!' came the muffled response. 'I'm trapped and the fire's in here!'

'Step back! I'm breaking down the door.'

'Hurry!' the watchman cried through the door.

'Let's do it,' Griffin told Bennett.

They wielded their axes quickly, but the door was stubborn

and it took several strokes before they jarred it enough for them to pry it open just wide enough for Griffin to squeeze through.

He walked into an inferno of flame and smoke and heat. The watchman had stepped away from the door, but overcome by smoke, he'd collapsed in a heap against the wall. Instantly Griffin took off his oxygen mask and fitted if over the man's nose and mouth. Then he lifted him in the traditional fireman's carry and moved back to the partially open escape door, trying to breathe shallowly.

'Here, take him.' Griffin passed the awkward weight of the unconscious man through the narrow opening to Bennett. 'Got him?' he called.

'Got him, Capt.!' Bennett grunted.

'Get him outta here. I'll be right behind you.'

'Roger, Capt!'

Griffin watched him disappear into the smoke. He started to squeeze through the doorway, and then all hell – literally – broke loose. The explosion threw him at least ten feet. He landed on his back. The air was knocked out of his already strained lungs. Still he struggled to gather himself and regain his feet. Then a noise much like the screech of a dying bird pulled his attention up just in time to see the railing of the curved metal staircase come loose and hurtle in slow motion toward him. He couldn't move. He couldn't do anything except brace himself for the impact of the twisted, melting metal.

Pain seared the left side of his body. Then, thankfully, blackness took him into its cool darkness . . .

Vulcan was deeply asleep. So deeply that he thought his mother's voice was just part of a dream.

'Vulcan, you must awaken.'

In his sleep he sighed, pulling Pea closer to his naked body.

'Son. Awaken.'

Vulcan frowned, beginning to move groggily toward consciousness.

'Vulcan! Now. Wake up!'

The God of Fire opened his eyes.

'Finally. You always have been a heavy sleeper. I don't know where you got that – neither your father nor I could sleep through the dropping of a pin.'

'Mother?'

'Yes, yes, yes, it's me, Hera, Queen of Gods – your mother. And I insist you awaken.'

Vulcan carefully extricated himself from Pea's still soundly sleeping form and sat up. Sure enough, his mother was standing in Pea's bedroom, her ivory-colored robes glistening as if they held a light of their own.

'Mother, what has happened?'

'There's a fire. You must go.'

At the word 'fire' Vulcan was already moving. Instantly he called the garb of an ancient Roman warrior to him.

'Yes, you are wise to prepare for battle. Come with me.' Hera took his hand and the two of them disappeared.

When they reappeared it was in the middle of fiery chaos. They were inside a burning building. The flames could not harm Vulcan, and automatically he added his own protection to his mother's aura. He would never allow fire to harm the Queen of Gods.

'Look there.' Hera pointed to a spot of burning rubble that the main area of flames was just about to engulf.

A weak movement caught Vulcan's sharp eye.

'Griffin!' he cried, and strode to the fallen mortal's side, flinging back the flames that were in his path. When he reached him,

Vulcan assessed the damage quickly. With one hand he flung the iron railing off the man's body. Griffin's eyes fluttered and then opened.

'Who are you?' he gasped. Then his gaze shifted and his eyes widened when he saw the beautiful woman standing in a halo of light beside the . . .

'A goddess!' Griffin said, his voice barely above a whisper.

'Yes,' said the man who knelt beside him. 'And I am a friend of Venus. Be still, breathe slowly. I will get you free of this inferno.'

'It is too late, my son.'

Griffin's eyes shifted from the god to the goddess who stood so serenely beside him. Amazingly she smiled and called him by name.

'Griffin DeAngelo, I am Hera, Queen of Gods.'

'Hello, Hera.' Griffin thought he said the words in a normal voice, but a raspy whisper was all that managed to escape his mouth.

'You must listen carefully to me, Griffin,' she said. 'We have little time. You see, you are dying.'

Griffin thought he should feel fear or, at the very least, shock at her words. Instead he was surprised that a sense of peace enveloped him.

'The watchman . . . is he saved?' Griffin whispered.

'He is,' Hera said. 'You did well.'

Griffin sighed. If this was to be his end, then at least he'd done his job, and done it well. Grayness began to tunnel the edges of his vision. He thought about his sisters and his mother, and he felt a knife of sorrow for the pain he knew his death would cause them. Then he thought about Venus, and how sorry he was for what he'd said to her. But she was a goddess . . . maybe she would somehow be able to know how he felt . . . even after he died . . .

'Not yet, Griffin DeAngelo! I command your spirit not depart yet!' Hera shouted.

Griffin's eyes shot open and, almost against his will, he blinked his vision clear.

'Mother, I can carry him from here. Surely we can . . .' the god began, but Hera lifted her hand and commanded silence.

'It has gone too far. His body has been too gravely damaged. Forgive me, mortal man, I misjudged the time Fate had allotted you. I meant to provide you with more of a choice in this.'

Griffin wanted to tell her she was forgiven, but his voice was beyond obeying him. The goddess turned to the god.

'There is only one way to save him, my son. You and he must switch souls. In doing so, you will become mortal and, with the aid of my power, there will be enough of your immortal essence left to heal his broken body and survive. But you will then be mortal – in all ways. Do you understand?'

Vulcan nodded. 'I do, Mother.'

'Do you understand that if you do this you will live one mortal life and only one, here in the modern world, and that when you die your body will return to dust and your spirit will descend to the Elysian Fields.'

'And I will spend that life with the mortal woman I love, and when she, too, dies, will she be allowed to enter Elysia?'

Hera bowed her head. 'I give you my sacred oath that her spirit will find a home there.'

'I understand and I agree.'

'Very well, my son.'

Hera approached Griffin's fallen body and knelt beside him. She touched his face. He thought how cool and soft her hand felt. 'Listen well, mortal man. My son is Vulcan, God of Fire, husband to Venus, whom I believe you love. He can save your soul and your life, but in doing so he must take possession of your body and your mortal life. You, in turn, will become him – one of the Twelve Olympians, God of Fire. You will retain your soul and your memories, but for eternity you must guard the sacred forge and the pillar of flame. You will become the God of Fire. Do you understand?'

With a mighty will, Griffin forced words through his damaged body. 'Does Venus know?'

Hera shook her head. 'No.'

'If I say no, I die?' he rasped.

'You will surely die, but you should know you have nothing to fear from death. You have been a good man. I can assure you a warrior's afterlife in the Elysian Fields.'

Griffin's fading eyes turned to the god called Vulcan. 'My sisters . . .' He gasped.

Vulcan dropped to his knees beside Griffin. 'I know of your sisters. I would cherish and protect them as if they belonged to me. They will never know that I am not their beloved brother.'

'Your oath on that,' Griffin said.

'You have my oath.'

Griffin closed his eyes and whispered, 'Then I agree. I will exchange souls with you.'

Griffin heard Hera begin a chant, the words to which he couldn't understand, but the power of them pushed against his skin with more insistence than the flames that threatened them. And then he felt an enormous tugging, as if he had been caught in a terrible tornado. He opened his mouth to scream and scream and scream . . . and then he knew only the utter blackness of a night more complete than any he could have imagined as nothingness engulfed him.

Chapter Thirty

The ringing phone woke Pea. Groggily, she muttered, 'Vulcan, hand me that, would you?' Then she remembered he was an ancient god and he probably didn't know anything about a ringing phone. She opened her eyes, expecting him to be smiling at her, perhaps a little confused, but sexy and rumpled and warm beside her.

He wasn't there. Except for Chloe, who was blinking sleepily at her from the end of the bed, she was alone in the room. Frowning, Pea reached for the phone.

'Hello?'

'Is this Dorreth Pea Chamberlain?' a tense male voice asked.

'Yes.'

'Miss Chamberlain, this is Robert Thomas from the Midtown Fire Station.'

'What time is it?' Pea asked the question without thinking.

'Five a.m., ma'am. Uh, I'm calling on behalf of Griffin DeAngelo.'

'Griffin!' A horrible sense of foreboding flushed her body. 'Has something happened to Griffin?'

'Yes ma'am, I'm afraid so. The captain has been injured on the job. He's at Saint John's, getting ready to go into surgery. His one request was that we call you and have you come directly to the hospital.'

'I'll be right there.'

She hung up and grabbed the jeans and discarded sweater that were lying over her vanity chair. 'Vulcan?' she called. No answer. 'Vulcan!' This time she yelled his name. Pea hurried through the house. Had he gone back to Olympus? Why hadn't he woken her first? And why had he left in the middle of the night?

She threw the T-Bird into gear and gunned it out of her driveway. Griffin was hurt. Of course he'd had her called. Clearly he understood she was his link to Venus. So she needed Vulcan to get word to Olympus that Venus was needed back here ASAP. But where was Vulcan?

Pea's stomach felt sick. Something was wrong. Something was terribly wrong.

She rushed through the emergency entrance of Saint John's Medical Center and almost ran straight into a soot-covered fireman.

'I'm Pea Chamberlain. They called me for Griffin DeAngelo.'

'Right this way, ma'am.'

Pea followed the somber young fireman into the bowels of the ER. A nurse stopped them.

'This is the woman the captain's been asking for,' the fireman explained.

'Then come with me, miss. You must hurry. They're taking him to surgery. You'll only have a moment with him.'

'How is he?' Pea asked, as she hurried to keep up with the nurse.

'It's not good,' the nurse said, without looking at her.

She led her to a glass room that was alive with people. Pea was glad everything was happening so fast. If she'd had time to think she might have gotten sick or, worse, fainted. She would have never recognized Griffin. His face was black and bloody. His lips were cracked and swollen. The left side of his body from his waist down was tented, and she thought he had tubes and wires coming out of every unburned surface on his body.

'Two minutes, miss,' the nurse said.

Pea made herself approach the head of the small ER bed. 'Griffin? It's me. Pea.'

His eyes fluttered twice and then opened. His blue eyes met hers and she felt a shiver of something . . . something she couldn't quite identify. She moved closer to him. His swollen lips began to move. Pea leaned forward.

'. . . love you, little one . . .'

She gasped as the truth slammed through her. 'Vulcan!' She gasped.

Relief relaxed his face. He smiled and closed his eyes with a contented sigh.

'I must ask you to leave, ma'am. We're taking him to surgery.'

Numbly Pea let them show her to the surgical waiting room. She sat on an overstuffed chair and nodded automatically when a fireman asked if she wanted coffee. Griffin wasn't Griffin. He was Vulcan. Of that she had absolutely no doubt. But how had it happened? Suddenly she felt claustrophobic.

'I—I have to get some air.' She ignored the concerned looks of the fireman as she ran from the room, down the hall and rushed out the automatic doors, where she leaned against the side of the hospital, drawing in deep breaths and trying not to throw up.

'You love him very much, don't you?'

Pea looked up to see an exquisitely elegant woman standing in a little halo of light beside her. She reminded her of Venus, even though she looked nothing like the Goddess of Love.

'If you mean Vulcan, then yes I do. I love him very much,' Pea said.

The woman nodded her head. 'I knew it. You are his eternal love – the true mate of his soul. I am Hera.'

Pea didn't need a schoolbook knowledge of mythology to know who this goddess was, she only needed the instincts of a woman. 'You're Vulcan's mother.'

The goddess smiled. 'I am. And I owe you a debt of gratitude, Dorreth Pea Chamberlain. Before Vulcan knew and loved you, he was only partially alive. You saved him from eternal loneliness and more. You have given him a happiness I never thought he would know. I find his immortality a small price to pay for such a blessing.'

Pea wasn't sure she'd heard the goddess correctly. 'His immortality? What does that mean? What happened tonight?'

'My son is not the only immortal who has been observing your modern world. I knew Griffin DeAngelo had become beloved of Venus. Tonight DeAngelo was dying. I saved him by having my son take his place. Vulcan breathed the one remaining spark of immortality that clung to his spirit into his mortal shell. Now Vulcan is Griffin – a mortal man. He will live one mortal life. And Griffin has become Vulcan, God of Fire, for eternity.'

Pea's body began trembling. 'He remembers? He's still Vulcan?'

'In all but body, yes he is.'

'And he'll live?'

'Yes. My son will live a long and happy life. You and he will have many children. I will be a grandmother and great-grandmother over and over again, and for generations the spark of the God of Fire's spirit will shine in the DeAngelo family.'

Pea began to cry. The goddess approached her and touched her face. 'My son chose wisely.'

'What about Venus and Griffin?' Pea said, wiping her eyes while she still tried to comprehend the enormity of what the goddess was telling her. 'What will happen to them?'

'That, my sweet mortal daughter, will be up to the new God of Fire and the Goddess of Love.'

A commotion in the parking lot interrupted Pea's next question for the goddess. The two of them glanced behind them in time to see four distraught young women hurrying toward the ER entrance.

'Griffin's sisters. The oldest and most reasonable is called Sherry. Speak with her first and the rest will follow her lead,' Hera said. 'Now go to them. You will soon be a part of their family.'

'You aren't leaving, are you?'

'There is nothing more for me to do here, but do not worry. I will return often to visit my grandchildren.' The goddess raised her hand regally. 'May my blessing stay with you eternally.' Hera silently disappeared.

Pea drew in a deep breath, willing herself to be calm. Vulcan would be okay. She had a goddess's word on it, and that was good enough for her. She met the four girls as they got to the ER doors.

Pea picked out the woman who looked the most in control of herself. She had long, dark hair and Griffin's startling blue eyes. 'Sherry DeAngelo?' she asked.

The four women stopped short. 'I'm Sherry DeAngelo. Who are you? Do you know what's happened to our brother?'

'I do. He's been in an accident.' The women gasped, and the one who was clearly the youngest started crying. 'They've taken him to surgery, but he's going to be okay. Everything's going to be okay. I promise.'

'Who are you?' Sherry asked.

'My name is Dorreth Chamberlain, but everyone calls me Pea. And I'm the woman your brother loves. He and I are going to be married.'

All four sisters gave her mirror looks of confusion. Pea smiled. 'I know it seems odd. You probably thought he was in love with Venus, the beautiful blonde, right?'

They nodded in tandem.

'Well, it's a long story. Actually Venus is a good friend of mine. But our little soap opera isn't what's important right now. What's important is getting Griffin well. Come on. Let's go together to the surgical waiting room; we'll talk more there.' And Pea led the confused sisters into the hospital while she hurriedly concocted a reasonable 'Griffin and Pea' love story.

Well, one thing was certain – her overactive imagination was certainly going to come in handy. Maybe she even had a future in writing fiction.

'Goddess, Zeus and Hera send word that they will see you now.' The nymph bowed low as Venus swept past her.

Where was Vulcan? It had been a full day. She'd sent word to his realm that his parents had agreed to hear their petition this evening during the gathering of the immortals in the Great Hall. But had Vulcan deigned to send her a response? Even a brief message via nymph or satyr or wood sprite saying that he'd be there? No. How totally annoying.

Of course if she were being honest with herself, she would admit that everything in the past twenty-four hours had annoyed her. The opulence of her temple bothered her. Her servant nymphs got on her nerves. The wine was too warm. Or too cold. Prayers from her subjects had stacked up until the very air around her was filled with a deafening cacophony of irritating sound. But all of that chaos could have been borne if her heart and her spirit hadn't been pining for Griffin.

Venus had to admit it: She missed him dreadfully, and it had taken all of her will to go on about her divine duties and not rush directly back to Tulsa and confront Griffin again. Give him another chance. Try to show him that she hadn't changed, she hadn't misled him, she was still the woman he'd fallen in love with. But she hadn't gone back. She'd stayed in Olympus and pulled her pride around her like an expensive robe.

The Goddess of Love did not chase after any man.

The Goddess of Love did not bear insult well.

The Goddess of Love had pride and dignity.

Venus's sigh was soul deep. 'The Goddess of Love is miserable,' she muttered.

The Great Hall of Olympus was crowded with glittering, golden immortals and exquisite nymphs of all types dressed in diaphanous scraps of clothing. Venus even recognized several lesser deities, like Hebe, Goddess of Youth; Iris, Goddess of the Rainbow; and the Muses and Graces. Persephone gave her a saucy wink as she walked past her, which Venus tried her best to return with good humor.

Well she supposed she should be pleased that apparently all of Olympus was there. Everyone could witness the dissolution of her marriage with Vulcan. It would save her having to repeat herself over and over again.

Maybe after this was finished, she would return to Tulsa with Vulcan. She'd only been away from Pea for a day, but already she missed her mortal friend. No, she corrected herself gloomily. Vulcan and Pea would want to be alone. They would probably begin planning their wedding. And she was happy for them – really she was.

She was also thoroughly depressed.

'Venus, Goddess of Love, and Vulcan, God of Fire, we shall hear your petition now.' Zeus's voice boomed across the enormous room.

Venus began picking her way to the raised dais, which held the two glittering thrones on which sat the king and queen of Olympus. Discreetly she let her eyes sweep the room. Where was Vulcan? She could do this without him, but if she did it would seem meanspirited and disrespectful. Unless he was there to show that the dissolution of their marriage was mutual, no matter how she put her request, it would appear that Love had discarded Vulcan. His name would be spoken with even more disdain. Perhaps she should wait for him and ask to come before Zeus and Hera another day.

No, Vulcan wouldn't want that, and neither would Pea. And what did Vulcan care about what the immortals thought of him? He'd found his love. Pea was all that mattered to him. Venus stopped before the dais and curtsied low with such fluid grace and beauty that she called the attention of everyone in the room to her.

'What may we do for you, Goddess of Love?' Zeus asked. Then, with a frown, he added, 'And wasn't the request for petition made by you *and* our son?'

'It was my lord,' Venus said. 'But it seems Vulcan has been detained, so I will present the request for both of us.'

Zeus snorted, but Hera responded with a gracious, 'Go ahead, Venus. We will hear your request.'

Venus lifted her chin and spoke in a clear, confident voice that carried throughout the Great Hall. 'It is no secret to any of you that my marriage to the God of Fire has been an unusual one, and it is that marriage that is the subject of our petition today.' Venus paused, waiting for the curious whispers to fade. 'Vulcan and I have been good friends, but we married under false pretenses. Ironically our marriage has lacked love. We would now like to rectify our mistake. Marriage should be based on more than convenience, so Vulcan and I ask that—'

'You stand witness to the recommitment of our marriage.'

With the rest of the crowd, Venus gasped with shock at the interruption. She looked around the enormous room until she caught sight of Vulcan's tall figure making his way toward her. Surely she'd misunderstood his words. She looked up at him as he joined her before the thrones of his parents.

'Vulcan, what are you talking about?' She kept her voice low for his ears alone.

He smiled at her, but instead of answering he faced his parents and bowed to them.

'Zeus, Hera,' he said. 'Thank you for hearing our petition today, and forgive me for being late.'

'That's quite all right, son,' Hera said, beaming a smile at her favorite child. 'Go ahead with your request. Your father and I are ready to hear it.'

'Venus was quite right. We started our relationship together in a loveless way. But now I would like to rectify that. If Venus will agree, I want to recommit to our marriage, and this time it will be a real marriage.'

He ignored the disbelieving whispers and the sarcastic laughter that was the response of the watching immortals and turned to Venus. Then he further shocked her by taking her in his arms. When he spoke he didn't lower his voice. The entire Hall could hear what he was saying, but his words were confidently

317

spoken and they seemed to brush her soul with the depth of their passion.

'Who knew Love could be intimate with loneliness?'

'What? I–I don't understand, Vulcan,' she whispered.

Again he spoke from his heart to her, but he made no attempt to speak quietly. 'You've been lonely, wife.'

Numbly, not understanding what was happening, she automatically replied the same words she'd spoken days earlier during a bizarrely similar conversation. 'I have. We should have never married. We've both been unbearably sad. Friendship can only be an addition to, not a substitute for, true love.' Venus held her breath, hoping against all reason that she knew what his next words would be.

'And neither is waiting and searching. Is there any way we can reconcile? How can we make this better for both of us?'

When she heard the familiar response, from the night of the masquerade party, Venus began to tremble. And suddenly the Great Hall seemed to fade around them, and it was replaced by an Oklahoma night when the man who looked into her eyes had been wearing a different kind of mask.

'Is it you? How did this happen?' she whispered.

And then he did lower his voice so that Venus alone could hear him. 'It's easy, my goddess. I found the courage to accept your love.'

With a glad cry Venus threw her arms around Griffin's neck and melted against him as he lowered his mouth hungrily to hers, and Vulcan, God of Fire, formally and officially, possessed Venus, Goddess of Love, with Mount Olympus as his witness. The Great Hall exploded in pandemonium. Somewhere in the back of her mind, Venus realized that the noise around her was made up of joyful shouts and cheers as the Olympians acknowledged the glimpse they had been given of true love. But that was something she would consider and be glad of later. Just then she was too busy feeling her soul leap in joyful acknowledgment that it had been granted the miracle of living for eternity with its mate.

Epilogue

One year later

'Darling, you don't have any lamb. Would you mind terribly if I zapped up a succulent young leg of lamb for the grill? I have such a taste for it.' Venus was peering into Pea's refrigerator as if she actually expected to find a freshly butchered carcass of lamb hiding between the milk and orange juice.

'Venus, we're having buffalo steaks. I've been marinating them since last night. They'll be delicious – trust me on this. Plus they have less fat and cholesterol than beef, let alone lamb.' Venus's beautiful face was a total question mark. Pea rolled her eyes. 'Buffalo is better for you.'

The goddess thought for a moment and then her expression changed so that she looked like she had just taken a large bite of something distasteful. 'You mean it's *healthy*?'

Pea laughed.

'Are you terrorizing the immortals again, little one?'

Venus watched Vulcan (*no, Griffin*. Sometimes it was still hard to remember she must always call him Griffin) walk slowly to his wife. His leg was getting better, she thought. The wound had been dreadful. His entire left leg had been crushed. Venus remembered how during one of her numerous visits to Pea in the months following the accident and the bizarre exchange of their lovers' souls, her mortal friend had talked about the doctors

320

and their opinion that Vulcan (who was now living the mortal Griffin's life) would never walk again. Pea and Venus had shared secret smiles over that. They knew the doctors had underestimated the soul within the mortal shell. He still walked carefully and slowly, but he walked.

Pea was laughing again and telling her husband that terrorizing immortals was one of her favorite pastimes, when the God of Fire materialized in the kitchen. Pea let out a little shriek and pressed her hand to the very pregnant swell of her belly.

'I don't know why I can't get used to that,' she said, under her breath.

'Sorry, Pea.' The god looked chagrined. He bent to kiss Pea's plump cheek, then the two men greeted each other. 'It's still weird,' said the immortal, who used to be mortal.

'I believe it will always been disconcerting,' said the mortal man who used to be God of Fire.

Venus noticed that, as always, they shook hands warmly. The two men honestly liked and respected each other. That, the Goddess of Love thought, proved that there was something intrinsically honorable and good about each man's soul. Then her husband walked around the table to her. By Circe's huge tits, she loved him! Venus didn't think she would ever tire of the unique spirit that sparkled in his dark eyes or of the way he made her body sing beneath his hands. He was incredibly strong and powerful, and during the past year that Griffin had resided within Vulcan's immortal frame, the God of Fire had completely lost the limp that had caused him so much anguish for eons. Ironic, really, that the wound followed the man's soul more than his body. Then Venus could only think about how warm his lips were as she pressed herself against him, returning his kiss.

'Hey there, my goddess,' he whispered. 'Did you miss me?'

'Oh, jeesh, you two. Please. She's only been here for one day without you,' Pea said, shaking her head good-naturedly at them.

'I would miss you if you were gone for a day.' Vulcan bent to nuzzle Pea's neck, which made her giggle and shiver.

'Stop that! We don't have time. Your sisters will be here any second, and I still have lots to do so that we can eat and be ready to leave for the grand opening of Fabio's boutique.' She turned her stern look on Venus. 'You know he'll be crushed if you're late.'

'Darling, remind me what he decided to call his little shop,' Venus said.

'*Fit for a Goddess*.' Pea grinned. 'He said you inspired the title.'

'Of course I did.'

'Want me to light the charcoal for the grill?' Vulcan asked her.

'You know that I could very easily do that for you,' the new God of Fire said.

'Thanks, but I still like to start a fire or two every once in a while.' Vulcan lifted his now mortal hands and wiggled his fingers, doing an excellent impression of how Venus liked to zap things into being. 'Even if these don't work so well for me anymore.'

Venus snorted at him, but secretly she thought that mortality had been good for his sense of humor.

'Well, God of Fire, if you want to make yourself useful, you can get a box for me from the pantry. It's on the very top shelf, and I'm not feeling like climbing the step stool right now. I think I put a bag of special mesquite wood chips in it, and I want y'all to add it to the charcoal as more seasoning for the steaks.'

'She's feeding us healthy food.' Venus muttered.

'I heard that,' Pea said.

'No problem.' Griffin grabbed the box from the pantry and put it on the kitchen table.

'Venus, would you get the chips out of there for me?'

'Yes, darling, as long as you don't try to make me eat them,' Venus said sweetly.

'Very funny.' Pea went back to chopping celery for the potato salad while Venus searched through the box.

'Pea, darling, isn't this the book you used to summon my aid?'

Pea turned. 'Yep, that's it. Wonder how it got in that box?'

'So this is what started it all.' Griffin took the ornately bound leather book from Venus. '*Discover the Goddess Within – Unleash Venus and Open Your Life to Love* by Juno Panhellenius. Now that's a mouthful.'

As if someone had punched her in the stomach, all of the air left Venus's body.

'What?!' She and Vulcan gasped the word together.

He hobbled over to the table and took the book from Griffin. Venus was shaking her head over and over and over. 'I had no idea. Absolutely no idea.'

'You'd never seen the book until now?' Vulcan asked her.

'Never. Pea was reciting the invocation from memory. I simply can't believe this.'

'What is it?' Concerned, Pea had joined them at the table. 'What's wrong?'

Venus looked at her mortal friend. 'It's the author. I know her.' She faltered and added, 'And him.'

'We know them,' Vulcan said. 'Actually Griffin knows them now, too.'

'What are you two talking about?' asked Griffin.

Venus pointed at the name, printed in beautiful raised metallic script across the cover of the book. 'Juno is one of the many names Hera uses. And Panhellenius means "God of all the Greeks." It's one of Zeus's epithets.'

'The old manipulators! They were behind this all along,' Vulcan said incredulously.

'We've had their blessing this whole time, and we didn't realize it,' Venus said.

Pea looked at her beloved husband, who had gone through so much to find his happiness. 'That means they love you, they still love you, very, very much,' Pea said.

'Actually,' Venus added, wrapping her arm around her mortal friend's shoulder. 'It means they love all of us, and that we all have the blessing of the king and queen of the Olympians.'

And as the four friends smiled at one another, thunder rolled playfully across the cloudless Oklahoma sky.